#1 ***New York Times***

#1 ***USA Today***

#1 ***Wall Street Journal***

#1 ***Chicago Tribune***

#1 ***Entertainment Weekly***

#1 ***Publishers Weekly***

E #1 BESTSELLER EVERYWHERE

THE BLACK BOOK

WOW!!
SOMETHING
ELSE!

TRULY ONE
OF HIS (J.P.)
BEST

WFE
7-4-18
HAPPY 4th @ LAKE —

THE BLACK BOOK

JAMES PATTERSON

AND DAVID ELLIS

NEW YORK BOSTON

Grand Central Publishing
Hachette Book Group
1290 Avenue of the Americas, New York, NY 10104
grandcentralpublishing.com
twitter.com/grandcentralpub

Originally published in hardcover and ebook by Little, Brown and Company in March 2017
First oversize mass market edition: May 2018

Grand Central Publishing is a division of Hachette Book Group, Inc. The Grand Central Publishing name and logo is a trademark of Hachette Book Group, Inc.

ISBNs: 978-1-5387-2908-3 (oversize mass market), 978-0-316-46414-7 (ebook)

Printed in the United States of America

OPM

10 9 8 7 6 5 4 3 2 1

THE PRESENT

ONE

PATTI HARNEY stops her unmarked sedan two blocks shy of her destination, the narrow streets packed with patrol cars, the light bars on top of the units shooting a chaos of color into the night. Must be twenty squad cars at least.

Patti ditches her car, puts the lanyard around her neck, her star dangling over her T-shirt. The air outside is unseasonably cold for early April. Still, Patti feels nothing but heat.

She runs a block before reaching the yellow tape of the outside perimeter, the first officer stepping forward to stop her, then seeing her star and letting her pass. She doesn't know that perimeter cop, and he doesn't know her. All the better.

Getting closer now. The sweat stinging her eyes, the T-shirt wet against her chest despite the cold, her nerves jangling.

She knows the condo building even without following the trail of police officers to the place where they're gathered under the awning outside. One of those cops—a detective, like Patti—recognizes her, and his face immediately softens.

"Oh, Jesus, Patti—"

She rushes past him into the lobby of the building.

It's more like a funeral than a crime scene, officers and plainclothes detectives with their eyes dropped, anguished, their faces tear-streaked, some consoling each other. No time for that.

She works her way toward the elevator, casting her eyes into the corners of the lobby for security cameras—old habit, instinct, like breathing—then sees a group of techies, members of the Forensic Services Division, working the elevator, dusting it for prints, and she spins in her gym shoes and pushes through the door to the stairs. She knows it's on the sixth floor. She knows which apartment.

She takes the stairs two at a time, her chest burning, her legs giving out, a riot breaking out in her stomach. Woozy and panicked, she stops on the third-floor landing, alone among the chaos, and squats down for a moment, grabbing her hair, collecting herself, her body trembling, her tears falling in fat drops onto the concrete.

You have to do this, she tells herself.

She motors up the remaining stairs, her legs rubbery, her chest burning, before she pushes through the door to the sixth floor.

Up here, it's all business, photographs being taken, evidence technicians doing their thing, blue suits interviewing neighbors, and Ramsey from the ME's office.

She takes a step, then another, but it's as if she isn't moving forward at all, gaining no ground, like she's in some circus house of horrors—

"Can't go in there."

"Patti."

"Detective Harney. Patti!"

A hand taking hold of her arm. As if in slow motion, her eyes move across the face of the Wiz, the bushy mustache, the round face, the smell of cigar—

"Patti, I'm—Mary, mother of God—I'm so sorry."

"He's...he's..." She can't bring herself to finish the sentence.

"They all are," he says. "I'm sorry as hell to be the one to say it."

She shakes her head, tries to wrangle her arm free.

"You can't go in there, Patti. Not yet."

The Wiz angles himself in front of her, blocking her from the door.

She finds the words somehow. "I'm a...I know how to...handle a crime scene."

A crime scene. Like this is just another act of violence she would encounter in the course of her job.

"Not this one, Detective. Not yet. Give us a chance to—Patti, c'mon—"

She bats away his hands, drives him backwards. He struggles for a moment before he braces her shoulders.

"Patti, please," he says. "Nobody should see their brother like this."

She looks into his eyes, not really seeing him, trying to process everything, thinking that he's right, that she doesn't want to see him, because if she doesn't see him he won't be dead, he won't really be gone—

The *ding* of the elevator.

But—the elevator's been taken out of service. The boys with FSD were dusting it. Who's using the elevator? Someone must have pulled rank—

Oh—

"Chief of Ds is here," someone says.

She looks over Wizniewski's shoulder.

The tall, angular figure, those long strides, the beak nose—which she did not inherit.

"Dad," she says, the word garbled in her throat, feeling every ounce of control vanishing.

Her father, chief of detectives Daniel Harney, a sport coat thrown over a rumpled shirt, his thinning hair uncombed, his eyes already shadowed. "Baby," he says, his arms opening. "Oh, my little angel."

"Is it true, Dad?" she speaks into his chest as he holds her tight, as if he would know, as if she's a toddler again, looking to her father for all the answers in the universe.

"I want to see him," says her father, not to her but to Wizniewski. He locks arms with Patti, as if escorting her down the aisle, and turns toward the door.

"I understand, sir," says the Wiz, "but it's—it's not—brace yourself, sir."

Her father looks down on her, his face bunched up, a dam holding back a storm. She nods back to him.

His voice breaks as he says, "Lead the way, Lieutenant."

TWO

SHE CLICKS off something in her mind and flicks on a different switch. She will be clinical. She will be a detective, not a sister. She will view a crime scene, not her dead twin brother. Clutching, clinging with all her might to her father's arm, stepping onto the tiled entryway of the condo.

She knows the place. It opens into a great room, a small kitchen to the left, bedroom and bathroom in the back. Pretty standard high-rise condo in Chicago, anyway, but she knows this one in particular. She's been here before.

The first time was yesterday.

The apartment goes immediately silent, as if someone raised a hand for quiet. Everyone busy at work dusting or photographing or collecting samples or talking—everyone stops as the chief of Ds and his daughter, a detective in her own right, enter the room.

Patti does her detective thing. No sign of struggle in the front room, the main room. Furniture in place, the tile shiny and clean, no sign of activity other than what the detectives and technicians are doing.

Someone had turned the air conditioner on full blast, the air good and cool, which should moderate lividity—

Lividity. My brother's dead body.

"It's in the bedroom," says Wizniewski, leading the way. "Now, I can't let you go in there, Chief, you understand that. You're the immediate family of one of the—"

"I just want to see. I won't walk in, Lieutenant." Her father, in that precise, resolute way he has of speaking, though she is probably the only one who recognizes the tremor in his voice.

Patti's eyes moving about, seeing nothing. Amy kept a clean apartment. She's seen, in her time, plenty of attempts to clean up a crime scene, and this shows no signs of recent scrubbing or spraying or incomplete attempts to wipe away smears or vacuum up debris. No violence happened in the great room or the kitchen.

Everything that happened happened inside the bedroom.

Red crime-scene tape, the inner perimeter, blocking access to the bedroom.

Her father delicately positions himself ahead of Patti, a protective gesture, allowing him the first look inside the bedroom. He leans over the red tape, takes a deep breath, and turns to his right to look inside.

He immediately squeezes his eyes shut and turns away, holding his breath, immobile. He swallows hard, opens his eyes—now deadened, filled with horror—and turns back and looks again.

He murmurs, "What in God's name happened here?"

She hears Wizniewski breathe a heavy sigh. "The position of the bodies, everything—it looks pretty much like what it looks like, sir."

Patti steels herself and angles past her father, looking into the room.

Three dead bodies. Kate—Detective Katherine Fenton—lying dead on the carpet, her eyes staring vacantly at the ceiling, a single gunshot wound over her right eye. A pretty clean shot, only a trickle of blood running from the wound, the rest of the blood following gravity's pull, probably leaving through the exit wound in the back of her skull, soaking the carpet beneath her, obscured by her auburn hair. Her Glock pistol lying just outside the reach of her left hand.

She focuses on Kate—not because she's never seen a dead body (she's seen dozens), and not because she liked Kate (she didn't), but because it's preferable to what else there is to see in the room, something that thus far has only leaked into her peripheral vision.

Two bodies on the bed—her brother Billy and Amy Lentini, each of them naked. Amy with a GSW to the heart, a single shot. Her body sprawled out, her head almost falling off the bed's left side, a large bloodstain barely visible behind Amy, where she bled out.

And then—

Billy. She fixes on him, her heart drumming furiously, heat spreading across her body as she looks at her twin brother sitting upright on the bed, blood streaked down the right side of his face, his head lolled to the side, his eyes closed and peaceful.

Take away the blood, the wound, and he could just as easily be sleeping. He could do that in a way she never could. She's always had to sleep on her side, a pillow between her legs. Not Billy. He could sleep all night in a chair or sitting up in bed. He could catch some shut-eye in the middle of geometry class without making a single sound, without snoring or jerking or anything that would give him away—he could sleep in secret just as he could live in secret, just as he could do just about anything in secret. He could hide his fears, his emotions, his thoughts, his sorrows behind that implacable, genial expression of his. She was the only one who knew that about him. She was the only one who understood him.

You're just sleeping, Billy.

Please. It's me, Billy, c'mon. Pop open those eyes and say, "Surprise!"

Please be sleeping.

"Too early to know, of course," Wizniewski says to her father. "Sure looks like Detective Fenton walked in—on this, on them—and opened fire. Billy shot back. They killed each other. A fuckin' shoot-out at the OK Corral right here in the bedroom."

"Ah, Jesus."

No, Patti thinks to herself. *That's not what happened here.*

Her legs giving out, her head dizzy. An arm pulling her away, her father, and just as much as she dreaded seeing Billy, even more so now she dreads taking her eyes off him.

Her father pulls Patti back into the main room. The officers all stop what they're doing and stare at father and daughter as if they were museum exhibits.

Behind Patti, medical personnel slip past and head into the bedroom with body bags.

Body bags. She can't stomach the thought.

"We do this by the book," her father says to the room. "That's my son in there, yes, but he was a cop. Before anything else, he was a cop. A damn fine one. Honor him and Detective Fenton by doing this case right. By the book, people. No mistakes. No shortcuts. Be at your best. And get me—"

Her father chokes up. Solemn nods all around. Patti's chest is burning, so hot she struggles to breathe.

"Get me a solve," her father finishes. "Solve this crime."

Suddenly feeling claustrophobic, Patti turns and heads for the door. *This isn't real,* she decides. *This didn't happen.*

"Oh, my God."

Just as she's at the door, she hears the words. Not from her father. Not from any of the officers in the main room.

From the medical personnel in the bedroom.

"We have a pulse! We have a pulse!" the man shouts. "This one's still alive!"

THE PAST

THREE

DETECTIVE BILLY Harney rubbed his hands, his breath lingering, frozen, in front of him, a wispy reminder of how cold Chicago can be in the middle of March. Three hours was long enough inside the SUV. He hated stakeouts. Even though this one was his idea. His case.

It started with a dead undergrad, a junior at U of C. The area around the campus—Hyde Park—had some rough spots, and everyone chalked up the murder to urban violence. But they didn't know what Billy knew from a download of the data on her cell phone—that this young woman made money in her spare time as an escort. She worked through an Internet site that was taken down the day after her death, but her text messages indicated that she had one particular client who had some unusual needs and was willing to pay top dollar for them.

In a nutshell, he liked to choke her during sex.

He was a trader, married with kids, who made more money in a week than Billy made in two years. The kind of guy who could buy an army of top-shelf lawyers to defend him. Billy wanted this asshole to drop his guard, to relax, so he leaked some news that a suspect was in custody for the undergrad's murder, that it looked like another garden-variety attack in Hyde Park. And then Billy followed the scumbag trader.

Precisely one week ago, at 9:00 p.m., the trader entered the brownstone down the street. Billy got him on video but wasn't sure what was happening inside, so he laid low. A little recon work told him that this place was a high-rent brothel.

So assuming that this guy had a regular appointment—and Billy was willing to lay down good money that he did—tonight should be the night. Catch him with his pants down and offer a simple trade: no arrest for the prostitution if you answer a few questions about a dead undergrad. Billy could take it from there. Always better to start a Q and A with the subject sweating his ass off and eager to please.

He pushed back the sleeve of his overcoat and checked his watch. Half past eight. He blew warm air into his hands.

"Sosh, how we doin'?" he said into his radio to Soscia, the cop in one of the other vehicles, two blocks down, staking out the brownstone from the east.

The response came through Billy's wireless earbud. "Ready, willing, and able," Sosh said. "Just like your sister."

"My sister wouldn't touch you with a six-foot pole. And neither would Stanislowski."

"Who the fuck is Stanislowski?"

"A six-foot Pole."

"Harney, get back in the car." This from his partner, Katherine Fenton, sitting in the warm car just next to him.

"Sosh, how's your rook holding up?" Soscia had a

new detective working with him, a nice kid named Reynolds. "You know I bought him lunch today."

"Yeah, I fuckin' know. He said putting extra pinto beans on the burrito was your idea. And I've been stuck in this truck with him for three hours."

Billy smirked. Stakeouts weren't *all* bad. "Hey, Crowley, you still awake?"

The third car, Crowley and Benson.

"Yeah, just dyin' from all this excitement. How many cops does it take to rope one lowlife?"

Sosh and Crowley had both raised that point. But this was the hoity-toity part of town, the Gold Coast, and he didn't need any mistakes. He wanted old hands like Sosh and Crowley on this.

"What, Crowley, you got somewhere better to be? I know your old lady isn't home, 'cause she's in the car with Sosh right now."

"Well, then, Sosh won't be getting no action, neither."

It was freakin' cold out here. Ten minutes out of the car and he felt the sting in his toes. "Hey, Fenton," he said to his partner. "What do you call a clairvoyant midget who escapes police custody?"

He opened the passenger door and climbed into the warm SUV. Detective Fenton—Kate—shot him a sidelong glance.

"A small medium at large," said Billy.

Sosh liked that one. Kate not so much.

"Hey." Billy stiffened in his seat. "Two o'clock. Our first action."

"Right." Kate talked into her radio. "White male traveling northbound on Astor in a brown coat, brown cap."

Katie, Billy thought to himself, *always so intense, so*

keyed up. He's the only person out here walking; they can probably spot him.

But he let it go. Telling Kate to calm down was like throwing a match on a pool of gasoline. "You got him, Crowley?"

"Aw, yeah. He's smilin' nice and pretty for the camera."

"I know that guy," said Fenton. "Right? That's that guy from that show."

"What show—"

"That show—that movie-critic thing...*Front Row* or something."

"Right." He'd seen it. *The Front Row with*... couldn't place the name. "We should arrest him for that alone."

"Yeah, it is—that's him," said Sosh. "Brady Wilson."

They sat tight as the film critic waltzed up the steps of the brownstone. Before he pressed the buzzer, a man in a dark suit opened the door and ushered him in.

"Fancy," said Crowley. "Do we think he's here for business?"

"Definitely," said Billy. "One guy owns all three floors. He claims to live there, but I haven't seen any signs of anyone living there since I started sitting on it. Three floors, probably eight or ten bedrooms."

"So this could be a real party we got going on."

"Maybe we should call in Vice," said Billy, knowing the reaction he'd receive.

"Fuck Vice," said Katie. "This is ours."

"Jesus Christ," said Sosh. "Jesus H. Christ on a popsicle stick."

"Talk to me, Sosh."

"You're never gonna believe who just walked past me. Crowley, you guys got video on this?"

"Roger that, we've got—holy mother of God."

"Will you guys tell me already?"

Billy wished he had a high-powered scope. He wasn't expecting this. He fished binoculars from the backseat and trained them on the steps of the brownstone as an elderly man trudged up toward the front door.

"Well, well, well," said Billy. "If it isn't His Excellency the Most Reverend Archbishop Michael Xavier Phelan."

"Lord, he is not worthy; Lord, he is not worthy."

Billy couldn't decide if he was excited or disappointed. His partner, Kate, had made up her mind—she was all in. This had just become a heater case.

"Everyone take a breath," said Billy. "He's probably just going in to hear confession."

A black SUV, not very different from the one Billy was in at the moment, pulled up at the curb outside the brownstone. The windows were tinted, as best as Billy could tell through binoculars in poor light. That was odd, because tinted windows were a no-no in this state, with only limited exceptions.

Exceptions such as vehicles that transport government officials.

Billy moved his binoculars down to the license plate, then back up.

"Oh, shit," he said. "I better call the Wiz."

"Why?" Kate asked, almost bouncing out of her seat.

Billy shook his head.

He said, "Because the mayor of Chicago just got out of that car."

FOUR

BILLY CLIMBED into the sedan a block away from his stakeout point. The car reeked of cigar smoke. Wizniewski carried that odor on him at all times.

The Wiz turned his round face toward Billy. "How many inside?"

"We've seen twelve people go in," said Billy. "No two of them at the same time. Like it's all synchronized, so nobody sees anyone else. As discreet as discreet gets. Seven of them we can't ID. One of them is my suspect in the undergrad's murder, the trader. One of them is this film critic who has a TV show, Brady Wilson. Another is a male black who Sosh's partner says is some rapper named Chocolate Q."

"The fuck does *that* stand for?"

Billy looked at the Wiz. "When I arrest him, I'll ask him."

Wizniewski rubbed his eyes. "And you're sure about the archbishop?"

"Positive."

"And the..." Wiz's lips came together to make an *m* sound, but he couldn't bring himself to say the word.

"It's the mayor. No question. His security detail dropped him off but didn't go inside. The car is parked down the block. How we doin' on numbers?"

"I have ten uniforms ready to assist on my call," said the Wiz.

Ten plus the six detectives should be enough.

"You don't have to do this," said Wizniewski. "You know that."

He meant that Billy didn't have to arrest everybody. He could do what he came there to do—arrest the suspect in the undergrad's murder and avert his eyes to anything else.

You chickenshit. The Wiz was always thinking of tomorrow, always looking to climb the ladder, always playing office politics. This thing could fall either way, Billy realized. The police superintendent, after all, was appointed by the mayor. The supe might not be too happy about the mayor getting bagged; if the mayor went down, he might, too. Billy could get a gold star on his report card for this or he could see the effective end of his advancement in the department. And the Wiz could, too. This could be the best thing that ever happened to their careers or it could be the worst thing. A guy like the Wiz, always weighing the political consequences, avoided risks like this.

But Billy wasn't wired the same way as the Wiz. He kept it simple. It came down to three words for him—*Do your job*. Any consideration beyond that made you lose your edge. It blurred your focus and made you less than the cop you were supposed to be.

Do your job. He had probable cause to believe a crime was in progress, and that was all that mattered.

"Are you calling me off?" Billy asked.

"No, no." The Wiz drew a line in the air. "Absolutely not."

Absolutely not, because that would be even worse for the Wiz, telling a detective not to investigate a crime because it involved a high-ranking public official. That could mean dismissal from the force, maybe even criminal charges. The Wiz was far too cautious a politician to ever let something like *that* go on his record.

"Everything you do from this moment on will be carefully scrutinized," said the Wiz. "Reporters, BIA, the IG, defense lawyers—everyone's gonna put you under a magnifying glass. You get that, right? I'm just saying it's okay with me if you don't wanna push this. If you wanna stick with the murder suspect and leave everything else alone. We're not Vice cops. We don't make a habit of arresting johns and hookers."

Billy didn't respond, just waited him out.

"You fuck this up," said the Wiz, "it could be the last arrest you ever make. It could tarnish your father. And your sister. You could get into all kinds of hot water over this. You don't need it, Billy. You got a bright future."

When it was clear his speech was finished, Billy turned to the Wiz. "Can I go do my job now?"

The Wiz dismissed him with a scowl and a wave of the hand.

Billy got out of the car into the sting of the cold air and headed for the brownstone.

FIVE

BILLY AND his partner, Detective Kate Fenton, approached the black SUV parked by the corner, the one carrying the mayor's security detail. Billy approached the driver's-side door, his star in hand.

The tinted window rolled down. A burly middle-aged man turned toward the detectives as if annoyed.

"You're parked in front of a fire hydrant," said Billy.

"We're security for the mayor."

"That exempts you from traffic laws?"

The man thought about that answer for a minute. "You want we should move?"

"I *want* you and your team to step out of the car."

"Why do we have to get out of the car?"

"You have to get out of the car," said Billy, "because a police officer told you to."

The back driver's-side window rolled down. "I'm Ladis," the man in the back said. "Former CPD."

"Good. You can explain to your friends the importance of obeying a lawful police order."

It took a moment, but all three men emerged from the car. Billy settled on the former cop, Ladis. "How do you contact the mayor? Or how does he contact you?"

Ladis didn't like the question but reluctantly answered. "He hits the Pound key twice on his phone, or we do the same."

"Who has that phone?"

Ladis looked at the others. "The three of us and the mayor."

"Give me your phones. All three of them."

"Can't do that."

Billy stepped closer to Ladis. "We're taking down that brownstone," he said. "And we don't need anyone getting advance notice. Hand over the phones or I'll arrest you for obstruction, failure to obey, and whatever else I can think of between now and when we pull you up to Area 2 with about a dozen reporters waiting."

Ladis found that reasoning persuasive, so he and the others handed over their phones. A young officer in uniform jogged up to the SUV. Billy said, "This officer's gonna stay with you in the car. He's gonna be upset if any of you try to use any form of communication. Text, e-mail, phone call, anything at all. Just sit in the car and listen to the radio. You get me?"

"I get you," said Ladis.

"And one more thing," said Billy. "Lemme borrow your coat."

Billy approached the brownstone and started up the stairs. He hit the buzzer and waited.

"Hello?" A voice through the intercom.

"Mayor's security detail," Billy said, making sure the emblem on his coat was front and center for any cameras that might be watching. "I need to talk to him."

"The mayor isn't here."

"We drove him here, dumbass. I need to speak with him."

The light in the foyer came on. A tall, wide man in a

suit approached the door. There was a bulge in his jacket at the hip. He was armed. And he probably didn't appreciate being called a dumbass.

The man opened the door slightly. "Why don't you call him?" he said.

"See, that's the problem," Billy said as he leaned in and pushed the door fully open. He stepped forward and drove a quick jab into the man's exposed throat. He expelled a wet choking noise before losing the capacity to make any noise at all.

"Green, green," Billy called into the radio attached to his collar while simultaneously seizing the big man, throwing him up against the railing of the stairs and keeping the door propped open with his foot.

The other detectives, followed by blue suits, swarmed up the stairs.

"Keep your hands on the railing, feet apart," said Billy before handing the big guy over to one of the uniforms. "He has a piece on his left hip."

And a sore throat.

Billy led the way inside. The lighting was dim, and the air smelled of incense. A staircase led up to the second floor. Next to it was a door to what looked like a closet. The faint sound of music—a thumping bass—came from below.

"Crowley," said Billy, "clear the main floor. Sosh—"

From behind a curtain straight ahead, a man emerged, holding a shotgun upright. Before Billy could yell *Police—don't move,* Katie was on him. She braced the shotgun, kneed the guy in the balls, then, when the man bowed forward in pain, drove her other knee into his midsection. The man crumpled to the ground with nary a sound, Katie triumphantly holding the shotgun.

Well, there's that.

Another man came through the curtain—this was like clowns in a circus car—and once again, before Billy could say anything, Katie swung the butt of the shotgun into the man's face, knocking him backwards off his feet.

Don't fuck with Katie.

Billy directed officers forward and upstairs. He walked over to the door by the staircase and opened it up. It was, in fact, a closet, but an odd one. There was no horizontal bar for hanging coats. Nothing on the floor. No hooks, even.

But the thumping bass was more audible.

Billy stepped into the closet, placed his hand against the back wall, and pushed. It gave immediately. A false wall. This was the door to the garden level.

Billy motioned for some uniforms to follow him. He took the stairs down to the lower level slowly, his gun raised, the music pounding between his ears.

Wondering, *Did they hear the commotion upstairs?*

But he thought not. It seemed like the place was soundproofed.

The music was loud, the female singer's voice sultry, almost a moan over the pounding bass. Billy hit the bottom stair and spun, gun raised.

The lighting was dim, a purplish glow. A stripper pole in the center of the room, a lithe, naked woman working it, upside down, her legs interlocked around the shiny steel beam. Around her on all sides, women in various stages of undress or erotic costumes—naughty nurse, Catholic schoolgirl, dominatrix—and men, some in costumes, all of them wearing masks of some kind to obscure their faces.

Caught up in their fantasies, nobody noticed him

right away. The bartender, at three o'clock, was the first one, and he was a threat, obscured behind a small bar.

"Police—don't move!" Billy shouted, his gun trained on the bartender. The bartender showed his hands as Billy shuffled toward him.

And then it was chaos—Billy's team behind him, shouting commands, forcing everyone to the floor. The participants had nowhere to go; their only exit was cut off by the police, and none of them was in a position to challenge the authority of a half dozen cops with firearms trained on them.

Billy counted six men. Twelve had entered the brownstone.

"Crowley, how we doin'?" he called into his radio.

"Main level clear. Fenton took care of the only two goons."

"Sosh, the top floor?"

"All clear. Only one up here's the manager."

Twelve men had entered the brownstone, not including the three oafs they had subdued. They weren't upstairs or on the main floor. So where were they?

Then he noticed another door in the corner of the room.

SIX

BILLY PUSHED the door open. It was thick, as was the wall—more soundproofing, he figured. It would make sense for a sex club…or whatever the hell this was.

He walked into a long hallway with three doors on each side.

Six more men to find, six bedrooms.

He signaled Sosh, Katie, and some uniforms into the hallway, everyone taking a door. Everyone with guns drawn, the detectives with their stars hanging from their necks.

Billy gave a nod, and all at once, six members of the Chicago Police Department kicked in six different doors.

"Police—don't move!" Billy said, entering a dark room illuminated only by the glow of the street lamp outside. He saw movement on a bed. He flicked on the light and yelled his command again. Two people scrambling to cover themselves, naked, the man on top of the woman. But unarmed. They posed no threat, other than to their own dignity.

The woman looked young. Very young. Possibly underage.

The man was three times her age.

"On the floor! Both of you! Facedown on the floor."

They complied. Billy cuffed the man behind his back. "Miss, how old are you?"

"Twenty-two," she said, her voice shaky.

He didn't really want to, but he cuffed her as well. "You're twenty-two like I'm the king of Spain. And you, sir, what's your name?"

"What?"

"What is your name, sir?"

"My name is…John Barnes."

Billy squatted down next to him. "John Barnes, you say?"

"Yes…yes."

"Okay. My mistake. For a minute there I thought you were Archbishop Phelan. But this city's highest-ranking member of my church wouldn't be soliciting a prostitute. Especially one who, it seems to me, is underage. Because that's worse than a prostitution beef. That's statutory rape."

"Oh, no. Oh, God. Oh, God, help me…"

"Yeah, so good thing you're John Barnes instead."

Billy backed up and peeked out into the hallway. By now it was filled with police. He motioned over a uniform to secure his room.

Detective Soscia, stepping out of another room, nodded to Billy. "The mayor wants to speak with the man in charge," he said, a smile spreading across his face.

Billy popped his head inside. The mayor, Francis Delaney, was sitting upright against the bed, a sheet wrapped around his waist, his hands cuffed behind him, what remained of the hair atop his head sticking nearly straight up. His ruddy complexion was flushed, maybe from the sex but more likely from the humiliation that was quickly enveloping him.

"You're the detective in charge?" the mayor asked.

"I am."

"Could you close the door?"

Billy shrugged. "I could, but I won't. You already had your jollies tonight. And no offense, but you're not my type."

The mayor didn't see the humor in Billy's remark. "This is... this is a sensitive situation."

"For one of us it is."

"Well—I was wondering if I could get any consideration here."

"Consideration? I *consider* you a moron for putting your job in jeopardy for some cheap thrills. I *consider* you a selfish asswipe for betraying the people who elected you. Will that do it?"

The mayor dropped his head. "I'm a good mayor for this city. I am."

"You mean when you're not cutting coppers' pensions to balance the budget?"

The mayor looked up, sensing an opening. "Maybe we should talk about that," he said.

"Sure. Let's grab coffee sometime."

"No. I mean—maybe that's something you and I could work out right now."

Billy squatted down so he was face-to-face with the mayor. "Are you saying if I let you walk, you'll change your position on our pensions?"

The mayor, ever the politician, his chubby, round face gaining fresh color, looked hopefully into Billy's eyes. "Well, what if I *did* say that?" he asked.

"If you said that," said Billy, "I'd arrest you for attempted bribery, too."

Billy left the room and found Sosh, a sheen of sweat across his prominent forehead, jacked up over the night's events. "And here I thought this would be a boring stakeout," he said. "Wanna go meet the manager of this place? She makes Heidi Fleiss look like a Girl Scout."

SEVEN

BILLY SPENT the next hour overseeing the cleanup. Making sure the scene downstairs was captured on video, getting each arrestee on camera, processing names (shockingly, several people gave false ones), and beginning the search for records inside the brownstone.

Once the arrestees were all inside the paddy wagon and the uniforms had their marching orders, Billy found himself with Sosh on the main floor.

"The manager," Billy said. "Let's go see her."

Coming down the stairs, just as they were heading up, was Goldie—Lieutenant Mike Goldberger, Billy's favorite person on the force, his "rabbi," his confidant, one of the only people he truly trusted.

"*There* you are," Goldie said, slapping his hand into Billy's. "Big night for you. Just wanted to say congrats. Thought you'd be up there taking the praise."

"Up there?"

"Oh, yeah. The deputy supe's up there."

"He is?"

"Sure. This thing is spreading like wildfire. The Wiz is making it sound like he spearheaded the whole thing. You'd think it was a one-man show starring him."

"What a prick," said Sosh.

"Get up there," said Goldie. "Get some spotlight. I tried to throw your name in there, but the Wiz has sharp elbows. Congrats, again, my boy."

Gotta love Goldie. Billy and Sosh headed upstairs.

On the top floor, as Goldie said, the deputy superintendent of police was beaming widely, shaking the Wiz's hand, the other hand clapped on the Wiz's shoulder. The deputy supe was passed over for the top job by the mayor, so he wouldn't be the least bit unhappy at seeing the mayor get pinched. No cop would be after the mayor tried to cut police pensions.

The Wiz nodded at Billy and Sosh but didn't say anything, didn't acknowledge them to the deputy supe. Sosh mumbled something unflattering under his breath, but Billy didn't really care. *Do your job*. Keep it simple.

They passed by an office, and Billy stopped briefly and looked in. It was immaculate—a beautiful maple desk with several stacks of papers, neatly organized, on top. But no computer. Kate was in there with a number of uniforms, searching the place high and low, opening every cabinet, leafing through the pages of books on the shelves, pulling back the carpet, everything.

"How we doin'?" Billy called out.

Katie walked up to him. "You know the Wiz is over there taking all the credit for the bust."

Billy shrugged. "Did you find anything in the office?"

She shook her head. "No records. No computer. The paper shredder's even empty. There's a lot of cash, but that's it."

Not terribly surprising. Computer records were almost as bad as e-mails and text messages—once created, they could never be truly erased. These guys were pros. They would have records, of course, but only of the pencil-and-paper variety.

"No little black book?" Billy asked.

Katie shook her head. "No little black book. There's gotta be one. But it's not here."

Billy nodded toward the next room. "Let's go meet the manager."

They moved one room over, where Crowley was sitting with a woman who didn't look very happy. She was a nice-looking woman, middle-aged, thin, with bleached blond hair. She was wearing a sharp blue suit.

"Meet Ramona Dillavou," said Crowley, who looked like he was up past his bedtime, which he probably was. "She's the manager of this place. Isn't that right, Ramona?"

"Fuck you," she said, crossing her arms. "I don't have to say shit to you."

"I read her her rights," said Crowley, rolling his eyes. "I have a feeling she already knew 'em."

Billy approached the woman. "Where's your computer?" he asked.

"I don't have to answer that."

"I'm gonna find it anyway. Better if you tell me." Billy removed a small pad of paper from his inside pocket, a pen clipped to it. "I'll even make a note that you were cooperative. And I'll draw a smiley face next to it."

"Fuck you," she said.

"Then how about your book?"

"Which book is that? My Bible?"

"C'mon." Katie kicked a leg on the woman's chair, turning her slightly askew. "Tell us."

"I don't have a computer. I don't have a book."

"Listen, lady," Katie said.

"My name's not Lady. My name's Ramona. And I'll call you cop slut."

Sosh bit his knuckle. Katie was not the right gal to piss off.

"Never mind," said Ramona. "You probably couldn't even get a cop to fuck you."

Billy winced. Sosh squeezed his eyes shut.

"I see your point," said Katie. "On the other hand…"

Katie slapped the woman hard across the face, knocking her from the chair.

"That was my other hand," she said.

Billy inserted himself between Katie and the woman, now on the floor. "Get some air," he said to Katie.

"I'll fucking sue!" Ramona cried. "I'll sue your slut ass!"

Billy offered his hand to the woman. She gave him a long glare before she took it and got back in the chair. "Ramona," he said, "we can tear this place apart looking for it, or you can tell us where it is and we won't have to. Now, I know you have a boss. You think he's gonna be happy with you if you make us break through walls and rip up carpets?"

A little good cop, bad cop. It was only a cliché because it was true.

Ramona, still smarting from the slap, a sizable welt on her cheek, shook her head as if exhausted. "You're not gonna find a little black book," she said.

"We'll search your house next. We'll have no choice."

"I want a lawyer," she said.

Et voilà! Thus endeth the conversation.

"Keep the uniforms here until they find it," said Billy to Sosh. "Let's find a judge and get a warrant for her house. We'll find that little black book sooner or later."

EIGHT

A BIG bust, so a big night out to follow. Billy and Kate went to the Hole in the Wall, a cop bar off Rockwell near the Brown Line stop. A couple of retired coppers bought the Hole ten years ago, cleaned it up, got word out about giving cops discounts on drinks, and the place thrived from day one. A few years ago they set up a stage in the corner and put up a microphone and sponsored an open-mike night that was so popular it turned into a regular thing. Now the place drew more than cops and the badge bunnies who followed them; some people came for the comedy. A lot of people, Billy included, thought this place rivaled the comedy clubs on Wells Street.

When Kate and Billy walked in, they were greeted like royalty. The two of them were quickly separated in the rugby scrum, everyone grabbing Billy, slapping him on the back, putting him in a headlock, lifting him off his feet with bear hugs, messing up his hair, shoving shots of bourbon or tequila in front of him—which he accepted, of course, because he wouldn't want to be rude. By the time he and Kate had found a table, he was half drunk, his hair was mussed like a little kid's, and he was pretty sure he'd pulled a muscle or two.

"I think they heard about the arrests," he said to Kate, who was similarly disheveled.

Two pints of ale appeared in front of them on the tall table, with a stern direction that their money was "no good here tonight." Billy raised the pint and took a long swig, savored it. Yeah, it was a big night. The reporters were all over it. The archbishop? The mayor of Chicago? Too big for anyone to pass up. Half the cops in the joint right now were passing around smartphones, reading news articles and Facebook and Twitter posts. The mayor hadn't been friendly to the cops' union or to their pensions, so nobody was shedding a tear over his downfall. The archbishop—that was another story. Some people were upset, especially the devout Catholics on the force, of whom there were many, while others used the opportunity to rain some cynical sarcasm down on the Church, some of which bordered on the politically incorrect. Several cops noted that at least this time, a priest was caught with a female, not an altar boy.

Kate was enjoying herself. She was an action junkie, much more so than Billy. If you gave that woman a desk job, she'd put a gun to her head within the hour. She enjoyed detective work, but she really enjoyed the busts, the confrontations, the thrill of the moment. She became a cop for the right reasons, the good-versus-evil thing, but it was more than that for her. It was a contact sport.

He looked at her standing by the table they'd secured, her eyes up on the TV screen in the corner, which was running constant coverage of the arrests. She was wearing a thin, low-cut sweater and tight blue jeans. She cut quite a figure. She'd been a volleyball star at SIU and, more than ten years later, still had her athletic physique. The tae kwon do and boxing classes she took probably helped, too. So did the half marathons she ran. Sometimes Billy got tired just thinking about all the stuff Kate did.

But not tonight. He wasn't tired. He was buzzing, like Kate, from the arrests. He always told himself that one arrest was like another—do your job, regardless—but he couldn't deny himself a small thrill after the action tonight.

People kept coming up to him, offering their congrats and their jokes about the mayor and archbishop, which grew cruder as the booze continued to flow. At one point he turned toward Kate and saw Wizniewski, the Wiz, with his arm around her and whispering into her ear. Kate had a smile planted on her face, but Billy knew her as well as anyone did. He could see from her stiff body language and forced grin that she would sooner have an enema than deal with the Wiz's flirtation.

Oh, the Wiz. The same guy who tried to talk Billy down from executing the arrests in the first place, the politician who was afraid that this bust might upset the status quo, who turned around and took full credit with the deputy superintendent, and here he was yucking it up with the brass as if he were just one of the guys.

"There you are. The man of the hour."

Mike Goldberger—Goldie—in the flesh. Goldie was a pretty low-key guy who, unlike Billy and his pals, didn't do a lot of drinking and carousing, so it was unusual to see him at the Hole.

"Don't get too drunk," he said, wagging a finger at Billy. "You could be part of a presser tomorrow."

It had occurred to Billy that the press conferences

would continue over the next few days, but he was pretty sure Wizniewski would be the one standing behind the police superintendent, not him.

"How you feelin' about everything?" Goldie asked. "Tonight. The bust go okay?"

Billy nodded. "I think so. Pretty by-the-book. No question I had PC."

"Okay." Goldie didn't seem surprised. Probable cause to search was a low barrier. "Nothing unusual?"

"The mayor tried to bribe me."

Goldie recoiled. "Seriously?"

"Well, he was on his way to it. He said maybe we could work on that pension problem we have. Maybe, if I let him walk out the back door, he'd change his mind on cutting our cost-of-living adjustments."

"You shoulda said yes," Goldie said with a straight face.

"I tried to work in some free Hawks tickets for myself."

"Don't even..." Goldie drew him close. "Don't even joke about that."

"I know, I know."

"I know you know, but—Billy, seriously. This could get ugly." He lowered his chin, looked up at Billy. "Some of the city's most powerful people got mud splashed on 'em tonight, and if you haven't noticed, people with power don't like to let go of it. They'll do whatever they have to do. They'll go after whoever they have to go after. Including the cops."

"Fuck 'em."

"I'm already hearing questions," he said. "Questions about the inventory of evidence. Questions like 'Where's the little black book?' How could that have disappeared?"

"We searched that house top to bottom. There isn't—"

"Christ, *I* know that, Billy. I'm on your side."

That much Billy knew. Goldie had been Billy's guardian angel since he joined the force. Maybe Goldie was overreacting. But he had a nose for this kind of thing in the department.

"Watch yourself," Goldie said, whispering into Billy's ear. "From here on out, drive the speed limit. Help little old ladies across the street. Rescue drowning puppies from Lake Michigan."

He gave Billy a firm pat on the chest.

"You're under a magnifying glass, my friend," he said. "Don't give anyone a reason to burn you."

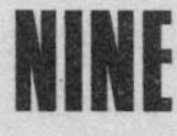

NINE

PATTI HARNEY watched her brother Billy stumble toward the makeshift stage in the corner of the Hole in the Wall. He was the man of the hour, though he didn't seek out the spotlight. He never did. She couldn't remember one time in their lives when Billy tried to call attention to himself or bragged or promoted himself. The attention just seemed to come naturally. People gravitated to her twin brother in a way they never did to her.

A couple of cops practically pushed Billy to the microphone. He wasn't at his best tonight—a half dozen shots of bourbon and a handful of beers was probably a low estimate—but everything Billy did seemed effortless. Like this, for example: grabbing a mike and telling jokes off the top of his head. Patti would be absolutely terrified of doing something like that, but Billy had a what-the-fuck attitude about the whole thing. Did they really come out of the same birth canal seven minutes apart?

"I'm Harney," Billy said into the mike as the crowd quieted. "You know you got to laugh sometimes. Or you'll go fucking nuts in this town. Let's do a little laughing."

"You the man!" said one of the cops standing just a

few feet away from Billy, a patrol officer who worked the West Side, a man who looked like he doubled as a bodybuilder. Billy waved the guy up on stage. Whatever the burly officer might have been wearing when he arrived at the bar earlier tonight, he was now down to a tight white undershirt that showed off his ripped muscles and his shiny bald head.

Billy put his arm around the guy. "I'd like to thank Mr. Clean for coming tonight," he said.

The crowd roared. Some of the younger cops probably didn't get the reference.

"Mr.—can I call you Mr.? Mr. here has been fighting grime in this city for decades."

How does he improvise like that? Patti wondered. She made her way through the crowd and found Detective Katherine Fenton, who was standing by a tall table, laughing and watching her partner up on stage.

"Hey, Kate," said Patti.

Kate's expression broke just slightly, betraying her reaction before she recovered and smiled vaguely. "Hi, Patti."

On the surface, Katherine Fenton was a good partner for Billy. They smoothed out each other's edges. Kate was intense and aggressive, while Billy was laid-back, less defensive, more self-assured, always searching for the humor in a situation.

But Patti and Kate—they'd never hit it off. It was hard for Patti to pin down why. Patti was always polite with Kate, never spoke a harsh word to her. She couldn't name one thing she'd ever done that would make Kate dislike her.

This was what she figured: somehow, in some way, it had become a competition between them over Billy.

Kate wanted to be closest to Billy, but she couldn't because of his twin sister.

You'll never know him like I do, Kate. It will never happen.

"Congrats on the big night," she said to Kate.

"Thanks," Kate said, her eyes still on the stage.

"I go to church at least once a month to seek absolution for my sins," said Billy to the audience. "Tonight was the first time a *priest* confessed to *me*."

The crowd liked that—big whoops and exaggerated groans. Everyone liked Billy. He played to the crowd well. He was playing to his phone, too, perched upright on a stool on the stage. Billy recorded his comedy routines on his phone and uploaded them to some Facebook page he shared with a guy named Stewart, whom he'd met at the hospital three years ago, back when Billy went through all that horrible stuff.

God—three years ago? It still felt fresh to her. And look at Billy, still going strong after all that shit, tragedy that would have broken most people. It would have broken *her*. But Billy, he just kept motoring forward with that placid expression, like the entire shitstorm that came his way just slid off him, no problems, no worries.

It changed him. It must have, in ways even Patti couldn't understand. But you could put a gun to Billy's head and he wouldn't let on.

She watched Kate watching Billy and didn't like what she saw. Kate, she had to concede, was drop-dead gorgeous, her reddish-brown hair pulled back, her large green eyes, her hard, athletic body—the kind of beauty that would render her unapproachable to most men. Billy was pretty easy on the eyes, too, tall and well built, with that killer smile that came so naturally. The thought had occurred to Patti more than once that he and Kate could be a thing. But she'd never actually seen either of them flash any sign of that until tonight, until right now, when she was looking into Kate's eyes as she listened to Billy on stage.

Yes, there it was, in her eyes, while her guard was down, while the alcohol tangled with her emotions, while she thought nobody was watching.

But I'm *watching, Kate.*

When Billy was done, he raised his beer in a salute, and everyone applauded. When it died down, Patti put her drink on the table and got close to Kate.

She was so near now that Kate couldn't ignore her without being rude, so Kate reluctantly turned toward Patti, raising her eyebrows.

"Billy's one of the good guys," Patti said.

"He's the best," Kate agreed.

"He's still getting over everything, y'know."

Kate pulled a sip from her bottle of beer and set it down. "I know that."

"You do?"

"Yes, Patti, I do."

"Don't hurt him," said Patti. "Don't hurt my baby brother."

Kate drew back. "What is *that* supposed to mean?"

"You know what it means. And you better know I'm serious." Patti wanted to say more, but she'd had a lot to drink herself, and who knew what might come out of her mouth if she didn't disengage? Her insides burning, she set down her drink and headed straight for the exit.

TEN

BILLY TOOK one of the tables at the back of the bar and considered the beer and the shot of whiskey before him. He couldn't remember the last time he drank so much. Someone had put a plate of fries out, too. He couldn't imagine eating them. The grease would probably make him puke.

Kate dropped down next to him, and he scooted over. The place was dying down now. It was past three in the morning. The place closed at four. It was last call.

"What a fuckin' night," he said to her.

"I know, right?" Kate's hand touched his leg underneath the table.

Her hand...on his leg.

"Hey!" Some drunk guy—in this bar, that was a redundant phrase—plopped down across from them. "What was the mayor like?"

"He was a gentleman throughout the process," said Billy. "He accepted his fate with grace and dignity."

The guy laughed. So did Kate.

Her hand slid upward. Billy was drunk and beaten down, but another part of his anatomy sprung to attention.

"That must have been a thrill and a half, catching him like that," said the guy.

Kate turned to Billy, who wasn't sure what kind of facial expression he was sporting at the moment. "Was it?" she asked, her hand moving farther up his leg. "Was it a thrill, Detective?"

Billy looked into Kate's eyes. There was no misunderstanding. That hand sliding up his leg was no accident.

"I would call it unexpected," he said.

Her hand moving again, getting close to pay dirt in his lap.

"Unexpected in a good way?" she asked. "Or a bad way?"

And...bingo. There it was, Kate's hand finding his main artery, wrapping her hand around it, squeezing it, stroking it.

"It could be bad," he said, watching the guy across from him, the drunk cop who was more interested in the french fries.

"That's true," said Kate, nodding as if nothing was going on beneath the table while she artfully unzipped his pants and slid her hand inside. "It could be *very* bad." Still stroking the throttle. If she kept going like that, it was going to be blastoff.

"I need to take a piss," said the drunk guy, who scooted out of the seat and left them alone.

"Bad can be good sometimes," said Billy. His right hand reached down and found Kate's leg, her blue jeans. At that moment, he wished it had been a skirt. Kate's legs, together under the table, parted, and Billy accepted the invitation, sliding his hand upward.

"If it's just one time," said Kate. "If it's not complicated."

Billy was having trouble breathing now. He wasn't blind. He knew Kate was a knockout. He'd just never let himself go there. She was his partner. He had just closed his mind to it.

But now that barricade was coming down. Of course—of course the thought had passed through his mind. You couldn't look at Kate every day, spend eight-hour shift after eight-hour shift with her, and not have it cross your mind. Look at her.

Which he did. But now he wasn't picturing Detective Katherine Fenton. He was picturing *Kate,* naked, her back arching, her hair in her face, her legs wrapped around his back, a primal moan escaping her lips, her body writhing in response—

"We don't need complications, do we, partner?" she said.

"No...no complications." He could hardly speak he was so aroused. He was about to launch, right here in front of a handful of drunken cops, none of whom seemed to notice, thank God in heaven.

Then they were waving to the rest of the crowd and making their way to the exit.

"Just one time is no big deal," he said.

A row of cabs waiting outside. They got into the first one.

"Not a big thing," he said.

"No?" She put her hand back where it had been when they were sitting in the booth. "It felt pretty big to me."

When the cab sped away from the bar, he was on her, tearing at her clothes, shoving his hand inside her blue jeans, her breath hot in his ear.

Just one time, he told himself. *No big thing.*

ELEVEN

"OH, SHIT. Holy fuck."

Billy stirred in bed, moaned, rolled over, and opened his eyes to a squint, the pain ricocheting through his skull.

"You gotta see this, Harney."

He felt the bed depress, Kate falling onto it. She was wearing running gear, the shirt wet against her chest, her hair pulled back, gym shoes still on.

Figures. Rain or shine, big night of drinking or not, Kate is up at the crack of dawn doing her miles.

"Look at this." Kate held her phone in front of his face.

He could hardly state his own name much less read something off a small screen. The lasers of sheer agony crisscrossing through his brain made him briefly consider whether someone was reenacting a scene from *Star Wars* between his ears.

Then his eyes focused on it, and he concurred with Kate's initial impression: holy fuck.

It was a headline from *ChicagoPC,* an online newspaper-blog—the concepts were merging these days—that covered politics (*P*) and crime (*C*) in Chicago. The byline was credited to Kim Beans, an investigative reporter whom Billy had met on a few unpleasant occasions. *Unpleasant* was an understatement. Kim Beans had the tenacity of a pit bull and the charm of a rattlesnake.

The headline: GREEN BAY PACKERS QB A REGULAR AT SEX CLUB?

Wow, thought Billy. *That didn't take long.*

"Video footage," Kate says. "It says they have video footage of him visiting the club."

"Not last night, though. He wasn't there last night." He read through the article. It said that *ChicagoPC* had "come into possession" of video footage of the starting quarterback from Green Bay walking into that brownstone sometime last summer.

The article also promised that there was more video, of more celebrities, to come.

"This isn't good," Kate said. "It's all going to be about this little black book that we didn't recover. You know they're already asking questions about it, don't you? Wizniewski even said something to me last night, the little prick."

Goldie had said the same thing to Billy. But to Billy, the more interesting question was, who took this video? And why?

"This is bad," Kate said.

"Look on the bright side," said Billy.

"There's a bright side? What's the bright side?"

"This might give the Bears a shot at the NFC North this year."

"Jeez, Billy, you don't see this as a problem?" She directed her finger back and forth between them. "This is going to be your and my fault. We were in charge of the investigation."

"I was in charge," Billy corrected. "It will be my fault."

"But I was in charge of the inventory, the search."

Trying to stop Kate from worrying about something was as easy as trying to stop a freight train at high speed. Kate did everything fast and hard. There was no second gear for her.

"The mayor needs to deflect this," she said. "He needs the story to be about something besides him. He wants it to be about us."

"So," said Billy, "we'll find the little black book today at the manager's house." Last night, after they interviewed the manager of the sex club—Ramona Dillavou—and searched the brownstone without any luck, Billy sent uniforms over to Dillavou's house to seal it off.

"We better." Kate bounced off the bed. "Or we're dead."

TWELVE

"WE'RE DEAD," said Kate.

"We're not *dead*. You're overreacting." Billy peeled off his rubber gloves. He was standing in the foyer of Ramona Dillavou's house in Lincoln Park. Managing a house of prostitution must pay well, because her three-story brownstone on Belden was gorgeous—shiny hardwood floors and expensive artwork, updated fixtures and appliances, a cinema-size TV screen in the basement, complete with rows of the type of chairs you'd find in a movie theater, a master bathroom with a full-size sauna and a shower the size of Billy's living room. This house had everything you could ever want.

Everything, that is, except a little black book.

It could be anything, Billy had said to the officers and technicians assisting in the search. It could be an actual book, or it could be a computer or tablet, or it could be something on a flash drive or an SD card. It could look like a phone directory or an accounting ledger. It could be in code. It could be scribbled in pencil on the back pages of a novel sitting on a bookshelf. It could be anything. It could be anywhere.

But after eight hours, they had found nothing. Ramona Dillavou had an iPad and a personal computer, and the technicians had downloaded the contents of each onto an external hard drive for later review, but an initial examination by one of the techies showed nothing helpful.

Billy chugged another bottle of water. His mouth felt like the Sahara desert. He tried to think strategically, as Ramona Dillavou would. *If I had something valuable like that, something I wanted to keep totally confidential and untraceable but couldn't lose, where would I put it?* The problem was that his thoughts and ideas were navigating through a storm of lightning strikes and clashing cymbals and jackhammers trying to blast through the interior of his skull. The worst hangover ever.

"Oh, this is great. Look at this."

Kate handed Billy her phone, this time displaying an online article from one of the city's mainstay newspapers, the *Chicago Tribune.* Billy scrolled through the headlines, all of them about the arrest.

WILL MAYOR RESIGN?
MAYORAL WANNABES LINING UP
ARCHDIOCESE STATEMENT VAGUE

But amid those stories, this gem:

QUESTIONS RAISED ABOUT POLICE CONDUCT

There wasn't much new in the article. The second half was a cut-and-paste job, a summary of the arrest and all the prominent people busted. But the first three paragraphs said that the mayor had hired a lawyer, a high-powered attorney who served as the nation's attorney general under the first George Bush, who was claiming that the police "turned innocent conduct into criminal behavior and stormed into a private residence without any cause to do so."

Billy smiled and shook his head. His default reaction to bad news. His general view of things, after everything that had happened three years ago, was that he'd taken the worst life had to offer, and everything else had to be put in perspective.

But this was his job, and it mattered to him. It was all he had now. And as much as Kate tended to exaggerate, she wasn't the only one sounding alarms about what might be coming down the road. Mike Goldberger had, too, and Goldie had a sense for things like this more than anyone Billy knew.

"It'll be fine, Kate," Billy said, trying to convince himself as well as her.

And then a buzzing sound in Billy's hand, and on Billy's belt, too, where his own phone was encased. Both of them had received a text message at precisely the same time. Billy felt a chill pass through him.

He handed Kate her phone while he checked his. It only took them a second to read the message and realize that they both got the same thing.

A text from Wizniewski:

Report to 5th flr of Daley Center in 1 hr.

The fifth floor of the Richard J. Daley Center was the principal location of the Cook County state's attorney's office, the top prosecutor of all crimes in Chicago and the county's surrounding suburbs.

Kate looked at Billy. "We're dead," she said.

THIRTEEN

"THE STATE'S attorney will see you now." The man pushed open the blond-wood door. The first thing Billy saw through the picture window in the large corner office was the darkness outside. Then he saw photographs and keepsakes lining the walls—vanity photos, not surprising for a politician.

Then he saw two people in the room: the superintendent of police and the Cook County state's attorney.

The police superintendent, appointed by the mayor, was a man named Tristan Driscoll, whom the mayor had hired away from his previous job running the police department in Newark, New Jersey. Driscoll's brother was a lobbyist and fund-raiser who had raised millions for Mayor Francis Delaney in the last election, so even though the mayor heralded the fact that he was bringing in an "outsider" to "clean house" in the Chicago PD, he was also bringing in the brother of one of the people to whom he was most indebted for winning his reelection. Welcome to Chicago.

Next up, the Cook County state's attorney, Margaret Olson, who had served as an alderwoman for three terms before she decided that she wanted to be the county's top prosecutor. She'd only practiced law for a couple of years, but she won the race after receiving significant support from—take a wild guess—Mayor Francis Delaney.

Aware that many people doubted her qualifications for the job, Margaret Olson decided to be the toughest, most aggressive prosecutor the county had ever seen—never dropping a case, always refusing plea bargains. It quickly earned her the nickname "Maximum Margaret" for her tendency to seek the harshest sentences for all crimes. The judges hated her. Civil rights advocates protested her. Cops didn't appreciate the fact that every single case, no matter how slam-dunk, no matter how small, required their in-court testimony because Margaret wouldn't cut deals. The only people who liked her were defense lawyers, because Maximum Margaret was good for business.

A third person was in the room, a woman, fairly young, probably Billy's age, dressed smartly and focused like a laser on them, staring at Billy so intently that he thought she was trying to read his mind.

If she *could* read his mind, this is what she'd take away:

Superintendent Driscoll is a soulless asswipe. State's Attorney Olson is a political hack who'd indict her own mother if it would boost her favorables by a single percentage point. And both of them owe their positions to the mayor, whom I just humiliated and ruined. And what's your story, gorgeous? Italian, I'm guessing. Maybe Greek, with that silky ink-black hair and those haunting dark eyes. You look like Kate Beckinsale with a law degree. That's the good news. The bad news: you seem about as pleasant as a case of genital warts.

"Detectives," said Margaret Olson, sitting behind

her walnut desk, her graying hair cut short. "You know the superintendent, of course."

Sure, I know Tristan. Hey, Tristan, what the fuck kind of a cop's name is Tristan? Were your parents hoping for a girl?

"Of course," said Billy. Kate only nodded, didn't speak.

"This is assistant state's attorney Amy Lentini," said Olson, nodding to the beauty queen with the steely expression in the corner.

Italian. That was my first guess.

"She handles special investigations for my office. Sit, Detectives, sit."

Billy and Kate took the two seats in front of the desk. They were flanked: the top cop to their left, the top prosecutor dead ahead, and Amy Lentini, the special investigator, to the right.

Okay, Billy thought to himself. *I know you're all eager to thank us for doing a good job last night. Who wants to go first? Raise your hand!*

Billy glanced at Kate, who was visibly shaken. Her reaction prompted one in him. It pissed him off that they were being treated this way, this obvious attempt at intimidation. He felt his protective instinct take over and reached for Kate's hand, but then thought better of it.

"We have some questions for you about last night," said Amy Lentini. "We assume you'll want to help us understand a few things."

That was a nice way to put it, a friendly, we're-in-this-together offer delivered by a woman who looked like she wanted to lop off their heads.

"Why were you there in the first place?" she asked. "The Gold Coast isn't your jurisdiction."

Billy said, "I was investigating a homicide. The one by the U of C campus, the girl who was strangled. I had a suspect. I saw him go into this brownstone the week before, and I sat on the place long enough to figure out that it was some kind of brothel."

"A Vice case," she said.

"Sure, a Vice case, except I didn't like it for a Vice case. I wanted to catch my suspect there."

"Why?"

"Have you ever been a cop, Amy?"

She recoiled. Billy wasn't sure what bothered her more, that he turned the questioning on her or that he used her first name.

"See, Amy," he went on, "when you have a suspect like I had, a guy with all the money in the world, it's easier to get him to talk if you have something on him. If I caught him with a prostitute, I'd have leverage over him."

Amy Lentini opened her hands. "You thought if you caught him with a hooker, he'd up and confess to murder?"

"Okay, so you answered my question."

"What question did I answer?"

"You've never been a cop." Billy sat back in his chair and crossed a leg.

"This will go easier for you if you cooperate," said Tristan Driscoll, the superintendent—Billy's boss, ultimately.

How about you, Tristan—have you *ever been a cop? A real one, I mean?*

Billy coughed into his fist. "If I just hauled this guy in off the street, he'd lawyer up in two seconds flat," he said. "But if the conversation began with him being terrified that his wife and kids would find out about a hooker, I could make him an offer he wouldn't refuse. If he could answer a few questions for me, maybe I would forget about this hooker thing. No, he wouldn't answer the *big* question, the did-you-kill-her question. But I could have made him admit that he knew the girl, that he'd sent her text messages, that kind of thing. I could have started laying the groundwork."

Lentini stared at him, blinking a few times. "And how'd that work out for you? Did your plan work?"

"No," Billy conceded.

"No," she said, mimicking him. "Because your suspect lawyered up right away. Because the media heard about this massive bust—this Vice arrest, made by a *homicide* detective—before he'd even made it to the police station. So this concern he might have had about his wife finding out—that ship had already sailed."

It was true. But once Billy saw all those men go inside the brownstone, he couldn't ignore it. He wasn't *supposed* to ignore it. He was a cop, witnessing a crime in progress.

But Lentini had made her point. Once Billy rounded up all the men and the prostitutes, his plan to interrogate the murder suspect had been blown.

Lentini had him on that point, and everyone in the room knew it.

Billy felt the first chill through his body.

"Let's talk about the little black book," said Lentini.

FOURTEEN

"WHERE IS it?" Amy Lentini asked. Not *Have you been able to locate it? Do you have any leads?* She was saying it as if Billy already knew the answer.

"I don't know," said Billy. "We stripped down the brownstone and the manager's house. We searched her laptop and her iPhone. There must be some record. They'd have to keep a list of clients. Maybe not a book, but a disk, a flash drive, even a pad of notes. There must be something."

"I agree."

"Good," said Billy. "I'm glad we can agree on something."

Lentini didn't think he was funny.

"We have reason to believe it *was* there," she said. "In the brownstone."

"You do? How?"

"We're not at liberty to discuss that."

"You're not at liberty to…" Billy almost came out of his chair. "What does that mean—you're not at liberty to discuss it? I'm the investigating detective. If we have a lead, I need to know about it. We're supposed to be working together."

Lentini didn't answer. The superintendent and state's attorney kept faces of stone.

"What the hell is this?" Billy said, this time popping up from his chair. "Since when does the state's attorney's office not share information with the police department?"

"Since now, apparently," said Kate, speaking for the first time, the color drained from her face.

"It's no longer your case," said Lentini. "You've been removed."

"You don't get to decide that. The state's attorney doesn't—"

"*I* decided," said the superintendent.

Billy looked at Tristan Driscoll, a slow burn coursing through his chest.

"What do you know about that video that surfaced today?" asked Lentini. "The one showing the Packers quarterback visiting the brownstone this summer?"

Billy took a moment to recover, his legs feeling unsteady.

It could be the last arrest you ever make, Wizniewski had warned him.

"I saw the video on that website," he said. "That's all I know."

"Did you *shoot* that video, Detective?"

Billy finally took his eyes off the superintendent, turned back to Lentini. "What the hell are you talking about? Why would *I* shoot that video?"

"Would you consent to a search of your house and personal belongings?"

Billy moved toward the special investigator, who stood as he approached. He faced off with her, almost nose to nose. She was almost daring him to do something, to make a situation that was already spiraling downward worse. He could feel the Irish rising within him, an anger that closed his fists and drew heat to his face.

"Now, why would you want to search my house, Amy?" he hissed.

And then the door to the office opened. Lieutenant Mike Goldberger walked in with another man, a man wearing a suit—a civilian, Billy thought.

What the hell was Goldie doing here?

"I'm sorry to interrupt, Mr. Superintendent, Madam State's Attorney," he said.

The superintendent did not look pleased. "Lieutenant, what in the—"

"I heard about this meeting, and I just wanted to make sure you were properly covered, sir." Goldie motioned to the man next to him. "This is one of our union reps. Since this is an inquiry into a police officer's conduct, obviously the detectives here are entitled to union representation before being questioned. I didn't want there to be any reason for you to come under criticism."

Billy, in spite of everything, couldn't help but smile. Goldie to the rescue, rushing in with the equivalent of a lawyer, but pretending he was doing it for the superintendent's benefit.

"This—Lieutenant, you're out of line," said the superintendent. "And for your information, this is not a police department inquiry."

"Then what *is* it?" asked the union rep, a man on the short side wearing a crew cut and a defiant expression. "Sure looks like an inquiry to me."

"This is an investigation being conducted by the state's attorney's office," said Amy Lentini.

"But with the police superintendent present. Oh, so you tried to circumvent the detectives' right to union representation by technically calling this a *state's attorney's* investigation?"

That's exactly what they did, Billy realized.

"That—no, that wouldn't look so good, either," said Goldie. "That's why I figured it was better to protect you, Mr. Superintendent."

Billy marveled at how Goldie could keep a straight face during all this. *When I grow up, Goldie,* he thought to himself, *I wanna be just like you.*

"Probably better to reschedule," Goldie suggested. "Make sure all our *t*'s are crossed and our *i*'s are dotted."

Driscoll looked at the state's attorney and Lentini.

Billy and Kate walked out with Goldie and the union rep.

"Harney," Amy Lentini called out, following them into the foyer.

Billy stopped and turned. So did Kate.

"You're the comedian, right?" she said. "We'll see how funny you are when I'm done with you."

Kate, who was white as a ghost, decided to answer nonverbally. She gave Amy Lentini the finger.

"That sounds about right," said Billy. He flipped her the bird, too, before they walked out.

FIFTEEN

"THE PLAYOFFS are different," said Sosh, dropping his pint on the table with a splash. "You gotta have a shooter and a goalie. We got Kane, but I'm not so sure about Crawford."

The Blackhawks, the favorite topic in the Hole in the Wall. Detective Soscia was giving Billy a tutorial on the key to winning the Stanley Cup. It was the same lecture he gave Billy last week, but Sosh was too drunk to remember that.

The Hole was jumping, as always. It was colder than a landlord's heart out there, but the coppers wouldn't be deprived of their drink. Cops hung together even more these days because it was becoming an increasingly us-against-them mentality. Especially now with smartphone cameras and videos. For every video someone took of a cop being too aggressive, there were ten they didn't take of cops who had to chase an offender down a dark alley or go through the door on a domestic disturbance with no idea whether someone had a hand cannon waiting for them. It was very easy to judge a cop but not so easy to understand one.

Billy stuck to beer. No shots, no clear liquids—not tonight. Kate was somewhere around here sulking, fearing the worst about what happened last night in the state's attorney's office. But then she always feared the worst, always jumped to the worst-case scenario.

"You should be the coach, Sosh," said Billy, deadpan. "Seriously. You should turn in your badge and coach hockey."

"I don't know enough about the fundamentals," he said, as if Billy were serious.

"That never stopped you from being a cop."

Sosh wasn't listening anymore. "Hey, Romeo," he said, his chin down. "You got a bunny at three o'clock makin' some serious eyes at you."

Billy never really understood the badge bunnies—the women drawn to cops. Why would a woman want to hang with a cop? Cops deal with the dregs, the shit, with death and violence and sorrow all day long. Then they come home, and they're expected to say, *Hi, honey, how was your day? That meat loaf smells delicious!*

That's what Billy told himself, anyway. He'd never get married again.

Billy lifted his pint and looked to his right.

"Other side, Einstein," said Sosh. "Three o'clock."

Billy emptied his pint and set it down. "I think you meant *your* three o'clock. Which is my *nine* o'clock. See? Because we're sitting across from each other. Maybe you should have another pint."

"I gotta piss. If you don't make a move on that bunny, I will. She looks like a fuckin' movie star."

Sosh almost fell off his stool. Billy looked to his left, his nine o'clock.

Yep, a beautiful woman, with her eyes directly on him.

Assistant state's attorney Amy Lentini. Her dark hair pulled back, dressed for a night on the town. She gave him an ambiguous smile. Then she gave him the finger.

He made a point of looking surprised, even turning to look behind him, as though the gesture must have been directed at someone else. Then he looked back at her, placed a hand on his chest. *Me?*

But no, he wasn't going to take the bait. If she was here for him—and she must have been; Amy Lentini wasn't a typical Hole in the Wall gal—she could make the first move.

"The fuck is *she* doing here?"

It was Goldie, looking out for him, as always.

"She thinks I'm a dirty cop," said Billy. "You could appreciate that."

Lieutenant Mike Goldberger started running the Bureau of Internal Affairs a few years back. IA was the least popular branch of the CPD for obvious reasons, but Goldie built a reputation for being fair and straightforward. If you fucked up, you got caught, but nobody got railroaded. He'd never be voted cop of the year, but generally cops respected Goldie for his approach to the job.

"I catch bad cops," he said. "I don't smear good ones. That's the difference between her and me."

"It's not the only difference," said Billy. "She's not losing her hair."

"Don't talk to her," he said. "She's trying to catch you with your guard down."

Billy got up to refill his glass and get one for Sosh, too. "You ever know me to let my guard down?"

"I don't think you know how."

"Exactly," said Billy, but his tongue tripped over the word. Okay, maybe he'd had a few too many. So one more wouldn't make that much difference.

By the bar, he found Kate talking to a group of patrol officers, all men, as always. They were taking turns trying to impress her, sucking in their guts, trying for that one wise comment that would make her swoon into their arms. It wasn't going to work, but Kate could use the distraction, being so worried about everything. At least these guys all were managing to keep their tongues in their mouths.

Kate made eye contact with him and motioned, with her eyes and a nod of the head, in the direction of Amy Lentini. Billy made a zipping motion across his mouth, giving her the same advice that Goldie gave him—don't talk to her.

Goldie was right. She was trying to strike when his guard was down. He shouldn't talk to her. Absolutely not. Goldie was spot-on with that call.

He heard his name, someone calling to him. Then another somebody, and then they were chanting his name. "Har-ney! Har-ney!"

He knew what they wanted. He wasn't really in the mood, but he knew he'd give in sooner or later, and if it was much later, at the rate he was downing the pints, he might not even know his last name.

On his way up to the mike, he passed by her table. She was clapping, along with the rest of the bar.

After I do a few on the mike, he thought, *I'll talk to her.*

SIXTEEN

"BY THE way, I'm sorry I was late tonight," Billy said into the microphone. "There was a hostage situation downtown at the American Bar Association. The ABA was holding its annual convention, and a bunch of guys stormed the place and took all the attorneys hostage. They were pretty tough with their demands, too. They said if they didn't get a million dollars and a plane to Mexico, they'd release one lawyer every hour."

The crowd seemed to like that. Billy took a drink from his pint and set it down, careful not to block his phone, perched on the opposite chair, recording his routine. "Nah—actually, I just came from a cemetery. I was paying my respects to an old friend. On the way back to my car, I saw a tombstone that said, 'Here lies a lawyer and an honest gentleman.' And I thought, y'know, that's really great. I didn't know they could fit two people in one grave."

Lawyer jokes: it was like shooting fish in a barrel.

"I should be nicer," he said. "You can hurt people's feelings. This morning, I yelled at one of the prosecutors at 26th and Cal outside court. I said, 'All lawyers are assholes!' This other guy comes up to me and says, 'Hey, that comment really offended me.' I said, 'I'm sorry. You're a lawyer?' And he said, 'No, I'm an asshole.'"

He could feel his tongue getting furry and his words becoming syrupy, so he put down the mike. He picked up his phone and hit the button that would instantly upload the video to the Facebook page he shared with Stewart.

Stewart, the old man who stayed with him at the hospital all those nights three years ago. It was no time for laughing back then, but later, Billy started visiting Stewart at his nursing home and had him in stitches the whole time. He started uploading all his routines onto their shared Facebook page, which Stewart's granddaughter had taught Stewart to access. She once told Billy that the first thing the old man did every morning was check his computer for a new video.

He got off the stage, his eyesight adjusting again, and found himself heading toward Amy Lentini's table.

"You lost or something?" he said on approach. "Or just slummin' it?"

She smiled. It wasn't a warm smile, but at least it wasn't as cold as the temperature outside.

"I heard there was good comedy here," she said.

He shrugged. "Should I have a lawyer present, Amy?"

"I'm a lawyer," she said. "One's plenty."

"One too many."

"Yeah, I got that drift from your monologue. Very funny, by the way. Your reputation is well deserved." She leaned closer to him. "We don't have to be enemies," she said. "I just want the truth."

Oh, you're gonna "good cop, bad cop" me, Amy? I fucking invented that game.

"And you're sure you know what the truth is?"

"Pretty sure," she said. She put her mouth over the straw in her drink, something colorful, flavored.

That mouth was nice. It was the first time in Billy's life that he wished he were a straw.

She was dressed to kill, too. Overdressed, in fact, for this place.

"Are you checking to see if I'm wearing a wire, Detective?" she asked.

He blinked and looked away. Better not answer that one.

She got off her stool, her purse over her shoulder, her arms out. "Would you like to pat me down?"

Well, aren't you a piece of work? Using every trick in your bag tonight, aren't you?

"So you think I've been videotaping that brothel to blackmail people," Billy said.

That dangerous mouth curved into another smile.

"Why would I do in the mayor? And the archbishop? See, Amy, once you arrest them, you can't really blackmail them anymore. How does that help me?"

"Okay," she said. "Play it your way. And I never said it was you, Detective. Definitely a cop, though."

"Well, I'd like to catch the guy as much as you."

"Who said it was a guy?"

He didn't have an answer for that one. He wouldn't give her one, anyway. She was trying to turn him against his partner, Kate. She was trying to fuck with his mind.

She was enjoying herself, too, with that mischievous smile. What the hell was her angle? She couldn't possibly expect him to up and confess—not that he had anything to confess, but still. What was she hoping for tonight? Those were bedroom eyes she was flashing at him.

He felt heat come to his face. She was good.

He leaned into her ear. Her hair smelled like berries.

"This flirtation thing you're doing, it's not working," he said. "It's not gonna happen, and we both know it."

"Oh, c'mon, Billy, don't be such a pessimist."

He drew back from her. What was with this lady?

"You like to live dangerously, is that it?"

"Same as you," she said, holding eye contact.

"You think I'm bent."

"I know you're bent. And you know what the best part is?"

"Tell me, Amy."

"The best part is you're going to admit it to me. Forty-eight hours, tops, you're going to be spilling everything to me. Either you or Kate. One of you's going to be begging me for mercy. That's a race you don't want to finish second in, Billy."

Billy had given a variation of that speech a hundred times to suspects. *The first one to talk gets the sweetheart deal.*

"You don't know me very well," said Billy.

"Oh, I know you better than you think. There's not a move you can make that I won't see coming."

"You sure about that?" Billy backpedaled, winking at her as he made his way through the crowd. He grabbed his coat and went outside. The air actually felt good, at least temporarily. He stomped his feet and stuffed his hands in his pockets and waited. It wouldn't take long.

A moment later, Amy Lentini came bursting out of

the Hole, looking around urgently until she saw Billy. "Okay," she said. "Where is it?"

"Where's what, Amy?"

"My badge," she said. "It was in my purse. Now it's not."

"Well, I did see a prosecutor's badge over there in that puddle. Could that be what you mean?"

She gave him a hard look, then bent down and fished her badge, encased in leather, out of the slush, holding it up with two fingers. "I'm going to enjoy sending you to Stateville," she said.

"I hear Joliet's nice this time of year." Billy flagged a cab turning onto Rockwell. "Say, Amy," he called to her as she headed back inside.

She turned back to him.

"If you're gonna hit me, you better hit hard," he said.

"And why's that?"

"Because I hit back," he said before climbing into the cab.

SEVENTEEN

BILLY NAVIGATED the winding streets of Hyde Park, near the University of Chicago campus. The U of C was a beacon of prestige, a globally renowned institution with state-of-the-art facilities surrounded by one of the most dangerous neighborhoods in the city. Some of the world's finest minds came here to teach and study, to probe the limits of science and mathematics and law and medicine, but they required security escorts back to their cars so they wouldn't get mugged.

Billy and Kate were still investigating the death of the sophomore who was strangled not four blocks from where they were driving. Billy was trying to re-create her whereabouts on the day of her murder, and they'd made a visit out here to talk to one of the faculty members in the biology department who had sent a few ambiguous text messages to the victim in the week leading up to her death.

It hadn't led them to anything, and they were driving back empty-handed. Kate was still distracted, playing on her phone, pulling up story after story about the sex scandal that threatened to take down the administration of Mayor Francis Delaney, rock the Catholic Church, and oh, by the way, end the careers of Detectives Billy Harney and Katherine Fenton.

"You're gonna go crazy reading that shit," said Billy.

"How can the mayor not resign?" she said, her eyes on her phone.

"He's doing the Bill Clinton shuffle. 'It's just a sex thing. People elected me to do a job, and I'm not gonna let 'em down.' Like he's doing it for us."

"I guess."

"Hey, long as we're down here, let's hit Morry's. I'm so hungry I could eat the crotch out of a leper's undies."

"Morry's? So you can get a Polish?" Kate, consistent with her psychopathic workout regimen, didn't eat fast food if she could help it. The body's a temple and all that.

"For your information, Detective," he said, "I wasn't going to order a Polish sausage."

"No? Then what? A chef salad? A yogurt parfait?"

"I was thinking a double Polish."

"I don't know how you can think about food, anyway." Kate's knees were bobbing, her feet playing a constant beat in the footwell of the Tahoe. She was nervous. She couldn't get this stuff out of her head.

"I gotta keep up my strength so I can vigilantly fight crime," said Billy.

"Doesn't anything ever get to you?"

Billy looked over at her. He knew Kate pretty well, but he wasn't used to seeing this side of her. She was an ass kicker, an adrenaline junkie, and a damn fine-looking one at that. The vulnerable thing played on her a lot differently. For some reason, it seemed to flip a switch inside Billy, make him view her as a completely different person.

Don't start, Harney. Don't even start. That was one time.

"We're gonna be fine," he said. "We didn't do anything wrong."

She let out a bitter laugh. There was a lot in that single grunt, maybe more than he could read. It wasn't always that simple, she was saying. It didn't always matter that you were right. You could still be in the wrong place at the wrong time.

"I'm not going to let anything happen to you, Kate. No bullshit. That's a promise."

She turned to him. They made eye contact. It was brief—Billy didn't want to lose control of the Tahoe on these brutal streets—but meaningful.

Not again, Harney. That was one time.

It was pretty great, sure, but it was one time.

He looked at her again. She was still eyeing him, this time with a lot in her stare.

Okay, the sex was mind-blowing, I admit.

"We keep our secrets, don't we, partner?" she said.

Billy nodded.

"I didn't enjoy seeing those eyes that prosecutor was throwing your way last night. I got a little jealous."

"She's a shark."

"Yeah, but last I checked, you like swimming in deep water."

"A little danger can be fun," he said.

"It can be," she said. "Especially over the lunch hour. Before we're expected back."

No, Harney. Absolutely, positively not.

"Take our mind off things," he said.

"Right."

"Therapeutic and such."

"Exactly. You up for a little therapy?"

Billy changed course, found Lake Shore Drive, sped the Tahoe up toward the Belmont exit.

Kate owned a condo in a building off Lake Shore Drive in the Lakeview neighborhood. It was no more than seven hundred square feet, but it had a killer view of the lake. Today the view was probably beautiful, the lake so serene and majestic—but how would Billy know? He didn't look out the window. They were at it the moment they entered the apartment. He threw off her body armor, pulled up her sweater, unbuttoned her blouse, and ran his hands inside, feeling lace.

Then she was naked, that hard athletic body, her skin radiating heat, sweat on her face, her tongue violent inside his mouth, her breath a powerful mint. She took over from there, her mouth on his nipple, sucking so hard it hurt, then lowering herself to her knees and removing his underwear with her teeth. She didn't need to rev him up any more than he already was—his rpm's were well into the red—but she spent some time down there anyway, her hand caressing the undercarriage, her mouth working the throttle, and goddamn it, he was out of car analogies—

He pulled her to her feet, spun her around, and threw her against the back of the leather couch. It was how they taught him to do an emergency takedown at the academy. She liked it, being bent over the couch, pushing her rear end up against him with an approving, kittenish hum. "Gee, Officer, whatever are you going to do to me?"

This wasn't normally Billy's thing, but what the hell. He landed his open hand on her butt, a good smack.

"Is that the best you can do?" she said. "I've been a very bad girl."

Well, okay—in for a penny, in for a pound. He spanked her again, harder.

"Spank me again."

That sounded like a good idea, so he complied.

"I'm placing you under arrest," he said.

"Then I better spread my legs. So you can check for concealed contraband on my person."

Well, sure, that would be standard protocol.

So he checked, probing between her legs as she let out a low moan like none he'd ever heard.

Dear Penthouse: *I never thought this would happen to me…*

For good measure, he bent down to make doubly sure she wasn't concealing a weapon. She liked that even more, breathing like an animal in heat as he worked his tongue. At this point, she wasn't concealing a single thing.

"Officer," she said, "I think you need to fuck me now."

EIGHTEEN

WELL, THAT was interesting.

Billy looked up at the ceiling in Kate's bedroom. He was so drained and sore that he wasn't sure he could even get out of bed. He knew Kate was a volleyball player and martial-arts aficionada, but he had no idea she was an amateur gymnast, too.

And he got to be the pommel horse.

"Just this one time," she said to him.

"Definitely. Never again."

"Makes things too complicated."

"No question about it. Glad we agree on that."

He looked at her. She looked at him. Neither of them kept a straight face.

"Seriously," he said.

"I'm serious, too."

And then the simultaneous buzzing of their cell phones, an unwelcome alert. Last time they got text messages at the same time, they were being hauled into the state's attorney's office.

Billy checked his phone. *Fuck,* he thought.

"We are so fucked," said Kate, reading her phone.

"Now partner, don't leap to the worst-case—"

"We've been summoned to the supe's office, Harney. You think this is good news?"

He didn't. All the way on the drive, Kate threw out one theory after another, rehashed the whole incident, tried to discern the various motives of the various players in the story. Billy didn't bite. Whatever it was going to be, it was going to be, whether they predicted it accurately or not. He'd learned long ago that when bad news was going to come, it was going to come.

They waited inside the superintendent's suite while Mr. Big Shot was in his office behind a closed door. When the door opened, Amy Lentini peered out.

"The superintendent will see you now," she said, not even pretending that she didn't enjoy it.

Superintendent Tristan Driscoll was in uniform—God only knew why; maybe he wanted to pretend he was a real cop today—and seated behind his desk.

"Detective Harney, Detective Fenton."

He didn't ask them to sit, so they didn't.

"You're being placed on administrative leave with pay, pending the completion of the state's attorney's investigation."

Kate dropped her head. Billy didn't move.

"Surrender your badges."

Kate seemed to be waiting for Billy.

"It was my arrest," said Billy. "Not Kate's. Take my badge. Don't take hers."

Driscoll peered at him, his eyes narrowed. "Surrender your badges," he said.

"I'll surrender it to a cop," he said.

The superintendent turned his head, as though he didn't hear right. "Are you suggesting that I'm not a *cop,* Detective?"

"I'm not suggesting anything," said Billy. "I'm saying it outright."

The blood rushed to Driscoll's face so fast it was like his head had been placed in a microwave. "You want to go for *unpaid* leave, Detective?"

"You don't have cause to put me on unpaid. If you could've, you would've. You try to do that, you'll be embarrassed. We both know it." Billy stepped forward, put his hands on the supe's desk. "You're a politician trying to save his own ass. If the mayor goes down, you're out of a job, too. You're no cop. You're a fucking coward."

Billy dropped his badge down on the desk so hard it popped off the desk and fell to the floor. He watched Kate painfully surrender hers, too, without a word.

"Let me know when you're ready to talk," said Amy Lentini with a gleam in her eye, having the time of her life.

"Oh, I'll be in touch, Amy," he said on his way out. "You can count on that."

NINETEEN

BILLY STOOD inside the coffee shop on Ohio Street, staring at the storefront real estate agency across the street. In the window was a picture of a smiling racially mixed family, the father shaking hands with the agent who just sold them a home with a nice white picket fence, the family about to live happily ever after.

He remembered happily ever after. It didn't end so happily.

Goldie passed by the window, walking carefully on the treacherous sidewalk, still slick with ice, his breath trailing behind him like smoke from an engine.

He walked into the coffee shop and sidled up to Billy without a word.

"Rough day," he said. "Sorry for your troubles."

"It's okay. I've been meaning to catch up on my needlepoint."

"You talk to your pop yet?" he asked.

Billy shook his head. "Four voice mails from him."

"He's worried sick about you. You should call him back."

Maybe. Billy's father, Daniel Harney, the chief of detectives, prided himself on two things—that two of his kids were cops and that neither of them used nepotism to get there. *Everything you earn, you earn on merit, not because your dad's a superior.*

That was fine. Billy wouldn't want it any other way. But sometimes Pop took it too far—his desire to avoid favoritism at all costs created a distance, a canyon between them. When Billy made the big arrest earlier this week, every cop he knew showered him with praise, either at the Hole or in text messages, phone calls, shout-outs—everyone except his father.

"Anyway," said Billy. "You got anything for me?"

Goldie blew out a sigh, which meant no. "The place is tighter than a nun's legs right now. Best I can tell, it's what we've been thinking. The supe is trying to save the mayor, and the only way he knows how is to cook you and Kate."

"I don't even get that," said Billy. "Even if I did steal some little black book, it doesn't change the fact that the mayor had his dick where it didn't belong."

Goldie didn't answer. Didn't even draw a breath. Billy looked at him.

"Even if," Goldie mimicked. "You mean, like, hypothetically."

Billy resumed his stare out the window. People bundled thoroughly from head to toe, shoulders tight, heads down, like they were under attack from the elements.

"Even *if* you stole a little black book," Goldie said.

Lieutenant Mike Goldberger was the smartest man he knew.

"Let me ask you something," said Goldie. "How well do you know Kate?"

"Better than she knows herself."

"You trust her?"

"Yeah." Billy thought more about that, nodded. "Yeah, I do."

"You don't like her for this black book?"

"No. I don't see her taking it."

"She had opportunity. She handled the search, right?"

That was true. Billy remembered seeing Kate in the office upstairs in the brownstone, going through the cabinets and drawers.

"I don't see it," said Billy.

"How well does she know you?"

Billy shrugged.

"You know what I'm asking," Goldie said.

"She doesn't know about me." Billy shook his head. "Nobody knows. Nobody but you and me."

Outside, on Ohio Street, a cab screeched to a halt just short of the truck in front of it.

"You sure about that?" Goldie asked.

"Yeah, Goldie. I think I would remember if I'd told my partner that I work undercover for Internal Affairs. I think that would, y'know, stand out in my mind."

"Okay, okay." Goldie put a hand on Billy's shoulder, gripped it tight. "What about your sister?"

"No," he said. "Patti doesn't know."

"Your pop?"

"You tell me, Goldilocks."

Goldie drew back. "If your father knew that you were my guy inside the detectives' bureau, he'd string my undies up on a coat hook."

Billy looked at Goldie. "You think that's what this is all about, though? You think someone knows I'm with you? You think this thing with the mayor is just an excuse to stop me?"

That, of course, was the sixty-four-thousand-dollar question. Goldie returned a poker face.

"I sure as hell hope not," he said. "Because if it is, losing your job is the least of your worries."

THE PRESENT

TWENTY

"IT JUST doesn't make sense," says Patti Harney as she paces back and forth, making herself crazy, unable to contain her thoughts or control her emotions. The last two weeks she's felt like a pilot trying to navigate through meteors hurtling at her from every direction. Even though it's the middle of June, she hasn't seen sunlight for more than a week and sometimes loses track of whether it's day or night.

"Well, this is definitely not my area." Her brother Brendan, the oldest child in the family, is a financial planner who moved to Dallas when he fell in love with a Texas girl after college. Brendan rolls his neck and grimaces. He's been sleeping, if you can call stretching out on a chair and catching a couple hours of shut-eye "sleep." He's wearing a shirt he's had on for the past two days, the collar and armpits stained with sweat, his hair sticking up like it used to when they were kids after a wrestling skirmish between him and the second oldest, Aiden. They used to spend entire days trying to pin each other to the basement floor.

Speak of the devil: Aiden comes out of the bathroom, having splashed water on his face and run some through his hair—as always, too long for Patti's taste, as if anyone asked her opinion. Aiden is divorced and lives in Saint Louis, where he manages a gym. Why he didn't move back to Chicago after he split with his ex Patti never understood.

"What's not your area?" Aiden asks.

"How all this happened," says Brendan. "The shooting."

"We still talking about that?"

"She is." Brendan flips his hand toward Patti. "Pop says it's obvious what happened. Kate walks in on Billy in bed with this woman Amy, and she goes crazy and starts shooting. She kills Amy, but Billy manages to get a round off before she shoots him."

"I don't believe that," says Patti. "I just don't."

"Does it matter?" Aiden wipes a towel over his face. He's a workout fanatic, which makes the choice of managing a gym a good one for him. His gray Russell Athletic T-shirt is probably two sizes too small for him. He has the bent ears of a former wrestler and looks like he could still be one. He walks over to the bed in the room and gently grips Billy's ankle over the bedsheet. "All that matters is that our boy is way too tough to let a single fuckin' bullet keep him down."

Patti looks over at Billy, who looks like another person—not her brother, not Billy—his head wrapped, hooked up to tubes and machines and monitors. A portion of his skull was removed to lessen the swelling in his brain. These people actually have part of his skull on ice somewhere in this hospital.

Please come back, Billy. You got this far. You survived this much.

It's been two and a half months since it happened. Two surgeries. The prognosis grim. The doctor explained it to all of them, the whole family—Patti and her brothers and her father—as though he were teaching a class. *With a brain injury,* he said, *it's like real estate. Location, location, location.*

Nobody thought that was cute.

Some good news here, the doc said. *The bullet traveled a straight front-to-back trajectory. It didn't cross the midline, didn't hit the brain stem or thalamus. It looks like it injured only one hemisphere and only one lobe. It was a low-velocity bullet, and the path was quite linear. There was no yaw,* he said. *Think of a football moving through the air in a tight spiral versus wobbling. This bullet was a tight spiral, with no wobble.*

Patti had furiously scribbled down these words like a secretary taking dictation, not that she really knew what any of it meant. The only words that really registered with her were *some good news.*

The bad news, the doctor said, is that Billy actually lost brain activity for quite some time, as much as thirty minutes, which was why the responding police officers and paramedics initially thought Billy was dead. He *was* dead. And then he came back to life. It happens, the doctor said, but not very often.

The long and short: Billy has already beaten tremendous odds. But the truth is that he's very unlikely to survive, and if he does, we have no way of knowing what kind of damage was done to his brain. We can guess, but we won't really know until he regains consciousness.

"He's going to make it," says Patti. "And he's gonna be better than ever."

"Damn straight," says Aiden.

"He'll probably be a bigger pain in the ass than ever," Brendan adds.

"He'll be like Rain Man or something. He'll be doing multiplication tables in his head. Like he wasn't already smarter than the rest of us combined."

That last part is true. Billy had a mind that never stopped calculating, always ten steps ahead of everyone else—

No, he has *that mind, not* had. *He's coming back. He's going to come back. He has to.*

"I can't sit here doing nothing," she says.

"You're not doing nothing," says Brendan. "You're staying with Billy."

"I'm gonna get some air." She pushes open the door and comes upon her father in the hallway.

"Check again," he says into his cell phone. "I said check again. I don't care. That can't be right." He punches off the phone and turns and sees Patti. "Oh, sweetheart—"

"What can't be right?"

Her father tucks his phone into his pocket, as if hiding the phone will hide the secret.

"Patti, go home and take a shower. Get some sleep. I promise I'll—"

"What can't be right, Dad?" She holds her ground.

Her father looks terrible, just as run-down as the rest of the family. The last two weeks have aged him considerably.

"Ballistics," he says. "It must be a screwup."

"Tell me, Dad."

"I...they...it...it can't—" Her father takes Patti in his arms. He's hugged her more in the last two weeks than he has in her entire life, even when Mom died, six years ago.

He whispers in her ear. "I'm sure it's a mistake," he said. "Ballistics came back on the shooting. Amy Lentini wasn't shot by Kate's gun. She was shot by Billy's gun."

Patti pushes herself away from her dad. "What?"

Her father nods. His eyes fall to the ground. "They say the first person to fire a gun in that room was Billy. He shot Amy, then turned the gun on Kate, who fired back at the same time."

She feels herself backpedaling. "No...no...I...no."

"It can't be right." Her father, the chief of detectives, runs a hand through his grimy hair. "It just can't be right."

TWENTY-ONE

PATTI LOSES track of time, marching the hallways of the hospital, not wanting to roam too far from Billy but unable to sit still.

None of this is right. The whole scene at Amy's apartment. And now they're saying *Billy* fired first? Billy killed Amy Lentini?

No, it can't be. She knows it's not true.

Now you really have to come back, Billy. You have to say what happened. You have to clear your name. You can't let this be how you're remembered. You have to come back, you have to come back, or all this will be my fault—

Wait. How long—how long has she been gone? What if the doctor comes? That would be just her luck—she sits in that damn room for more than ten hours, but then the fucking doctor shows up in the brief window of time when she walks out. *I'll bet that happened. I'll bet he decides to waltz in while I'm gone—*

She finds the elevator and stabs at the button so many times she's sure she's killed it.

"Come on!" she shouts at the elevator. Heads turn all around her.

Screw you guys. You try losing your brother, the only

person who ever really understood you, the only person you've ever trusted in this miserable world, and tell me how well behaved you'd be—

The elevator doors slide open. Two elderly patients inside in wheelchairs, younger family members behind them.

Please don't leave me, Billy. And now—what they're saying about you. I know it's not true. Help me clear your name. Come back to me, Billy; please come back, please come back, or all this will be my fault—

The door pops open. She races down the hallway, knocking into a tray of food, mumbling an apology—

At the door, at Billy's door, a woman in scrubs. African American, cornrows, a petite figure.

"Doctor," she calls out.

The woman turns. Dressed in surgical scrubs, yes, but she's no doctor.

She's Kim Beans, the reporter for *ChicagoPC,* the online newspaper covering politics and crime in Chicago. The rag that, last winter and this spring, dripped out a name each day, one at a time—celebrities who were caught patronizing the now infamous brownstone on the Gold Coast where the mayor was arrested.

"Patti!" she says. "Hi!"

"You." Patti's hands ball into fists.

A beautiful woman, yes, once destined to be a major star on the Chicago television news scene before it was discovered that she got a little too cozy with the subject of a story she was handling, a local kidnapping. She probably figured the brownstone-brothel story was going to get her back in the good graces of the Chicago news media.

If all Kim did was leak celebrity names from that

brownstone, Patti would just chalk her up as another media jackal.

But she will never forgive Kim for what she did to Billy.

"Hang on, Patti. I'm on your side."

"You're not on anybody's side but your own." Patti gets up close and personal with Kim. "You have five seconds to walk out of here, or I'll have you arrested."

"You're gonna arrest a reporter?"

"You mean a trespasser. Disguised as a surgeon. A reporter who doesn't have the right to barge into the ICU to interview the family. Or to snap photos of a man in a coma—"

"I just want your side of it."

"Five seconds," says Patti. "One…two…three…"

"Patti—"

"Four…"

"Listen to me, Patti."

Patti slaps Kim hard across the face, a satisfying, full-palm smack. Kim almost falls over in the process, looks back at Patti with fire in her eyes.

"Five," says Patti.

"I can be your friend or your enemy," Kim says. "Don't forget that."

Patti watches Kim walk down to the elevator and get in. Then she lets out a breath and walks into the room.

Aiden and Brendan are laughing.

"…and Patti was playing Mary, holding the baby Jesus. And you're Joseph. All you have to do is sit there while the three Wise Men bring their gifts to the baby Jesus. I don't even think you had a speaking part. Right?" Brendan, sitting on the right side of the bed, his hand holding Billy's, looks across the bed at Aiden, who has the left side covered.

Aiden can't even speak, he's laughing so hard.

Patti feels her face warm. She remembers this all too well. She and Billy were six, in CCD, putting on a little Christmas story for the parents. All Billy was supposed to do was sit silently through the whole play.

"So right there in the middle of the play, Mrs. Ginger is sort of whispering to you guys what to do, and all the parents are sitting there in those shitty folding chairs, and all of a sudden you raise your hand and say, "Mrs. Ginger? How'd Mary have a baby if she was a virgin?"

Aiden and Brendan lose it. Patti does, too. It feels so good, the release. And it gets better.

Aiden wants to tell the next part. "So Mrs. Ginger, she's trying to shush you, she's like, 'Billy, shh, Billy, shh,' and some of the parents are already giggling, and before she can get to you, you say, 'My pop says Mary must have had a hell of a time explaining that one to Joseph.'"

They all erupt. What a moment. Mom was mortified. Her father even more so. He wasn't exactly a God-fearing Catholic—he said the job took all the faith out of him—but their mother was a churchgoer 'til the day she died.

Aiden has tears in his eyes. As the laughter subsides, the emotions ride the inevitable roller coaster. Brendan, the big brother, always the one trying to pick everyone else up, pats Billy's arm. "You remember that, don't you, buddy? You brought down the whole room."

Aiden pushes himself away from the bed, tears falling. Such a big, muscle-bound guy with tears running down his cheeks—she remembers him crying when Mom died, but she can't remember any other time. "It seems like just yesterday Billy was in a hospital just like this one."

"I know," says Brendan. "It was three freakin' years ago. Can you believe it?"

Aiden shakes his head. "He was starting to get back on his feet, y'know? I mean, he was just recovering from all that, and *this* happens."

"Well, if it isn't the Four Stooges." It's Mike Goldberger—Goldie—entering the room, dusting off the nickname that everyone used for the Harney kids when they were growing up.

Her brothers greet Goldie, whom they've known for years, and he tells them he'll take the next shift; they should go get something to eat.

Brendan grabs Billy's ankle and says, "You hang in there while I'm gone, baby brother, or I'll kick your ass."

When they've left, Goldie gives Patti a once-over.

"Your pop told you about ballistics," he says.

She nods.

"It's bad," he says. "And it's about to get worse."

TWENTY-TWO

"SO HOW'S our guy doing?" Goldie talking.

"Oh, you know with these doctors." That's Patti. "It's all probabilities and prefacing every remark. Honestly, as much as I hate to say it—they're saying he's not going to make it."

That doesn't sound good.

"They're saying it's a miracle he got this far. I mean, he was actually dead for a while."

I was?

"Yeah, I remember."

Well, with all due respect to Mr. Twain, reports of my death have been greatly exaggerated.

Although I don't feel alive, either. I can't feel anything, not my arms, not my legs. I can't see anything, either. I can hear them, though, their voices muted like I'm inside some enclosure. Floating like a fetus inside a womb.

"And they say there's no telling how he'll come out of it if he does."

A drooling vegetable?

"He could have a completely different personality."

Some people might say that's an improvement.

"He might not have any memory."

Well, I remember you, Patti. And Goldie. And Mark Twain.

And my badge number. And pi to ten decimal places.

But I don't remember how I got here.

"I hear the surgeries went well," says Goldie.

"As good as they could, yeah. You know they removed part of the back of his skull to reduce the swelling."

Hold up—part of my *skull* is missing? What the fuck happened to me? Yo, Patti-Cake, you wanna do a little background for those of us who are just tuning in?

"They say the bullet didn't hit the left hemisphere," she says. "The part that controls speech and language."

Ah, okay. I got shot in the brain? The right side, sounds like.

So I'll be in a wheelchair the rest of my life, but at least I'll have my "speech and language," so I can coherently ask the nurse for more applesauce.

"Well, that's good."

Nurse! I want more applesauce! Who do I have to kill around here to get more applesauce?

"Anyway, my dad told me about ballistics. It can't be right. It's not right, Goldie."

"I know, I hear you—I mean, your pop's got 'em redoing the entire testing. But really, when is ballistics ever wrong?"

"Billy's not the shooter," she says.

I shot someone? Who'd I shoot? The guy who shot *me,* I hope.

"I'll bet this'll make the mayor happy," says Goldie. "Or at least his lawyers."

The mayor? Why would Mayor Francis Delaney care about me?

Did I shoot *him?*

Think back, guy. What do you remember?

I remember…a murder. A college girl. University of Chicago, I think. Then…then what?

Then—nothing. Nothing but a fuzzy screen.

I remember Stewart…

…sometimes, during the worst parts, I'd rest my hand over his, and we wouldn't look at each other… both of us holding back tears, too proud to admit it…

…the jokes…the old man laughing so hard he sounded like a busted car engine, like he was about to expel a lung…

…laughing so we wouldn't cry…

I remember when it was over. Feeling like…

…like I wanted to die, too.

I don't want to remember anymore. I don't want to remember anything.

"What was that? Did you hear something? Was that…Billy?"

"Billy! Billy, can you hear me?"

I can hear you, Patti, but I want to go away now…

"Stewart," says Goldie. "I thought I heard 'Stewart.' Who's Stewart?"

"Stewart was the old guy in the hospital, remember? Back when Billy practically lived at Children's Memorial—"

"Yeah, of course."

"Stewart's grandson was hit by a car. They waited together for weeks. They got real close."

I don't want to remember that…

"Billy, are you there, pal?"

"Billy, it's me. It's your sister. Can you hear me?"

"Hey, Brendan, it's Goldie. We think maybe we heard Billy speak. Okay, hurry."

"Billy, you need to come back to me. Please, Billy. You can do it."

I don't know how…I don't know if I want to…

"Do it for me, Billy. I need you. We love you, Billy. The family's all here. Brendan and Aiden are here. Dad's here. Goldie's here. Come back to us, Billy. We need you to come back."

I feel something.

Patti's tear on my cheek.

And light—blinding, searing light in my eyes.

TWENTY-THREE

"I KNEW it." Patti's eyes, welled with tears. "I knew you'd come back."

My eyes moving slowly, as if filled with sand, around the room. Brendan and Aiden. Pop. Goldie. All of them surrounding me, each of them touching me, as if they want to embrace me warmly but at the same time recognize my fragility.

I feel removed from the whole thing, like I'm watching this happen to someone else, my family surrounding me and placing their hands on me, like they're examining a museum object ("Go ahead, you can touch it") or participating in some religious revival ("Touch me and you shall be healed").

I try to speak, but nothing comes out.

Am I dead?

Everything goes black.

My eyes open again. The same people surrounding me. Patti still crying. Aiden, the musclehead with the big heart, teary-eyed.

"You're in a hospital," says Patti. "You were shot. But you're gonna be fine."

So I heard. At least the part about getting shot. If memory serves, Patti, you told Goldie I might never be the same again.

"A bullet's not gonna keep this one down." Brendan, my oldest brother. Always the cheerleader of the family.

Everything goes black again.

Am I dead?

Light again. My eyes adjusting. The same people in the room. Pop and my siblings, the Three Stooges plus me, the fourth. Plus Goldie. All hovering over me.

"Not yet," Patti is saying.

"She's right." Brendan.

About what? I try to speak but can't. I can think just fine—but I can't translate it to my mouth.

"We need to know." Pop.

"Not *yet*." Patti, more firmly. "He's just waking up."

Aiden leans over me. "How you doing, pal?"

I can't answer.

"Say something for me. Say this: 'The Cubs… fucking…suck.'"

Brendan: "Say, 'You're under arrest.'"

Aiden: "How about 'Kiss my white Irish fanny?'"

"Hey, I came all the way from Dallas," Brendan says to me. "The least you can do is say hello to your big brother. Or maybe I should crack you one?"

"Don't listen to that ingrate," Aiden comes back. "You did him a favor. You ever been to Dallas? They wear cowboy boots and big hats."

"Coming from a guy who wears a tank top and shorts to work."

"Least I don't say 'y'all' or 'howdy.'"

Yeah, this is definitely my family.

"You could do us all a favor, Billy," Patti says, "and tell your meathead brothers to shut the fuck up."

"Who you calling a meathead?" says Brendan. "I graduated top of my class."

"From Wesleyan," says Aiden out of the corner of his mouth.

"Yeah? And what's Roosevelt University? The Harvard of the Midwest?"

Definitely my family.

My lips part. Patti, watching my every move, notices it and holds out a hand for silence.

I feel like an infant whose parents are hovering over him. *He's going to speak! He's going to say something!*

And my first words come out, with all eyes on me, everyone leaning in for the big moment.

"Goo goo ga ga," I say.

Nobody knows how to react—frozen, confused, eyebrows arched, foreheads furrowed, everyone holding their breath.

I open my mouth again. They lean in further still, as if examining the contents of a petri dish.

"Just...kidding," I whisper.

A collective release of tension—relief and good humor sweeping the room.

"Oh, you piece of shit." Aiden, shaking his head, bursting into tears.

"Well, you're definitely back." Brendan gently shakes my arm. "He's back! The comedian's back!"

"You did it," Patti whispers to me, overcome with emotion. "You did it, Billy."

TWENTY-FOUR

IN AND out. Light and dark. I drift in and out of consciousness, no concept of the time of day or the day of the week, none of the usual sources to prompt me. My vision isn't yet good enough to make out the digital clock on the opposite wall. I'm in an interior room in the ICU, so there is no sunlight or nightfall. I'm being fed by a tube, so it's not like my meals vary from scrambled eggs to chicken with rice. And it's still hard for me to summon the strength and focus to speak, so I try to reserve that effort for questions more burning than whether it's three in the afternoon or two in the morning.

I measure the passage of time instead by my sister's changes of clothes. Since I first opened my eyes, Patti has worn three different outfits, so either I've been out of the coma for three days or she likes to change up her wardrobe a whole lot.

Pop is here less often; being chief of Ds is a big job, and he can only delegate the daily duties for so long. My brothers have stuck around the hospital but spend a lot of time out in the hallway calling home or opening laptops and sending things back and forth to Dallas and Saint Louis.

The two constants have been Goldie and Patti, who

have been by my bedside pretty much every time my eyes are open.

Everyone has kept it light so far. I've asked questions but received no answers, just a lot of evasive responses like *Just focus on getting better* and *We can talk about that later*.

I've asked what happened to put me here.

I've asked who shot me. I've asked who it was I shot.

But the question I ask most often is, where is Kate?

I can think in full sentences—at least I think I can. It doesn't translate when I open my mouth. The connection between my injured brain and my mouth is like the signal I receive on my phone when I'm driving through the South Side. Sometimes it works; sometimes it's fuzzy; sometimes it completely disconnects.

I'm not paralyzed, either. Everything works. Not well, not yet, but I'm okay.

I remember arresting the mayor now. That memory came back when my sister was wearing a green shamrock T-shirt. Today she's wearing something brown. So I think it was yesterday. Yesterday the bust came back to me, along with the shitstorm that followed. I remember the superintendent was pissed off, and the state's attorney appointed a woman—a real knockout—to investigate me and Kate, to look into whether I stole the little black book at the brownstone.

Every day, every change of Patti's clothes, I remember a few more things.

I remember the name of the investigator: Amy Lentini.

I remember being suspended. Kate, too.

I remember talking to Goldie at a coffee shop, thinking that this whole thing was a lot bigger than a stupid black book, that it was an excuse to get to me. I remember thinking that someone had figured out that I worked undercover for Internal Affairs and that whoever it was used the mayor's bust as an excuse to silence me.

Cut! That's it. That's where it ends in a cloud of smoke, like my memory is a car speeding away, leaving me in the dust.

My doctor, an Indian guy named Pameresh, said most things will come back to me sooner or later, but probably not the traumatic events themselves. *You'll probably never remember the shooting or the events that immediately preceded it,* he said. *It's called retrograde amnesia.*

Patti is working her phone, humming to herself, unaware that my eyes have opened again. She looks so tired, so pale, so wrung out.

It was hard for Patti growing up. She was mostly coddled, three brothers hovering over her, protecting her, but she never shook the insecurity that gripped her, especially when she was compared to me, her twin brother. I never knew what was so special about me, but in her mind, I exceeded her in every way—smarter, more athletic, more popular, better looking. I never understood it. Something grabbed hold of her at a young age and never let go, something that told her she wasn't good enough.

But it never came between us. Whatever she felt about me, she never held it against me. We've been together during highs and lows. When everything happened three years ago, Patti took it as hard as I did; it was almost as if it had happened to her.

"Kate," I say, not even trying to put together a string of words.

Patti looks up from her phone. "Morning, sunshine." She leans over and carefully kisses my forehead. My head is shaved and heavily bandaged—the top of my skull is still sitting in a mason jar somewhere—and I'm still connected to tubes and electrodes and machines. They're feeding me, monitoring my brain and heart functions, even massaging my limbs with electric pulses so I don't lose circulation.

"Kate," I say again, my eyes level with hers. "Please."

Patti's eyes drift about, considering the question. We are alone in the room. Not even Goldie's here.

She tries to touch my face, my head, but there's nowhere to place her hand. Her eyes well up with tears. She has probably cried enough to fill Niagara Falls. I'm sorry to do this to her, but I need to know, and I know she'll tell me if nobody's around to stop her.

"Kate's dead, Billy. The shooting. You survived, she didn't."

Something expels from my mouth. A low moan.

I thought this was coming. It was hard to think of another reason why Kate wouldn't have been here to visit me. But hearing it—confirming it—something snaps inside me like a twig.

"We aren't sure what happened," she tells me.

I let her down. I was supposed to cover her back. That's what a partner does. I didn't do that.

Oh, Kate. Oh, Kate…

"Who…who…"

Patti watches me, dreading the question. Injured brain or not, I can read her like a book. She knows what I'm trying to ask: *Who killed Kate?*

"We don't know what happened," she repeats, this

time less convincingly, a robotic repetition, like a shield against further inquiry. "We don't know."

The more she says it, the clearer it is to me that she's lying. And why would she lie about that? Why wouldn't she want me to know who shot Kate?

No. No. It can't be.

Poison through my veins, a weight crushing my chest, stealing my breath. Some of the machines start making noises, bells and whistles. Patti pushes a button and calls for the nurse.

The door pops open, and doctors and nurses rush in.

Before Patti steps aside, she leans into me.

"Whatever anyone tries to tell you about what happened," she whispers, "don't believe it."

TWENTY-FIVE

"THIS IS a bad idea," says Patti. "It's a terrible idea."

It's the best idea I've had in the fourteen weeks I've been here.

I fit my arm through the sleeve of my button-down shirt. "I don't care. I'm not spending another night in this place."

Nothing against the hospital, which has treated me more than well. The room to which I was transferred had a window overlooking the lake, which was nice, though it reminded me of the view from Kate's condo in Lakeview. The people doing my rehab were good souls, too, exhibiting more patience with me than they would with a child, coaxing me into "one more step" or one more bicep curl with a ten-pound weight or one more recitation of "Peter Piper picked a peck of pickled peppers" or one more round of counting backwards from 20.

It was brutal at first, but they got me back on my feet. I can dress myself and feed myself and walk (albeit with a cane). I can speak in full sentences and read and write. My vision is almost as good as it used to be. My sense of humor, for better or worse, is still intact.

And my skull is fully reattached, thank you very much. My hair is growing back a little straighter than it was before and right now is the length of a buzz cut. I have lost about twenty pounds. I have a scar where the bullet entered my brain, but the rest of the repairs the doctors did to my noggin are covered by hair. Yes, if you look closely enough, you can see scars that read like a road map all across the top and back of my skull, but I can live with it. The fact that I can live at all, I realize, is a small miracle.

So I'm leaving! Ninety-eight days after taking a bullet to the brain.

"You need another month of rehab, at least," Patti says.

"So I'll do it as an outpatient. Or I'll do it at home. It's not like I'm going back on the job right away."

I need medical clearance before they'll let me back to work, even at a desk. A lot of coppers I know would take the disability leave without complaint, as though it were a paid vacation, but not me. I can't bear the thought of watching game shows and daytime talk shows and soap operas. I'll think of something. Mostly I'll work on getting myself back in shape to get back to my job.

But none of that is why I want to go home.

Yes, I'm stir-crazy in here. Yes, I want to be a cop again.

But the real reason is that I want control again. My family—Patti in particular—has controlled my access to information and the news. All I know about the shooting, after fourteen weeks, is that three people were found shot, and two of them—Amy Lentini and Kate—were already dead. I was clinging to life. And I know that the shooting happened in Amy Lentini's apartment.

And though neither Patti nor anyone else has ever

actually confirmed it, it sounds like everyone thinks I shot Kate.

I haven't pushed the issue. Once I came up against resistance, once everyone started deflecting the issue, I decided to lay low. That's where I'm at my most effective, when I've receded into the background, when I'm the funny, harmless guy, the comedian, the baby brother, the fourth stooge. I'm at my best when everyone underestimates me.

So that's what I'll do. I'll be the guy recovering from the brain injury. The guy with the limp. The guy who moves and acts and thinks slowly. The guy who probably, likely, will never be the same again. The guy who's no longer a threat.

Let them all think that.

I don't know how I got to Amy's place the night of the shooting. I don't remember any of the circumstances leading up to it. I've lost days and weeks before that point in time. And I can't for the life of me figure out why on God's green earth I would shoot my partner.

But I'm going to find out.

TWENTY-SIX

"DETECTIVE." THE woman who enters the room is tall and thin, with ash-colored hair pulled back, wearing black-rimmed glasses and a sleeveless red dress and heels. I try not to stare, because I'm a gentleman.

"I'm Dr. Jagoda," she says.

I rise from my seat and shake her hand. "Billy Harney."

She sits across from me. Lush, high-backed leather chairs. Like something in a reading room somewhere. All we're missing is a fireplace and a snifter of brandy.

She doesn't just look nice—she also smells nice, her perfume fresh and clean, not overpowering.

On the dark walls: diplomas from Harvard and Yale, certificates from various psychology associations.

"So how does this work?" I ask. "I tell you my mommy didn't show me enough affection? And then I realize..." I shake my fists and bite my lip, as if in a moment of self-discovery. "I realize that...I'm not a bad person! And then we both have a good cry, and I go find happiness."

She observes all this with a poker face. No tell whatsoever. "How do you want it to work?"

"The truth?"

"Preferably."

"I don't want to be here at all."

"I never would have guessed."

"But I have no choice. The department says I gotta see a shrink. Y'know, on account of my traumatic experience and all."

Her eyes narrow. That psychologist-appraisal thing. "You did this before," she says. "Three years ago."

"Three years ago I didn't wanna do it, either."

"But did it help?"

"Not really."

"So." She claps her hands and leans forward. There is a table separating us, a small round wooden job with a design on it that looks Middle Eastern. "What do you hope to get out of it this time?"

"I hope to get out of *here,* period," I say. "No offense. But I don't need a shrink."

"Why don't you think you need a shrink?"

I look at her. "Do you just ask questions? Do you ever make affirmative statements?"

"Do you want me to?" She allows a small curve of a smile, her face otherwise deadpan. At least that time she was joking

"What kinda name is Jagoda?"

She sits back in her chair, crosses her legs. "Polish," she says.

"You know how many Poles it takes to screw in a lightbulb?" I ask. "Three. One to hold the bulb and two to rotate the chair he's standing on."

"You know how many cops it takes?" she replies. "Three. One to screw it in and two to violate the civil rights of a black guy standing nearby."

Well played. "You wanna know the thinnest book

ever written? *The Complete List of Polish War Heroes*."

"Oh, but the Irish have made a real contribution to the world."

I could mention beer and potatoes, but I don't.

"How about you just give me a diagnosis and send me on my way?" I say. "Let's go with post-traumatic stress disorder. Write me up a prescription, and I'll promise to take my meds."

She cocks her head. "I'm good at what I do, Detective, but somehow I don't think I'm prepared to make a full diagnosis after meeting you for five minutes and simply reading your file."

"I'll settle for a partial diagnosis, then."

"Oh, a partial one? That's easy," she says. "You're batshit crazy."

I actually let out a laugh. The first one I can remember. Okay, she's good for a chuckle or two, but this is still a waste of time.

I get out of my chair. "See you around, Doc," I say.

"You're extremely intelligent," she says as I'm headed for the door. "Far more so than you're willing to let on. You're emotionally wounded, probably from what happened three years ago as well as what just happened, but you bury it all underneath this facade of being the smartass, the comedian. Humor is your shield. You're hiding. You've probably been hiding for so long that you don't even realize it anymore."

I don't respond. I don't move.

She turns and looks at me, eyebrows raised. I break eye contact.

"You're broken," she says. "You know it, and I know it. But I can help put you back together. Who knows? I might even help you get your memory back."

I look at the door, even reach for it with my hand.

"Go ahead and walk if you want. I won't stop you. Make a decision, Billy."

I draw my hand back from the door. I slowly swivel around and look at the shrink. Then I return to the chair and sit down.

"You can get my memory back?"

"No guarantee," she says. "But I'm your only shot."

THE PAST

TWENTY-SEVEN

"MORE BAD news for us," said Kate as she drove the Tahoe with me in the passenger seat. I pulled up the website on my phone and immediately spotted it. Another story from the online rag *ChicagoPC,* once again courtesy of Kim Beans, the formerly disgraced TV reporter making a spirited comeback with the photographs she obtained from the brownstone brothel.

The heading of the article read PEEKABOO, FRANCIS! The photo captured Mayor Francis Delaney walking up the steps of the now infamous brownstone, only he wasn't bundled up; he was in a light jacket and wearing a baseball cap. It was taken in warm weather, in other words—not during the night two weeks ago when we made the bust. The point being that the night I caught the mayor of Chicago with his pants at his ankles was not the first time he'd visited the brownstone.

"You're right: this is absolutely outrageous," I said. "How could the mayor wear a *Cubs* cap?"

Kate shot me a look. Not funny.

See, Kate considered this photo of the mayor bad news because she considered *anything* in the news about this story to be bad. And she was right. In the two weeks that had passed since we arrested the mayor and everyone else at the brownstone, the national media had caught wind of this story, and once it did, it held on like a pit bull on a mailman's leg. When the 24-7 news outlets—CNN, Fox, MSNBC, Bloomberg, whatever—sink their teeth into a story, they demand further juicy details and gobble up every little nugget, big or small, verified or unverified. It turns up the heat on everyone under the microscope.

Consider, for example, our state's attorney, Margaret Olson. Last week a reporter from CNN looked at her campaign-contribution reports and realized that she owed her election as the top prosecutor to Mayor Delaney, who provided her with significant financial support. Under a news segment entitled "Conflict of Interest?," the anchor questioned whether Maximum Margaret would go easy on the mayor because of all he'd done for her.

That prompted the state's attorney to hold a news conference in which she announced that she would be accepting no plea bargains for any defendant accused of soliciting prostitutes that night in the brownstone, whether that person was someone of prominence (read: Mayor Delaney or Archbishop Phelan or the Green Bay Packers QB) or an ordinary Joe. And she would be seeking maximum sentences for all of them.

The sex-club case was headed to trial soon, and everyone involved was hunkering down, bracing for the next splashy revelation to emerge, hoping that it wouldn't be their ox that got gored.

And every news outlet, every reporter covering this case, was looking for the little black book that mysteriously disappeared from the brownstone that night.

So things were tense, but Kate needed to look on

the bright side, too; there'd been some good news. The disciplinary board that oversees police-officer cases ordered that Kate and I be reinstated to duty while we waited for the hearing on our alleged misconduct. The police superintendent, Tristan Driscoll, had suspended us immediately, on the spot, but the board said we got to remain on duty until he proved his case against us.

So after taking an unplanned two-week vacation, I was a cop again—at least for now—and so was Kate.

"I can't believe we have to go and play nice with that bitch," she mumbled.

Amy Lentini, she meant—the special investigator assigned to the sex-club case, who'd been trying to prove for the last two weeks that either Kate or I or both of us stole the little black book naming customers at the brownstone brothel. Since Kate and I were the arresting officers, we would be required to testify at the trial and prepare for it with Lentini in advance. Personally, I'd rather have my wisdom teeth pulled without Novocain, but nobody asked me my opinion.

"It won't be so bad," I said.

"Oh, I'm sure *you* won't mind." Another look shot in my direction. "The Italian beauty, fluttering those eyes at you."

"That's not fair at all, and you know it," I said. "It's her ass I like the most."

"This isn't a *joke,* Billy."

There it was again, that jealousy thing. Kate and I had been partners for years, and I never seriously considered anything between us. Then it flared up after the brownstone arrests, and I admit it was pretty great—crazy and kinkier than I was used to, but great. But then we were suspended, and though we talked every day for those two weeks, nothing else happened. It was like the suspension of our official relationship pushed the Pause button on the sex part, too. Now that we were back together as cops, I wondered if we would hit the Play button again. And I couldn't decide if it was a good idea or not.

"Amy Lentini is a wolf in sheep's clothing," said Kate. "She'll draw you in nice and close, then stick in the knife."

Kate pulled the car over next to Daley Plaza. Parking wasn't ordinarily allowed there, but the cops looked the other way for one another. That was one of the perks of the job. The pay sucks, the pension is shaky, people curse at you and try to goad you into anger while recording you on their smartphones, and you never know when someone might stick a gun in your face—but hey, the parking is great.

"Watch yourself around her is all I'm saying," Kate warned me as she threw the car into park. "You could get us both in trouble."

TWENTY-EIGHT

"DETECTIVE HARNEY, Detective Fenton, good morning." Assistant state's attorney Amy Lentini was all business when we walked into her office. She was decked out in a crisp blue suit that hugged her nicely, a perfect blend of professionalism and flattery. She cleaned up good, I had to admit.

She showed us to seats and stood by the window, overlooking Daley Plaza. The fact that she had an office with a window said something about her status here. I still didn't know her story, how she moved up the chain, whom she knew. Hell, for all I knew, she got where she was on her merits. There was a first time for everything.

"Congratulations on your reinstatement," she said with no trace of irony.

"It's only temporary, until the board rules on the merits of our case," I said. "Something about the presumption of innocence. I think we have that in this country."

"That sounds familiar," she replied, deadpan.

"Some people still want us kicked off the force. Oh, wait." I snapped my fingers. "That someone is you."

Her head inclined to the right, the beginning of a smirk on her face. "It's a delicate situation."

"A delicate situation," Kate said, mimicking her. "You really are a lawyer."

"I'm a lawyer who's not going to lose this case," said Amy. "And you, Detectives, are my case, whether I like it or not. So putting this business about the little black book aside, we need to be ready for the attack." She opened her hands. "Although believe me—any time you want to tell me what happened to that black book, I'm all ears."

Sure she was. She must have assumed that other celebrities and politicians and power brokers were featured in that tell-all book. She was an ambitious prosecutor who had stumbled on a career-maker of a case. The bigger the fish, the bigger the boost to her career.

"We don't know what happened to that book," said Kate.

Amy narrowed her eyes at Kate but didn't answer. Nothing was going to be resolved between her and us, probably ever, on that score. "You're going to be attacked," she said. "The defense doesn't have much else to say. The mayor, the archbishop, all the men you caught—they have no defense to this crime. You caught them, in some cases literally, with their pants down."

Yeah, it wasn't the archbishop's finest moment. I didn't remember the mayor coming off so well, either.

"So their only avenue is to attack the police," Amy went on, pacing by the window. "They will challenge the constitutionality of your entry into the brownstone. They'll say you lacked probable cause."

"Piece of cake," I said. "I had information that that brownstone was a brothel. They weren't going in there to play bingo."

"Oh, okay, so this case will be easy," Amy said, dripping with sarcasm.

I sat back in my chair. "Easy as Sunday morning."

"So you won't mind if I ask you a few questions about it?"

"Shoot."

"Okay." Amy looked up at the ceiling, as though she were recalling events. "So you went to that brownstone to confront a man whom you suspected of murdering that student at the University of Chicago."

"That's how it started. That's why we were there in the first place. But then it all changed."

"Suddenly you were a Vice cop. Suddenly you didn't care one iota about that suspect. Suddenly you wanted to bust up a prostitution ring."

"Yeah, the focus changed. I was witnessing a crime in progress—"

"What crime did you witness in progress? Did you see some prostitute screwing some guy? Did you see money changing hands?"

"Obviously not," I said.

"Obviously *not*. You were outside in your car. So you saw a bunch of individual men walking into a brownstone."

"A brownstone I knew to be a brothel."

"Run that by me again—how'd you know it was a brothel?" She scratched her cheek in mock curiosity.

"I had been following my suspect. I saw him going in there the week before. I had a suspicion about what he was doing, but I wasn't sure."

"You weren't sure because all you saw the week before, when you were trailing the suspect, was a man walking into the brownstone and then coming back out later."

"Right."

"It's not a crime to walk in and out of a brownstone, is it?"

"Obviously not."

"You didn't hear him say, 'Gee, I just had sex with a prostitute.'"

I gave her a cold smile.

"He wasn't wearing a sign around his neck that said 'Just got a blow job,' was he?" she asked.

"It was more like one of those sandwich boards," I said. "One side said 'I just paid someone for sex.' The other side said 'I also killed a U of C undergrad. Arrest me!'"

She stared at me.

"You're correct, Counselor," I said. "When I was following the suspect, all I saw was him going in and coming out."

"So you had no idea what was going on inside that brownstone."

"But then I sat on the place," I said.

"You did recon."

"Sure, recon. I sat on the place. I saw young beautiful women going into the place and older men going in, too."

"Did you know for a fact that any of those young women were prostitutes?"

"For a fact? No. But the way they were dressed made me think so."

"Well," Amy said, opening her hands. "How were they dressed?"

"Like hookers," I said. "Showing a lot of leg. Hair teased up. Lots of makeup."

"So all women who dress provocatively are hookers?"

"Of course not."

"*Most* of them are?"

"No," I said, leaning forward. "But I watched maybe a dozen young women walk into that place and then a bunch of much older men."

"How do you know they didn't go to separate floors of that brownstone?" Amy asked. "How do you know that the women weren't having a party in the garden apartment and the men weren't a bunch of old college buddies watching the Bulls game together in a different apartment?"

I shook my head. I was playing a hunch that night, the law of probabilities, going with instinct. That's what cops do. No, I wasn't *positive* that brownstone was a brothel, but it sure as hell looked like it.

Still, I had to admit she had just tied me in knots. I was beginning to think I'd underestimated Amy Lentini.

Amy moved away from the window, came around the desk, and stood against it, facing me head-on. "And I was being gentle," she said. "The mayor and the archbishop have hired two of the best defense lawyers in the country. If you didn't have probable cause to enter that brownstone, our whole case is gone. And they won't blame *me* for that."

No. Everyone would blame me, the cop who muffed the search.

"So believe it or not," she said, "*like* it or not, I'm on your side."

TWENTY-NINE

TWO HOURS later, Kate and I were in the elevator, heading out of Daley Center. Another person got in with us but checked out two floors below, leaving us alone.

The moment the doors closed and it was just us, Kate punched me in the arm.

"Ow. What's your problem?"

"You're my problem," she said.

I rubbed my arm. The kid could pack a punch.

When the elevator door popped back open, we walked through the lobby, full of lawyers and cops and sheriff's deputies—even a small group protesting police brutality, which was probably allowed to come inside because it was so freaking cold out in the plaza.

I zipped my coat up to my neck and pushed through the revolving door.

"So how am I your problem?" I asked. "Because I 'played nice' with the prosecutor?"

"Because you're an idiot," Kate answered, walking so fast I could hardly keep up with her.

"Hey," I said, stopping, hoping she'd stop, too.

She did, turning around, something in her eyes suggesting concern, maybe hurt.

"My ass is on the line," I said. "If the search gets

tossed and I blew the arrest on the mayor of Chicago, then I *really* look like an idiot."

"I see. So the prosecutor is helping you."

I nod. "I thought she had a point, yeah. She's smart. She's thorough."

"Oh, she's smart, I'll give her that."

I opened my arms. "So..."

Kate smiled, but not a smile of happiness—more like a grin-and-bear-it smile. "She is playing you like a fiddle, Detective."

"Oh, now it's 'Detective.' Not Billy?"

Kate walked over to me. "In case you hadn't noticed, *my* ass is on the line, too. And my fate is basically in your hands. Which means I have to sit and watch while she leads you around wherever she wants you to go. You have a serious blind spot."

"I don't see that," I said.

She leaned in nice and close, her mouth next to my ear. "That's why they call it a blind spot."

She stepped back and shoved me, this time in the shoulder.

"So yeah, now it's 'Detective,'" she said. "We're partners on the job, and that's all we are. We always said it was a one-nighter, right? Even if it was more than one night."

She tossed me the keys to our car, still parked in the fire lane on Clark.

"C'mon, Kate," I said. "You're not even going to ride with me?"

She started away but turned again, facing me, giving me a good long once-over. "Did you take the black book?" she asked.

"What?" It felt like a punch to the gut. "I can't believe you'd even ask me that."

She was only about five yards away from me, but suddenly it felt like the distance between us was measured in miles. The woman who rode with me for almost five years, who went through doors with me, who solved murders and rapes with me, who cried in my arms when her father died two years ago, who spent hours in the hospital with me three years ago, when everything happened—that woman was gone. Now all I had was a partner who didn't trust me.

"Did *you* take it?" I asked back.

I felt something break between us. She did, too. Her reaction wasn't anger but sadness, loss. She broke eye contact with me and walked away.

And she never answered the question.

But then again, neither did I.

THIRTY

"THERE HE is," Lieutenant Mike Goldberger said. "The newly reinstated detective."

We met at a pub by the station, though it was for lunch only, not beers.

"Congratulations," he said.

I bumped fists with him. Goldie was saying all this as though he'd just heard the news. I seriously doubted that. I had a sneaking suspicion that Goldie had something to do with my reinstatement. Did he know somebody on the police disciplinary board? I wasn't sure, but it wouldn't surprise me. Goldie had a gift for networking. His current position, heading Internal Affairs, was really a perfect fit for him. He was the consummate behind-the-scenes player. He never sought credit, but you always knew that when things happened, somewhere behind a curtain, Goldie was turning the levers.

And if he did know someone on the disciplinary board, if he did pull a string or call in a favor to get me reinstated, he'd never tell me. It wasn't his way.

I never thought I'd work for BIA. Most cops don't. Most cops, you put a gun to their head, they wouldn't work in the bureau that investigates other cops. I was resistant myself—I only agreed to do it because it was

Goldie who was asking and because he promised that it wouldn't involve rinky-dink stuff. My job wasn't to catch cops doing little things like fudging a time sheet or tardiness or missing a court appearance or uttering a politically incorrect word or two at the station.

No, we would stick to the important stuff. Major crimes. Big-time corruption.

As far as I knew, nobody but Goldie and I knew that I was undercover. Not even my sister, Patti, or my father knew. Nor did Kate. It felt odd not telling those people closest to me, but really, I was doing them a favor. I was working on something that could be pretty explosive, and if my role came out, a lot of shit would hit a lot of fans. My family and Kate would be better off claiming, truthfully, that they never knew a thing about it.

We sat at the bar and ordered corned-beef sandwiches. The bartender put a wicker basket of popcorn in front of us. We dove into it, stuffing handfuls into our mouths.

"I had two weeks sitting on my suspended ass, doing nothing but thinking about this," I said. "And all I could think was, this whole thing with the little black book isn't about a little black book at all. It's about *me*. Somebody made me. Somebody knows I'm undercover. Somebody knows what I'm investigating. And whoever it is wants to stop me."

"Nobody knows what you're investigating. Nobody but me. Your name isn't anywhere." Goldie looked over at me. "You told me you never told anyone. Not your sister, not your partner—"

"I didn't."

"Then nobody knows but you and me. You're a ghost, as far as that's concerned." He whacked my arm with the back of his hand. "How'd your meeting go with the prosecutor?"

I drew back. "What, you know everything I do now?"

"Kid, I know what you had for breakfast today."

That was Goldie. Eyes and ears everywhere. I couldn't have a better person looking out for me.

"This trial's gonna be a bitch," I said. "She's afraid they're gonna punt the whole thing on probable cause."

"Translation: it would be your fault," Goldie said, cutting right to the chase.

"No fuckin' foolin'."

"Ride it out," he said. "You never know when the winds might shift."

I looked at him. Goldie never opened his mouth without a reason.

"Talk to me," I said.

He shrugged. "I'm just sayin'—the state's attorney's golden girl, Lentini, the one who two weeks ago was trying to make you for stealing the ledger."

"The little black book."

"Right. Now she's the one trying the brownstone case. Now she needs you. That strike you as odd?"

It did, actually. "What do you think it means?"

"Maybe our good state's attorney is recalculating. Maybe Maximum Margaret is taking a lay of the land and seeing things different."

"How so?"

"Well, her first reaction was, you took down the mayor, and the mayor's her Chinaman, right? He's the reason she became state's attorney. So she was trying to smear you."

"For sure."

"But now?" Goldie threw up his hands. "Maybe she's thinking, hell, the mayor doesn't have a prayer now—he's going down for this thing. So she might as well make the best of it." Goldie looked at me. "Somebody's gotta take the mayor's place, right?"

I hadn't thought of that. "Maximum" Margaret Olson could be the next mayor. Sure. Of course.

"This Amy Lentini," Goldie went on. "She's their ace. She was a federal prosecutor up in Wisconsin. You remember a couple years back, that US senator up there went down for taking a bribe?"

"She did that case?"

"Yep. She's the real deal."

"Wisconsin. Huh."

"Yep. Born in Appleton, went to Madison for undergrad, Harvard Law."

Our sandwiches arrived: corned beef piled high on rye, a huge spear of a pickle, and thick potato chips.

"Why am I not surprised that you know all about her?" I said.

"It's my job." Goldie took a massive bite of his sandwich. I did the same. "The situation's fluid, is all I'm sayin'," he went on. "Nobody knows which side to be on. So just ride it out for now."

That sounded about right.

"Stay close to Amy Lentini," he said. "Keep an eye on her."

That wouldn't be hard. I didn't really have a choice, anyway.

"But more important than any of that, solve your problem," Goldie said, running his tongue over his teeth. "Find that little black book. That's the key to everything for you. You find that thing, your problems are solved."

Damn straight. Now that I was back on the force, that would be my priority.

"How's our thing going, by the way?" he asked.

My undercover investigation, he meant. The one that only Goldie and I knew about. The one that, if it came out the way I thought it might, would turn the Chicago Police Department upside down.

"I'm close," I said.

"How close?"

"Soon," I said. "Very soon."

THIRTY-ONE

"WELCOME BACK, sport." Soscia smacked me on the back as he passed by my desk.

"You miss me?"

"I got no one to talk to. My new partner, he doesn't like hockey. How do you not like *hockey?*"

He meant Reynolds, his partner, the rookie in the detectives' bureau.

The cops with me on the raid that night were Detectives Lanny Soscia, Rick Reynolds, Matt Crowley, and Brian Benson.

But it was hard to imagine Sosh, whom I'd known since we were cadets in the academy, doing anything like that. Reynolds was so green I wasn't sure he was even toilet trained yet. Nice kid, but he didn't know detective work from needlepoint. Crowley? The guy was pushing retirement. I was pretty sure he was in adult diapers by this point. And Benson? I mean, a great guy, good for a laugh, and he'd have your back when it got sticky out there, but he didn't have an original thought in his brain.

And really, none of those four detectives had volunteered for the assignment. I asked them to come along only because I had a hunch that busting into a Gold Coast brownstone might get a little messy. I didn't realize *how* messy, but the point is that none of these guys had any idea I'd ask them to come along until earlier that day.

Whoever took that little black book didn't do it on the spur of the moment. He was thinking things through. He had a plan.

He or *she,* that is.

As if on cue, Kate walked in, throwing her bag down on her desk without a word to me or even a glance in my direction. I felt the temperature plummet.

"Harney." Lieutenant Wizniewski—the Wiz—my supervisor, wiggled his fingers at me.

The Wiz was there that night, too. He tried to talk me out of the bust.

It felt like an old-school Agatha Christie novel: *One of the people in this room is the thief! One of you took that little black book.*

The corned-beef sandwich sat like a brick in my stomach. I needed some coffee. The coffeemaker, a glass container that was probably purchased during the Eisenhower administration, held only a trace of burned sludge at this point in the day, and I didn't feel like going to the effort of making more, so I passed it without stopping.

"Yeah, Lew," I said, leaning against the doorway of Lieutenant Wizniewski's office.

Wizniewski's desk looked like a hoarder's paradise, with piles of paper threatening to topple over. The place reeked of cigar smoke, and he had a half-smoked stogie resting on the corner of the table.

"No smoking, boss," I said. "Maybe you hadn't heard."

"You see me smoking it?"

Wizniewski was a politician first, a cop second. If what Goldie said was right, and nobody was sure which way all this was going to play out, the Wiz must have been reading tarot cards at night.

If that was all I could say about the Wiz, I could live with him. There are politicians in every police force, ass kissers, suck-ups. But word was that the Wiz was a dirty cop.

And he was on my radar in the undercover investigation I was doing. He just didn't know it yet. I was very much looking forward to the day he did.

"I just wanted to give you some friendly advice," he said to me.

"Yeah? What's that?"

"Don't fuck up again."

"That's good advice, Lew. Hang on." I patted my pockets. "You get a pen and paper? I wanna write that down before I forget it."

The top of his head turned red. It always did when you got a rise out of him, which wasn't hard.

"Always the comedian, this one." He seemed like he was looking for something amid the clutter on his desk. He couldn't find something on that desk if it were set on fire.

"I'm gonna find that black book," I said, staring at him.

He stopped what he was doing and looked up at me. "Yeah? Why you telling *me* that?"

"I just thought you'd want to know."

Seemed like he took it for the accusation it was. I didn't think that forehead could get any redder.

"Best of luck with that," he said evenly.

THIRTY-TWO

RAMONA DILLAVOU walked out of her house just past seven. She looked like the wealthy woman she was, wearing an expensive long fur coat and matching hat, her bleached-blond hair hanging down in a stylish bob, her head held high, a confident strut to her walk. She didn't go far. There was a car waiting for her outside, an average-looking Chevy sedan. Uber, probably, or maybe someone she knew.

I was in my car, so I followed behind. Parking in Lincoln Park is tricky, so this could pose a problem for me; if she was in an Uber car, as I suspected, she could just be dropped off, and I'd have to park my unmarked vehicle somewhere.

Ramona Dillavou was released on bond after her arrest two weeks ago at the brownstone. As the manager of the brownstone brothel, she was the best lead to the little black book. That night she denied its existence in a profanity-laden tirade that took some of the polish off her sophisticated veneer, but the point was that she didn't tell us squat. She lawyered up almost immediately and refused to answer our questions at the police station, too. The five thousand dollars she had to come up with to get sprung was probably chump change to her.

I didn't have much to go on. She had a record consisting of two priors—one for prostitution and one for promoting it. She had graduated into the big time with the brownstone brothel and its exclusive clientele, but I didn't know much else about her. All I knew for sure was that we had put her brothel out of business and she'd be looking for another way to make some money.

The car dropped her off in the Gold Coast, south of Lincoln Park, on Rush Street. Tyson's was a high-end restaurant with a bar where on occasion one might find an aging, unattractive man with an uncommonly beautiful woman on his arm.

I double-parked my car and took my time crossing the street. I had no idea what I was going to find. More than likely she was just meeting someone for dinner and drinks, in which case I'd strike out—just as I'd struck out the other times I had followed her over the last two weeks. So far no luck, but a Boy Scout keeps trying.

The place was packed, the circle of people around the bar three deep at least, all sorts of merriment and chatting. The lighting was dim, and there was some kind of jazz-swing music coming over the speakers. Loud and crowded was a good thing. It made it easier for me to disappear.

I pulled out my phone for a couple of reasons. One, if I needed to duck my head quickly to avoid detection, I'd have an excuse for staring downward. And two, I might need the camera on the device.

I looked around the place and didn't see her on a first pass. She could be in the dining area, which would be harder for me. She was wearing a fur coat, though she might have taken it off by now.

That reminded me of a joke, and I hadn't sent my friend Stewart anything for a week or so, so I put my iPhone camera on the video setting and spoke into it.

"A guy named Jerry gets out of the shower at his country club," I said. "The cell phone by his locker is ringing, and he answers it. 'Honey,' the woman on the other end says. 'I just saw a fur coat I've been dying to buy. It's five thousand dollars.' Jerry says, 'Wow. Five thousand for a coat—that's a lot. But go ahead; it's okay.' She says, 'Well, since you're in a good mood, I just passed a Mercedes dealership, and there's a new model I just love. But it's a hundred and fifty thousand.' Jerry says, 'A hundred and fifty grand for a car? Jeez, I guess so. Sure, go ahead.' She says, 'You're the best, honey,' and hangs up. Jerry hangs up the phone and puts it down. His buddies at the gym say, 'Jerry, we had no idea you had that kind of cash.' Jerry says, 'I don't. I'm flat broke. By the way, any of you know whose cell phone this is?'"

I punched the Facebook icon next to the Video button on my iPhone, which transfers the video immediately to the Facebook page I share with Stewart. My sister, Patti, who understands these contraptions better than anyone I know, somehow configured that Facebook button onto my camera so I could automatically upload videos. Otherwise I'd be clueless as to how to do it.

I hadn't visited Stewart in his nursing home for months. I met him at Children's Memorial Hospital three years ago, when we both sat in the ICU for weeks. For Stewart, it was his grandson, who'd been hit by a car and was clinging to life. Making him laugh at my corny jokes was the only thing that got me through it all.

Somehow sending him my stand-up routines at the Hole in the Wall and posting the occasional joke like this made me feel like I was doing a good deed. His granddaughter once told me that he checked that Facebook page every single day, first thing in the morning.

I looked up from my phone and immediately looked down again, having caught a glimpse of Ramona Dillavou's shiny blond hair. So she *was* in the bar area, seated on the opposite end from me. I turned away and moved between two businessmen, which wasn't hard in this rugby scrum, so I could get another look from a hidden vantage point.

I raised my eyes and saw enough to see Ramona turned to her left, talking to someone. She seemed to be keeping her voice down, showing some discretion.

But I couldn't see the person next to her because the bar was wrapped around the liquor station in the middle, the bottles of booze obscuring my view.

So I moved to my left to get a better angle, to see the person with whom she was conversing. I was hoping that it would be a man—that Ramona Dillavou, now out of a job as the manager of the brownstone brothel, was returning to her previous calling as a prostitute; that I could catch her in the act and make her an offer she couldn't refuse. Tell me where the black book is or violate your bond and go back in the clink.

I positioned myself behind some people and shot another look across the bar at Ramona.

I peeked and looked back down at my phone.

Then I peeked again.

My heart kicked into overdrive. I couldn't believe what I'd just seen.

Maybe, I told myself, it was the dim lighting. Maybe I just didn't get a good look.

I looked again, holding my stare. Even though I might be recognized. Even though I knew what I'd seen.

Dim lighting or not, I hadn't made a mistake.

Ramona Dillavou wasn't talking to a man. She was talking to a woman.

A woman I knew very well.

THIRTY-THREE

"PATTI," I mumbled to myself.

I worked my way through the crowd and out the door into a throng of people. I pulled up my collar as I walked down the wind tunnel that was Rush Street, the question buzzing through my head.

What was my sister doing with Ramona Dillavou, the manager of the brownstone brothel? I couldn't make it fit. It just...didn't make sense.

I pivoted suddenly and turned back toward the restaurant, almost colliding with a couple right behind me who didn't appreciate my sudden stop. I stepped back and looked toward the restaurant, as though if I stared at it long enough, something would change. I considered returning to the bar and taking yet another look, but of course that made no sense, either. I'd seen what I'd seen.

What the hell are you doing, Patti?

I continued south toward my car, navigating through the crowd of lively pedestrians, the sounds of car horns blaring and drivers yelling and tipsy people laughing and chatting.

I pulled out my car keys, a natural thing to do, since I was heading toward my car. I bumped into a man coming toward me on my right and let my keys fall behind me. I mumbled an apology and bent down, creating a small space as people navigated around me.

"Excuse me, excuse me," I said. "Sorry."

I grabbed my keys off the wet sidewalk, righted myself, turned back, and headed to my car.

It was double-parked on Rush. It was a small miracle that it was still there. I had pushed my luck.

I was hoping that I had a little bit of luck left. Because I was going to need it.

Or so I thought. It's a cliché for a cop to talk about his gut, his hunch, but clichés aren't always wrong. It's part experience and part intuition. It didn't hurt that I'd been working undercover with BIA for the last three years, either. It helped me know how to pick up the signs.

It's not hard to do. If you're in that mode, it's almost automatic. You stop and glance over your shoulder when a pretty woman passes. Or you stop at a corner, waiting for the traffic light to change, and turn back.

Or you allow yourself to bump into someone and pretend to drop your keys.

Any excuse to take a look behind you. You don't look directly at any one person. You don't make eye contact. No, you just take in the crowd. You look for any tickling of a sensation that someone is moving as you move, stopping as you stop, shadowing your movements.

I couldn't be sure. I couldn't swear to it. But I had a pretty good idea that somebody was tailing me.

And now I had to decide what to do about it.

THIRTY-FOUR

I GOT in my car and drove north, the only direction I could go. I made a quick left and then another onto State Street, now heading south, navigating potholes and death-defying pedestrians who zigzagged through traffic to cross the street. (In Chicago, obeying Don't Walk signs is usually considered optional.)

The distractions forced me to train my focus forward, on the road, though my eyes continually shot into the rearview mirror to see what was happening behind me. Traffic was thick, and in the dark it was all headlights behind me. That helped when I was following Ramona Dillavou. She never could have made me for a tail. But apparently it hindered me, too, because I didn't notice at the time that somebody was following *me*.

And the traffic hindered me now, too. I couldn't make out the colors or even the makes of cars in my rearview mirror, much less see their occupants. But that was okay. There was more than one way to sniff out a tail.

Traffic behind me dissipated as I moved west and south, away from the Gold Coast, but it was still pretty heavy, giving my tail sufficient cover.

I wanted to go home. I wanted to pace around my

town house, pour myself a stiff drink, and ponder why in God's name my sister, Patti, would have been meeting with the manager of a brothel, presumably the guardian of the prized little black book.

But I couldn't go home. Because I didn't want my tail to stop following me. If he knew me—and he must have—then he knew where I lived. Once he saw me pull up to my building, he'd assume I was going in for the night. He'd keep his distance. He might even call it a night himself.

And I didn't want him to call it a night. So I didn't go home.

From Chicago Avenue, I turned right onto Damen and kept my car at an even speed. Damen probably wasn't the best choice, because as I drove north, the area became crowded again, with restaurants and bars and some pretty high-end boutiques, too, once you got north of North Avenue. Fifteen years ago, this was the cool place to live, where the artists and hipsters hung out. That crowd was still here, but it had attracted more yuppies and even some families, people who could afford the sky-high property values.

But I didn't care about the gentrification of Wicker Park or Bucktown at the moment. I was more interested in the sedan three cars behind me, which thus far had made every turn I had made. See, the route I'd taken was unusual. I'd started on Rush Street, going north, then done a loop to head south on State Street to Chicago Avenue, then I drove west to Damen, and now I was heading north again on Damen to Armitage, which was a mile north from where I originally started—my double-parked spot on Rush.

My route, in other words, made no sense. The guy who said that the shortest distance between two points is a straight line? That guy would've said I was an idiot. Why go to all that trouble to head south when I could have just kept going north from Tyson's on Rush Street? I'd gone completely out of my way. Instead of a straight line, my route looked like a humpbacked serpent.

You know what I looked like? I looked like either (1) a tourist who didn't know his way around Chicago or (2) someone who was trying to be surreptitious about his movements.

And my tail knew I wasn't a tourist.

But the other benefit was that I could now say the same thing about the guy following me. The only reason for him to take this route was to tail me.

With my right hand on the steering wheel, I used my left to slip my piece out of my side holster, ejecting the magazine to check the clip. I had enough bullets. It usually only takes one.

Not that I planned on using it. I'm a lover, not a fighter. I'm a sweetheart of a guy. Confrontation is never my first choice. But sometimes you can't avoid it. And a Boy Scout is always prepared.

I turned left off Damen onto Dickens, driving west again. We were in an area that still hadn't decided if it was going to be upscale residential or semi-industrial. I drove another mile or so before I hung a right. Now I had three blocks of driving ahead of me, straight north on a quiet street, so I could see behind me pretty clearly.

There in the distance, a good city block behind me, the sedan made the same turn.

It was no coincidence. We'd left coincidence in the dust miles ago.

I pulled into an abandoned lot that, once upon a

time, was home to a bank with a drive-in wing on the side. Some stray garbage was littered about. No reason—no good reason—for anyone to be here this time of night.

I pulled up next to the drive-through lane and stopped. I wanted to make sure that my tail had a good look at me. I put the car in park but kept it running. I fished through the glove compartment until I found an empty envelope.

The sedan drove past on the road. It slowed a bit as the driver, I assume, was trying to get a look at what I was doing. If he had any kind of a scope and could see into my car, he would probably think I was waiting for somebody.

The sedan drove on. He didn't have much of a choice. He was too conspicuous, on a side street that wasn't busy. With me sitting idly in an abandoned parking lot, he couldn't stay where he was.

I scribbled a note on the envelope, took a photo of it with my phone so I wouldn't forget the details, and got out of my car.

It was colder than a mother-in-law's glare out here. The wind, in open space, came at me from all directions. I made a point of looking all around me, as though I were making sure that nobody was watching.

Then I walked over to the slot by the teller's window and placed the envelope inside it.

I jogged back to my car and got in and drove out of the parking lot, back to the street I'd originally taken, but this time driving in the opposite direction, south.

"Your move," I said, looking in my rearview mirror.

I drove a normal speed, my eyes glued to the mirror. I was more than two blocks down, almost at Dickens, and the car still hadn't come out from wherever it was hiding to follow me.

That's what I figured. He wasn't going to follow me.

He was going to see what I had dropped in that teller's slot.

THIRTY-FIVE

I MADE a right onto Dickens, which is the direction my tail would expect me to take if I were going home. I lived about two miles from this spot, to the south and west.

But I wasn't going home. I turned right on the next street and headed north, back to the abandoned bank, approaching it from the other side.

I picked this location for a reason. Many moons ago, when I first made detective, we caught a pickpocket who was working this neighborhood. We had several complaints in the span of a single week, and it didn't take Sherlock Holmes to quickly discover that the victims had one thing in common—the last thing they had done before their pockets were picked was withdraw money from the ATM at this bank. Not the drive-through window but the walk-up vestibule, encased in glass and locked in the evenings but open during the day.

The thing was, the thief didn't just steal the victims' wallets. He also went immediately to the closest ATM and emptied their bank accounts of the maximum amount the bank would allow for a single withdrawal.

How, I wondered, being the new, eager detective

that I was, *could the thief figure out the ATM password so quickly?* Sure, maybe he had some sophisticated computer software, but this was several years ago, before that sort of thing was as rampant as it is today—and besides, he was using the ATM card within minutes, if not seconds, of the theft.

So I did a wee bit more detective work and realized that one end of the bank's parking lot was bordered by trees. I decided to kill a bit of time in an unmarked vehicle down the street. It only took three hours until a white male, a teenager fitting the description of the suspect, climbed a tree and trained his binoculars on the ATM vestibule.

Well, I didn't need to climb a tree tonight. Binoculars wouldn't have hurt, but I didn't have any. So I crawled over to the shrubs and kept low. The view of the teller's slot was nice and clear. It was dark in the vacant lot, but if it was dark for me, it would be dark for him, too. He'd probably need a flashlight, and with any luck the light coming off it would give me enough illumination to see this asshole's face.

The sedan that followed me here pulled up to the intersection where the bank was located. The guy probably wanted to wait a while to make sure nobody was around, to be confident that I had left for good.

Then the car pulled into the parking lot and drove toward the teller window of the drive-up, just where I'd been. The car's headlights shone into my face. That wouldn't help. It would make things harder. But maybe he'd walk past the headlights, which would light him up nicely for me. All I needed to know was who he was, just a quick shot of his face.

The car stopped but kept running, the headlights still on.

"Come on," I whispered.

The car door opened. The interior dome light came on, which would have been my chance to see his face, but those damn headlights blinded me. So I needed him to walk around the front of the car, passing by the headlights.

No luck. He went around the rear of the car. With headlights shining in my face and no other illumination in the parking lot, I couldn't see much besides a figure—a figure bundled up in a heavy jacket and hat in the frigid evening air—heading over to the teller window.

I could hear just fine: the *ka-thunk* as the slot at the teller window opened and closed. Then a pause, while my new friend tried to read the note I had left.

"Flashlight," I mumbled. "Flashlight."

He used the glow from his phone to put some light on the note. But he was turned away, so the small amount of illumination from the phone didn't give me anything. I could see the piece of paper in his hand, but whoever this person might be was hunched over, reading it. All I could get was a heavy jacket and some kind of a hat on his head.

Then the glow disappeared. Another *ka-thunk* as my newest, bestest buddy closed up the slot on the teller window.

Then he got back in the car. I tried to get a look inside, but the headlights were still hitting me head-on, and when the car turned and the headlights swept away from me, I couldn't see my hand in front of my face.

I had my phone out, ready to hit the flashlight app so I could catch the license plate, but I couldn't risk giving away my position. The sedan left the parking lot and drove away.

So I struck out.

But that was okay. I'd have another chance soon.

Still crouched in the bushes, I clicked on my phone and looked at the photograph I took of the note I left in the teller slot.

It said: Tomorrow, 6 p.m. Red Line, Jackson stop, northbound platform. Bring it with you.

The guy tailing me had read the note. That much I could see. If he was curious about me already—and he must have been—he'd be very interested indeed in finding out whom I was meeting with and what that person was going to bring along.

He'd be there. And this time I would see him coming.

"See you tomorrow night, my friend," I said as the car disappeared from sight.

THIRTY-SIX

I SHOULD have gone home after that. I should have gone back to my town house and poured myself a stiff drink or six so I could think about the two questions I couldn't get out of my mind.

What was my sister, Patti, doing talking to the manager of the brownstone brothel?

And who the hell was following me?

But I didn't feel like making myself crazy just at that moment. So I went to the Hole in the Wall. It was full of cops and bunnies as usual. Most of them were well into their pints, which was fine with me. I didn't need conversation. I just needed the white noise of the crowd, the heat and animation. A couple shots of bourbon wouldn't hurt, either.

Detective Larry Soscia—Sosh—was over in a corner, holding forth with a few of his buddies, probably going on about the Blackhawks' second line, though I doubt anyone could understand half the words he was saying. He raised his pint in salute when he saw me, spilling some of the beer on his shirt. The best part was he didn't even realize it.

No, the best part was that he'd be at his desk at eight sharp tomorrow morning, ready to go. Sosh was one of those cops who drank a lot to get through all the shit he saw on the job, but he always came back for more. They'd have to pry his badge out of his dying hand, even if they might have to pry a bottle of Budweiser out of the other.

I took a couple of shots of Maker's Mark at the bar and then looked over the crowd. I heard a woman's laugh, and it registered with me. I turned and saw Amy Lentini sitting at a high table with some guy. A good-looking guy, I noted, also noting that I felt a small knot form in my stomach.

Well, shit, I thought. *Fair play to her.* She could have her pick of the litter. She probably had guys crawling out of the woodwork to ask her out.

I had to admit I had underestimated her. She was smart as hell, and apparently she brought some credentials to the job. A former federal prosecutor; a high-profile takedown of a US senator in Wisconsin. And she twisted me up like a pretzel when we did a mock cross-examination.

Watch that one, I reminded myself. *Watch that one closely.*

She caught my eye and froze for a moment. I nodded to her.

She gave me the finger. Then smiled. I felt something lift. Something that usually got me in trouble.

The guy she was with had sandy brown hair and a thick neck and shoulders—your basic high school homecoming king–varsity letterman guy who had done just fine in the professional world flashing that smile, knotting that tie just so, timing that joke perfectly. He probably secretly wore ladies' undergarments and still sucked his thumb when he curled up with his teddy bear at night.

That wasn't fair. I didn't even know the guy. He

could be totally different from that. For all I knew, he snuck out at night to screw barnyard animals.

And what the hell was my problem, by the way? What did I care what Amy Lentini did in her spare time? If she wanted to gallivant around with some eye candy who has the IQ of a tree stump, who's to tell her no? Certainly not I, I told myself as I downed my third shot of bourbon and asked for a fourth. I didn't care about Amy Lentini. Nope. Not one bit.

Then I saw Lieutenant Mike Goldberger moving my way. I felt a rush of relief. Goldie was my port in the storm. Everybody needs one. I needed one right now, in fact.

Goldie liked to have a cocktail now and then, sure, but that's not why he came to the Hole. He came here because this was where everybody talked, especially after too many pints of Guinness. He liked to lie low, say very little, gently prod the conversation forward, as if he were just being polite when in fact he was collecting and filing every piece of data. He knew more things about more cops than anybody I knew.

"How's things?" he asked, leaning against the bar, telling the bartender he'd have the same shot of Maker's Mark I was having.

I repositioned myself, turning away from the crowd and toward the bartender. I moved my head toward Goldie and held my words for a moment. He sensed I had something to say. He knew me well. He leaned a bit in my direction.

But how much to tell him? I didn't want him or anyone else to know about Patti visiting with Ramona Dillavou. Patti was my problem. She was my twin sister. She didn't need to go on anybody's official radar. No, I wasn't going to mention that part.

As if on cue, my sister, Patti, walked through the front door.

No, I decided: whatever Patti was up to, it would be my problem only.

But the part about my being followed? Goldie could help me with that.

"I think I have a shadow," I said. "I need your help tomorrow."

Goldie lifted the shot glass and drained the bourbon, signaled the barkeep for another, then pulled out a twenty from his roll and dropped it on the counter.

"Call me," he said, correctly reasoning that the conversation would require too much detail for a chat at the bar. He took the next shot, downed it, and walked away without another word.

I looked back at Amy's table. The guy sitting next to her put his arm around the back of her chair. She didn't seem to mind. I felt something burn inside me. Maybe it was the bourbon in my throat. Yeah, probably that was it.

I heard someone start up with my name, then the chant. *Har-ney! Har-ney!* I didn't really feel like doing a few at the mike, but I didn't have anything better to do, and my friend Stewart would probably appreciate a little stand-up tomorrow morning when he checked our Facebook page.

I passed Amy on my way to the stage, giving her the finger and a quick wink.

THIRTY-SEVEN

"A GUY walks into a confessional," said Billy, standing on the stage at the Hole. "He tells the priest, 'I just had the wildest sex of my life tonight. I met these three prostitutes...'"

Patti moved through the crowd as her brother did his thing. She spotted the prosecutor Amy Lentini, the one going after Billy. There was a guy with her. A drop-dead handsome man. Well, weren't they the perfect couple—the gorgeous Italian beauty and the Calvin Klein model.

"'We had sex all night,' he tells the priest. 'We tried every position. At one point, I was hanging from the chandelier...'"

But Amy didn't seem interested in her well coiffed beau. No, with her chin propped on her fists, her eyes were on Billy. Patti had seen that look before. The expression that went well beyond just listening to a stand-up comic and enjoying the humor. The flicker in her eyes that meant a lot more than simply thinking a comedian was humorous.

Sure, Patti had seen that look before. She'd seen it on Kate.

"'We used chains and whips; we dressed up in costumes; I played a prison warden and a doctor...'"

The male-model boyfriend glanced over at Amy, then up at the stage, then back to Amy. He saw it, too, the way Amy looked momentarily lost, transfixed on Billy. He said something to her. She nodded vaguely in his direction. Then he got off his chair, grabbed his coat, and headed for the exit. Amy didn't seem to notice.

"So finally the priest says, 'Okay, okay, I get the point—you had wild, kinky sex all night. So now you want absolution?' The man says, 'Oh, no, Father—I'm not Catholic. I don't even believe in God.' The priest says, 'Then why did you tell me all this?' The man says, 'Are you kidding, Father? I'm telling *everybody!*'"

The crowd roared in response. Everyone except Amy. Oh, she allowed for a smile, but it wasn't the raunchy humor that held her attention. It was the person delivering it.

By then Patti had moved close to Amy. She felt her body shaking. She approached the table but didn't speak.

Billy, on stage, picked up his phone and clicked a button, the button that Patti set up for him to allow him to upload his stand-up routines to that Facebook page he shared with his friend Stewart. Billy wouldn't know how to work that phone if you put a gun to his head. He needed Patti for that. He needed Patti for a lot of things. Even if he didn't know it.

With Billy's set over, Amy finally realized that Patti was standing next to her.

"Do you know who I am?" Patti asked.

Amy, taken aback, shook her head. "I'm sorry; I don't."

"I'm Patti," she said. "Patti Harney. Billy's sister."

"Oh, okay." Amy put out her hand. Patti didn't shake it.

"His *twin* sister," Patti said.

Amy drew back her hand with a questioning look.

"Billy's been through the wringer," said Patti. "Do you know his history?"

"I—I'm sorry...what is this—"

"You do, don't you? You probably know all about him. Because you're investigating him. You know what happened to him, his family?"

Amy didn't respond, but Patti could see the defensive shield go up.

"Can I help you with something, Patti?"

"You sure can, *Amy*. You can stay away from my brother. That will help me a lot."

By that time Amy had had the chance to readjust from casual-greeting mode to hostile-conversation mode. "Is that any business of yours?"

"It sure as hell is, Amy. And you better know I'm serious."

"Oh, that much I can tell."

"You ever have a pissed-off cop on your ass, Amy?"

Amy stepped off her chair and faced Patti. "No, as a matter of fact I haven't. Have you ever had a pissed-off prosecutor on yours?"

Patti let a smile play out across her face. Amy, for her part, held her stare.

"Stay away," said Patti, drawing out the words, "from my brother."

THIRTY-EIGHT

"I'LL BE here all week," I said before I clicked off the mike and placed it on the stand. I grabbed my phone, punched the icon to upload the routine onto Stewart's Facebook page, and stepped off the stage.

The bartender had a shot of bourbon and a beer chaser waiting for me, his little way of thanking me. He seemed to think my comedy drew people into the place. I didn't know if that was true. I usually did my routines to vent, to go off on something that bothered me, kind of the observational-humor thing. Other times, when I was less in the mood but felt some obligation to get up on stage, I went on autopilot and just drew from the reserve of jokes I'd accumulated over the years. My brain worked that way. Ask me my online password for my bank account, and I need to look it up every time. Ask me about a joke that Richie Stetsafannis told me in fourth grade, and I can recite it verbatim.

I downed the shot and chased it with the beer. A couple of guys I used to serve with on patrol were near the stage, and they pulled me to their table. I didn't really feel like talking to them, but my mother raised a polite boy. We traded stories about our days in patrol, stories that had changed significantly with the passage of time, allowing us to remember ourselves as brave and daring and decisive instead of the scared puppies we really were, praying that we wouldn't embarrass ourselves or, God forbid, shoot somebody.

I found a break in the conversation and told them I had to take a piss, which was a lie but the easiest way to break free. My eyes quickly moved to the table where Amy Lentini and her boyfriend had been sitting. The table was empty.

I looked over at the bar but didn't see her there, either.

I deflated. I couldn't deny my disappointment. I didn't understand it, but it was there. I was like a jealous schoolboy.

I had tied on a pretty healthy buzz, and I had a big day ahead of me tomorrow. According to the note I had scribbled on the fly and left in the bank-teller slot, I was going to meet somebody at a subway station tomorrow night, and I had to get this right—I had to flush out my tail, who surely would be there.

So I decided to skip out. I didn't have my car. I had dropped it off and taken a cab to the Hole. When I pushed through the door, the wind smacked me. It was so cold outside that a lawyer would have his hands in his *own* pockets. But it felt good. It woke me up. I decided to walk a few blocks and see how that went.

I made another decision, too. I pulled out my phone and, before I could talk myself out of it, dialed Amy Lentini's number.

She answered on the third ring.

"Well, well," she said.

My spirits lifted. She had me on caller ID. She had taken the time to input my name into her phone. I know, I know—I felt like I was in grade school. Next up I was going to pass her friend a note saying *Do you think she likes me?*

"Hope I didn't wake you," I said.

"No, I'm good."

I couldn't get much from her words. She wasn't out of breath, so at least she wasn't in the middle of mind-altering sex with the Chippendales dancer.

"I heard your routine tonight," she said.

"Yeah, I was gonna stop over, but you were gone. Too much excitement for one night?"

"Hey, I'm just a small-town Wisconsin girl. I have to get up early to milk the cows."

Yeah, right. But I liked that she downplayed herself that way, even if we both knew it.

"Your boyfriend seemed nice," I said.

I couldn't believe I said that. It was the half dozen shots of bourbon talking.

You should hang up right now, you moron. Cut your losses.

"He's not my boyfriend," she said.

"No? Does *he* know that?"

"He does now."

He shoots, he scores!

But I didn't say anything in response. I'd already made an ass out of myself, bringing up her date in the first place.

"Are you calling to confess, Billy? To admit that you stole the little black book?"

I crossed an intersection without noticing that a car was coming right toward me. The driver didn't even slow down. He just honked his horn and expected me to jog out of the way. He must have been born and raised here.

"No," I said. "I think I'm going to exercise my right to remain silent."

"And yet you called me."

She was a lawyer, all right. And she had a point. I'd called her. And I didn't know why. Or maybe I did but didn't want to admit it to anybody, including myself.

"You ever eat?" I asked, feeling my pulse jack up, putting it all out there.

"I—yes, I've been known to on occasion."

She wasn't going to make this easy, was she?

"Are you asking me to dinner?" she said.

"No. I'm just taking a survey on people's daily routines."

"Oh, I see."

"But if you wanted to have dinner with me, that would be fine."

She seemed to like that, a cute little chuckle. "Well played, Detective. So now *I'm* asking *you* out."

"And I accept," I said. "I mean, since you insist."

I punched off the phone to the sound of her laughter. I figured I should quit while I was ahead. I felt a little steam in my stride. The wind felt like a balmy ocean breeze.

You don't have the slightest clue what you're getting yourself into, I thought to myself. *But it will be fun finding out.*

THIRTY-NINE

THE NEXT morning was not so fun. I walked into the station feeling like I was carrying sand in my feet, like tiny anvils were hammering at the back of my eyes.

Kate was already there, looking alert and fresh. She sensed me before she saw me. Her head moved slowly in my direction.

When she looked at me, it was like we'd never met.

For a moment, that is, and then she nodded at me.

We hadn't parted on good terms yesterday, to say the least. We had all but accused each other of stealing the little black book, of not trusting each other. But she was saying, with her nod, that we still had a job to do, and we would do it.

So I nodded back. It was enough for now.

The day passed slowly. We had a murder on the South Side, which apparently started as a robbery and turned lethal when one of the three suspects pulled out a knife. We had a dead body and vague descriptions. Forensics would take a few days and might get us somewhere; there was a lot of blood spilled, not all of it the victim's, so if any of the offenders had records, we might have their DNA on file.

We started with interviews in the morning. When

it comes to most murders on the South Side, the word *interview* means "nobody saw nothing, nobody knows nothing." It's not that people don't give a shit. They do. Most people in any neighborhood, no matter how rough, want the criminals to go to prison so the good people can live peaceably. The problem is that the gangs have these neighborhoods so wired that people who talk to the police have to spend the rest of their days looking over their shoulders. I had a murder one time near Cicero and 79th that happened on the street just outside a 7-Eleven. A security camera inside the store caught some good footage, and the manager turned it over to the police. Three days later, the store was torched, burned completely to the ground, and the street gang's name had been scratched into the metal door to the back alley with a knife.

Plus, as you may have heard, some people don't trust the police.

Put fear and loathing together, and it's tough to get eyewitness testimony out here. So it was a tough day for us. By five o'clock, we shut it down. I would visit the victim's family tomorrow to see if they had any information.

"See you tomorrow," I said to Kate—without looking at her—as we split up. She might have waved but didn't say a word.

When she was gone, I checked my phone again—the picture I'd taken of the note I had dumped in the teller's window slot: Tomorrow, 6 p.m. Red Line, Jackson stop, northbound platform. Bring it with you.

I'd chosen the subway platform for this bogus meeting because it was hard to follow me there without giving yourself away. Whoever was tailing me couldn't hide in the darkness of a car with the headlights blazing, couldn't watch from a safe distance with binoculars. No, if this person wanted to know whom I was supposedly meeting with, he'd have to get himself on that damn platform. And for all he knew, I might jump onto an arriving train and he'd have to follow.

I picked six o'clock because it would be busy; if it was too late in the evening, the platform would be empty, and he'd be afraid to follow me down there because he'd feel exposed. At six, he'd feel comfortable in the knowledge that he could blend into a crowd while watching me and my supposed meeting partner.

The catch in my plan? There was no actual meeting, obviously, and nobody was bringing me anything. That part I had to improvise.

That's what friends are for. And my only friend was Goldie.

I made it to the platform at ten minutes to six. I went to the south end. I wanted to be conspicuous. I stood in the corner and faced north, so I could see the other people on the train platform. I could also see everyone across the tracks on the opposite platform—the people who were taking southbound trains.

The problem was that it was hard to actually see them. We were in the depths of a Chicago winter. Everyone was dressed for it, bundled up in hats and scarves, jackets zipped up to their chins. I couldn't get a good look at anyone's face. The lighting was pretty good, but you can't see someone hiding behind all that clothing.

Goldie wasn't going to come himself. He was going to send somebody. He said I wouldn't know the guy, but I should expect a tall African American man in a camel-colored overcoat.

At five minutes to six, a southbound train arrived, hissing to a stop. That meant everyone on the platform opposite me would get on. Anyone who didn't—well, that wouldn't make much sense, would it? The only reason people were supposed to be on the platform was to take that train.

When the train doors opened, a number of passengers got off, and the people waiting on the platform got on. Or at least it looked like that. It was a big crowd of people, and the train itself was between me and the passengers.

When the train sputtered forward again with a heavy sigh and grunt, I scanned the platform. Almost everyone was moving toward the exit.

Almost everyone.

One man hung back. Wearing a brown stocking cap and a thick, chocolate-brown coat with the collar zipped high. His back turned to me. I hadn't seen him on the platform previously. He'd just gotten off the train.

And he wasn't moving toward the exit. He was staying put.

I pulled out my phone and pretended to talk on it. That was my crutch; I could look at someone but pretend that I was doing so absently, that my focus was on the conversation.

In my peripheral vision, I saw someone moving toward me. I looked over and saw a big guy, African American, wearing a camel-colored overcoat and a colorful scarf. He made eye contact with me and nodded. He was my contact, the guy Goldie sent.

Then I looked back at the guy across the platform,

the stocking cap and chocolate coat. I watched him pull back his sleeve to look at his watch. His head crept up for just a moment, and his head turned in my direction.

I looked away just before he caught my eye. "I know," I said into the phone, my fake conversation. "I couldn't believe it, either."

The guy across the platform didn't see me looking at him, I was pretty sure. But I got a good look at his face in that nanosecond before I averted my eyes.

I knew him. He was my boss.

The man watching me from across the platform was Lieutenant Paul Wizniewski.

FORTY

MY HEART started pounding. The Wiz, my boss, was the one tailing me.

Did he know? Did he know I was Internal Affairs? Did he know that I was more than just a homicide detective, that I was working undercover for Goldie and BIA?

Did he know that *he* was one of the main targets of my undercover investigation?

The tall African American guy, he of the camel coat and colorful scarf, was making his way toward me now. Goldie had sent him, so he was almost surely BIA.

The man walked up and stood next to me as though he didn't know me—just another guy waiting to take a northbound train.

I kept up my bogus conversation on my phone. I shook my head as I spoke, like something in the conversation was frustrating me.

Yep, two guys just waiting for a train.

I mean, we had to make it look like we were trying to be surreptitious, right? My tail—whom I now knew was the Wiz—would expect nothing less.

As casually as I could, I turned around so my back was to the platform and, more important, so that I was facing away from Wizniewski. I wanted it to be easy for the Wiz to watch me, and if I had my back to him, he could stare all he wanted. He could even snap photos with his phone if he was so inclined.

Now it was time for the guy next to me, Mr. Camel Coat, to sneeze.

He did. Faking a sneeze isn't hard, especially when the person you're trying to fake out is across the train tracks from you. After he did so, Mr. Camel Coat turned away, an instinctive, polite thing to do, so he could blow his nose. He reached into his coat as he turned. He produced a handkerchief and a manila envelope, one large enough to hold a set of glossy eight-by-ten photographs.

At this point we both had our backs to the Wiz, and we made a point of keeping a small distance between us so the Wiz could clearly see the envelope pass from Camel Coat to me.

Camel Coat, without missing a beat, blew his nose, or pretended to, then folded up his handkerchief and turned around to face the platform again. He was good. I caught a whiff of his aftershave as he turned. But I never looked directly at him.

I stuffed the envelope into my coat and pretended to end my phone conversation. I turned around so that I, too, was facing the opposite platform again.

Just two guys waiting for a train. Eyes cast casually downward, in a fog after a long day of work.

Now that we were both facing the platform again and the Wiz could see our faces, it was time for Camel Coat to speak, just one word.

"When?" he said.

He enunciated the word sharply, so it would be easy to read his lips.

Now it was my turn to utter one word, and I did it the same way, pretending to be casual but making sure the word would be easy to read off my lips, as though I were serving it on a silver platter to Lieutenant Paul Wizniewski.

I said, "Soon."

FORTY-ONE

I MADE it back to my town house, stripped off my winter garb, dropped the manila envelope that Mr. Camel Coat had given me on the kitchen table, and poured myself a few inches of bourbon.

To summarize: my boss was surveilling me, my sister was secretly meeting with the manager of the brownstone brothel, and my partner distrusted and probably despised me. And a prosecutor whom I found incredibly attractive, and whom I could not stop thinking about, wanted to put me in prison.

Other than that, things were looking up.

I carried my drink and the manila envelope up the stairs. I was anxious to put everything together, but I'd learned over the years that you can't always force these things. Sometimes you have to sit still and let everything move around you until the pieces lock into place.

My undercover investigation was a good example. I had stumbled over it, really. Nobody assigned me to it. It was just something that came my way when I wasn't looking.

Here's what happened: around eighteen months ago, I was investigating a homicide in Greektown, some oily Mediterranean type who took a bullet in the wee hours of the night out on Adams Street near all the restaurants. You know—the ones with lots of white stucco, blue accents, flaming cheese, and waiters chanting *Opa!*

Anyway, the murder itself was pedestrian. No big deal, right? It was the investigation that I found interesting. I had a couple of suspects, one of whom was a young guy whose parents owned one of the restaurants. So I ran a sheet on him and found that he'd been arrested eight—count 'em, eight—times, but none of the charges ever stuck. Not one. Eight arrests, zero charges filed. A few of the times, he'd been released before a prosecutor even weighed in on possible charges—he was let go, in other words, by the cops on their own, which was unusual.

As it turned out, this suspect wasn't my guy for the murder, but I kept a copy of his rap sheet and stared at it for weeks. How did this guy manage to get such favorable treatment? Especially when the cops never even referred the case to the state's attorney—when the cops just released the guy from his jail cell and sent him on his way?

It first hit me then: someone was protecting this guy. Someone was making sure he didn't get in trouble.

The cases on this guy's rap sheet went back several years, and as I looked back at the supervising officers and the top badges in that district, one name stuck out like a glass of ice water in a desert. The name was Paul Wizniewski, who since had been promoted to lieutenant and transferred to my district.

The Wiz, I thought, was running a protection racket. *You stuff a few bills in my pocket, I make your arrest go away*—that kind of thing.

It's not hard to do, really. Prosecutors depend, first

and foremost, on the cops, who are the engines that drive the criminal justice system. If the cops say the guy didn't do it, or if the victim isn't credible, or if there isn't enough evidence to charge, the prosecutors rarely push back. Why would they? They aren't out there on the streets with us. If a cop calls a case bullshit, the prosecutor usually goes along; they have plenty of other cases to charge.

So I could see it happening. I saw it eighteen months ago. That's how this whole undercover investigation started—with that one suspicious rap sheet. I had no clue how high this thing went or how many people were involved. All I knew was that I had to investigate.

I went to Goldie and told him we had to open a file on this. Goldie, of course, said yes. We both knew it was sensitive, as touchy as a case can get. Goldie also said something to me that I never forgot.

If you wanna do this, he said, *you damn well better be right.*

Take your time, he told me, *and be sure you have a case before you make it.*

So that's what I've been doing in my spare time. Over the last year and a half, in between trying to figure out who stabbed that woman or shot that guy or strangled that baby, instead of reading fine works of literature or taking up pottery or learning a foreign language, I've been trying to figure out if members of the CPD are on the take, handing out get-out-of-jail-free cards to people in exchange for some pocket money that never gets reported to the IRS.

I've been investigating Lieutenant Wizniewski, in other words, while I'm right under his nose, working for him as a homicide detective.

I thought I'd been discreet. I thought there was no way he would know. It wasn't like I rifled through his desk or put my ear up against the window of his office or opened his mail. I'd been subtle. I was reading old files and looking up rap sheets and monitoring people who seemingly had managed to get off scot-free from serious charges while under the Wiz's watch. I was cautious. I was sure that he'd have no idea what I was doing.

Apparently I was wrong.

Apparently Lieutenant Wizniewski knew I was investigating him.

I ripped open the manila envelope. I knew Goldie would put something inside the envelope to give it some heft, to make it look legit—for anyone watching me on the subway platform, it probably looked like the envelope contained photographs.

When I looked inside, I saw three or four blank pieces of paper, just as I expected. But Goldie had scribbled a note on the first of those papers. There was no signature, but I'd recognize Goldie's handwriting anywhere.

CALL WHEN YOU CAN, it said. AND WATCH YOUR BACK.

FORTY-TWO

I POPPED awake, sitting upright on my bed. It took me a moment to orient myself, to separate the real from the unreal: the dreams fading away, images of Kate, of Amy Lentini, of sweat and moans and laughter, of bullets and blood and terrified shrieks.

The noise from the television I'd turned on at some point last night before passing out, the chatter from news reporters about "breaking news overnight."

And the pounding at my front door, in sync with the drumming of my heart.

I looked at the clock on my bedside table. It was nearly four in the morning.

I grabbed my gun, blinked out the cobwebs, and looked at my phone. Goldie had called me twice. He'd left me two text messages saying Call me.

A new text message popped up while I was holding the phone. Also from Goldie.

It said, Open your fucking door.

I got off my bed, still in my clothes from last night. On the TV, the reporter was talking about a dead cop. "Authorities describe the shooting as execution-style," she breathlessly reported.

My gun at my side, I went down the stairs and looked through the peephole. Outside, standing beneath the glow of my porch light, Lieutenant Mike Goldberger was dancing in place, trying to stay warm.

I opened the door to an arctic rush. I grabbed my coat. "Saw the news," I said.

"This is bad," Goldie said. I locked the front door behind me and followed him to his car. Goldie violated about twenty traffic laws on the way, but the predawn streets were basically empty.

I rubbed my eyes. Five minutes ago I'd been dead asleep. Now I was speeding toward a crime scene in the middle of the night.

"So did you flush your tail out last night?" he asked.

"I did," I said. "It was Wizniewski."

"Ah, shit. I was afraid of that. Are you sure?"

"Oh, yeah. It was him on the platform, stealing glances at me. He was good, too," I said. "He came in on a southbound train and slow-walked his way to the exit. He timed it perfectly so he was there right when I was supposed to meet your guy with the camel-colored coat."

"So he knows," Goldie said. "He knows you're investigating him for the protection racket."

"Or he suspects."

"Not good." Goldie looked over at me. He took his foot off the accelerator as he turned onto Jackson about a mile west of the river and Union Station. Large media trucks had assembled—the rainbow colors of NBC 5 and the local Fox, ABC, and CBS affiliates; reporters in their makeup positioned near the crime scene, speaking into microphones.

I stepped out of the car. It was colder than a witch's nipple in a brass bra. I couldn't feel my toes.

I had my star out, and Goldie had his around

his neck. We stepped under the police rope and got within ten feet of the crime scene—a gold sedan parked by the curb on Jackson. The passenger door was open all the way, allowing us a view inside.

The windshield and dashboard were splattered with blood.

The driver, an African American, still with his seat belt on, had slumped to the right as far as the seat belt would allow, like a human version of the Leaning Tower of Pisa. Blood had spilled from the exit wound on his right temple, covering the seat and floorboard with thick, dark, and now frozen fluid.

The right side of his camel-colored coat was soaked in blood, too.

Mr. Camel Coat had met with me last night on the train platform, and before the sun came up on another day, someone had put a slug through his brain.

And I didn't think it could feel any colder out here.

FORTY-THREE

WE STOOD there a while, Goldie and I, the breath trailing from our mouths, staring into the car at Mr. Camel Coat while lab technicians went about their work securing evidence. Reporters were speaking to the cameras, and the few curious onlookers there were at this predawn hour stopped to gape.

"His name was Joe Washington," said Goldie. "Sergeant. He was a good man. One of my best." He shook his head, cleared his throat. He gestured toward the car. "They found the driver's-side window rolled down. Joe must have been meeting with somebody."

"Somebody he trusted," I said. "Or he wouldn't have rolled down the window."

"Right. But when he rolls down the window, instead of offering a friendly word or some interesting information, the other guy pulls a gun and puts one right through his left temple. He had bled out the right side of his head by the time we found him. Christ, he was probably dead on impact."

"When was he shot?" I asked, but I knew what was coming. When it's chilly, it's almost impossible to use the traditional methods of time estimation—lividity, rigor mortis—because getting shot on a night like this is like being killed inside a refrigerator.

"The best the ME can estimate, offhand, is ten o'clock. But who fuckin' knows?"

I took a deep breath. "So he was shot about four hours after meeting me," I said.

Goldie moved closer to me and spoke in a whisper.

"How sure are you about your investigation?" he asked. "How sure are you that Wizniewski's running a protection racket in the CPD?"

"Pretty damn sure. I've got a list of people who seemed to have immunity from prosecution. People who got picked up and released in the blink of an eye. There's a protection racket, Goldie, I'm sure of that much. There are dirty cops letting people off the hook for no good reason."

"But you can't prove it was Wizniewski running it."

"Not yet, no. But I'm close."

"Okay, now question number two," he said. "How sure are you that Wizniewski was the one who saw you two together on the train platform last night?"

"A hundred percent sure."

Goldie nodded, shook out a chill. "But you can't prove that, either."

That was the thing. He was right. I couldn't. "He was on the opposite platform," I said. "And he kept his head down. There's gotta be video down there in the subway, but ten gets you twenty he kept his face off it."

"Yeah," said Goldie. "Yeah, fuck. Fuck, fuck, fuck."

That seemed like a good summary of the state of affairs.

I tried to think it through, but it wasn't easy.

"Where did Camel Coat—Joe Washington, I

mean... where did Joe go after meeting me at the subway?" I asked.

Goldie shook his head. "I don't have the first clue. We're starting at square one. I don't know what he did or where he went. I don't know who he talked to. I can't put a single person next to him last night."

That wasn't entirely true, and both of us knew it.

"You can put *me* next to him last night," I said. "And I didn't keep my head down in the subway. I kept it up. I *wanted* to be seen. I'll be all over that video. There will be nice clear shots of me with a guy found dead a few hours later."

Goldie let out a pained sigh. "That's not good."

"Tell me something I don't know."

"Maybe it's time to go public on this thing," said Goldie. "Maybe we announce that Internal Affairs has been investigating the Wiz, and now we think he killed the guy he thought was your informant."

"No." I shake my head. "No way. I make that public now, and everything I've been doing the last eighteen months goes up in smoke. I'm not stopping now. I'm gonna nail the Wiz and anyone else helping him protect criminals. And while I'm at it, I'm gonna nail the Wiz for this murder, too."

Goldie made a face like he'd just swallowed vinegar. He peeked up at me.

"You see the problem here," he said. "You're on the subway video last night with Joe only hours before somebody pumps lead into his brain. And I'm guessing you have no alibi for last night after you left the subway."

"My alibi last night is me, myself, and I," I said. "I went straight home."

"So if you don't explain that you're Internal Affairs

undercover, you got no answer for why you and Joe were talking last night. You become suspect number one."

"I don't care." I shoved my hands in my pockets. "Fuck it. I'll take my chances."

Goldie pinched the bridge of his nose, like a major migraine was coming.

"Well, isn't this a shit sandwich?" he said.

FORTY-FOUR

LATER THAT same morning, news of Sergeant Joe Washington's murder rippled through the department like electricity through water. Homicides in Chicago come by the bushel, sure, but it isn't every day a cop gets shot. Morale in the department was low enough already. Our pensions were under attack. Crime on the West and South Sides was pandemic, but nobody blamed it on the breakdown of families or unemployment or bad schools—it was always the cops' fault. And everybody with a smartphone, which meant everybody, was ready to hit the Record button on their cameras every time a cop confronted a defiant civilian on the street. Half the time it felt like people were daring us to overreact so they could get their video on MSNBC, where talking heads who never spent a single day on patrol, who never once were in fear for their lives, could cluck their tongues at us.

And now this—a cop murdered execution-style only a mile from the river, from Union Station and downtown.

So I was looking forward to my date with Amy Lentini that night. Something to get my adrenaline going in a positive way. Or at least I hoped it would be positive. An objective observer might say I was crazy asking out a prosecutor who suspected I was a crook. And it wasn't like I gave it a lot of thought before I asked her. It was an impulse—a drunken one, at that.

But when she walked out the front door of her apartment building, I knew I'd made the right decision.

Her hair was pulled back, and some strands had been teased out on each side. They brushed her cheeks gently. There was probably a fancy term for that hairstyle, but *sexy* and *classy* were the only ones that sprung to mind. She wore a gray hat and a long gray coat that was appropriate but somehow formfitting at the same time.

"Our big date," she said as I tried to fold my tongue back into my mouth.

We hit an Italian restaurant on the North Side with valet parking so I wouldn't have to sweat the parking situation. Dinner was awkward at first, which was weird, because if there's one thing you can say about me, it's that I can talk. I was nervous. And it had been a long time since I'd been nervous.

We ran through some small talk—the murder of Sergeant Joe Washington being the hot topic, but I played it as if I'd never met the guy—until we hit our second glass of wine, when we both loosened up. There was a twinkle in her eyes, a soft flush to her cheeks from the booze.

"You didn't like me at first," she said.

I let out a small laugh, took a drink of the Pinot. "Memory serves, the first time we met, you were trying to tear my head off."

"I was asking you straightforward questions," she said with no trace of apology. "Questions I thought you should be able to answer. If you were telling the truth."

"So here we go again," I said. "The little black book."

"Here we go again." But I saw a trace of amusement in her expression. Like she enjoyed busting my balls. She leaned forward, elbows on the table. "Okay, Detective, I'll tell you what. Maybe there is a small possibility that I came on a bit too strong."

"A *small* possibility," I repeated. "A *bit* too strong. Wow, Counselor, don't go overboard."

She raised her eyebrows. They were nice eyebrows, not thick, but not so thin that they looked fake. She didn't need to fake anything with her looks. She gave the impression, at least, that it was effortless.

I cleared my throat. "Okay, Amy, since you were so forthcoming," I said. "There is an infinitesimal chance, so small that you'd need a microscope to spot it, that I can be kind of a horse's ass every now and then."

"No."

"It's true."

"I don't believe it," she said. "You?"

The food arrived. She got some rotini dish with vegetables and red sauce. I got the chicken parm. I liked the fact that she didn't just order a plate of lettuce or something.

"But I'm honest," I said. "I'm a good cop."

She paused, narrowed her eyes. Then she sunk her fork into the pasta.

"Don't feel the need to comment," I said.

She looked at me again, as though she were trying to find the words. I waited her out. I didn't want to change the subject. I wanted to hear what she had to say.

After she drained her glass of Pinot, she wiped her mouth and looked at me. "I haven't really figured you out," she said. "And that's weird for me. I usually can size up somebody like that." She snapped her fingers.

"I'm a riddle wrapped in a mystery inside an enigma."

She cocked her head. "Who said that?"

"I just did."

"No, I mean—"

"I think it was Joe Pesci."

A wry smile played across her face. "I think it was Churchill."

"I haven't seen his movies."

She found that amusing, or she pretended to. "No, I'm saying my judgment tells me that you're a good person. But then I have these suspicions about what happened at the brownstone that night. Hey," she said, reading my expression. "I've been up front about that. I haven't hidden that."

"No, you've been clear about that. You think I stole that black book."

"I suspect you might have."

I didn't answer.

"Did you?" she asked.

"Why would I do something like that?"

"That's not an answer. That's responding to a question with a question. It's a way to manipulate a conversation. You're very good at that, did you know that?"

"Me?" I shrugged. "I'm just a simple cop."

"And I'm just a farm girl from Appleton." She wagged a finger at me. "Whatever else you may be, Detective Harney, you're not simple. I suspect, in fact, that you're quite intelligent. Far more than you want anyone to realize."

"Which allows me to manipulate."

She started to respond, then opened her hand. "Exactly."

"How is everything here?" the waiter said, pouring the last of the wine into our glasses.

"Great," I said. "I'm learning a lot about myself."

I ordered a second bottle. Amy smiled to herself. I could imagine what she was thinking—I was trying to get her drunk.

When the waiter left, I said to her, "If you think I stole the black book, then why are you here with me? Why would a pristine, well-credentialed attorney with a bright future want to mingle with a crooked cop?"

Amy thought about that for a while, her eyes dancing, chewing on her bottom lip. I could see the hint of a smile, but she was forcing it down.

"I don't know," she finally said. "I've been trying to figure that out myself."

FORTY-FIVE

I PULLED up in front of Amy's building and threw it into park.

"I'll walk you to your door," I said.

She looked at me, an eyebrow raised.

"Just to the door," I said. "To be a gentleman and all that."

"Chivalry," she said.

"There you go."

It was cold out, but I didn't feel it much. I was pretty charged up.

At the security door to her building, Amy turned to me. "This was fun," she said. "I don't do this very—"

Then I kissed her. The element of surprise, I guess, except I was as surprised as anyone. I couldn't help myself. I'd been wanting to press my lips against hers from the moment I laid eyes on her, even when she was grilling me, trying to put an end to my career, trying to put me behind bars. I didn't know why, and I was tired of trying to figure it out.

She let me do it. Another surprise. She parted her lips only slightly, no tongue, no major make-out session outside her building. But enough to be intimate, to let me know that it was welcome, that she wanted it, too.

She put a gloved hand to my face, and I drew her against me.

Okay, so maybe it was a make-out session. She drew a breath and opened her mouth. I kissed her deeply. Our tongues found an easy rhythm. I ran my hands through her hair and knocked her hat askew on her face until it was about to fall between our noses, at which time she grabbed it and tossed it away. She came at me even harder, moaning softly.

I mean, kissing like that was so intimate. I'd had a few flings over the last three years, including with Kate, but it was mostly greedy, horny, animal stuff—groping and grinding and thrusting—nothing like this, a galaxy far, far away, opening myself up again, letting someone in, surrendering to another person. I hadn't felt like this since, well…

Since my wife. Since Valerie died.

The thought of her shot through me like poison. I felt myself withdraw. For a moment, I thought my heart was going to burst through my skin.

I didn't think Amy noticed. She probably thought I was just coming up for air. She took a long breath, too, and put her face against mine. Then she quickly drew back to get a look at me.

"You're…crying," she said.

"No." I wiped at my cheek. "Just the cold. Just the cold."

She looked at me differently, like she was searching my eyes, discovering something about me.

"Just the cold," I said again.

She didn't buy it, but she didn't challenge me, either. Both of us were surprised.

Get hold of yourself, Harney. What's your freakin' problem?

"Billy," she whispered.

"My eyes tear up in the cold," I said.

She nodded, still with that look on her face, trying to read me.

"I...okay, look," I said. "There's something you don't know about me. I used to be married. Three years ago, there was...we..."

"I know," she said. "I know all about it."

I blew out air. "Okay. So it's a little weird for me..."

We both took a moment to decelerate. But what had just passed between us—wow. It would take me hours to fall asleep tonight.

She put her body against mine. "I know what happened," she said. "And it's none of my business. I have no right to say this. But I'm going to say it anyway. Even though I wasn't there. I'm just going to say it anyway."

I was still trying to catch my breath. She drew my face to hers, as if she were going to kiss me again. But she didn't kiss me. She just held my face in her hands and whispered the words to me.

"It wasn't your fault," she said.

She planted one last soft kiss on my lips and walked into her building.

FORTY-SIX

I DROVE back to my town house in a fog. I should have been more careful. I knew that. Wizniewski was watching me closely, and I was sure that he'd just killed Camel Coat, the guy I'd met in the subway. There was no reason he would stop there. If he was trying to put the kibosh on my investigation, I would be next.

Still, I was so shaken by everything that had happened with Amy. It was just a harmless dinner and a good-night kiss, but— no, it wasn't just a kiss. It was some kind of connection, something that didn't come from a word or a gesture but from something deep inside of us, something each of us repressed, that we released in that kiss.

Jesus, Harney, what are you—a poet all of a sudden?

I got into my town house and dropped my keys and coat and walked upstairs like a zombie. I walked into my bedroom, saw the king-size bed, the right side of the bed (my side) rumpled, the comforter turned back, the pillow turned sideways. The left side of the bed (Valerie's, once upon a time) immaculate.

It wasn't your fault, Amy said to me.

A nice thing to say. But what did she know?

My hand, trembling, reached for the bottle of

bourbon, half full, on my bedroom dresser. I opened my throat and emptied the bottle. It was dumb, a terrible idea, but I needed this night to end.

I dropped the empty bottle and heard it break on the floor. I took a deep breath and waited for the alcohol to kick the ever-loving shit out of me. It didn't take long.

I staggered down the hall to the small bedroom by the hallway bathroom. Inside was a toddler bed in the shape of a princess carriage, shades of pink and purple. A pink toy box on the floor filled with stuffed animals and princess dolls. The walls painted a light green, matching the area rug, pink with green polka dots. I remember it took me an entire afternoon at Menards to match up the wall paint to those polka dots.

Lying on the bed was a tiny skirt, lavender and frilly, and a white T-shirt that read, in glittery purple letters, MY DADDY LOVES ME.

I fell against the wall and dropped to the floor. I let it all out. I couldn't stop. I made a small puddle on the floor. I cried so hard that my lungs seized up, my stomach twisted into knots.

I cried so hard that I couldn't breathe.

I cried so hard that I didn't hear the front door open.

I did hear the footsteps, though, coming down the hallway. I recognized them. Funny that footfalls can have such a rhythm, such a sound, that you can attribute them to a person. I guess when you've heard them your entire life…

Patti walked in and tucked in her lips, folded her arms.

"Oh, my," she said. "Okay, handsome, come on."

I wiped at my face with my shirt sleeve. She helped me to my feet, like a parent would for a child, and walked me to the bedroom. The half bottle of bourbon had now combined with the wine I drank at dinner to turn everything upside down.

"Sleep is what you need," she said as she tucked me into bed, pulling the comforter over me. "Everything's going to be fine now."

I closed my eyes and waited for sleep to come. I heard Patti go downstairs then come back up and sweep up the broken glass from the Maker's Mark bottle. Then I felt her breath on my face.

"Everything's gonna be fine now, little brother," she said. "Everything's going to be okay."

Sleep hovering over me from all directions, swatting away images that shot before my eyes—

—a little girl in a birthday hat, blowing out a single candle on a purple cake—

—Valerie, with tears in her eyes, showing me the first ultrasound photo—

It wasn't your fault

—the whirl of police sirens—

—my friend Stewart sitting with me in the intensive care unit, telling me to keep the faith—

—but focusing on my sister's words, fighting off all other images and gripping tightly to Patti's words. *Everything's gonna be fine now.*

When I opened my eyes again, my alarm was screaming at me. Unforgiving sunlight was piercing through my window. Patti was gone.

But the television was on. The same news channel I typically watched.

A TV reporter, standing outside a house in Lincoln Park, with police tape behind her, police officers and

Forensic Services technicians moving up and down the stairs.

"...authorities believe she was tortured before she was killed..."

I knew that house. I had *searched* that town house, top to bottom.

It was the house that belonged to Ramona Dillavou, manager of the brownstone brothel.

FORTY-SEVEN

I PULLED my car within two blocks of Ramona Dillavou's house. It was the second morning in a row that I'd arrived at a crime scene filled with media trucks and reporters. A patrol officer was trying to direct early morning rush-hour traffic around the barricades.

The first person I saw was Goldie. Of course he was there. The guy was everywhere. He nodded at me and waved me toward the front door.

"The maid found her this morning," he said. "She died sometime last night."

We took the stairs up to the second floor. Ramona Dillavou was staring right at me, sitting in a chair, her head lolled to the right, a hopeless grimace on her face, her eyes lifeless.

Her mouth was bloodied. I thought maybe part of her tongue had been cut, but that was just a guess.

She was wearing a silk blouse that was unbuttoned. Her bra had been removed. One of her nipples was missing, replaced with dried blood. She had cuts all over her midsection—not slashes but slow, careful, painful incisions.

Her hands, tightly gripping the arms of the chair, had been butchered, too. Several of her long polished fingernails had been removed entirely. Her left pinkie had been cut off at the knuckle.

But her bare feet were in the worst condition. Several of the painted nails had also been removed, and several of her toes had been smashed so hard that they looked like mashed potatoes.

It didn't take a whole lot of detective work to realize that Ramona Dillavou had been brutally tortured.

"Someone went Guantánamo Bay on her," said Goldie.

I moved closer, taking care where I stepped. I saw ligature marks on her wrists and feet. They were thin, not wide. They'd cut through the skin.

"He handcuffed her wrists and ankles to the chair," I said. "Made it easier to torture her."

"Somebody really wanted to find that little black book," said a voice behind me.

My body went cold. I turned and saw Lieutenant Paul Wizniewski. He was staring directly at me, the words he'd just spoken an accusation.

"We might have some questions for you about this," he said, nodding toward the victim.

Yeah? Well, I have plenty of questions for you, Wizniewski.

And then it hit me. Maybe it was seeing the Wiz in the same room as Ramona Dillavou. But suddenly it smacked me like a roundhouse punch I should have seen coming long ago.

I remembered the night I first met Ramona Dillavou, the raid on the brownstone brothel.

The raid that the Wiz tried to talk me out of making.

I wasn't supposed to raid the brownstone that night. Nobody knew I was going to. Hell, *I* didn't even know. I wasn't a Vice cop. I was a homicide detective. I only went to that brownstone because that's where my suspect in the University of Chicago murder had gone.

I had accidentally stumbled upon a brothel where Chicago's elite and powerful came to get their jollies.

It had always struck me that it was incredibly risky for these prominent people, these millionaires and politicians, to visit a house of prostitution. But now I realized why they didn't consider it so risky.

They knew they wouldn't be arrested. Because they had protection.

And then suddenly I show up, unannounced, investigating a murder with a small band of my trusted fellow cops, and I arrest the whole lot of them.

That's why Wizniewski tried to stop me from raiding the place that night. When I insisted, he had no choice—too many of us had seen too much—but first he tried very hard to talk me out of it.

We're not Vice cops, he said to me that night. *We don't make a habit of arresting johns and hookers.*

You fuck this up, he'd warned me, *it could be the last arrest you ever make. It could tarnish your father. And your sister. You could get into all kinds of hot water over this. You don't need it, Billy. You got a bright future.*

I thought he was just being a chickenshit, trying not to ruffle feathers by arresting prominent politicians and the archbishop. I thought he was just playing it safe.

But he wasn't playing it safe. He was trying to help the people who were *paying* him for help.

The brownstone brothel was part of his protection racket.

Nobody knew that better than Ramona Dillavou.

She knew the cops protecting her, and she knew the brothel's clients who were being protected. She had a treasure trove of information in that brain of hers.

And now she was dead. Now she could never talk about a protection racket. Now she could never name names.

I stared into Wizniewski's eyes. I knew he killed Camel Coat, the guy from the subway. No way was that a coincidence.

And now, I realized, he probably did Ramona Dillavou, too. He was tying up all the loose ends.

"Let's start with this question," said the Wiz. "When was the last time you saw the victim?"

The last time I saw Ramona Dillavou? Well, the last time I saw her she was secretly meeting at Tyson's, a bar on Rush Street, with my sister.

As if on cue, as if a director had called into his headset *Enter stage right,* my sister, Detective Patti Harney, walked up the stairs and looked at the dead, tortured victim.

Then she looked at me.

Everything's gonna be fine now, little brother, she said to me last night in my drunken, self-absorbed stupor. *Everything's going to be okay.*

No, I thought to myself. No. It couldn't have been Patti. Not Patti.

"I'm waiting for an answer," said the Wiz.

I looked at Wizniewski, then back at my sister.

What the hell was going on?

THE PRESENT

FORTY-EIGHT

THE SMELL of bratwurst sizzling on the grill moves my stomach in a positive direction. And the sound of my brother Aiden cursing when some brat juice squirts in his eye as he hovers over the grill takes me back to a comfortable memory.

"Almost ready," Aiden announces, stepping off the deck into the soft grass in the backyard, wiping sweat off his forehead. "They're gonna be *perfect*." He makes an okay sign with his fingers.

"Like brats are hard to cook," Brendan mumbles out of the side of his mouth as he hurls a football in Aiden's direction. "Hey, Chef Pierre, just burn the shit out of 'em and throw buns over 'em."

It's my father's sixty-first birthday. We're keeping it low-key, just a backyard barbecue with immediate family, Brendan flying in from Dallas and Aiden driving up from Saint Louis. Pop said he wanted nothing special, as we had a big blowout for his birthday last year (the big six-oh), but I know the real reason is me. Everyone looks at me—the baby brother, the victim of a traumatic brain injury, and oh, by the way, the sole survivor of a double murder that took the lives of Detective Katherine Fenton and assistant state's attorney Amy Lentini—as though I were a fragile porcelain doll. *Let's not have a big party,* they probably said to one another. *Billy's not ready.*

Physically I'm back to—well, maybe not normal, but decent. I can walk without assistance. I'm up to eleven push-ups. I can sleep for five hours without interruption. My appetite has returned, though I'm unable to eat vegetables, or at least that's what I tell Patti every time she puts them in front of me.

Mentally—that's another story. I do miss Kate, because she was such a part of my life for so long. She was my partner, my friend, and for a brief window even a friend with benefits. I saw her almost every day for years. But things got weird near the end. Our relationship was strained. We stopped trusting each other.

And then—Amy. The last thing I remember about her is the night we had dinner. At the end of the night, we kissed, and I felt something explode inside me, like there was electricity on her lips; I felt moved in a way I'd never felt since Valerie died. I remember that it rattled me, that it scared the shit out of me. I remember feeling like Amy felt the same way about me.

And now all I have is a dull ache. A pain I can't locate or identify. Is it the ache of losing someone with whom you were falling in love? Or the sting of betrayal?

I wish I could remember.

"We spend all winter bitching about the cold, then we can't stand the summer heat." My father, holding a bottle of Bud Light, wiping at his face. Even as the sun begins to disappear behind the trees in Pop's backyard, it's still a sweltering mid-July evening.

That's Pop, though, holding back. This is how he shows concern. His idea of checking in on me is to comment on the weather. It's the Harney way. We aren't a touchy-feely bunch.

"How's the investigation?" I ask.

"Which one?" he says. As the chief of detectives, my father is involved in countless cases at the same time. He basically oversees all of them.

I give him a look. "The double murder," I say. "You might remember it. The one where I caught a bullet in the brain."

Pop stiffens. "Nobody tells me anything," he says.

Since the investigation involves me, his immediate family, my father is not allowed to participate or even supervise.

"If I remember correctly," I say, "your ears still work."

Between Pop and Goldie, it's hard to imagine they couldn't snoop into the investigation if they wanted to. And they want to.

"I'm sure you're gonna be fine," he says, not answering the question, clearly trying to pacify me. "Me, I think the evidence looks exactly like what it is. Kate walked in on you and Amy, she went into a jealous rage, she opened fire on you, and you returned fire. Two people died in the process, and you got lucky. To me, the only one committing a crime in that room was Kate, and she's dead. I'd close the file without charges if it were up to me."

The hope in his voice is obvious. But he still hasn't answered my question.

Pop looks at me like he has something to say and is trying to decide whether to say it. I wait him out while he wrestles with it.

"Ah, shit," he says. "I didn't want to bring this up now. Not tonight."

"Bring what up?"

He blows out air. "They—there's a new cop running the investigation."

"Who?"

He shakes his head. "Wizniewski," he says.

I take a step backward. "How—"

"He requested it. He went to the superintendent."

"The superintendent who wants my head on a platter."

"That one, yes."

"He turned the investigation over to the Wiz? The guy who's been running a protection racket? The one who tried to talk me out of raiding the brothel because he was protecting the politicians I caught? The one who killed the brothel manager so she couldn't point the finger at him? The one who killed the cop who met me on the subway platform because I was getting too close—"

"Billy, Billy." Pop raises a calming hand. "We don't have proof of any of that. I know you're right. But what *I* think doesn't matter. We have to *prove* that Wizniewski's dirty."

Pop throws down his beer bottle. Luckily, it bounces on the grass instead of shattering on the porch.

"I'd quit the force the way they've treated you," he says. "But how does that help you? I'm no help to you as a private citizen. Even if they're holding me at bay, maybe there's *something* I could do."

Patti comes through the back door carrying a salad in a huge glass bowl. None of the men will eat it, unless maybe Patti draws her firearm, which is always a possibility.

"You guys are both missing the point," she says as if

she's been part of the conversation all along. I look behind me and notice the open window into the kitchen, where she must have been listening.

"What's the point?" I ask.

"The point," she says, "is you have to get your memory back. Until then, you're at the whim of Wizniewski."

FORTY-NINE

DR. JILL Jagoda narrows her eyes, peering at me in concentration. She leans back against the high-backed leather chair, crosses a leg, and removes her black-rimmed glasses. Tucks a strand of her ash-colored hair—hanging down today to her shoulders—behind her ear.

"That's it?" she says. "That's all you remember?"

"That's it," I answer.

"You had a date with Amy Lentini that stirred up a lot of emotions for you. You went home and drowned your sorrows. Your sister came over. She has a key?"

"To my house? Yeah, of course. Patti has a key."

"And the next morning, this woman who ran the brothel, Ramona Dillavou, was found dead. Tortured."

"Correct."

"So over the course of two days, two people—that woman and the cop who met with you on the subway platform—were killed."

"Right. Like someone was trying to clean up a mess."

"And then..." She leans forward in her chair.

"And then—nothing," I say. "I don't remember a single thing. The curtain comes down. End of story.

Hope you enjoyed the show. Thanks for coming. Drive safely."

Her eyes drift upward. "That's . . . two weeks before you were shot."

"I'm aware of that."

"You lost two whole weeks of memory?"

I make a fist, then flay my fingers open. *"Poof."*

"You don't even remember the sex-club trial?" she asks. "When the mayor and the archbishop and all the others caught in that brownstone were prosecuted—"

"No," I say. "I mean, I've read about it since, like everybody else in the damn country. But it's like I'm reading about another person. I don't have the slightest memory of that trial."

"I . . . okay." The Ivy League–educated shrink bites her lower lip. Another long, sleeveless dress for her, today royal blue. She dresses up for work, I'll say that much. Don't see a wedding ring, either. Just basic detective work, basic instinct . . . it's not like I'm interested in her in that way. Maybe under different circumstances.

"Talk to me," I say.

"Well, it's just—memory loss has a physiological and a psychological component," she says. "Memory loss proximate to a traumatic injury is typically physiological. You get into a car accident but you don't remember the collision. You were knocked unconscious and you suffer retrograde amnesia."

"That would be the physical part."

"Yes. Or neurological amnesia—memory loss suffered because of a brain injury. That's physiological, too. You could lose your entire memory from something as severe as the injury you received."

"I could," I say, "but I didn't."

"Exactly. You didn't. Your memory loss is very specific, very contained. You seem to have a strong, vivid memory that suddenly—almost violently—disappears in the snap of a finger. You go from a full-color, 3-D memory to an absolute black hole."

"That's right. I remember being at Ramona Dillavou's apartment, and then, like I told you, *poof*."

"That's not physical," she says. "That's emotional. It's not that you *can't* remember, Billy. Whatever happened... you don't *want* to remember it."

FIFTY

I DRIFT through the streets—or, as I like to call it, undergo physical therapy, which means walking two miles a day, if my halting limp qualifies as walking. I move my feet and arms and hope that collectively they will jar something loose in my brain and suddenly it will all become clear. I haven't gone more than a block before sweat is covering my face, my shirt sticking to my chest.

Losing your memory is like misplacing something, except not only can you not find the thing you lost, you also don't even know what it *is* you lost. So you drift through the fog, hoping you'll bump into something and recognize it when you do.

Or, as I said, you go through physical therapy.

It's summer, so kids are everywhere, throwing baseballs across the street to one another, dancing through the gushing water of an open fire hydrant, sliding and climbing and playing in sandboxes in the park down the street. Everywhere I look there are yard signs, or posters wrapped around light poles or tied to fences; the ones I see the most are the kelly-green ones with huge white letters saying MARGARET FOR MAYOR.

When Mayor Francis Delaney was forced out of office in disgrace, and the state legislature passed a law calling for a special mayoral election, everyone figured that the front-runner for the position was a congressman who represented the North Side. Congressman John Tedesco, silver-haired and handsome, had served in the House of Representatives for fourteen years. He had millions in his campaign coffers and favors owed to him that had accumulated during his time in public office. But he cited declining health and begged out of the race, throwing his support behind his friend the state's attorney Margaret Olson.

Maximum Margaret currently leads a crowded field in the special election to replace Mayor Delaney. Three aldermen and two county commissioners have also declared their candidacy, but Margaret is the only woman. She also has far more money than anyone else, and her slogan—"A crime fighter to end corruption"—seems to be carrying the day.

Margaret Olson is everywhere—on TV, on the Internet, on laminated brochures in my mailbox. The most vicious and ambitious prosecutor the county has ever seen is almost certain to become the next mayor of Chicago.

I spend more than an hour walking. I brought a bottle of water with me, but by the half-hour mark I've emptied it. I make it to the three-way intersection of North, Damen, and Milwaukee, where well-dressed yuppies and hipsters hang outside at the outdoor cafés or carry their shopping bags from their trip down Damen.

I'm still young, but I feel old. I've been through a marriage and a near-death experience, and I move like an octogenarian, limping and moaning while I wait for myself to get back to good. By the time I reach my block, I'm ready to collapse.

Then I stop in my tracks.

Three squad cars and two unmarked sedans are parked in my driveway and along the curb. Five cars full of cops. That can mean only one thing.

As I approach, a few officers who know me nod with apologetic looks on their faces. I nod back. It's not their fault. They're just following orders, doing their jobs.

When I reach the cavalcade of law enforcement, Lieutenant Paul Wizniewski gets out of one of the sedans and holds out a piece of paper. He could at least pretend not to be so happy about it.

"William Harney?" he says, like we haven't worked together for years. "We have a warrant to search the premises."

"Gee, I wish I'd known," I say. "I could've tidied up the place. Made some cookies."

Wizniewski steps even closer, so we are almost nose to nose. "You might think about making some omelets," he says. "We're going to be here all day and all night. I'm going to find it, Harney, sure as I'm standing here."

FIFTY-ONE

PATTI HARNEY gets out of her vehicle and rushes toward the squad cars outside Billy's building. She sees a young officer she recognizes, not by name but by face. "Where is he?" she asks. "Where's my brother?"

"In the car, Detective," the officer says, nodding toward a rust-colored sedan parked along the curb.

She finds Billy in the backseat, leaning his head against the headrest. He looks utterly depleted. A lot of that is simply physical. He still hasn't recovered his stamina. The doctors said it could be a full year before he can do everything he used to do.

She raps her knuckles lightly on the window. Billy's head lolls over, and he looks at her. She opens the door.

"You wanna get some fresh air?"

"I better stay here, keep an eye on things," Billy says.

Patti gets into the car and shuts the door. She sits close to him. They lean their heads toward each other until they touch.

"You doing okay, little brother?"

He shrugs. "I'm in a fog, Patti. I don't know if I'm supposed to be nervous or angry or sad or… what."

"I know, I know. It's gonna be okay. This is just Wizniewski getting his jollies."

Through the window, she sees officers leaving the house, carrying boxes. One of them is holding an old computer in his arms.

"I'll be lucky if they don't pull the stove out of the wall," says Billy.

Sarcasm like that makes her think that Billy is becoming himself again. But he is a long way from back. He used to always wear a smile—everyone's friend; the comedian; the glass always half full, as though the sun were following him wherever he went. Now it's like he's haunted. The glass is half empty, and the sun, which always trailed him, is covered by a black cloud.

Now you know how I feel, Billy. Not so fun, is it? Life ain't so grand when things don't fall into your lap, when people aren't constantly telling you how funny and smart you are.

"I never asked you," Billy says. "I've wanted to, but...I don't know."

She turns to him. "Asked me what?"

"One night back before I was shot," he says. "I followed Ramona Dillavou. I found her with you at Tyson's, on Rush."

Patti stiffens.

"Why were you meeting with her? I never asked."

But you did, Billy. You did ask me that question. You just don't remember.

"I was trying to get the little black book," she answers. "I was trying to help you."

"By buying her a drink? You thought that's all it would take?"

She lets out a sigh and runs a soothing hand over his leg. "Billy, Billy," she says. "Always pushing away the people who want to help you. Always drawn to the people who don't."

"That's not an answer to my question."

Patti shakes her head and looks out the window again. Another officer, carrying another box out of his town house.

"Don't worry about a thing," she says, stroking his arm. "I won't let anything happen to you. Your sister will protect you."

"I don't need protecting. I just need the truth."

She turns again and looks at her broken, damaged baby brother, even if he's only younger than she is by a few minutes. She's the elder, but it's always been as if it were the opposite, as if *she* were the baby, as if *she* needed assistance, propping up, protection from the world.

"Remember," she whispers. "Don't say a word to Wizniewski. Don't tell him anything."

FIFTY-TWO

I SIT in an interview room, the irony not lost on me—this is a room where I have questioned dozens of suspects over the years. I know where the creaks are in the floor. I know where to seat a suspect so he's right under the air-conditioning vent or, depending on the time of day, so he's right where the sun will angle through the blinds and hit him squarely in the eyes.

The door opens, and the chubby face and cigar odor of Lieutenant Paul Wizniewski greet me. He is carrying a plain brown box and places it on the table between us.

"You understand you're not in custody," he says. "You understand you're free to leave."

"I understand you're saying that so you don't have to read me my Miranda rights and so you don't have to turn on that video recorder." I nod in the direction of the camera perched on a tripod in the corner of the room.

A wry smile crosses Wizniewski's face as he takes his seat.

Whether I'm read Miranda or not, I obviously know my rights. And I know what Patti, Pop, and Goldie have all said to me—don't talk to the police.

But here's the thing: I'm on the outside now, looking in. I can't just pick up the phone and ask the Wiz about the status of the investigation. They won't even tell my father what's going on. So this is the only way I can get the cops to talk—by agreeing to an interview.

"Whatcha been doing these last couple of days, since I last saw you?" he asks.

"Since you ransacked my house? I've been trying to clean it up. Three days of cleaning, and it still looks like it was hit by a hurricane."

"Yeah, that's a real shame. Hey, I want to show you something," he says. "It's a video taken in the subway station at Jackson." He picks up a tablet and turns it so I can see it, hits the Play button.

I haven't seen the video, but I remember meeting with Camel Coat—Sergeant Joe Washington. The video shows us doing what we did that night, pretending we were meeting in secret, cloak-and-dagger stuff, the handoff of an envelope.

"Do you know who that person is?"

I don't answer.

"Sergeant Joe Washington," says the Wiz. "You might recall that the same night you were seen with him doing a James Bond routine, he was found dead from a GSW to the noggin, parked in his car on Jackson. Anything you'd like to tell me?"

"I'm not a big fan of your aftershave," I say.

"If memory serves, you were at the crime scene later that morning," says Wiz. "Come to think of it, I saw you at Ramona Dillavou's crime scene, too, the day after that. Anyway, let's stick with Joe Washington for now. You and him on the subway platform."

"If memory serves," I say, mimicking him, "I recall

seeing you on the platform across from us, Wiz. Watching the whole thing."

His face lights up with a smile. "Is that a fact?"

"Yes, it is."

"Hmph. Camera didn't seem to pick that up."

Yeah, because you were hiding in the shadows with your head down.

"Anyway..." As if he doesn't have a care in the world, the Wiz reaches into the evidence box sitting on top of the table. He pulls out a handgun in a clear plastic bag, which he holds at the top, letting the gun dangle in front of me.

"Look familiar?" he asks.

"Based on my years of detective training, I'd say that's a firearm."

"Yeah, but *this* firearm, it so happens, I found inside an old cigar box in your basement."

I do a slow burn.

"Took us a bitch of a long time to find it. You had it tucked away nice and good."

"Not my gun," I say.

"We got ballistics back," he says.

"That was fast. Three days and you have ballistics results?"

"Yeah—go figure. See, our state's attorney, you mighta noticed—old Maximum Margaret—is running for mayor."

"Yeah. I might have seen a yard sign or two."

"Right. Sure. 'Margaret for Mayor.' And this is a priority for her. Y'know, Amy Lentini was one of her top people. She was grooming Amy. Had high hopes for her."

Wizniewski draws a long, delicious breath. "Anyway." He holds up the bag with the gun again. "So ballistics comes back on this gun we found in your basement. And guess what? You're never gonna guess in a million years. I tell ya, you could've knocked me over with a feather."

I pinch the bridge of my nose. I know what's coming. Wizniewski is far too happy for it to be anything else.

"Let's get this over with," I say.

"This gun," he says, shaking the bag, "which we found in *your* basement, came back positive for the GSW to Sergeant Washington. This is the gun used to kill Joe Washington."

"Let me guess," I say. "No fingerprints."

He wags a finger at me. "Correct. You were smart enough to wipe it down."

"But dumb enough to leave it in my basement."

He opens his hands, shrugs. Oh, is he enjoying himself. "One of the mysteries of the world, what people do. Maybe, deep down, you wanted to be caught, Harney. Y'know, atone for your sins and whatnot."

I don't say anything. He set me up. We both know it. But there's nothing I can do, sitting here, that will improve my situation. Let him have this moment. I'll have mine later. At least that's what I keep telling myself.

"Maybe that's why you didn't dispose of this, either," he says, reaching into the evidence box again, producing another clear bag, this one holding an ordinary kitchen knife, the kind you'd use to cut an apple. Only this one is caked with blood on the tip.

"And what would that be?" I ask in a flat tone.

"I asked myself the same question," says the Wiz, pointing a finger to his head. "I said to myself, 'Why would Detective Billy Harney tape this kitchen knife under the lid of his basement toilet?' But see, then we ran some tests on the knife, too. DNA tests, to be specific."

"DNA results in three days," I say.

"There you go again with Maximum Margaret rushing the results. We actually got back DNA before ballistics. This case is just fulla surprises."

He holds up the bag for my inspection. "Three guesses what I found."

I push myself away from the table.

"The blood on this knife belongs to Ramona Dillavou," he says. "This dull kitchen knife was used to torture and murder the manager of the brownstone brothel."

Keep your powder dry, I tell myself. *You don't gain anything by responding.*

"And you know the best part?" Wizniewski asks. "This knife *does* have your fingerprints on it."

FIFTY-THREE

LIEUTENANT PAUL Wizniewski watches me expectantly, his eyebrows raised, the joy in his expression evident. He wants me to deny this. He wants me to say things that could tie me up later.

There are so many things I want to say to him. *That's not my gun, and that's not my knife. You framed me, Wizniewski. You knew I was close to nailing you for the protection racket you're operating, and this is your way of stopping me.*

Your second way of stopping me. Your first way was shooting me.

But I didn't die. And I'm not going down this way, either—not without a fight.

But I don't say a word. It won't do me any good. My hobbled mind needs to stay focused. I can't stop what's coming next. But there is a bigger game being played here.

"Let's talk about Amy Lentini and your partner, Kate," he says.

He removes a folder from his evidence box and drops crime-scene photos in front of me.

Kate, lying dead on the carpet near the doorway.

Amy, lying dead in the bed, rolled over, with her back to the camera, almost falling off the bed.

I'm not in the photos. By the time the photos were snapped, I'd started up a pulse again and had been whisked away from the scene by paramedics.

"We rechecked ballistics, as your daddy requested," he says. "Same result. Your gun, the one found in your hand, was used to shoot Amy and Kate."

I shake my head. That just can't be true.

I squeeze my eyes shut, as if the memory of it all will just vomit into my brain. But there is nothing but fog.

"Take a look at Amy's back," he says. "See the blood spatter?"

I open my eyes. I see it, of course, along the middle and small of her back.

"That's your blood, Harney," he says. "You know what that means, don't you?"

Of course I do. It means that Amy was already rolled over, probably dead, before I was shot and spattered blood. Otherwise the blood would have hit her in the front.

"You see how the sequencing shakes out," he says. "You shot Amy first. Then Kate shot at you, and you returned fire. She died; you survived. So that bullshit story that everyone's trying to get me to swallow—that Kate walked in on you and Amy having sex and went into some jealous rage—it's a load of crap," he says. "You shot first. You started the shooting."

What he's saying makes sense. But it can't be true.

I need my memory back.

Wizniewski comes around the table, stands over me, hovering, one hand planted on the table next to me, the tobacco smell overwhelming the aftershave.

"Kate confronted you," he says. "Amy was there; she heard everything, so she was just as much of a liability as Kate. You had to kill 'em both. Me, I would've shot Kate first. She was the one with the gun. You gave her time to draw her weapon and shoot you back. That was a mistake. But people make mistakes, don't they?"

"It didn't happen that way," I say.

"I thought you had no memory of this, Harney."

"It couldn't have happened that way."

He leans down, speaking almost directly into my ear. "Kate made you. She figured out what you were doing."

"And what was I doing, Wiz?"

He lets out a small chuckle, like we both know the answer. "You were selling your badge," he says. "You were offering protection. And you were about to be exposed."

"No," I say.

Wizniewski stands up straight, takes a breath. "No?"

"No," I repeat.

"Y'know, we never recovered Kate's cell phone. You know that."

"I know that."

"And yours was smashed to pieces on the carpet."

I look down at the crime-scene photos. Next to the bed, by the side where I was shot, lay my phone, the screen broken badly, the phone itself cracked in half.

"I know that, too," I say.

"So—what?—you tossed her phone out the window or something? And you smashed your own phone? You figured you'd destroy the evidence?"

"Evidence of what?" I ask.

"You must have been really desperate, Harney. You had to know we would eventually recover all the text messages. Even if the physical phones were destroyed. It's called technology."

I shake my head, but inside me, something sinks into my gut.

"Text messages?" I ask.

Wizniewski lets out a bitter chuckle. "Like you don't know."

"I don't know. I don't remem—"

"Well, you do know that the coroner places the shootings at around ten o'clock that night, don't you?"

"Yeah," I say. "Right."

"Well, just get a load of this exchange of text messages between you and Detective Kate Fenton just minutes before that."

Wizniewski drops down a sheet of paper, a log of text messages generated by some computer. The log breaks down the time, the sender, the recipient, and the content of the messages. My eyes move down to the day of the shootings at 9:49 p.m.

Kate, to me: Need to talk to u

My reply: Not now

Kate: I'm right outside her door open up

My reply: You're outside Amy's apt?

Kate: Yes open door right now

My reply: Why would I do that

And then, finally, Kate's last text to me:

Bc she knows u idiot. She knows about u and so do I

I throw down the log and jump from my chair. Wizniewski takes a protective step backward.

"No," I say. "That's not possible. Something's...that can't be right."

Lasers shooting through my brain, everything upside down, shaking out words and facts and blips of memories and dumping them into a black hole—

"Still think this was a jealous-rage shooting?" Wizniewski sneers. "Doesn't sound like one to me. Nope, it sounds to me like Amy Lentini figured you out, and so did Kate."

"No...no." I feel myself falling, literally, to the floor. Figuratively, I feel everything slipping from my grasp. I need it back. I need my memory.

It's not that you can't remember, my shrink said to me. *You don't want to remember.*

"Billy Harney," says Wizniewski, "you're under arrest."

THE PAST

FIFTY-FOUR

I WALKED out of Ramona Dillavou's house, now a crime scene, now the site of a brutal torture-murder. In the time I was inside the house, fighting off questions from Wizniewski and staring down my sister, the press arrived, gathering in droves outside, running their cameras and tossing out questions to anyone who would respond. I could hardly blame the media for assembling here. The madam, the manager of the brownstone brothel, the same week that the sex-club trial was to begin, was permanently silenced.

Patti, who slipped out before I did, was walking quickly down the sidewalk past the media horde toward her car. I picked up my pace and called out to her. She didn't respond. So I started walking faster. She wasn't going to start running; that would look too strange, especially in front of the reporters. Eventually I caught her. I grabbed her arm and pushed her toward the walkway of another house, more than half a block away from the crime scene.

She looked at me, her eyes wide and intense, her mouth opening slightly, air slithering out of her mouth like smoke.

"Looks like the woman with the little black book is

out of the picture now," she said to me, a hint of accusation.

"Yeah, it sure does. You have something to say to me, Patti?"

Her eyes narrowed, her jaw tight.

"You were looking pretty messed up when I saw you last night," she said. "Drunk and upset. Crying in your daughter's room. You're not a crier, Billy."

"And just why were you there?" I asked. "Why did you come to my house last night? What—just in the neighborhood?"

She nodded her head, not saying yes, just taking in what I said, thinking about it. "You should be glad I did," she said.

"Why's that?"

"Because I'm your alibi," she said. "I can say you were at home last night. That you didn't kill Ramona Dillavou."

I stepped back from her. "What?"

"People are going to think that," she said. "Don't be naive, Billy. Everyone's on your case about the little black book, and suddenly the person who kept that book is dead? I saw the way Wizniewski was looking at you in there. He thinks you killed her."

I felt heat throughout my body.

"So you're my alibi?" I asked.

She nodded. "Damn straight I am."

"I guess that works both ways," I said.

"What does that mean?"

"It means," I say, "that I'm *your* alibi, too."

Her eyes lit up, her body tensing. She looked to her right, at the glut of cameras and microphones.

"Is that why you came to my house?" I asked. "So I could cover for you? So I could say, 'Gee, Patti was with me most of the night, tucking me into bed, cleaning up the mess I made, singing lullabies to me and holding my hand'?"

Patti angled her head, as though she were trying to get a better look at me.

"You're tired," she said. "Strung out. Saying things you don't mean."

"Well, here's something I do mean," I say. "The other night, I followed Ramona Dillavou. Just basic surveillance to see what I might find. And guess what I found, Patricia, at Tyson's, on Rush Street. I saw Ramona Dillavou having drinks with *you*."

She turned to stone for a moment, no movement. Breath creeping from her mouth. Her cheeks the color of cotton candy.

"I was trying to get her to give up the little black book," she said. "Trying to help you. Is that a crime?"

"No," I answered. "*That's* not a crime."

"Did anyone else see me with her?" she asked.

"Just me."

"Did you take pictures?"

I shook my head no.

Patti lunged toward me, grabbed both of my arms. "Tell me the truth—did you snap any photos with that phone you wouldn't even know how to use if it weren't for me?"

"Jesus, no." I pushed her away. "But maybe I should have."

"Maybe you *shouldn't* have," she said, catching herself, the volume of her voice, and lowering it. "Maybe it's time you start figuring out who's on your side and who isn't." She emphasized the point by thrusting her index finger into my chest.

"And you're on my side, is that it?"

She looked at me again, her eyes looking moist but her face tight, controlled. "You're my twin brother," she said. "You're family. We always stick together. We don't tell our secrets. Do we, little brother?"

I shook my head. "This goes beyond family."

"*Nothing* goes beyond family. Nothing."

"Did you kill her, Patti?"

It was her turn to step back, just a small step, to get a better look at me.

"I come to your house late last night and find you completely unraveled, distraught, a shattered empty bottle of Maker's Mark on the floor—looking like you've just been through something horrifying—and you're asking me if *I* killed her?"

I nodded my head. "That's what I'm asking," I said.

"That's the wrong question," she said.

"Yeah? And what's the right question?"

Patti looked again to her right, toward the crime scene and the gaggle of reporters.

"The right question," she said to me, "is would you turn me in if I did?"

I started to respond, but then I heard my name being called, and we both turned and saw Kim Beans, the reporter, jogging our way with a recorder in her hand.

Patti drew close to me. "Just so you know, baby brother of mine," she whispered, "I would never, ever, turn *you* in."

She pivoted on her heels, showing me her back, and continued walking down the street.

FIFTY-FIVE

"BILLY HARNEY."

"Kim Beans," I said as I watched Patti walk down the street, hustling away from the reporter, who had caught up to me. Then I turned to Kim, the beautiful former television reporter now working for the online newspaper *ChicagoPC*. Her mess of kinky hair was tamed by a wool headband that covered her forehead and ears. Her long black wool coat was buttoned to her chin. We were surrounded by the gray of the cold.

"So," she said. "Ramona Dillavou. Any comment?" She held out a small recorder.

"Background only," I said.

"Oh, come on, handsome. Something on the record. This is huge. The trial of the decade is this week, and one of your star witnesses was just murdered. I'm hearing she was tortured."

I looked at her. "Background only," I said. "Turn that damn thing off."

"*You're* no fun." But she complied, turning off the recorder and stuffing it into her pocket.

"I've enjoyed your photographs of all the big players parading in and out of the brownstone brothel," I say. "Where'd you get them?"

The photos had continued to spill out online under

Kim's byline. An alderman from the West Side. The commissioner of streets and sanitation. A corporate bigwig at one of the big tech companies in Chicago. *The walk of shame* she had called it in her stories, the photos always showing these people approaching the brownstone in a surreptitious manner, heads down, eyes furtive. The brothel had apparently done amazing business until I came around and spoiled the party.

Leaks of the photos had slowed down in frequency; initially Kim was putting them out on a daily basis, but now it was once a week. Every week, on the day Kim's column appeared, people all around Chicago—and the country—eagerly went online and clicked on *ChicagoPC* to see the latest VIP who was walking up the steps of the infamous brownstone brothel.

She gave me a coy smile. "I'm supposed to ask *you* the questions. You know I have to protect my source."

"The pesky First Amendment," I say.

"Right. But I'll tell you this much," she said. "The photo coming out this week? It's gonna blow your socks off."

Maybe. I didn't really care, but it had definitely captured the imagination of this city. Kim had done an expert job of teasing her readers, drawing out the story to its maximum length for maximum effect—and promoting herself in the process.

"So Billy, what does this do to your case? With Ramona dead."

I shrug. "She wasn't going to testify anyway. She hadn't said a damn word to us. She lawyered up and hadn't opened her mouth. Another one of those pesky amendments—the fifth."

Kim frowned, as though she didn't believe me, as though I were holding back. "I'm hearing different," she said. "I'm hearing that the prosecution offered her immunity if she'd talk. You know that hellcat prosecutor the state's attorney put on the case? The hotshot they brought in from Wisconsin after she took down that US senator? Amy Lentini."

I felt something stir inside me. "What about her?"

"I'm hearing she offered Ramona a get-out-of-jail-free card if she'd turn over the little black book. Total immunity."

I gave her a blank look, or at least I hoped it was blank. But this was something new. First I'd heard of it.

"I'm hearing this whole thing, this whole case, is really just about the little black book," Kim went on. "That this prosecutor, Lentini, went to every single one of the people who were arrested—even the mayor—and said she'd drop the charges if they could tell her about the little black book."

I shook my head, but I wasn't saying no. It just didn't make sense.

But then—it did. After I arrested everyone that night at the brownstone, all that Amy Lentini wanted to know was the whereabouts of that little black book.

"Even...the mayor?" I asked. "She offered the mayor immunity?"

Kim nodded. "My sources say that that prosecutor, Lentini, told the mayor that if he could get her access to the little black book, and if he would agree to resign from office, she'd drop the charges."

I ran my hand over my mouth but didn't speak.

"You didn't know," said Kim, a conclusion, not a question. "You're the main witness in the case, and you didn't know."

No, I didn't, and it burned in my chest.

I could understand why Amy might consider the little black book important, but more important than prosecuting the people caught in the brothel? What—she hadn't caught big enough fish? The mayor and the archbishop weren't big enough heads to mount on her wall?

Who could possibly be bigger?

I started walking away from Kim to give myself some space, to work this through. I wasn't sure what bothered me more—that Amy never shared this information with me or that I cared so much that she didn't.

Kim walked along with me. "So now you owe me one," she said. "C'mon, sport. This is the biggest story in years around here. The mayor's blood is in the water. I'm hearing Congressman Tedesco is just waiting for the conviction before he announces he's running. That'll be quite a race, don't you think? Congressman Tedesco against Maximum Margaret."

I stopped and looked at her. "What do you mean, Maximum Margaret? For *mayor?*"

"Wow, you really *are* out of the loop." Kim smirked at me, pleased with herself. "I hear her political machinery is already gearing up. She's going to convict the mayor and then run for his job. Oh, she'll wait until the trial's over before she announces. You know, the crime fighter, the corruption buster, the tough broad who's gonna clean up this town—that whole angle."

It made sense, I supposed. But it hadn't occurred to me. Sure, I'd lived in Chicago my whole life, and I followed the circus of politics from a distance, but I was no insider, and I didn't want to be.

"Are you sure you're working on this case, Billy?"

Kim asked. "Because I seem to know a lot more about it than you do."

She certainly did. Amy was Margaret Olson's prized subordinate, her right-hand aide, and I'd never heard a single utterance about political ambition or any talk of plea deals. Maybe, I tried to tell myself, it was none of my business; she didn't mention it because I didn't need to know.

But it burned all the same. Every time I thought I'd figured Amy out, I learned something new.

And if she was willing to keep this information from me, what else had she kept from me?

FIFTY-SIX

I WALKED into Amy's office at our scheduled time, ten o'clock—preparation for the big trial. My head was still ringing from all the booze I'd drunk last night. And from what Kim Beans had just told me. And from my conversation with my sister, Patti, at the crime scene. Take your pick.

Amy greeted me formally outside her office—*Good morning, Detective, so good of you to come*—but when she closed her door, when it was just the two of us, she put her hands on my chest. "Hi, there," she whispered.

I drew back, surprising her. Last night we'd kissed, but it was more than a kiss; it had unleashed things in me I hadn't felt in years. She felt it, too, or so I thought. She read the look on my face and waited for me to explain.

"I need to ask you something," I said.

She looked at me as though she didn't understand. She also looked, by the way, radiant, dressed in a light gray suit, her hair pulled back professionally. She was smart—very smart—and beautiful, a deadly combination for me.

"Did you offer Ramona Dillavou immunity if she turned over the little black book?"

Amy blinked, just once, but otherwise didn't flinch. "Yes," she said.

"And the other defendants? The archbishop? The mayor? The celebrities and businessmen—did you offer them immunity if they could help you find the little black book?"

"I did," she said.

"And you never mentioned it to me?"

She shook her head. "I'm the prosecutor. You're the witness. It isn't my job to keep you apprised of every step of my trial strategy." She angled her head at me. "Anyway, that was before. Before I got to know you. Before I started to..."

"To what?" I asked, realizing how much I want to hear the words.

"To trust you," she said. "And care about you."

How badly I wanted to give in to that, to believe that, to let down my guard and let her in. But I didn't speak. I saw the look of hurt on her face when I didn't respond, but I needed more answers.

"You know I suspected you took the little black book," she said. "I never hid that from you. I wanted that black book. I didn't care how I got it."

"Do you still?" I asked.

"Do I still what?"

"Do you still think I took the little black book?"

She paused, just one beat of my heart, before she said, "No, I don't."

"But you still want it. You still want your hands on it."

She raised her eyebrows. "Actually, no. I mean, *I* do, but it's not up to me."

"What does that mean?"

She tucked a strand of hair behind her ear. "Well,

I've been told it's not a priority anymore. I was told to drop it for now and just focus on winning this sex-club trial."

"And why's that?" I asked. "Why the change?"

"Why? Because the entire country is following the sex-club case. It's a heater case. And we don't want to lose. Why else?"

"Maybe you want to win so your boss, Margaret Olson, can take the mayor's job after she convicts him."

Amy made a face. "That's ridiculous. Margaret's not going to run for mayor."

"No?"

"No. And I don't appreciate your questioning my motives. I'm prosecuting this case because I believe in it." She thought for a moment. "Who told you Margaret wants the mayor's job?"

I shook my head. "I can't say."

"Well, whoever told you is wrong. Margaret Olson will not run for mayor. You want me to say it again? Margaret Olson will not run for mayor."

I didn't know where to go from there. She confirmed one thing Kim Beans told me and denied the other. I wanted to trust Amy. I wanted to more than I'd wanted anything in a long time.

"When the sex-club case is over, I'll go back to finding that little black book," she said. "For now, my plan is to win. And with Ramona Dillavou dead, you're more important to the case than ever."

I nodded. That much was true.

She approached me again, put her hands on my chest again. "Y'know, after that moment we shared last night, I wasn't expecting to be greeted with an interrogation this morning. I was expecting something like this."

She leaned up and kissed me softly. I felt everything melt away.

She drew back just enough to speak, her lips so close to mine I could still feel them.

"So," she said more quietly. "Are we still okay?"

My heart was racing. I drew her in and kissed her, this time not softly.

Amy Lentini, for better or worse, had cast a spell on me.

FIFTY-SEVEN

AFTER PREPPING for the trial for two hours, I left the Daley Center and walked through the plaza, worn out, my stomach rumbling, hungry for lunch. It was dreary and cold today, pedestrians walking with their heads low, bundled from head to foot. Among the government vehicles parked alongside the plaza, I spotted a fire-engine-red Corvette.

Not very hard to notice. It was like spotting a ball of fire against a dark sky.

Nice ride. The kind of thing I'd never be able to afford. You didn't become a cop for the money.

The driver's-side door opened, and who got out but my partner, Detective Katherine Fenton.

It took a moment, though, to register. The lithe, athletic figure; the stylish coat cinched at the waist; the long legs, the knee-high thick-heeled boots—that was the same, that was Kate. But from the neck up, different. Her hair was cut very short, no bangs, the ends curling severely along her cheeks. The color was different, too. Less of the flash of the red. A deeper, darker crimson. More like the color of blood.

And a Corvette.

She saw the look on my face. "Like it?" she said, but not in the way that indicated she was fishing for a compliment. It was more of a challenge, more like *Fuck you if you don't*.

I wasn't sure if she was referring to her new ride or her new look. Probably both. Probably asking what I thought of Kate 2.0. "Sure," I said. "You inherit some money or something?"

She kept walking toward me, that confident strut she had, the heels clicking loudly on the pavement, her mouth set in a come-hither smirk. Her new tough-chick look, to my mind, was overkill. Look, she couldn't have had a better body if she tried, and the curve of her face and those high cheekbones—she had *sexy* oozing off her at all times, day and night. But it worked for her, I always thought, because it was so effortless. Now she was making an effort. She was practically wearing a sign around her neck.

She used her remote to lock her Corvette. "Last I checked," she said, "I don't need your permission to buy a new car." She stopped in front of me, daring me to be unimpressed. "So no more Ramona Dillavou," she said. "Who do we like for it?"

Whom did we suspect in Ramona Dillavou's death? Well, nobody had asked my opinion so far, and it wasn't my case. I didn't want to think about it, didn't want to confront it, but I knew deep down that I hadn't crossed my own sister off the list.

Still, it seemed pretty obvious that Dillavou's murder was tied to the little black book, and I also hadn't ruled out Kate's taking it from the crime scene.

Which meant she was on the list, too.

"No idea," I said. "You?"

"How would *I* know?" Again, the hostility, the challenge in her voice. She nodded toward the Daley Center. "How was your prep session? I'm up next."

That made sense. She was a witness, too, in the sex-club trial. It just highlighted the distance between Kate and me that I didn't even know she had the appointment. We still partnered every day, but it was all business, no talk in the car, no sharing of thoughts or secrets. Not long ago, I knew everything about her. I knew what she had for dinner the night before, her plans for the weekend, every thought or opinion that cascaded through her brain. Now I didn't even know when she was meeting with the prosecutor on one of our cases.

"Is your girlfriend Amy in a good mood today?" she asked.

I rolled my eyes.

"Well, at least you're not denying it anymore," she said in a strange way, like she'd won a small victory but wished she hadn't.

I couldn't think of anything I could throw on that fire that would douse it, so I let it go, didn't say a word.

"Please tell me you didn't just fuck her in that office," she said. "I have to *sit* in there." Still no response from me, because she didn't need any help. "A little dangerous office sex, people standing just outside the door, you've got her bent over the desk—"

"Kate, for crying out loud."

Her eyes stayed on me. "Just checking. I know Billy likes it a little kinky every now and then."

A reminder of our recent past, our fling, delivered with icy relish. But it felt like cover for her hurt. *Do you really like Amy more than you like me?*

There wasn't anything I could do with that, standing in the cold in the middle of Daley Plaza, the wind punishing us. Not the place for an intimate chat about our feelings. Only time for a hostile confrontation.

I had to leave, head back to the station, but she wasn't done with me.

"She still on your back about the little black book?" she asked. "Should I be prepared for another inquisition?"

"Nope," I said, relieved to change topics. "Just the facts of our case. They put the little black book on the shelf for now."

Kate went silent, looked at me, tried to read my facial expression. Gray fog escaped from our mouths. The wind whipped up and slithered inside my coat.

"She doesn't care about the little black book anymore?" she finally asked. Her words had an edge, though she was trying to sound casual. "I thought that was the only thing in life that motivated our Miss Amy. Now she doesn't care?"

I shrugged. It wasn't my job to speak for Amy.

"Well, Billy, congratulations on getting her mind off that. You must be fucking her good and proper."

"Kate, enough."

She cocked her head, an eyebrow rising. "Don't tell me she's playing hard to get. The innocent, doe-eyed girl from Wisconsin? Saying she wants to take it slow, wants to wait for the right moment, it's a big deal for her! Leaving you high and dry at the end of the night, stringing you along like a pup—"

"I'm done with this," I said, moving past her. "I'm not playing this game."

"No," she called out to me. "You're playing *her* game. And you don't even know it."

FIFTY-EIGHT

LIEUTENANT MIKE Goldberger carved up his eggs with a knife and fork, like a general executing some divide-and-conquer strategy. He was fidgety, which was unusual for him, and the eggs were paying for it. We used to do this a lot—breakfast at Mitchell's before work. It had been a long time, but Goldie wanted to rekindle our tradition this week, probably because it was the week of the sex-club trial.

"So what's the latest on Ramona Dillavou?" I asked. "And Joe Washington? Any leads on those murders?"

"He was good, whoever he was," said Goldie. "Pristine crime scenes. No forensics, no nothing. Almost professional."

He moved on to his sausage, carving the links up like his life depended on it.

I picked up my cup of coffee and put it back down. "Jeez, Goldie, you're making me nervous. I'm the one who has to testify."

"That's what's worrying me," he said, and he rarely said things like that. Goldie didn't show worry much, usually going with the cucumber-cool thing. "If this case goes south, if the judge says you had no probable cause to enter that brownstone—well, it's on you, Billy Boy. Nobody else will take the blame."

"You think I don't know that?"

"Then act nervous, kid." He waved his hands at me. "You're sitting over there like you don't got a care in the world. You always do. You always *have*. When you were a kid, your brothers, they'd share every single thought that came through their brains. And Patti? Patti was a freakin' mess, always stressed out over this or that, always seeking approval—but there you were, cracking wise but never showing a damn thing, like you had every fuckin' thing already figured out. It's annoying is what it is."

It was just my way. I should have been a poker player.

"I *am* nervous," I said. "But Amy thinks we have a good shot. Me, I'd say I just went with my gut when I raided the brownstone, but she's got my testimony sounding like I drew up some flowchart of reasons before I busted through the door. She's good, Goldie. She's a great lawyer."

He wiped his mouth with the cloth napkin and gave me a sidelong glance.

"That look you're giving me." I sat back in the booth. "Speak."

"Why don't you just admit you're in love with that girl?" he said.

A quick denial, an easy retort, came to my lips, but I didn't say it.

"Y'know, which is fine," he went on. "Dandy. Great. About time you got back on your feet after Valerie. Nobody's happier for you than me, my boy."

I leaned forward. "I sense a 'but' coming."

He let out air. Took a sip of coffee, set the mug

down. "But," he said, "does it have to be Amy Lentini? No offense intended, but the lady's a shark. She'll chew you up and spit you out."

"No offense intended? What was that, a compliment?"

"Hey, look." He held up his hands in surrender. "The lady's drop-dead gorgeous. On a scale of 1 to 10, she's a hundred. No question about it. Have a good time with her. But Billy, that woman does not have your best interests at heart."

"No?"

He thought for a moment, then leaned forward. "She's going to find that little black book eventually. You said she put that on hiatus until the trial's over—but the trial's this week. And when it's over, she's back to looking for it. Am I right?"

"Yes," I conceded.

"And she thinks you took it. Am I also right?"

"She says no."

"She says no. She says no." Goldie shook his head. "And you believe her, of course, because she's never held anything back from you."

A fair point. But I did believe her. I could separate my brain from my heart.

"You think I have it," I said. "You think I took the little black book. That's the only reason you'd be worried about it."

Suddenly Goldie took a keen interest in his coffee, draining the mug and adding some more from the copper-colored pot the waitress had left on the table.

"I never asked you that," he said. "Never once."

"Go ahead and ask me."

He shook his head. "It doesn't matter. Whether you did or not, you're the best cop I know and a credit to the force and one helluva fuckin' kid, by the way." A flush of red came to his face, genuine emotion in his eyes. Goldie never had kids of his own. His wife died of cancer at age twenty-nine, and they never got around to having children before she got sick. He was Pop's best friend and our surrogate uncle. But he was still a copper's cop, the tough exterior, not one to show emotion like this. I had to admit it disarmed me.

"Sounds like you're writing my obituary," I said.

He allowed a brief smile. "If you did take it, you had your reasons, and I don't wanna know them. Okay? Leave it at that."

"Ask me," I said. "Ask me if I took it."

"Shut the fuck up already. I'm not gonna ask ya." He put a hand on the table. "Just do me this favor, okay? Don't let anyone else ask you, either. Not Patti. Not Kate. And *definitely* not Amy."

Without having taken a single bite of the food he had so viciously sliced up, Goldie picked up the check and threw some cash down. I tried to add a ten, but he batted it away as though it were an insult.

When he had settled the bill, he looked me squarely in the eyes. "Just remember that someone's out there killing people to find that little black book," he said. "So if you have it, my friend, you better watch your back."

FIFTY-NINE

WHEN I left Goldie, I headed to my car, ready to go to work. I checked my phone almost automatically, just as everyone does these days. In my case I was checking the news online.

I stopped in my tracks. Kims Beans had posted a new photo, her weekly scandalous pic of a client entering the brownstone brothel. She had promised—what had she said to me?—that the next photo would blow my socks off.

She was right.

In many ways, there was nothing different about this photo. Most of the poses were the same—head down, surreptitious, not wanting to be noticed. There were dozens of them by now, celebrities and power brokers, some famous, some not so famous.

This photo was of a member of the Chicago City Council, which would make, by my count, four of them caught on camera—in still photographs, anyway—and publicly exposed by Kim Beans. I didn't recognize the person by face or by name. There were fifty members of the council altogether, and I didn't know the roster by heart. According to the article, this one represented the Northwest Side.

So there would be the usual buzz, the usual denials.

A photograph doesn't prove anything; walking down the street in the Gold Coast isn't a crime; I don't specifically remember that night—I may have been shopping. One guy caught on camera, an appointee to the Chicago Board of Education, claimed he was walking his dog—off the leash, of course—and that the photographer had cropped the pooch out of the photograph. Another person caught, a B-list actor, someone who was a child TV star but failed as an adult, claimed that his picture had been Photoshopped and that his face was put on someone else's body.

This one, too, would likely come up with some version of a denial, specific or otherwise. Nothing unusual about that.

But there was one thing unusual about this particular photograph, which was why Kim had made her comment.

This one was a *woman*.

Alderwoman Patricia Bradford, who, according to Kim's article, was a divorced mother of three and in her fourth term on the city council.

A woman. Well, why not? Why would a sex club, where people go looking for a discreet place to play out their fantasies, be limited to men?

SIXTY

I STARTED to stuff my phone in my pocket, but then my thought of the Gold Coast and shopping reminded me of a joke. I hadn't left Stewart a joke in a long time, and the poor guy checked our shared Facebook page every morning in the nursing home, according to his daughter, Grace.

I hit the Record button on my phone, the one Patti had installed for me, and spoke into the microphone.

"A guy walks into a store and says to the female sales clerk, 'I'm looking for a pair of gloves for my wife, but I don't know her size.' The sales clerk, a real good-looking lady, says, 'Here, I'll try them on.' She sticks her hand inside a glove and says, 'It fits me. Is she about my size?' The man says, 'Yes, she is about your size, so that's very helpful, thank you!' The sales lady says, 'Anything else?' The man says, 'Yeah. Come to think of it, she needs a bra and panties, too.'"

I pushed the icon again, instantly sending it to our Facebook page and deleting it from my phone. Not the funniest joke I've ever told, but Stewart liked that kind of humor.

My cell phone buzzed as I held it. I almost dropped it.

The caller ID said Stewart.

Wow, that was weird. Weird that he was just on my mind and weird that Stewart would call me. He never called me. He would sometimes post a comment on the Facebook page, but our interactions were mostly limited to my visits to the nursing home. It was up north, in Evanston, and these days I rarely got out there.

Anyway, I answered the phone. "Stewart?" I said, propping up my voice with cheer.

"Billy?"

A woman's voice. His daughter?

"It's Grace," she said. Yep, his daughter, Grace, the one whose own daughter was in the intensive care unit back then.

"Hi, Grace," I said, as a chill of dread spread through my chest.

"Billy, I have some bad news. My father passed."

"Oh, Grace. Oh, I'm so sorry."

"Listen, I'm sorry for the late notice—I couldn't find your number. You're unlisted. I finally figured out that Dad had your number in his phone. It's just that—he never used that phone, and we were distracted—"

"Grace, it's no problem."

"Well, the wake is tomorrow," she said. "He died four days ago, and I'm just now calling. I think... well, considering how you two met and what you went through, I think he'd understand if it was too hard for you to come. But I wanted to give you the choice."

Tomorrow. Bad timing. Amy and I were going to do an entire run-through of my direct examination at trial and then a complete cross-examination. But that didn't matter.

"Of course I'll be there," I said.

SIXTY-ONE

THE FUNERAL home in Winnetka was like all of them, everything muted and clean and tasteful. The people working the place were wearing gentle, noncommittal expressions. The walls were painted soft shades of purple or pink. Flowers were arranged just so.

The large photo of Stewart resting on an easel when I walked in was striking to me because it didn't look like the Stewart I remembered; it was a black-and-white photo from his wedding day, I presumed, taken in the early fifties. There were hints of the Stewart I knew in that photograph—the eyes, that crooked smile—but here he had a head full of hair and athletic shoulders.

I learned a lot about him over those several weeks in the ICU. I knew he married his college sweetheart, Ann Marie; they were married forty-six years, had four children and thirteen grandkids. At the time I probably could have named all seventeen of the offspring. The names escaped me now, three years later, and for some reason it made me feel guilty.

The place was full, which made me feel glad for Stewart. Times like these, I always asked myself questions incapable of being answered, like whether any of this meant anything; whether Stewart even knew we were gathered here for him; whether he was looking down on us or was just a dead body in a coffin.

Stewart once told me, when we got around to discussing funerals—a morbid topic but an unavoidable one at the time—that funerals weren't for the dead, they were for the living, to give them an outlet to grieve.

But I wanted to tell myself that I was doing this for him. I didn't want to be here, but I owed it to him. In many ways, Stewart saved my life in that ICU.

I found Grace, his daughter, the one whose own daughter died in that ICU. Her face was washed out from so many tears, her body language showed she was worn down, but she smiled sweetly at me, and we hugged. She introduced me to her siblings, one of whom I'd met before. "This is the guy I was telling you about, the police detective," she said, and they all knew me that way. They all thanked me for the jokes. They reminded me, each of them, that the first thing Stewart did every morning when he got up was turn on the laptop computer and look for Facebook videos from me.

"You kept him going when Annabelle died," one of his sons said to me, pulling me aside, referring to the granddaughter Stewart lost. "He said he couldn't have made it through without you."

I made my way into the visitation room and waited my turn at the open casket. He looked like some semblance of my Stewart, a bit waxy and artificial, but the makeup artist did a pretty good job. I touched the casket and said a prayer, not knowing if it made a difference but covering the bases all the same. Then I took a seat in one of the chairs and sat quietly. I didn't know anybody else there and didn't plan on staying long. I needed to leave, in fact, but I wasn't ready to let go just yet.

I thought of what Stewart's son said to me. It didn't

feel like I was propping Stewart up in the ICU. It felt like the other way around. He gave me an outlet, someone to talk to, a shoulder to cry on. He let me crack off-color jokes so I didn't have to sit there every waking moment for more than twenty-three agonizing days—561 hours, to be precise—wondering how in God's name it made sense, how it was okay, how it could possibly be part of God's plan that my beautiful angel, my three-year-old daughter, had to die.

Oh, was Stewart a feisty, foul-mouthed ball buster. He used to demand the straight scoop from the doctors. *Stop coddling me,* he'd always say, *and just tell me what's what.* He always told me that at some point in your life you get tired of bullshit. You just want the truth. You just want what's real. Decide what matters in life, he said, and focus on that. The rest is bullshit.

I was wondering if I was reaching that stage myself, though I was less than half Stewart's age. I was so tired of the lies. It was enough that I spent my career chasing bad guys—and sometimes bad cops. The bad guys I could deal with. Somebody needed to separate *us* from *them,* and I was as good as the next person to do it.

But now people close to me were in my line of sight, and what was just as bad was that I was in their line of sight, too. Patti and I had all but accused each other of killing Ramona Dillavou. Kate and I had all but accused each other of stealing the little black book. Amy initially wanted to tear my head off, and now we set off fireworks every time we touched.

I didn't know whom to trust anymore. I didn't know how. I didn't know how to love. Even Stewart, my friend Stewart, even someone for whom I had nothing but the deepest gratitude and affection. Sure, I kept in touch, but I did it remotely, not visiting him in the nursing home and brightening his day, not taking him out to lunch or grabbing a beer or getting some fresh air. No, I sent him videos of my stand-up routines and random jokes, bringing sunlight into his day, sure, okay, but doing it from a distance, over the Internet. I was the comedian, the guy who made you feel good from a stage, holding a microphone and talking to a crowd shrouded in darkness or sending videos over Facebook. I felt good doing it—but it was nothing intimate, nothing up close and personal.

Everything from a distance. Because it hurt too much to get close.

I got up on shaky legs and turned to leave.

Amy Lentini was sitting in a row of chairs three south of mine, dressed in black.

I walked over to her.

"Just in case you needed someone," she said.

She put her hand in mine. I took the other hand, too, gripped them tightly, and looked directly at her. When the words came out of my mouth, they were rough, like sandpaper, coming as they were from a throat garbled with emotion. They came out as a whisper, maybe because of our surroundings, but more so because I meant them more than ever, and I was afraid of the answer she would give.

"Can I trust you?" I said. "I mean, really trust you?"

She peered into my eyes. She didn't know what was swimming through my head, but under the circumstances, knowing how I met Stewart, knowing my backstory, she could take a pretty good guess. She seemed to recognize the weight in my question, that I'd never said anything more serious in my life.

"You can trust me, Billy," she whispered. "I promise."

SIXTY-TWO

I DROVE my car behind Amy's, following her. Tomorrow the pretrial hearing would begin—the case of the brownstone brothel, which had ensnared the mayor and archbishop of the nation's third-largest city as well as a dozen other of its VIPs. The entire country would be watching. All eyes would be on the prosecutor, Amy, and me, the star witness, as defense attorneys from across the United States, some of the highest-paid lawyers in the business, took their turns trying to dissect my testimony like Lieutenant Mike Goldberger had dissected the eggs on his breakfast plate.

Those lawyers would spend today sharpening their knives, engaging in mock cross-examinations with their colleagues, looking for any hole they could find in the dam of my testimony, probing for any possible way to show the judge that I had no reason to raid that brothel, that my arrests violated the Fourth Amendment, and that all their clients should go free on a legal technicality.

So Amy and I were going to do a final practice round, too.

But Amy, heading down Lake Shore Drive from Winnetka, did not make it all the way downtown to her office. She turned off earlier, at Irving Park, and I followed her through some of the side streets in Wrigleyville until she parked.

She got out of her car, hiked her purse over her shoulder, and walked up to a low-rise condo building. I got out, too, and followed her. She typed a number onto a pad, and her door popped open with a buzz.

I followed her without saying a word. We walked through the foyer to the elevator, then took it up to the sixth floor. We walked down the hallway to her apartment. She opened the door and walked in. As soon as she was inside, she turned to me and pressed her lips against mine.

We undressed slowly, savoring it, my hands running over her shoulders as I eased the blouse off her. Dropping to my knees to slide off her pants, running my hands up the curve of her leg. She smelled so fresh, not a particular scent I could identify, but fresh, clean, new.

We walked together, her forward, me backward, into the bedroom and fell into bed. We kept our slow pace, enjoying every moment, every touch of the skin, every gentle moan. She held me in her hand and left it there, just feeling it, feeling me, taking it all in, before it was time to accelerate. But I didn't want to accelerate, didn't want to speed this up; I wanted to remember every moment, wanted time to stand still so this could be all that was happening in my life—not the lies, not the suspicion, not the pain. Just this.

She sucked in her breath as I entered her, looking me in the eye until her head lolled back and her breathing escalated. I felt so much heat, so much energy inside me that I felt like I would explode, but as we moved in sync, as our bodies rose and fell together,

I felt something else, too, something I could only describe as peace.

I felt safe, for the first time I could remember.

When it happened, when I couldn't hold back any longer, I fought off the urge to push the pace. Instead I let it happen on its own, allowed it to slowly release from me. I heard myself cry out while Amy did the same. It was less like we were engaged in sexual intercourse than like we were hanging on tight while the roller coaster plunged downward, out of control.

"Oh, my God," she whispered when it was over.

We didn't get a lot of practice in that afternoon or evening. We were ready for their best shot, Amy told me, and she was probably right. Instead we ordered Chinese food and ate kung pao chicken and noodles on her couch. We talked about things other than the trial, about music and literature and travel. I learned that she was once a concert violinist, that she spent a year studying abroad in Florence, that her younger brother qualified for the Olympics in speed skating, that she didn't know how to swim and was too embarrassed, at her age, to take lessons.

It was the best afternoon I'd had in a long time.

We had another go-round in bed, this time less tentative, more familiar, but very different, more confident, more animal aggressive. I had the distinct feeling that every sexual encounter with Amy Lentini would be an experience all its own, every one unique, like a snowflake.

We decided it was better not to spend the night together. We had to be ready bright and early the next day for the hearing, so we made plans to meet at the courthouse at 26th and Cal an hour beforehand.

I drove back to my town house, a song on my lips,

my limbs rubbery, feeling weightless. Something felt different now. It felt like maybe I had "turned the corner" that everybody, with good intentions, had promised me I would turn sooner or later.

When I got home, I pulled my mail from the slot. Perched against my door was an envelope, the full-size, eight-and-a-half-by-eleven kind. Blank, nothing written on the outside.

I set down the mail and slid my finger under the envelope's flap. Inside was a single glossy photograph. It didn't take me long to recognize the brownstone and the steps leading up to it. It was another one of those scandalous pics, the ones I'd seen previously under Kim Beans's byline. The individual in the photograph was trying to be discreet, head down, coat collar pulled up high, not wanting to be seen or noticed.

But the camera wouldn't be denied. The photographer got a nice zoomed-in shot of the person's face.

There was no denying who it was.

The person in the photograph, taking her first step up the stairs of the brownstone brothel, was none other than Amy Lentini.

THE PRESENT

SIXTY-THREE

"HERE. EAT."

I glance at the bowl of pasta Patti sets in front of me. I nod at her but don't reach for the food. She's trying to distract me, more than anything, from what I'm seeing on television.

Margaret Olson, front-runner for the race for mayor, before a bank of microphones, the white and blue stripes and red six-pointed stars of the city's flag behind her. She looks like a pro, scrubbed and coiffed, her blue suit impeccable, trying for the perfect combination of serious crime fighter and chief executive.

"While my candidacy for mayor will continue in full force," she says, "my job as the Cook County state's attorney has not ended, and I won't allow politics to get in the way of my duty. The crimes committed by Detective Harney strike at the heart of the problems in this city. When a sworn police officer not only breaches the trust of our citizens but also kills to cover up that breach—I can think of no greater crime. I have vowed to stop this kind of corruption."

"Why don't you vow to stop your mouth from running?" Patti says to the screen.

"For this reason, I will be personally prosecuting

the case against Detective William Harney," says Margaret Olson.

Her words zap through my family room, a quick flash of lightning, and then there is nothing but silence for a palpable beat, even from the TV, as though she were talking directly to me and wanted the words to sink in. *I'm coming for you, Harney. You're mine.*

"William," Patti sneers, like that's the most intriguing part of what she just heard. "Who the hell ever called you William?"

The press has taken to using my formal name, too. Even Kim Beans, whose career has rebounded nicely since the night of the sex-club raid, who now has a spot as a crime reporter on the local NBC station, whom I've known for several years and who has always called me Billy, now refers to me as *Detective William Harney*. Sometimes I prefer it that way, as if it's happening to someone else, not me. William Harney? No, I'm Billy. That must be another guy who's charged with killing four people and facing life in prison.

"Mom called me William," I say. "When she was pissed."

"At you? Mom was never pissed at you. You were her little angel."

It was supposed to come out as a compliment, a supportive boost, but her comment turned sideways at the end. Patti always thought I spent my life gliding along a smooth, paved road, as if my feet barely touched the ground, while she struggled to traverse a path of potholes and sharp curves. I never really figured it. We had the same life. We did the same stuff.

"That's not a good development," says my father, just walking into my family room, leaning against the wall. Leave it to Pop to shoot straight, never to mince words.

Patti waves him off. "What does Margaret fucking Olson know from trying cases? She's a politician. She's not a trial lawyer."

Pop doesn't bother arguing. Quibbling with Patti can be exhausting. When she gets an idea in her head, she won't let go. The more unreasonable her position, the tighter she clings to it.

And on one level, she's right. Margaret Olson isn't some veteran trial lawyer. She was an alderwoman who was elected the county's top prosecutor. She's no Clarence Darrow. But that's not Pop's point. His point is that if she's putting herself out there front and center, she can't lose the case. She *can't*. She'll be putting her entire candidacy for mayor on the line. If she loses my case, she'll look like an amateur, not the trusted corruption buster who will "Save. This. City!"

Pop casts a look in Patti's direction but can't summon any anger or frustration. All of us are pretty beaten down. It's been a rough seven weeks since I was arrested and charged with four counts of first-degree murder. I was released on a million-dollar bond, which was the only good news, because a lot of murder suspects are denied any bond at all. The best thing I had going for me, ironically, was my physical condition—the fact that I was still in recovery from a gunshot wound to the head. The county lockup ain't exactly the Mayo Clinic, and one of my doctors told the judge that I still needed weekly therapy.

Anyway, Pop put up his house for bond and got me out. For the first couple of weeks afterward, I was hunkered down in my house or his, reporters waiting to pounce at any sight of me. Getting the mail every day was an exercise in stealth and misdirection.

Now, nearly two months since my arrest, things have died down a bit; they are on to their next set of stories: another weekend of double-digit homicides in the city, the city's pension crisis threatening to strangle the government, and God knows the mayoral race is a daily headline—one candidate made a stupid comment, another candidate stepped in a pile of doo-doo. But they know that my trial isn't far away, just a few short weeks, and soon they'll have the chance to gorge on the feast once more.

"How's it going with the shrink?" Pop asks me.

I shrug. "We've tried everything. No luck so far."

Dr. Jill Jagoda and I have tried everything that could pop something loose, that might poke a hole in the wall that is blocking my memory. We've spent entire sessions breaking down my relationship with my father and mother and sister and brothers. An entire session about Kate. Multiple sessions dealing with Amy.

We even tried hypnosis. When it was over, when I came out of it, the look on Dr. Jill's face was blank. She just shook her head briefly. She still thinks my emotions are repressing my memory.

If that's true, then I must really, *really* not want to know what I did.

Pop mumbles something to himself as he leaves the room. Once he's gone, Patti touches my leg. "Hey," she whispers.

It feels like we're kids again, whispering behind our parents' backs, exchanging knowing glances and half comments, finishing each other's sentences. Twin stuff.

The screen cuts away from Margaret Olson; the anchor is talking about a storm coming our way. I turn to Patti.

"Maybe it's better you don't remember," she says.

"How so?"

"Well…who's to say your memory didn't come back?" she asks.

I don't know what she means. And then I do.

She makes a face, like she wants me to try on the idea, wear it around a little and see if it fits, before saying no. "Nobody can read your mind. If you say you remember, you remember."

I shift on the couch and face her. "And I suppose what I'm going to 'remember' is that I didn't kill anybody?"

She runs her hand over the pillow behind me. Doesn't make eye contact but keeps her eyebrows lifted, wanting me to consider it.

"It might be better than the truth," she says.

SIXTY-FOUR

I SIT forward in the leather seat of Dr. Jill Jagoda's SUV, eyes outside, scanning the streets—daytime pedestrians, teenagers, moms with kids, dog walkers, some people getting a start on happy hour—soaking everything in, concentrating, eyes narrowed, focusing on everything and nothing at the same time.

"Don't press," says Dr. Jill. "Make it come to you."

This is the neighborhood where Amy Lentini lived, though I only know that because people have told me. I don't remember ever going to her apartment. Don't even remember the building.

Amy, looming like a specter, her image so thin it's transparent, vanishing when I reach for it. Did we fall in love? Did we have sex?

It feels like the answer to both of those questions is yes. But those last two weeks before the shooting are still a black void. I know that I was found naked in bed with Amy when I was shot, so there's no denying that we were together, but that's nothing more to me than something I don't really *know,* something I have to take the word of other people for. There is an ozone layer, but I can't touch it or smell it. There are other galaxies out there, but I can't see them. Amy and I were lovers, but I don't remember it.

But those flashes keep returning, that longing, that deep sense of loss and ache. That much I can feel. It's like a mysterious illness, some amorphous pain for which doctors cannot find a source.

"I want to ask you something," Dr. Jill says.

"Shoot."

"Why are you demanding a speedy trial? I mean, some defendants delay their trials for months or years. You could do that. You're out on bond. It's not like you're in a hurry."

"You sound like my lawyer." My attorney has argued constantly that we should delay this trial, wait until Margaret Olson is elected mayor, let the media buzz die down—and give me time to regain my memory.

It makes sense. I know it. But I can't live like this. I'm out on bond, but I'm trapped, locked behind bars I can't see, full of questions I can't answer. It's worse than pure terror. Pure terror is something I've experienced—breaking through a door, expecting someone on the other side with a shotgun. Racing through an alley, chasing an armed suspect, knowing you're about to corner him and that it will come down to you or him. Looking into the eyes of a suspect you know has killed with premeditation, the suspect knowing that you know, the sides of his mouth curving upward, those eyes boring into you, telling you, *Yeah, I'm a killer. I have taken life, and it doesn't mean a damn thing to me.*

That I can handle. Not this. Not the constant uncertainty, the ever-present shadow, the grief gurgling through my stomach, the lingering suspicion that I did something truly bad and just can't, won't, allow myself to remember it; the hope that I'm wrong, that there is another explanation.

The fear that I'm reaching frantically for an answer I will not like, that I'm trying to break down a wall, but that when I do a scalding fire will engulf me.

"There." Dr. Jagoda curbs her Lexus and nods her head.

I look around me. "Where?"

"That condo building right there. The awning."

I look at the building. This is where Amy lived. This is where Amy and Kate were murdered.

Nothing. The black void. Just another building to me, one of a thousand condominium buildings in our city.

I stare at the awning, up at the windows overlooking us, trying to will the building to speak to me. *You walked through this door. You went up this elevator. You walked down this hall. You entered this apartment.*

I've seen plenty of photos of the interior of Amy's apartment; it was the crime scene. But it looked like they all do—the kitchenette, the single bedroom, the well-kept living room.

You went into this apartment. You and Amy…

Amy and I what? I don't remember even being in the apartment.

"Easy," says Dr. Jill. "Don't press."

I shake my head. "Let's go."

"Why don't we walk around? It's a nice—"

"I want to leave."

"Billy, this is about all we have left. We've talked about feelings and emotions and your childhood and your relationships. We've talked about your daughter and your wife and your hopes and fears—"

"Believe me, Doc, I know."

"Okay, so you need to use your other senses. Your mind is struggling. You need to touch and smell and hear. You need to put yourself back in this place. You need to try to reconstruct the events. It's our last chance to unlock the door."

"Let's leave," I say.

She pauses. I stare at the awning until it seems as if it's moving, waving at me, taunting me.

"It's okay to be afraid."

I turn to her. "I don't need a shrink to tell me it's okay to be afraid. I get that part. Afraid is about the only emotion I have anymore. I'm just—I give up. Okay?" I throw up my hands. "I fucking surrender."

"No. We have four weeks until your trial. I'm not letting you give up."

"You're not *letting* me? This is *your* choice all of a sudden?"

Her eyebrows move together. Without her horn-rimmed glasses, which she took off while driving, she seems younger, more innocent.

"I don't think you killed anybody," she says.

"Then I hope you're on the jury."

She doesn't think that's funny.

"Let's re-create it," she says. "It's all we have left."

"How far do we take it? Should I shoot you? Are you gonna shoot me?"

"It's tempting, the way you're behaving."

I look back at the building, at the awning, up at the windows. It could possibly work, a reenactment. She seems to think so, and she's the expert.

But I remember what Patti said to me.

Maybe it's better you don't remember.

Who's to say your memory didn't come back? Nobody can read your mind. If you say you remember, you remember.

Maybe she's right. Maybe my only chance is to say

whatever I have to say to save my ass. Make something up. Something good. I can do that, right? Sure I can. I'm the best liar I know.

It might be better than the truth.

"Thank you for everything," I say to Dr. Jill. "But I'll take it from here."

SIXTY-FIVE

I WALK the streets, my stride improving every day, less of a limp, my stamina increasing, too. The weekly therapy and my daily walks have helped. It feels good out here, the feel of late summer and early autumn, a crispness in the air as darkness begins its slow creep.

Fuck my memory. It feels liberating to be freed from that locked room. I don't need to remember what happened to win my case. I just need a convincing story.

By the time I hit Southport north of Addison, darkness has settled in comfortably. The crowd up here isn't as thick as it is downtown, but I find myself in a steady stream of people. I don't do much other than walk and just exist. Just existing is a gift, I realize; I easily could have died from that gunshot wound—in fact, I *was* clinically dead for several minutes. So anything after that experience is just gravy, right?

That's what I tell myself, that I'm lucky I'm still breathing, even if one day soon I may find myself living and breathing and existing in the Stateville penitentiary.

I glance over at a storefront and do a double take, sure, absolutely certain for just that moment, that I saw Amy staring back at me. Instead it's just a mannequin with short jet-black hair wearing a designer suit.

That happens to me sometimes, little triggers like that. I'm not seeing ghosts. It's not time for séances or exorcisms. But on occasion I will look this way or that and swear that I saw her.

And it's not the only thing I feel at this moment. I also feel something behind me, a shift in the pressure. Like some movement behind me ceased at just the time I did.

I whip my head around. Nothing but a jumble of people moving in my direction. Nobody dropping back, ducking down, averting his eyes.

Nobody following me.

Still, it sweeps through me like a chill.

So tired of looking over my shoulder.

So sick of playing defense, clawing for my memory and feeling helpless. Time to stop playing defense and start playing offense.

I hail a cab and head north.

The Hole in the Wall. I haven't been there for ages. Once upon a time it was the first instinct: you were thirsty and had an hour to kill, you went to the Hole.

I get out of the cab, the sound of the train passing overhead on the Brown Line, raining down some rust. I reach for the door of the bar and pause. Then I open it.

The place dies down when I walk in. Something out of a movie: the music stopping, conversations braking to a halt in midsentence, like the abrupt screech of the needle lifting off a turntable.

All eyes on me, none friendly. Nearly a hundred faces I recognize, people I've known and worked with on the job. At the bar, Patti has a bottle of beer hoisted to her lips, frozen in midair as she stares at me.

"This is a bar for cops," someone shouts. "Not cop killers."

My fists in balls, my jaw set, I cut an angle toward the corner that I once owned, where people once watched and laughed, where people once chanted my name. I step up on the stage and grab the microphone, click it on, pat it for good measure.

"We don't wanna hear your jokes," someone yells.

"This isn't a joke. I didn't kill any cops," I say into the mike. "I didn't kill anybody."

"What happened to 'I don't remember anything?'" someone shouts.

I scan the room again, my heart pounding, my stomach doing gymnastics.

"Well, I remember now," I say. "I remember, and I didn't do it."

I drop the mike, sending a booming *clang* across the room, and step off the stage.

"Hey!"

I turn on my way out. It's Wizniewski's chubby face coming my way. "You're not welcome here. You know what you did, and *we* know what you did."

"And I know what *you* did," I say, doubling down on my lie. I pivot and move toward him. He's ready for me, hands raised. On a good day, I might have a better response, but I'm still moving slowly, and before I can bat them away, Wizniewski's fingers wrap around my throat. He pushes me backwards against a table, my back arched, my eyes up at the ceiling. My head fills with a rush of anger and desperation as the crowd comes alive with a roar, as the Wiz's chubby face peers into mine, as I struggle to loosen his grip, but I can't, I just—

Bam. The table over which I'm bent backwards

rocks violently, glass shattering. The Wiz releases me and steps back. For a moment I don't know what happened. It was like an earthquake of great magnitude, but limited to the small table.

Patti, holding a baseball bat she must have grabbed behind the bar. Letting it rest against her shoulder, but elbow out, like she's ready to take a swing. Her mouth set evenly, like she's cool as ice, but her eyes on fire.

"You like picking on people with medical conditions?" she says to the Wiz, loud enough for everyone to hear. "Wanna try someone who didn't take a bullet to the brain?"

Wizniewski, chest heaving, face tomato-red, glares at Patti. "Hey, bitch on wheels, you really wanna bring a baseball bat to a gunfight?"

Patti takes the bat in both hands, holding it horizontally, and tosses it at Wizniewski's chest. He puts out his hands defensively, not trying to catch it, so it hits his palms and clangs to the floor at our feet.

Before I know it, Patti has drawn her gun and has it within an inch of Wizniewski's nose, her legs spread, in the pose.

"Who needs a bat?" she says. Like she doesn't have a care in the world. Like it wouldn't bother her in the slightest if she pulled the trigger.

The crowd isn't sure how to react. A crowd of cops, most of them off duty, most of them wearing their pieces. Most retreat or crouch. Some reach for their waists. This could go a lot of different ways. Some of them bad.

"The fuck you doing? C'mon, Patti," Wizniewski says, not really believing she'll use it. But still, she's an itchy trigger finger away from splattering his brains on the ceiling. It does something to a fella's attitude.

"We done?" she says.

"Fuck, yes, we're done, we're done."

"Then apologize to my brother."

"I apologize."

She lowers the gun and says, "C'mon." It's a moment before I realize she's saying it to me. We walk out of the Hole, now stunned into silence.

"What was that about 'I remember now'?" she asks me as we beat a path from the bar.

"What was that about drawing your weapon?"

"You first."

"Like you said before, who's to say I don't remember?" I say. "Fuck trying to regain my memory. I'll just remember whatever I decide I remember."

"Good; great," she says. "Doesn't mean you had to announce it to a roomful of cops. Was that smart?"

Maybe not, I think to myself as I raise my hand for a cab. *Maybe so.*

SIXTY-SIX

I LOOK out my bedroom window, watching a man and woman, young lovers, staggering home from a night of partying, the woman holding her heels in her hand, the man singing some pop song in a falsetto voice, trying to sound awful, the cool air filled with their laughter. I take a swig from my beer, but it tastes wrong, bitter, rancid. Booze has tasted that way since the shooting, since I recovered from the coma. Food has, too, as though the damage to my brain screwed up the connections to my taste buds, rearranged them while I slept.

I'm supposed to eat four meals a day to get my weight back, but I can hardly stomach three squares. Some days the only things I eat are plain pieces of bread and water. Maybe, in some weird way, I'm readying myself for prison, for the tasteless paste they will slop on my plate every day.

I look at the handgun on the bedside table. I won't deny that it's crossed my mind, at my darkest moments, when my memory loss drove me to the precipice, when I wanted to tear my hair out and peel off my skin and scream until I had no voice, when I was convinced that I must have committed murder, that the evidence didn't add up any other way, and that I will spend the rest of my life in a living hell of prison. I thought about tasting the steel on my tongue, the muzzle so deep in my mouth that I gag, squeezing my eyes shut and willing my thumb to pull the trigger.

I thought about it. But I'm too stubborn to do it. The Irish don't commit suicide; we just let ourselves be miserable forever.

I have a story. It's not what I remember, and it may or may not be true, but it's a story: Kate walked in on Amy and me having sex and opened fire in a jealous rage. That's what everybody thought at first, before the test results came back, before they had completed their investigation.

Before they discovered that *my* gun, not Kate's, was used to kill Amy.

Before they recovered the text messages from Kate's missing phone.

But it's the best story I can think up. It matches the crime scene to some extent, and it's pretty straightforward. A jealous rage, a woman scorned who happens to be heavily armed at the time of said scorn, doesn't require me to prove a number of different facts. Even if jurors might not do it themselves, they can understand the sting of betrayal and the temptation to act on it, to kill the person who stole your lover from your arms and shoot the cheating bastard, too. It's been the stuff of movies, of songs, of novels for a reason—everyone can relate to it on some level.

Either that or I put on no defense at all, a sure loser. Or I take the witness stand and sit there like a dumbass, shrug at Margaret Olson's questions, and simply say, *Good question; wish I knew. Don't remember. Can't argue with you there. Boy, I agree, that sure looks bad, but there might be an innocent explanation IF I COULD JUST FUCKING REMEMBER—*

Enough. Enough of that crap.

I look once more at the log of those text messages, the ones that Wizniewski showed me with such delight, the ones Kate sent as she stood outside Amy's apartment door only minutes before everything happened.

Open the door, she was texting me:

Need to talk to u

Why would I do that I said in response, as if Kate had picked a terrible time for a chat. And Kate's answer, those words, those simple words in black and white on the page I hold in my hand, but not black and white, full of fire and fury, rising off the piece of paper and floating in front of me, dancing and taunting me:

Bc she knows u idiot. She knows about u and so do I

I have tried to decipher this message for the seven and a half weeks since I was charged with murder. I've tried to remember, and I've tried to think logically. But the two things are sewn together. I can't fit the pieces together when I don't *have* the pieces, when I can't remember what happened. The more I call out for my memory, begging, pleading for it to return, the farther it burrows into the shadows.

I will have to learn to live with it, like a patient with a spinal injury who has to accept that he'll never walk again. I have to accept that I'll never remember, that I'll never really know, that it will lie buried inside me until the day I die.

So I'll be a good soldier. I'll learn to cope with it. But still I will wonder—every hour of every day, every day of every year I will wonder.

What did Amy know about me? What could I have done that was so bad?

THE PAST

SIXTY-SEVEN

"DO YOU solemnly swear to tell the truth, the whole truth, and nothing but the truth, so help you God?"

I do. Or at least that's what I told the clerk before I took my seat on the witness stand. I straightened my tie. I looked over the courtroom, so crowded with reporters and spectators that it felt like the walls would bend outward. The defense table was thick with lawyers, while their clients, including Mayor Francis Delaney and Archbishop Michael Xavier Phelan and a cast of other VIPs, sat behind them in the front row.

The first defense lawyer—the mayor's lawyer—stood and buttoned his jacket. This wasn't the trial itself; this was the hearing where the defense would try to convince the judge that I lacked probable cause to enter the brownstone. If they won, the arrests were invalid, and all these guys would walk free. This was their only shot. After all, we caught these defendants in various states of undress with young women. They had no plausible defense at trial—nobody was going to believe that they snuck into a discreet high-society sex club to play Parcheesi with scantily clad women. Their only hope was to wrap themselves in the Bill of Rights, the Fourth Amendment. Their only hope was to tear me to shreds.

Amy's eyes were on me, but I looked away when I saw her. It was all business now, so it wasn't the time for me to discuss other matters—other matters such as the glossy full-color eight-by-ten photograph of Amy walking up the steps to the brownstone, the photograph that someone put into a plain envelope and propped against my door last night. The photo that I brought with me today, that was too big to stick in my pocket, so I put it in my briefcase next to the prosecution table. It was hidden, tucked away inside a flap, but it felt radioactive, sending out signals to me that something was not what it seemed—

But no time for that now. Now was all business.

"Detective." The mayor's lawyer, Shaw DeCremer, once served under the first President Bush as his attorney general. He had since joined some powerhouse law firm—Readem and Weep, or maybe it was Woulda, Coulda, and Shoulda—and handled cases from coast to coast, usually high-stakes trials involving celebrities and politicians.

"You didn't have a warrant when you entered the brownstone, did you?" he asked.

"That's correct."

"Could you..." DeCremer waved a hand, strolled a bit in front of the defense table. "Could you describe the brownstone?"

I did my best. An old place, freestanding, sandstone and dark wood, arched entry, three stories.

"How many exits and entrances?" he asked.

"One entrance in the front, another in the back."

"Anything else? Secret tunnels? Any kind of elaborate escape routes?"

I shrugged. "Not that I knew of. But you never know."

"But the point is you *didn't* know. At the time of the raid, you didn't have any reason to believe there was some clever way that the people in the brownstone could escape or anything."

"That's correct."

"In fact, Detective, you'd never set foot in that brownstone, had you? Before the raid, I mean."

His point was fairly obvious if you understood the Fourth Amendment, which I pretty much did as a cop. Amy had hammered it into me during trial prep. If you don't have a warrant when you enter, you better have a good reason. The most common reason is that you're aware of criminal conduct—you saw drugs or weapons, for example, through a window—and you fear that if you don't go in immediately, if you take the time to go before a judge and secure a warrant, the offenders will have time to destroy the incriminating evidence if not escape altogether. DeCremer is trying to demonstrate that I didn't have any such concern the night of the raid.

"I had never set foot in that brownstone," I said.

"In fact," he said, wagging a finger, as though the thought had just occurred to him, "the reason you were there that night in the first place had nothing whatsoever to do with prostitution, did it?"

"No, it did not." I explained the initial reason for the stakeout—that I was investigating a murder, that I had a suspect, that I wanted to catch him in the act of sleeping with a prostitute so I'd have some leverage over him and get him to answer some questions about the murder.

"Sounds like a smart plan," DeCremer said. When a lawyer pays you a compliment, look up. There's probably a guillotine poised to drop down on your neck.

"Thank you," I said.

"So you had this murder suspect, and you had already followed him to this brownstone the previous week, and your plan was to catch him in a—a compromising position, shall we say?"

"That's correct."

"And yet having had this plan in your head for a week, you did not ask a judge for a warrant."

"I did not."

"You didn't ask the state's attorney's office to help you apply for a warrant."

"I did not."

"And that's because you weren't worried about making a case against this guy for prostitution. You were concerned about bigger stuff. A murder."

"Correct."

DeCremer nodded, glanced down at his feet, at his polished Ferragamo shoes. There was no jury for this hearing. If this case went to trial and he had twelve in the box, he wouldn't be wearing thousand-dollar shoes. He'd try to dress like a man of the people.

"If you *had* been trying to put a case on this suspect for prostitution, if that had been your plan all along, you'd have applied for a warrant, right?"

"Objection." Amy Lentini popped halfway up from her chair. She knew the question was proper, but she was trying to disrupt his flow and also signal to me, if I didn't already know, that the water was getting choppy.

"I might have," I said after the judge overruled the objection. "But you're making this sound like some elaborate advance plan. It wasn't. I'd been looking for a chance to confront this suspect about the murder. I saw this as an opportunity, and I took it. I asked a few of my fellow detectives to ride along for support. That's all."

DeCremer nodded as though he expected my answer. He neither expected it nor liked it, but he'd never admit to either one. These guys were as smooth as butter.

"Fair enough," he conceded. "Let's talk about how you knew this was a house of prostitution."

SIXTY-EIGHT

"LET ME see if I have this straight," said Shaw DeCremer. "The week before, you trailed this suspect to the brownstone. You saw him go in. You saw him leave an hour later."

"Yes."

"You stayed and watched the brownstone."

"Yes."

"You saw several attractive young women leave. Women dressed provocatively."

"Yes."

"You saw nobody engaging in sexual intercourse."

"No."

"Not a single person."

"I think I just answered that question. I didn't have X-ray vision, no. I was outside."

That was good enough for the lawyer. Amy Lentini flipped a pencil in her hand.

"Then you 'sat on,' as you put it—you sat on the brownstone a couple of times over the next week."

"Yes, correct. Twice that week, before the raid, I parked across the street and conducted surveillance."

"You saw the same types of things. Older men walking in. Young, provocatively dressed women walking in."

"Right."

"You didn't see anyone having sex?"

"Obviously not."

"Or exchanging money?"

"No."

"You didn't see which floors these people went to, did you? I mean, this was a three-story building."

"No, I didn't, but I saw an armed doorman greet each of them. The women he just let in, like he knew them. The men—he checked their names on a clipboard. I gathered from that—the way the men kept their heads down, acted like they didn't want to be seen, and basically had to sign in to get inside the place—that they weren't just making casual social calls."

"But you never actually saw what any of these people were doing inside—"

"Men were parading in and out of there, Mr. DeCremer. The women came and stayed all night. Most of the men stayed for one hour—like clockwork—and some stayed for two hours. Then they left, acting just as suspiciously when they walked out as they did when they walked in. Was this a secret meeting of the Freemasons? Was it a Tupperware party? Maybe, but it sure seemed like a house of prostitution to me."

"It *seemed* like one."

I turned, surprised to see that the judge was addressing me. The judge, with sharply combed black hair and a thick mustache, a guy named Walter McCabe, who'd been on the bench for more than twenty years.

The judge is allowed to ask questions. The judge can do whatever he wants. This is his tiny fiefdom. But it's uncommon for a judge to interject himself into the questioning like this. It isn't a good sign.

"It *seemed* like one," he said again, looking down on me, "based on the pattern of movement of the men, in and out by the hour?"

"And based on the way they behaved. And the young women."

The judge didn't look convinced. Had he ever been a cop? Had he ever had to play a hunch? And did anyone care, by the way, that everything my gut had told me ended up being one hundred percent spot-on *correct?*

Judge McCabe said, "Detective, at any time before the night of the raid when you were staking out the brownstone, or on the night of the raid itself—at any point in time did you witness a crime in progress?"

"Every time I saw a man enter that brownstone I witnessed a crime in progress."

"But you know what I mean, Detective. It's not a crime to walk into a building."

"It is if the building is a house of prostitution."

"But you didn't *know* it was a house of prostitution. It *seemed* like one, you said."

"But—"

"Did you see sex? Or money change hands? Did you ever see one of the young women with one of the men? Did you see them so much as touch hands or wave hello to one another? Do you even know if they were on the same floor of the brownstone together?"

"No, Judge. And if it had been just one guy walking in, or even a handful, I wouldn't have thought anything of it. But it was a steady stream. And the guard at the door, he was very careful about discretion. He made sure nobody was entering if someone was leaving. He would look out, make sure the coast was clear, and then someone would hustle out. There was nothing about this that looked normal."

"Maybe not normal," he said. "But criminal?"

"That was my judgment, yes. And I didn't have time for a warrant. By the time I could find a judge and get her to sign off, these clients would have left. There wasn't time. This is one of the crimes where you have to catch them in the act or you have no case. I had to move right away."

The judge sat back in his seat, looking unsatisfied.

For crying out loud, I thought to myself. Talk about second-guessing police work. Everything about the way that place operated smelled like an upscale house of prostitution. And I was right—it was. Didn't that count for anything? But here we were, in a pristine courtroom with walnut trim and shiny floors, listening to a guy in a robe who'd never spent a day on the street and a lawyer dressed in an outfit that I couldn't afford on two months' salary, who'd never spent a real day in the shit, either, acting like they knew better than me.

The hearing wasn't over, not technically. Amy hadn't even had her chance to question me yet. But I could see it on the judge's face. He wasn't convinced. He thought I lacked probable cause. He was going to invalidate my search. He was going to toss this case.

And my career along with it.

SIXTY-NINE

LIEUTENANT MIKE Goldberger closed the door gently behind him before turning to address me and Kate, who would testify tomorrow. We were in a witness interview room on the same floor as the courtroom where I had just had my head handed to me.

I stood and stretched; I'd been sitting all day. Seven hours of questioning from six defense lawyers, then Amy grilling me on every detail. Nothing seemed to make a difference. From the moment the judge addressed his questions to me, it was clear that he didn't like our case.

Goldie said, "Okay, so that didn't go so well," which was like saying the *Titanic*'s maiden voyage had some rough patches.

"It was a righteous search," I said.

"Hell, *I* know that," Goldie said. "But the judge isn't with us. That's obvious."

I shook my head. "Some clown in a robe who hasn't—"

"Who hasn't spent a day on the job; I know, I know," Goldie grumbled. "But we're past crying in our Cheerios. Time to fix this."

I looked up at him. Goldie didn't say things casually.

Goldie pointed at Kate. "Detective Fenton, you guys staked out the brownstone two nights before the raid. When the stakeout ended, Billy went home. What did you do?"

Kate said, without missing a beat, "I left, too, but then I drove back to the brownstone."

I spun around to face Kate. "Huh?"

Kate kept her eyes forward, on Goldie, avoiding my stare. "I drove back to the brownstone. I waited for the girls to leave. I followed two of them home."

First I'd heard of this. Because it never happened.

"And what happened next?" Goldie asked as though he were a prosecutor in court, as though he already knew the answer.

Because he did know the answer. This wasn't the first time he was hearing it.

"The girls went home to their apartment on the second floor," said Kate. "I walked up to their building and looked at the buzzer assigned to the second floor. There were two names next to it. Sanchez and Daniels."

"Bullshit," I said. "This is bullshit."

"There was a postcard lying on the walkway next to the mail slot," Kate continued. "An advertisement a sale at Macy's or something. But it had a name on it. Erica Daniels."

"So you had one woman's full name and a partial for the second," said Goldie. "What happened next?"

"Oh, for fuck's sake," I said. "Hell, even *I* can finish *this* story." I looked at Kate. "You went to the station and did a criminal background check. It turned out Erica Daniels had a prior for prostitution. And you did a search on Sanchez and found the same thing. Their mug shots looked like the girls you followed.

And suddenly—oh, my God, wouldn't you know?—we knew that at least two of the women who spent the evening in that brownstone were hookers." I threw up my hands. "Hallelujah! We have probable cause!"

Goldie leaned against the wall. "Couldn't've said it better, actually."

"Yeah, except for the minor detail that none of it actually happened. Kate didn't follow those women to their apartment." My arms came down by my sides. "I mean, guys, what are we talking about?" I turned to Kate again. "Did Goldie talk you into this? I mean, I know he wants to protect us, but there's a—"

"Who said it was Goldie's idea?" she replied, as if she were insulted that I'd attribute perjury to him and not her.

Kate stood up, face-to-face with me. "If we lose this case, it's all over," she said. "The mayor stays in office, right? Sure he does. He goes free. And his best buddy, the superintendent he appointed, Tristan Driscoll—he stays on the job, too."

Goldie said, "How long until the supe finds an excuse to run you off the force? Or, worse yet, he assigns you to traffic duty the rest of your career? If this case goes south, that's your future, pal."

"I'll take my chances," I said.

"Yeah, well, *I* won't take *my* chances." Kate shoved me. "This isn't just about you, partner. My career goes down the tubes, too. I don't get a say in this?"

I let out air. "Katie," I said.

"Oh, now it's 'Katie.'" She made quotation marks with her fingers.

I looked at Goldie. "When did this all come together? This little story of yours?"

He said, "You mean this little story that will save

the careers of not one but two police officers who are among the finest cops I've ever known? This little story that puts the bad guys where they belong? That little story?"

I deflated. Goldie's heart was always in the right place. He'd stand in front of a train for me. From his perspective, this was just a little gloss on the truth, a harmless twist, to prevent a miscarriage of justice—and, more important, to protect me. Always looking out for me.

"Kate," said Goldie, "give us a minute, wouldja?"

That seemed like a fine idea to her. She grabbed her bag and walked out in a huff, barely glancing in my direction.

Goldie raised a hand. "Just shut your pie hole and listen to me one time. I don't like this any more than you do. It wasn't my idea. It was Kate's. She's a grown-up. I couldn't stop her if I wanted to. I prayed like hell your testimony would come in solid and none of this would be necessary. But now it is. We're out of good choices here."

I shook my head, fuming.

"It gets us to the right result," he said. "It's justice. You did good cop work. Every instinct you had was correct. So why should it end up that the scumbags walk free and two good cops get knives in their stomachs? How the fuck is that justice?"

It wasn't my first time in court, and I understood the art of presenting information in a way that favored your side, but that was spin, that was the fight. This—this was literally making up evidence. This I had never done.

As if reading my mind, Goldie said, "Never in a million years would I have asked you to say this on the witness stand. Hell, I wouldn't have asked Kate, either. She came to me with this. I tried to talk her out of it. You ever try talking Kate out of something?"

I allowed for that. A pit bull was less stubborn than my partner.

"And listen, at the end of the day, when my head hits the pillow and I try to put right and wrong on a scale and see which side's heavier? All in all, I think what she's doing gets us heavier on the right than the wrong. That's the best I can do, sport."

I was still fuming, but there wasn't much I could do. I was done testifying. Nobody was going to ask me anything else under oath.

"It's not your decision; it's not mine," Goldie said. "Let her do it, kiddo."

SEVENTY

JUDGE WALTER McCabe adjusted his eyeglasses and looked over a courtroom filled to bursting. "The court is prepared to rule," he said.

The hearing had lasted three days. My testimony took up the first day. Kate's filled the second day and part of the third, as defense lawyers poked and probed and came at Kate ten different ways, trying to challenge her surprising revelation that she had followed two of the prostitutes home from the brownstone one night, gathered their information, and discovered their criminal rap sheets. *Why didn't you ever document that information?* they asked. *Why didn't you tell your partner, Detective Harney? Could it be that we're hearing this for the first time, suddenly, conveniently, after Detective Harney's testimony didn't go so well?*

The courtroom was still. I heard the static ringing in the air that silence often produces. Or maybe that ringing was inside my head. The judge's ruling would determine the rest of my career.

"The court finds that the search of the brownstone was valid," said the judge, reading from prepared text.

I released a long breath.

"The detectives' surveillance gave them some reason to suspect that the brownstone was not a residence but a brothel, a house of prostitution. More important, Detective Fenton's testimony—that she surveilled two of the women working at the brownstone, ran background checks, and determined that they were prostitutes—was credible, and it was sufficient to establish probable cause. On the night of the raid, the officers had probable cause to believe a crime was in progress, and they had reason to believe that, in the time it would have taken to secure a warrant, those men would have been gone and the evidence of the crime, so to speak, would have been destroyed. The court finds probable cause, coupled with exigent circumstances. The defense's motion to suppress is hereby denied. State?"

Amy Lentini rose from her seat. "State stands ready for trial, Your Honor."

"Mr. DeCremer?" the judge asked the mayor's lawyer, who seemed to be the de facto leader of the defense team.

Shaw DeCremer stood up. "Could we put off the jury selection until tomorrow, Your Honor?"

The judge gave a slow nod. He understood. So did Amy. There wasn't going to be a trial. They took their shot on a legal technicality and lost. If they went to trial, a dozen cops and a dozen prostitutes—all of whom had been granted immunity for their testimony—would take the stand and publicly reveal every little detail of what happened that night behind closed bedroom doors. Kinky, humiliating details. The embarrassment far outweighed the minuscule chance for an acquittal. Every one of them would plead guilty.

Already, Shaw DeCremer had approached Amy, followed by other defense lawyers. They were lined up like customers outside a Toys"R"Us on Black Friday, hoping to get their hands on the newest version of the Xbox.

"The mayor will be pleading guilty," said DeCremer, keeping his voice low, though I was sitting in the front row of the courtroom, so I could hear him whisper to Amy.

"I'll draw up the papers," she said, shaking his hand. She might as well have called out, *Next?* It happened one after the other, all these lawyers who had drawn their knives and tried to slash me to bits copping their pleas and hoping for mercy from the prosecutor on an agreed disposition.

I looked behind me at Kate, who got to her feet and mouthed two words at me.

You're welcome.

I should have enjoyed this more. The eyes of the nation were on this courtroom, and we had won. Maybe the path we took was a little rocky, but I had told nothing but the truth, and Goldie was right—justice prevailed.

But I still had my briefcase at my feet, and it still contained an eight-by-ten photograph of Amy Lentini walking up the steps of the brownstone. I hadn't yet said a word to Amy, because all our focus had to be on this hearing, but now the hearing was over, and I felt something in the pit of my stomach, splashing and simmering.

When the last of the lawyers had given his notice to Amy and the courtroom was otherwise empty, Amy looked at me, relieved but not satisfied. "I'd give anything to know how Kate's testimony came about," she said.

"I don't think you would," I said.

Her eyebrows twitched. "She swore to me it was true."

"I know she did. She swore under oath, too."

When Kate first told Amy what she planned to say under oath, Amy didn't take it well. She pressed Kate over and over. She told Kate she would not suborn perjury; she would not let Kate testify falsely. But Kate never backed down. She swore it was the truth. They went back and forth like that for more than an hour, and Amy was clearly skeptical, but she didn't—and couldn't possibly—know that Kate was lying.

Amy even pulled me aside and asked me if Kate was lying. But Kate, quite skillfully, had kept me out of it by saying that she never told me about her surveillance of those two women. So I didn't have to lie. I told Amy the truth: it sounded like bullshit to me; I was pretty sure she was lying, but I wasn't there. I'd gone home. I couldn't say for certain what Kate did or didn't do once I went home after the stakeout.

Amy ultimately decided to accept Kate's testimony. She didn't really have a choice.

From the look on her face, Amy had a pretty strong feeling that the card game she'd just won was played with a stacked deck, but she didn't know it for sure, and so she played the hand she was dealt.

"Well," she said, warming up to her victory, letting it wash over her. "Should we celebrate?"

I looked around the courtroom to ensure that we were alone. Then I reached into my briefcase, pulled out the manila envelope, and produced the glossy photo of Amy walking up the steps of the brownstone. I held it up for her to see, but when she reached for it, I drew it back. It was my only copy.

Her expression dropped, her posture stiffened. "Where did you—"

"Where did I get this photo? It's hardly the most important question. Hell, it's not even in the top ten."

Amy blinked hard and took a step back. Her eyes worked along the floor, but finally, after a long moment while my heart drummed so hard in my throat that I doubted I could speak, Amy's eyes drifted up to mine.

Her voice flat, her eyes hooded, she whispered to me.

"Not here," she said.

SEVENTY-ONE

I FOLLOWED Amy from the criminal courts building at 26th and Cal to her condo in Wrigleyville. I played talk radio in my car as I drove. With our split-second news cycle, everyone was already talking about the outcome of the hearing. Mayor Francis Delaney had announced, outside the courtroom, that he would be resigning today.

And just like that they were already talking about who would succeed him. A number of aldermen and county commissioners were interested in running for the mayor's seat, but the presumed front-runner would be Congressman John Tedesco.

All because of my case. I should have felt adrenaline, some sense of power or awe, but instead I felt dread.

We both found parking at the curb, went under the awning and through the downstairs door, took the elevator up to the sixth floor, and walked down the hallway to her apartment. All in silence, not a word spoken. We'd spent days, weeks, preparing for a case that we had just won, but we looked like we were attending a funeral.

It made me think of my friend Stewart, now freshly buried, reunited with his wife in heaven. What he used to say about reaching the point in life when you're sick of the bullshit and only want what's real.

But I didn't feel that way. At that moment, as the two of us walked in grim silence to her apartment, I didn't want *real*. I wanted the fairy tale. I wanted what Amy and I were building together. At that moment, I wished I'd never seen that photograph of her outside the brownstone. I wanted to will it out of my brain, pretend I never saw it, and we would live happily ever after—cue the music and roll the credits.

Amy entered the apartment and hung up her coat. She walked into the center of her living room and turned. Without any hint of remorse or embarrassment, she said to me, "I want to know where you got that photograph."

"No," I said. "It's my turn to ask questions. I want to know what the hell is going on."

Amy gestured toward my briefcase, where I had put the photograph. "That's a crime," she said.

"Tell me about it. I think we just convicted a dozen people for it."

Her eyebrows wrinkled, forehead creased. "*That's* not what I'm talking about. You think—what? You think that photograph shows me about to have sex with a prostitute? Really?"

I didn't have an answer. The truth was, I didn't have any idea what to make of this photograph.

"I'm talking about obstruction," she said. "Whoever gave you that photo is guilty of obstruction of justice."

It took a moment for that to sink in. "What are you telling me? This was part of an investigation?"

Amy dropped her head, placed her hands on her hips. Took a breath. Made a decision.

"Billy," she said, raising her head, "did you ever wonder why I was so hell-bent on finding the little black book? From the first moment after the bust, when we hauled you and Kate into Margaret's office, all we cared about was the little black book. Did that ever strike you as odd?"

"It did," I answered. "But I figured you were trying to smear us. To protect the mayor. Margaret Olson and Superintendent Driscoll—both of them had their jobs thanks to the mayor. They wanted to keep him in power so *they'd* stay in power."

She listened to all that and made a sour face, like those political shenanigans were beneath her. Then her expression broke, and her eyebrows raised. "Wow," she said. "You must have had a really low opinion of me."

And she of me. But we had gotten past that. We had sailed those treacherous waters and found something on the other side, something warm and soothing, something that made my heart go pitter-patter like a schoolboy kissing a girl for the first time. I couldn't deny it. I was all in. I was in love with Amy Lentini.

"Talk to me," I said.

She nodded, took another breath, confirmed her decision. "For the last year or so," she said, "the state's attorney's office has been conducting an investigation. We have reason to believe that Chicago police officers have been running a protection racket. Taking bribes to let people walk."

I didn't move. Didn't show a thing. Didn't mention the fact that I had been investigating the same thing as an undercover officer for Internal Affairs.

Two different law enforcement agencies investigating the same damn thing, not saying a word to each other.

"And this brownstone was front and center in our investigation," she said. "Powerful people, with a place to go to get their jollies, indulge their fantasies, whatever—but it needs to be a safe place, right? They can't be caught publicly. The shame would be too intense. A woman like Ramona Dillavou knows that. She's not going to draw the rich and famous to her club if they're afraid of a police raid, right?"

"Right," I managed.

"Ramona Dillavou was paying off cops. Protection money."

"Who?" I asked. "What cops?"

She looked at me dead-on. Held perfectly still. Like a breathtaking portrait, my Italian beauty, my work of art. All that was missing was the gold frame and the artist's signature in the corner.

"Who was Ramona paying off?" I tried again.

The longer Amy paused, stood frozen, the harder my heart pumped.

"Kate," she said. "Detective Katherine Fenton."

SEVENTY-TWO

I FELT a *No* reach my lips but didn't say it. "Kate?" I mumbled. My brain tried to keep pace with my racing heart, tried to connect the dots. "Are you sure?"

"I can't prove it, if that's what you mean," she said. "Process of elimination. It has to be her."

I brought a hand to my face. The woman with whom I'd partnered, shared so much over the years—she was on the take and I didn't know it?

"We were just about to find out," she said. "We'd been tracking Ramona's bank accounts, her cash withdrawals. We were about to close in. I was literally in the process of drafting a complaint for a search warrant. We were no more than days away from raiding the brownstone."

I slowly nodded. "But then I raided the place first."

"But then you raided the place first."

It was coming clearer now. "You thought the cops knew," I said. "You thought the dirty cops got wind of your investigation, so we raided the place for cover. Publicly exposed the VIPs. Got Ramona in the soup. Blew up the whole thing."

"And stole the little black book," she said.

Right. Exactly. The little black book, the ledger, the computer disk, whatever it was—Amy didn't want it for the names of other VIPs who frequented the place. She didn't care about the identities of the johns.

She wanted the names of the cops Ramona Dillavou was paying off.

"So you thought I was one of the dirty cops," I said. "You thought I was part of the protection racket." I said it with a hint of accusation, though I couldn't blame her. As much as it burned, I couldn't deny that her initial reaction was logical. Before she knew me, it was her first instinct—she's about to raid the brothel and secure the little black book, and *wham,* I beat her to the punch by a matter of days. And the little black book mysteriously disappears. Yeah, if I were in her shoes, I'd have suspected me, too.

"You or Kate," Amy said. "You were the detectives in charge. So yeah, I suspected both of you for the protection racket. And stealing the little black book. But now I've ruled you out."

"How? Why?"

She was taken aback, hurt by the question. "Because now I *know* you."

Too much. Overload. Too many emotions swirling in too many directions, blurring everything together. I needed to think straight, sort through everything.

"Kate was the evidence recovery officer that night," Amy said. "She would have had the easiest access to that black book. Easy as pie she could've pocketed it, and nobody would have known."

I thought back to the night of the raid.

Remembered Kate being so ginned up to go in.

Remembered my thought that maybe we should call in Vice, because this was their turf, and Kate's reaction: *Fuck Vice. This is ours.*

Remembered Kate leading the search upstairs of Ramona Dillavou's office.

She easily could have done it.

"Kate," I said again, only this time not as a question.

"That photograph you showed me, of me walking up to the brownstone? That just confirms what I thought," Amy said. "That photo was taken only a couple of weeks before your raid. It had to be, because that was the only time I was there. I just wanted to see the place for myself. We'd spent so much time investigating it, but I'd never actually gone there. I didn't go in. I just walked up a couple of stairs and looked at it." She wagged a finger. "But the photograph proves that somebody knew I was there."

"Whoever snapped this photo knew that you, one of the top prosecutors with the state's attorney's office, was interested in that brownstone."

"They knew we were close, Billy. The dirty cops knew we were coming. And then, suddenly, just before we made our move, you and Kate lead a squad of officers and raid the place. And the little black book goes bye-bye."

She was right. It all lined up.

"But Kate didn't act alone," said Amy. "This operation is too big for one person. Which brings me to my original question when you first showed me that photograph: Where did you get it?"

"Found it on my doorstep," I said. "Anonymous. Plain manila envelope, no writing, nothing but the photograph inside."

She thought about that, disappointed that I didn't know more, paced her living room.

"Whoever left me that photograph doesn't want me to trust you," I said.

Amy looked at me. "Whoever left you that photograph is in on this with Kate."

I removed the photograph from my briefcase, examined it, turned it so Amy, who walked over to me, could look at it, too. "This is just like the others," I said. "All the photos that Kim Beans has published. Same angle, same focus, same everything."

"Same photographer every time," Amy murmured.

We looked at each other. It registered with each of us at the same time.

"A cop's been feeding these photographs to Kim," Amy said.

I nodded. "We find Kim's source," I said, "and we find our dirty cop."

SEVENTY-THREE

"HAND TO hand," I said to Amy. "Kim's source wouldn't e-mail the photos or text them. Too traceable. The US mail wouldn't work—the photo could be damaged, and you can't control timing as much. He wouldn't FedEx it because he'd have to put down a credit card or walk into a store that has a security camera."

Amy thought about all that. She was a prosecutor, not a cop, but she'd worked some pretty big federal investigations, and she knew something about the cloak-and-dagger aspect of corruption.

"And you don't think Kim already has all the photographs?" she asked.

I shook my head. "I don't think so. Whoever this dirty cop is, he's using Kim for some purpose, and he—"

"Or she," Amy added.

"Right. The dirty cop—he or she—would want to maintain control over the situation. Handing over all the photos at once to Kim is not maintaining control; it's giving all the leverage to Kim, letting her do whatever she wants with the photos whenever she wants. No," I continued, "our dirty cop is smart. He'd want to keep Kim on a short leash. He'd want to hand her one photo a week, keep her nice and compliant and dependent on him."

Amy nodded, then looked up and squinted. "Well, Kim's next column comes out in three days. So if you want to catch her in the act of receiving a photo from her source—"

"I have to go right now," I finished. "I have to start my surveillance right this minute."

"I'll go with you," she said.

"No. I work better alone."

Amy's mouth curled downward. "Maybe Kate does, too," she said. "Maybe she's working alone on this. Maybe the person handing Kim those photos is the same person who stole the little black book—Kate."

"Or maybe Kate did neither of those things."

Amy raised her eyebrows. "I still haven't convinced you?"

"It doesn't matter whether I'm convinced or not," I said. "I'll find out when I shadow Kim. Speaking of which..."

"You need to get going." Amy nodded. "Promise me you'll be careful. People have been killed over this."

"Careful's my middle name," I said.

I left. I didn't want to get drawn into a long goodbye with Amy, because knowing me and my lack of willpower, we would end up with our clothes off, and I really needed to hurry. I needed to know the truth. Was Kate really behind this? Was she shaking down Ramona Dillavou? Did she steal the little black book the night of the raid? Logic and reasoning made her the most likely suspect. But Kate?

I got to my car and started it up. My cell phone

buzzed. A text message from...well, speak of the devil. The message was from Kate.

U never thanked me when do I get my present?

There was a photograph attached. It was a photo of Kate, a selfie, as they call it. She was lying in her bed, naked down to her bra and panties, an angle downward that maximized the cleavage shot, a come-hither look on her face, the hint of a devilish smile. Your basic male fantasy.

Was this real? Or was this some kind of ploy to draw me in? I didn't know if Kate was trying to rekindle that brief—and, in hindsight, ill-considered—fling we had or if she was playing me.

Was she jealous or devious?

"Well, let's find out, Katie," I whispered. "Let's see who delivers the photo to Kim."

SEVENTY-FOUR

MY SECOND full day of surveillance of Kim Beans. I spent yesterday following Kim to work, to a bar in Ukrainian Village, to the Whole Foods in Lincoln Park, and to a Bulls game last night (which took some effort, but I badged my way into United Center, one of the perks of the job). I saw no indication of any handoff, any passing of a photograph or anything else.

This morning, Kim arrived at her office, in Dearborn Park, at eight. No fancy downtown skyscraper; *ChicagoPC* was just an online news outlet, so a medium-size office with a plate-glass window sufficed.

I had a Thermos of hot coffee and a box of granola bars, ready to stay in one position for as long as it took. In the ninety minutes I'd sat on her office, I hadn't seen any cops enter or exit, but then I wouldn't expect them to. If you were an anonymous source, you wouldn't stroll into a newsroom. And nobody shuffling in and out of these doors since Kim arrived looked anything like a cop. Most of them were in their twenties and wore ponytails and nose rings and berets and headphones. The new age of journalism.

My phone beeped. A text message from Kate.

Another personal day for Billy? R u sick or is it 4 fun

It was my second day in a row skipping work. I thought that Kate might take time off, too, after the big trial, but apparently not. It was yet another reminder of how far we had drifted, partners who once shared everything now failing to even coordinate our work schedules.

Just some personal stuff, I replied.

U want some company? she came back almost immediately.

I wanted to keep this informal, casual, but after the porn photo she sent me the night before last, it was hard to play dumb. I hadn't even acknowledged that photo, hadn't replied to her at all.

I'm good just some errands, I typed. Then I added, Talk soon. My way of politely ending the back-and-forth. I hit Send and heard the *swoosh* of my phone as it volleyed my message through cyberspace to Kate.

Two hours later: Kim left her office on foot, braced against the cold, and hustled across the street to a deli that was only about twenty yards from my position in my car. It was lunchtime, and lunch was a good cover for a meet. I got out of the car and watched her from the sidewalk through the large window. She didn't contact anybody, didn't brush against someone, didn't pick anything up that someone else had left. She simply pulled a salad out of a refrigerated case, put it on the counter by the cashier, swiped her credit card, and left.

I got back in the car, disappointed. I had to piss, too.

My cell phone buzzed again. Another text from Kate.

You have the right to remain silent

Another photograph attached. Another selfie.

Kate, in her patrol uniform, which she hadn't worn for years, the shirt unbuttoned to her navel, maximum cleavage. Firearm on her hip. Handcuffs dangling from her finger. The sexy-cop thing.

Punching every button she could find, trying to get a rise out of me. Why? I mean, I was a swell guy and all, but I wasn't *that* great of a catch.

I put down my phone as if to make it all go away.

An hour passed. Kim took a cab to a beauty salon. Luckily for me, I could see her through a picture window as the hairdresser took an inch off her curly locks. I didn't make this for the drop spot. Possible but unlikely.

My phone buzzed again and filled me with dread. Yes. Kate again.

Don't make me beg

"Jesus, Kate," I mumbled inside my car as my phone buzzed again, then again, in rapid succession:

Unless you want me to beg LOL

On my hands and knees?

There was that brief time during our fling when I would have enjoyed this. But I wasn't having any fun at all.

I typed the word Stop but didn't send it. Stared at it. Didn't want to make matters worse. Didn't want to throw gasoline on a fire. But I didn't want to encourage her, either.

Ninety minutes later, Kim was back at her office in Dearborn Park. Another text from Kate:

This is bullshit

I was beginning to feel the same way, and my lack of progress on Kim's surveillance had me pretty agitated already. The word Stop was still typed into my phone from the last time Kate had texted me.

This time, I hit the Send button. And took a breath. Steeled myself for the counterpunch. I was pretty sure Kate wouldn't enjoy being told to stop anything.

Nothing, on any front, for the next ninety minutes, as the sun sank below the buildings in the South Loop and dusk began to cover the sky. Nothing from Kim, and nothing from Kate.

Then my phone buzzed again. Another message from Kate.

See anything u like?

Another photograph attached. Another selfie. Kate, inside her hot-red Corvette, naked except for a leather jacket spread open generously for a nice view. Yet again, a photo worthy of a porn website, the third one she'd sent me.

But this time there was one difference: in her right hand she was holding her service weapon against her temple.

It hit me hard, a clash of cymbals between my ears, a hot spear to my stomach. She knew very well how my wife had died.

Kate was coming unglued. Something was happening. I didn't know what. But I couldn't ignore it.

At that moment, Kim Beans left her office and walked to her car.

Shit. I had to stay with Kim. Tomorrow was the day her next photo was set to be published. If she was meeting her source, it would be between now and tomorrow morning. I couldn't leave her side now. Not *now*.

I typed, but erased, several messages into my phone.

That's not funny

I hope you're joking

Don't do anything rash

None of them felt right. I threw my car into gear as Kim sped away in her car. I hastily typed Talk soon I promise and hit Send. It wasn't the perfect message, but it would have to do.

I didn't know whether she was playing me or in real distress. I hoped that I would have the chance to find out.

SEVENTY-FIVE

I STEPPED out of the car, shifting my weight from one foot to the other, trying to keep warm. It was long past dusk, and the air stung my face. I couldn't remember the last time it had been so cold in early April. It was so cold that the prostitutes were charging money to blow on your hands.

I was in a strip mall at the corner of Ogden and Grand—West Town. One of my favorite areas. I knew the Twisted Spoke well. One of the best burgers in the city; thick, spicy Bloody Marys. I wished I was in there right now ordering a fatboy, debating between whiskey and beer.

But I was across the street, bundled to my chin, blowing frosty air out of my mouth, binoculars in hand. I had pretty good eyesight, so as long as Kim Beans just sat at her table inside the Spoke sipping her drink with her back against a window, I wouldn't use the binoculars and look like some pervert. Whenever anyone approached her table, the binoculars went up to my eyes. So far thirty minutes had passed, and the only person coming within ten feet of her was a surly overweight guy with facial hair and a bald head who took her order.

My car was running, headlights off, dome light off,

heat blasting. Every ten minutes or so I ducked into the car for a quick warm-up, never taking my eyes off Kim's position.

I stomped my feet in place and bounced up and down. I looked like an ice fisherman doing aerobics.

Inside the Spoke, Kim looked at her watch and nursed her drink, something yellowish, a fruity job. She'd been there now for forty-five minutes. I decided to get back in the car, because I could use my binoculars without being so conspicuous, and the view was good enough—the angle wasn't quite as good if I wanted to see anyone across the table from her, but I could see Kim just fine, and if she moved even an inch, I'd jump out and get a wider look. Until then, I didn't feel any particular need to get hypothermia.

An hour later, Kim hadn't moved an inch. She ordered something from the menu—hummus and pita, probably, just to keep up appearances and not piss off the owner by monopolizing a table without ordering anything.

By eleven thirty, Kim was drumming her fingers. Her back was to me; I could only see her face when she looked toward the door. But in those few moments when I could see her, I wasn't getting *angry* from her. Her eyebrows were knit together, her mouth tight. She was concerned.

I was, too.

By midnight she was looking pretty unraveled. There was absolutely, positively no way that she was waiting for a friend or a date. She wouldn't have stayed two hours past the meet time. And she would have made a phone call, one of those *Hey, I'm here: is everything okay?* calls, politely telling her friend or date to hurry the hell up.

But she hadn't made a call. Because whomever she was here to meet, she didn't have that person's phone number. Her source wouldn't want any kind of trail. No e-mail. No texts. No cell-phone calls.

Kim paid her bill and left. She hailed a cab and went back to her place in Lincoln Park. I followed her, watched her walk in and go upstairs to her apartment on the third floor. I was done for the night.

I hadn't gotten everything I wanted, but I had learned two things.

One: Kim had definitely been planning to meet her source. That part was easy and good. It meant I was on the right path.

The second thing was not so good. It was like an ugly growth: it could be nothing more than an unsightly blemish, but it felt more like a cancerous tumor that was slowly spreading its ugly poison, a tumor that grew larger and uglier the longer I watched Kim Beans wait in vain for her source.

My cell phone buzzed. Caller ID said Amy. My heart kicked up like I'd been hit with a cattle prod.

I reached for the button on my cell, considered not answering. Punched it anyway.

"How's it going?" Amy asked.

I waited a beat, thought about my answer.

"False alarm," I said. "She just had dinner and went home."

That was technically true, but I'd left out how long Kim had been waiting. I left out that I was sure she'd been waiting for her source, that I had no doubt.

Because the second thing I'd learned tonight was

that Kim's source, somehow, in some way, knew not to come tonight.

Somebody tipped off Kim's source that I'd be watching.

And the only person who would have known that piece of information was on the phone with me right now.

SEVENTY-SIX

NO, I thought to myself when I got home. I was pacing the floor in my bedroom. *Impossible.* Amy wouldn't have told anybody about my surveillance. But then how did the source know I was tailing Kim?

Wasn't I careful? Discreet? I was good at surveillance. It was my specialty.

But I must have blown it somehow. That was the only explanation. I wasn't careful enough. Kim's source did some reconnaissance of his own—or *her* own—and somehow made me and ditched out.

I blew it. And I wouldn't get another chance.

Yes, I thought to myself. *That must be it.* It wasn't Amy. It was my own negligence.

I checked my text messages. Nothing more from Kate since this afternoon, when I promised her I'd be in touch soon. No more pornographic photos. No more guns to her head. No more angry, flirtatious, unstable messages.

Dread suddenly filled me. One reason I hadn't heard from Kate could be a very, very bad reason. A reason that had something to do with putting a gun to her head.

Screw text messages. I dialed my phone and rang Kate.

Four rings before it went to voice mail. "Just checking in with you," I said. "Please call."

Then I added a text message for good measure: How are you doing?

I paced the floor with more urgency, like it was some kind of Olympic event, wondering if I should jump in my car and head over to Kate's. But it was almost two in the morning. That was crazy. Still, if she was thinking of harming herself, if by some chance she'd actually been serious when she sent me that photo with the gun—

Let me know you're ok, I texted.

—and then the panic began to rise in my chest, and I suddenly blamed myself, feeling guilty that I didn't take her more seriously when I first got that photo this afternoon, that maybe it was a cry for help and I was so caught up in my surveillance that I didn't pay sufficient attention—

—again, for the second time in my life, I didn't see the warning signs—

—call back, Kate, please call back—

I threw my coat back on and grabbed my car keys off the table by the front door. I went into the garage and popped open the garage door, a wave of chilly wind sweeping in, then I jumped in my car and started the ignition.

And my phone buzzed. I grabbed for it with such intensity that I fumbled it, the phone falling to the floorboard in my car. I reached down and grabbed it, read the face of it. It was a text message from Kate.

Fuck u

I breathed out. Never in my life had I been so glad to have someone tell me to fuck off. At least Kate hadn't... done the unthinkable.

I wiped sweat from my forehead, put my head against the steering wheel.

I typed a response into my phone. Do you want me to come over?

I wasn't sure if that was a good idea, so I added the words Just to talk. Then I hit Send and heard my message *swoosh* to Kate.

Within seconds, another buzz of my phone, then one more, another *rat-a-tat-tat* of messages from Kate.

Yeah I get that its just to talk u made it clear u aren't interested I don't have to be hit over the head

I don't need to talk to u

You had your chance. Remember that I gave u the chance

So now she didn't want to see me? Over the last two days, she was desperate for my company, trying everything in her power to woo me, and now she didn't want anything to do with me. What had suddenly changed?

Well, one thing had changed: I had just stopped tailing Kim Beans.

My body went cold. It felt like everything in the world skidded to a halt.

I killed the engine. Let the garage light go off. Sat in darkness inside the car.

Only Amy knew I was tailing Kim. She knew I was doing it, and she knew how long it would last. She knew specifically when it ended.

Kate had gone to rather considerable lengths to get me to pay her a visit over the course of that surveillance, from come-hither notes to angry words, from pornographic messages to suicidal references. Anything to get my attention. And then, the moment the surveillance was over, I was like a pariah to her, about as welcome as a case of the shingles.

In the long, dark, heavy silence of the car, I let out a chuckle. Because it was so implausible that it merited a good, hearty, mocking laugh.

There was absolutely, positively no way Amy and Kate were in on this together.

SEVENTY-SEVEN

I HEADED to work feeling hungover, though I hadn't had a sip of booze last night. Instead I'd spent the night trying to work it all out, trying to remain objective and logical, but hitting a brick wall at every turn.

It was time to talk to Kate once and for all. It was time to lock all this down.

On the drive in, at a stoplight, I pulled up *ChicagoPC* on my phone and found Kim Beans's weekly column. Sure enough, there was no photograph today, the first time in memory that Kim's column didn't contain a snapshot of somebody approaching that brownstone. Kim began her column with this:

> No pic today! Sorry! But hopefully absence makes the heart grow fonder!

Making a joke of it. Sounding cute and whimsical. She didn't look so carefree last night, when her source stood her up.

I wasn't feeling so carefree, either.

When I got to work, I found Kate's desk neat and orderly as always, the desk lamp turned off, her coat absent from her spot on the coatrack. She wasn't in yet. I checked my watch. I was a little late, which made Kate even later. Kate was never late.

"There he is."

I heard Soscia's voice.

"The big cop who won the big trial. Now he thinks he doesn't have to come in to work anymore."

Sosh was by his desk with my favorite lieutenant, Paul Wizniewski, both of them huddled over Sosh's computer.

"Where's Kate?" I asked, taking off my jacket.

"What, you guys don't ever talk anymore? She's taking a few days off."

Of course she was.

"Nice of you to show up," said the Wiz, nodding.

I had overtime up to my chin and hadn't taken any vacation all year. I had all kinds of time built up. But I didn't respond. Wizniewski would like nothing more than to write me up for insubordination.

"What's got your attention?" I asked, nodding to them as they focused on Sosh's computer. "Is there a new episode of *My Little Pony* today?"

"Nah," said Sosh out of the corner of his mouth. "We're all about to hear our favorite congressman tell us that he's going to do us the honor of becoming our next mayor."

Oh, right. Congressman John Tedesco, the presumed favorite in the upcoming mayoral race to replace Francis Delaney. Since the mayor's conviction and removal from office three days ago, the congressman had been saying he was "exploring" the possibility of running for mayor and "talking to constituents," all the bullshit things candidates say before they take the plunge.

I walked over to join them, getting a nice pungent

whiff of cigar for my trouble. Wizniewski didn't even look in my direction, which was fine by me.

I was just in time. The video was live-streamed, and Congressman Tedesco, silver-haired and handsome, had just approached the lectern, which was studded with microphones from various media outlets.

"I scheduled today's press conference to make an announcement about my intentions for the upcoming mayoral race," said the congressman. "Over these many weeks, I've spoken with many of you around this fine city..."

"Oh, fuck yourself. Just come out with it," said Soscia.

"But over the last few days, I have come to a different conclusion. I have looked at the state of this city, and I've decided it needs a clean sweep. It needs someone from a different generation. It needs someone who isn't afraid to make the tough decisions, to crack down on the corruption that plagues this city."

I held my breath. Tedesco wasn't running?

"This city needs Margaret Olson, the Cook County state's attorney."

No. What?

"Get the fuck outta Dodge," Soscia mumbled.

Congressman Tedesco held out his arm in invitation. Then Margaret Olson approached the bank of microphones and gave the congressman a warm embrace.

"You gotta be fuckin' kiddin' me," said Sosh. "Maximum Margaret?"

I couldn't believe it, either. Margaret Olson was running for mayor?

I looked at the Wiz, who didn't say a word. Didn't seem all that surprised, either.

"I am humbled beyond words," Olson said into the microphones.

"Looks like you did her dirty work for her," Wizniewski said to me. "You knocked the mayor out of office so she could take his job. What did she promise you?"

I didn't take the bait from the Wiz. In other circumstances, I might have, but I was still too stunned to speak.

"When Congressman Tedesco approached me about running, my first instinct was to decline," said Olson into the camera. "But then I thought about this city and its problems and whether I could be the one to clean it up."

"You're a fuckin' shark," Sosh said to the screen.

A shark. The same thing Kate said about Amy. The same Amy who swore to me, up and down, cross her heart, hope to die, that Margaret Olson wasn't prosecuting the mayor for political reasons and that Olson would never, ever run for mayor.

I felt something sink inside me—that feeling again, cascading through my chest, burning my throat, that I didn't have the entire story.

That feeling again, that I didn't know which way was up.

SEVENTY-EIGHT

AMY LENTINI got off the elevator at the Daley Center after hours, after darkness had long been settled over the city. Her eyes were down, intent, something on her mind, the weight of the world on her shoulders. She moved so swiftly that she almost didn't notice Patti.

Patti shifted so that she was blocking Amy's path.

Amy looked up, startled, and stopped in her tracks.

"Patti," she said simply.

"Amy, I've told you this before." Patti drew the words out. "I want you to stay away from my brother."

Amy snapped out of her fog. Eyes narrowed. Whatever had been bothering her before she saw Patti seemed to combine with this confrontation, and the mixture was toxic. Amy looked to be at a boiling point, at her wit's end.

Patti said, "Did you know that three years ago, his little girl died of a stroke? Did he tell you that? I'll bet he didn't. He doesn't like to—"

"He didn't tell me," said Amy, "but I knew. I looked into his history."

"And did you know that his wife, Valerie, couldn't handle it? Did you know that while Billy literally lived at the hospital for weeks on end waiting for his daughter to come out of that coma, his wife stayed away? Drank herself nearly to death?"

Amy studied Patti, shifted the bag on her shoulder. "I know most of that. I know she committed suicide afterward."

"*Right* afterward," said Patti. "Immediately afterward. Billy came home from the hospital, having just lost his baby girl, and found his wife dead in the bathroom."

"Patti—"

"She took Billy's service weapon out of their safe, walked into the bathroom, and blew her brains out with it."

"Okay, but—"

"So on top of losing his little baby, on top of literally *living* in the hospital for weeks, just on the off chance that his daughter might open her eyes one time, he also got the privilege of feeling *guilty* for doing that, for not taking better care of his wife."

Amy didn't answer.

"He's broken, Amy. It snapped him in half. He plays it like he's okay; he jokes around and does his job, he's everybody's friend, but he's not okay."

Amy stepped back from Patti. "So he can never have another relationship? Ever again?"

"Not with you," she said. "Not with someone who's using him."

The fire flared in Amy's eyes. Patti could feel the heat coming off of her.

"I'm using him?"

"You're *investigating* him," said Patti. "You always have been. Now your boss wants to be *mayor?* And I suppose there'll be a nice job in it for you, now that you did your part and cleared the path for her."

"Patti, listen to me—"

"I see that Congressman Tedesco stepped out of the way this morning," Patti interrupted. "How nice of him. How convenient. The clear front-runner decides that the job he's always wanted, mayor of Chicago—suddenly he doesn't want it so much after all. Oh, and he thinks Margaret Olson would be the *perfect* candidate!"

Amy didn't respond. Patti stepped closer to her, so tight they could feel each other's breath. "So how'd that work, Amy? What did you guys have on him? Was Congressman Tedesco in the little black book? Did you threaten to publicly expose him if he didn't step aside and endorse Margaret? Is that what all those photographs in Kim Beans's column were for? Threats to Tedesco? Weekly taunts? *You could be next, Congressman. You could be in next week's photo. Is that what you really want?*"

Amy, up close, so close Patti couldn't accurately gauge her expression, went cold, frozen like a statue.

"How'm I doing so far, Amy? Am I getting warm? Blazing hot?"

Amy still didn't speak, remained motionless. Her eyes avoided Patti's, looked off in the distance, but not a hazy stare—an intense focus, like she was trying to locate a fixed point far away.

You're wondering how I figured it out, Patti thought. *Maybe dumb little Patti, the little girl everyone had to coddle, the one who didn't quite measure up to her twin brother, the black sheep of the family, ain't so dumb after all.*

Patti grabbed her arm. They locked eyes. Amy could see it. Patti was sure of it. Amy could see that Patti was no longer joking, was no longer issuing a friendly warning.

"Stay away from my brother," she hissed. "It's the last time I'll say it."

Patti turned and left the building. She walked through the plaza, the brutal cold, the whipping wind. Then she stopped and turned back, looked through the large glass windows of the Daley Center.

Amy was still standing in the lobby, but now she was looking back at the elevator she had just gotten out of. She stood there a long moment, staring at that elevator.

Finally Amy started moving again. But she didn't leave the building. Instead she turned and disappeared back into the elevator, went up to her office, long past the time that everyone else had gone home.

It was too cold outside to wait. So Patti retreated to her car, drove it back around so she was parked alongside Daley Plaza.

And she waited. Two hours passed. Even longer.

It wasn't until close to ten o'clock, when downtown was frozen and desolate, that Amy Lentini appeared once again, walking quickly through the lobby, hailing a cab outside and jumping in.

Patti considered following Amy home, but she didn't bother. She already knew where Amy lived.

SEVENTY-NINE

IT WASN'T as hard as Patti thought it might be.

Amy Lentini left for work the next morning at seven—quite the early morning riser, but Patti wasn't surprised. Amy was the kind of person who always put in the extra effort, determined and ambitious and single-minded as she was. First to arrive at the office, last to leave—as Amy demonstrated last night, leaving near ten o'clock.

Getting past the locked front door of Amy's apartment building would be hard, but it just required the right timing and a few precautions. The timing part wasn't difficult. The apartment building housed young professionals on a budget as well as students from city colleges who kept irregular hours. People were coming and going at all times of day.

She waited until noon, accepting the fact that there would never be a perfect time to break into Amy's apartment. There was no such thing as perfect.

She screwed up her courage and got out of her car. The wind slapped her face, and the cold immediately penetrated her outer layers and chilled her skin.

But it only took a few minutes before someone came out of the front door. A student, presumably—

a young, squirrelly kid with a goatee and nose ring, a backpack over one shoulder.

Patti made sure she was there to catch the door. That was the timing part.

The precaution part: she was wheeling a carry-on suitcase behind her. Looking the part of a young professional returning from a trip. Looking nothing like someone breaking into an apartment.

And she held her phone up to her ear with her other hand, talking into it, saying, "I'm *finally* home! What a nightmare of a trip!"

Those things together, the suitcase and phantom phone conversation—and, yes, the fact that she was a woman—meant that she did not present the slightest hint of a threat to the college kid, who barely paid her any notice at all as he held the door open for her.

And then she was inside!

She kept up the ruse with the fake phone call, laughing into the phone—"You're kidding! She said that?"—in case anyone else was in the lobby.

But nobody else was. She was all alone. Her eyes scanned the spacious room. First she looked for security cameras—none. Shame on them, but good for her.

One wall was filled with locked mailboxes that looked like safe-deposit boxes at a bank. Some newspapers—the *Tribune,* the *Sun-Times,* and the *Wall Street Journal*—on the floor, wrapped in clear plastic.

A door to the left. Was it locked? Didn't hurt to try, not as long as the lobby remained empty. It might lead to something good.

It wasn't locked. And it led to something wonderful—a stairwell, the perfect way to get up to the sixth floor. Elevators were no good. There could be a security camera inside, and anyway it was cramped, confined, too easy to notice other people. The stairwell was far better. She picked up her suitcase by the handle—it was almost empty—and climbed the stairs.

She paused when she hit the sixth floor. Listened. Didn't hear anything. Opened the door and stepped onto the cheap carpeting. A long corridor.

She oriented herself, realized that Amy's apartment was right by the stairwell.

Picking the lock was the easiest part. A cheap pin-tumbler lock. A suspect she questioned once in a series of B and E's who wanted her to like him—a lot of suspects did; she had no idea why they thought it would help—showed her how to pick a lock. She held her breath as she went to work and listened intently for any sounds. If someone came out of one of the other apartments on the sixth floor, she would have to put on her game face, quickly raise the phone to her ear again, pretend to be on a call, chat merrily, tell her nonexistent caller *I can't find my damn keys,* and laugh. She would have to say and do things that wouldn't arouse suspicion.

She was good at this. So good it scared her.

She worked in private, nobody emerging from any of the other apartments. Patti gently opened the door to Amy's apartment and waited for the last hurdle—the possibility of an alarm.

No alarm. No sound when she entered. People in apartment buildings think their locked buzzer door on the ground floor is all the protection they need.

She closed the door behind her and felt relief swirl through her. She drew a long breath. Removed her winter gloves. Replaced them with rubber gloves.

Slipped out of her wet, slushy boots, too. They could leave footprints all over the apartment. Later, when it was time to leave, she would clean up the slush at the front door with paper towels and take the towels with her. She would leave no trace behind.

"Okay, Amy," she said to the empty apartment. "Let's get to work."

EIGHTY

SHE WASN'T sure where to start. A sock drawer. A kitchen cabinet. On the nightstand. Under a pillow. In a medicine cabinet. Under a rug. It could be anywhere.

She started unconventionally, assuming it wouldn't be anywhere obvious. She went through the bathroom cabinet and underneath the sink, feeling around the bottom, opening medicine bottles and jars of lotions. She looked under the bed and pulled back curtains. She quietly stomped her foot along the carpeting in the bedroom and on the hardwood in the main room, searching for false bottoms, secret compartments.

Nothing. She looked over at the small desk perched in the corner of the main room, a laptop resting on top along with some papers. A mini office in a cramped apartment. The obvious place. So obvious she didn't start there. But now it was time.

She pulled open a drawer and removed some notepads, a passport, some letters and other documents, a magazine open to an article about Amy's famed prosecution of the US senator in Wisconsin. Left inside the desk were a few pens and pencils and a small black thumb drive.

She picked up the thumb drive and stared at it, as if

it could tell her anything by itself. It had no markings, no label.

Patti felt a tremble in her limbs as she removed her laptop computer from the suitcase she'd brought with her. She sat in the chair by Amy's desk and carefully placed the thumb drive into the slot on the side of her laptop.

She held her breath as it booted up. A menu screen popped up, revealing the contents of the thumb drive. One document, in PDF format.

The title of the document was: LEDGER.

She felt a jolt of electricity sizzle through her as she clicked on the link and her laptop began its wrenching and tugging. The contents suddenly appeared on her screen.

"My God, this is it," she whispered. "This is the little black book."

EIGHTY-ONE

THERE HAD been various theories on what form it would take. Some people thought that Ramona Dillavou, the manager of the brownstone brothel, would steer clear of computers and simply write everything by hand on a pad of paper. Others figured she wouldn't have been able to resist the simplicity and flexibility of a computer.

But everyone agreed on one thing: Ramona Dillavou would absolutely, positively keep some record of the transactions inside the brownstone brothel.

The computer screen gleamed on Patti's face, the document lingering before her eyes like the Holy Grail. Hundreds of man-hours had been spent trying to find this document. Several lives had been lost.

It turned out that both theories were right—Ramona Dillavou had written down her entries in handwriting, on a pad of paper, but those pieces of paper had been scanned onto this thumb drive. Someone had made a copy.

There were more than forty pages of what looked like an accountant's ledger, organized by dates that began nearly three years ago. On each line there were codes—letters followed by numbers followed by what appeared to be a dollar amount for services rendered: "BBB-14-5000"; "JJ-21-7500"; "Q-17-10000." The entries went on for pages and pages. No names, just codes.

But at the end, after scrolling through nearly forty pages, she found the key to all the coded language. Each number referred to a different prostitute, her first name and last initial only. The number 14 was for a girl named Ava J. The number 21 referred to a Marnie B. In all, there were more than fifty prostitutes—Krista K., Courtney G., Leann L., and so on—who had worked at the brownstone brothel over the last three years.

Every letter was assigned to a client, his last name only, and once the alphabet was exhausted, the letters were doubled, then tripled. She found Archbishop Phelan under the letter *K*, which must have made him one of the earliest clients. *RR* was for Delaney—the now disgraced former Mayor Francis Delaney.

And *YY* was for Tedesco, which had to be none other than Congressman John Tedesco, the man who had just handed over the keys to the mayor's office to Amy's boss, Margaret Olson.

Patti read through the list of clients, some of whom had already been exposed by the flashy photographs that Kim Beans had published. But there were plenty more names, nearly a hundred in all.

When she got to the last of the client names, Patti paused. She was at page 40 of 42. There were two more pages to read. She wasn't sure what was coming next, but she had a pretty good idea. Ramona Dillavou had obviously been very conscientious in recording all her other transactions, the clients coming in and out of the brownstone, paying in anonymous cash for their anonymous fantasies. Why wouldn't she be just as diligent in recording the payouts she made to the cops to protect her illicit enterprise?

Patti took a breath and scrolled down to the next page. The heading of the page, in Ramona's handwriting, said, Payments Out.

Yep. The payoffs. The bribes. Ramona recorded them, all right.

And there was the same name, line after line, over the last three years, monthly payments, originally in the amount of $2,000, later doubling to $4,000, and by the end reaching $10,000 a month.

The same name on every single line, receiving every single payment.

"So Amy knows," she whispered to the empty room. "That's a problem."

Patti stared at the computer until the words began to blur, until they began to move and twitch on the screen. She kept staring even as the screen saver activated, asteroids hurtling across the black screen. She stared until darkness began to hover outside the windows of Amy Lentini's apartment.

She stared until she decided what to do.

Then she gently closed her laptop, as if it were explosive, and removed the thumb drive from the slot on the side.

She slipped the thumb drive in her pants pocket. "I think I'll be taking this off your hands now, Amy," she said. "Finders keepers and all that."

She placed the laptop back in the suitcase she had brought with her and zipped the suitcase closed.

"Don't you worry, little brother," she said as she put her boots back on. "I'm going to clean this all up. You can thank me later."

THE PRESENT

EIGHTY-TWO

"DETECTIVE KATHERINE Fenton was a woman scorned," says my lawyer, Stilson Tomita, leaning against the window ledge in his office, a view of the Chicago River and the Wells Street Bridge behind him. "A woman who wanted Billy Harney but couldn't have him. And if she couldn't have him, nobody could."

Wow. That's harsh.

"She had a brief affair with Billy, but she wanted more, and Billy didn't. Billy, in fact, started dating another woman, Amy Lentini. Kate couldn't handle it. So she lashed out. She tried everything. Think Glenn Close in *Fatal Attraction*. Except she's a cop who lives in a world of guns and violence. So instead of boiling a bunny on the kitchen stove, her version of getting back at Billy was murder. She killed Ramona Dillavou, knowing Billy would be a suspect. She killed Joe Washington after seeing him with Billy in the subway—again, knowing Billy would be a suspect. Then she planted the murder weapons in Billy's basement, knowing that would do him in. If he was going to ruin her life, she was going to ruin his."

And I thought his *opening* lines were harsh.

"Just a few days before the shootings, she was texting Billy half-naked photos of herself, including one with a gun to her head, threatening suicide if he didn't respond. And when he didn't return her affection, what did she text him? 'You had your chance. Remember that I gave you the chance.'"

I don't remember that text message. I don't remember those sexy photos she texted me, either. It's part of the black hole of my memory. The only reason we know about them is that the prosecution turned them over to us in discovery.

"Two days later," Stilson continues, "she goes to Amy Lentini's apartment, where Billy and Amy are in bed. It's the last straw. She draws her gun. Billy, whose gun is close by on the nightstand, reaches for it to return fire. His gun goes off, and Amy is hit by accident, in the heat of the moment, just before Kate and Billy shoot at each other."

Stilson pulls down on his tie, works his collar open. I've known Stilson Tomita since I was a kid, when he and my dad were rookie cops working a beat, before he finished law school and became a prosecutor, later turning to the defense side when he needed college tuition for his four kids. Stilson is a classic melting-pot Chicagoan: his father is a first-generation Japanese American who opened a tailoring business in Lincoln Park; his mother is a hundred-and-fifty-percent Irish South Sider who had cops in her family going back to the Depression. To look at him, you see more Ireland than Asia, but his features are dark enough to make it hard to place his heritage. He used to joke that people couldn't decide whether he was Italian, Greek, or Latino.

But regardless of nationality, he still looks like the cop he once was—the ruddy complexion, the deep-set eyes of someone who's seen the messy sludge of the criminal justice system, its ugliness and desperation and bitterness and, ultimately, its hopelessness. He has put away people, and he's defended them. Each side has its costs, and it shows on his weathered face.

I look around the room at the others, my trusted inner circle: my sister, Patti, my father, and Lieutenant Mike Goldberger, as close to a second father as anyone could get. Each of them is batting around what's just been said, Stilson's summation of my defense.

We are less than a week from trial, and the prosecution's evidence is all in. Stilson and I have kicked around defense theories for weeks, but now the rubber has met the road. Now we know everything they have against me. Now it's time to finalize our plan, then test it and retest it—kick the tires, so to speak, mold it like clay into the best argument we can make.

"My gun *accidentally* went off and shot Amy?" I say. "It was an accident?"

"Well, your gun killed Amy, not Kate's. They can prove that." Stilson shrugs. "If you have a better explanation, I'm all ears."

When your best explanation sucks eggs, things aren't looking up.

Stilson cocks his head, nods, seeing the look on my face. "We play the hand we're dealt," he says. "This is the best theory we have, Billy."

"It's the only theory," says Patti.

"No, it's not," I say. "They're saying I was a crooked cop, right? They're saying I shook down the brothel for protection money, that the state's attorney was investigating me, and that I killed everyone to cover it up. We could say the exact same thing about Kate. Or Wizniewski. Or both."

"But there's no proof of that." Patti pushes herself off the wall, uncrosses her arms. "There's no proof of a protection racket. There's no little black book. It's a fantasy."

"There's no little black book?" I say.

"They never found it," she says. "As far as the jury is concerned, it doesn't exist."

"I agree with Patti," says Stilson. "Listen, Billy. We start by saying the prosecution is full of shit. They can't prove a protection racket, and therefore they can't prove a cover-up of a protection racket. Then we give the jury a plausible alternative." Stilson grabs blowups of the photos that Kate texted me, the sex-kitten poses. "This is a woman whose heart has been broken, who's trying desperately to get your attention. All the jurors in that box, I guarantee you, at some point in their lives have had their hearts broken. They know the sting of rejection. They may not have committed murders and frame-ups as a result, I'll grant you that, but they can relate to how she was feeling."

I look at Goldie, who grimaces as he stares at the floor.

At my father, who narrows his eyes and brings a hand to his face.

At Patti, who nods in agreement.

"Kate was an unstable woman who went off the deep end," she says. "That's your story. There was no corruption. There was no little black book."

EIGHTY-THREE

PATTI RUNS north along the jogging path, violent wind slapping her skin, Lake Michigan lashing out like an insolent child to her right, the cars cruising by on Lake Shore Drive to the left. The weather is still warm, but this close to the lake it feels like a different climate altogether. It's one of the things she's always loved about Chicago—the ability to escape the concrete jungle and be so close to a beach and a massive body of water; the way the roiling lake waters and car traffic on the outer drive produce their own combination of sound, their unique symphony.

She is not alone, not physically. There are bikers and Rollerbladers and other joggers, gaggles of people hanging out along the concrete promenade, the smell of marijuana reaching Patti's nostrils more than once during her run.

But she is alone in every other way. She feels completely, utterly alone in the most important way.

She follows the path into Lincoln Park, the wind easing up, her feet appreciating the soft cinders in contrast to the unforgiving concrete next to the lake. Feeling a good runner's high now. The burn through her chest feels right, like punishment. Part of her wants to run until her legs catch fire, until her heart explodes.

Billy's trial starts in two days.

As she continues north, through Lincoln Park, past Lakeview, she veers off to Montrose Harbor. She takes a minute, catches her breath, her hands on her knees.

The harbor is still nearly full of boats, as summer has drawn to an end but the weather has stayed warm. Most boaters will try to wring every last temperate day out of the season before they put their boats away for the winter.

She walks along the dock, a thin sliver of concrete, a perpendicular extension a good hundred feet out into the water, a lighthouse at the end. Nothing out here but this narrow strip of pavement, the whipping wind, and the lake waters, deep and turbulent.

She stops and looks out. To the south, the city looms, massive and imposing. Overwhelming, too. Sometimes overwhelming.

And the lake water, an endless black hole beneath her.

I could do it, she thinks to herself. *Just one quick, impulsive surrender to temptation, and it would be over. Nobody would ever know.*

She and Billy came here once, after graduating from high school, so young and full of energy and hope. They sat on this very dock, opened a bottle of Johnnie Walker Red, and sipped it as their feet dangled over the side and the wind lifted their hair. They told each other they'd be cops like their father, and they'd work together, and they'd have each other's backs, always, forever.

She is shivering now, her body temperature cooling rapidly against the violent wind, the chilly air.

The lake, dancing up around her, calling to her.

I could do it. Nobody would know.

Yes, she decides. *I should have done it a long time ago.*

She reaches inside her running shorts, into that skinny front pouch big enough to hold only a key or a small wad of cash. Or a thumb drive.

The thumb drive she stole from Amy Lentini's condo the day before Amy's death. The thumb drive containing the little black book.

Just do it, she tells herself.

She holds the tiny thumb drive in the palm of her hand. Wraps her fingers around it, makes a fist. Cocks her arm back like a pitcher winding up, looking out over the dark, endless lake. The wind will catch it, but it's not so light that it won't sink when it hits the water. Sure, it's just heavy enough. It will sink deep down to the floor of Lake Michigan, a hundred feet below, carried away in the undercurrent, lost forever.

She cocks her arm back farther still. She always had a pretty good arm—*for a girl,* everyone would always add. But Billy was the better athlete.

Billy was the better everything.

But not anymore.

EIGHTY-FOUR

THE NIGHT before my trial is to begin, I go for a walk.

I walk north and east toward Bucktown, mingle among the crowd, searching out signs of life—the animated chatter in open-air restaurants, the smell of sizzling carne asada and onions, the squeal of car tires and the blaring of horns. Sometimes I still see a glimpse of Amy's face in the crowd or hear her voice in my dreams, but it's fading, less frequent and more distant as each day passes.

My legs feel good; my limp is nearly gone. My hips ache these days, mostly because I'm overcompensating for my bad leg, the docs say, but otherwise I move pretty well. Stilson, my lawyer, wants me to walk into court with my cane, limping and stooped. He wants me to look wounded—a victim, not a killer. Like all those mobsters who spend their entire lives robbing and intimidating and killing and when they finally get hauled into court, they're bent over in wheelchairs and using oxygen tanks.

I make it back to my neighborhood after a good four miles, more than an hour. I feel pretty good. The walk has loosened my muscles and massaged out some of the stress. But the specter of the trial weighs on my shoulders.

I know how this is going to end. We will put up a valiant battle, and the jury will probably believe that Kate went too far in her pursuit of me. But who's kidding whom? It will take a miracle to escape all four murder charges, to convince the jury that Kate was responsible for the murders and a frame-up, all because she couldn't have me.

That feeling again—

I stop dead on the sidewalk. Spin around. Nobody in sight. I can't put my finger on it. I don't see or hear anybody. But I *feel* it.

Somebody is following me.

I turn back around and keep walking. A gold SUV rolls up to the intersection, seems like it slows. Seems like maybe the driver casts a look in my direction. I don't get a good look at him, as dusk has settled in, and he drives away before I can confirm anything, before I can even make out the license plate.

When I turn the corner toward my home, I stop again.

Somebody sitting on the porch outside my town house.

I draw closer. It's just dark enough that I can't make out—

Oh. It's Pop. Didn't recognize him in the baseball hat.

"Mind if I join you?" he asks when I approach.

We keep walking past my town house. The air feels good. We don't always get this in Chicago. Usually we skip from summer to winter without much of an autumn.

"Your mother and I used to go for walks," he says to me. "After you and Patti were off to college and we were empty nesters. She said it calmed me down. It worked out all the demons I built up after a day on the job."

The wind kicks up, carrying the smell of rain. Pop twirls a key ring on his finger.

"I didn't want you to be a cop," he says. "Did you know that?"

I didn't. I assumed that nothing would make him prouder than to see his son follow in his footsteps.

"And then," he goes on, "once you were sworn in, I made a vow that I wouldn't do anything to interfere. I wouldn't pull strings to get you ahead. I wouldn't hover over you." He nods to himself, lets out a sigh. "I thought that was the best gift I could give you. To let you make it on your own merits, so you'd know that I didn't smooth your path. But I should've watched over you more. I should have made sure..."

I stop and turn to him. It takes my father a moment to look me in the eyes.

"Pop," I say, "I'm not a dirty cop. I never took a dime. I didn't offer anyone protection. I didn't kill anybody."

He looks me over, gives me one of those meaningful parental appraisals.

"I know that," he says.

"No, you don't. You *hope* that. Because if I'm a dirty cop, you think it's your fault for not watching over me on the job."

He doesn't respond to that. He works his jaw and narrows his eyes. For a moment I think he's about to lose it, burst into tears, which is not something my father does. But all our emotions are bubbling at the surface right now.

I can't imagine what it's like to see your child stand trial on murder charges. But I can guess. I can guess that Pop is reliving all those Little League games and piano recitals and school plays he missed because of the demands of his job, because of his ambition to advance in the force. All those times he could have taken me in his arms and told me how much he loved me instead of just giving me a stoic nod of approval or a clap on the shoulder.

He's playing that cruel game of "what if." What if he had spent more time with me? What if he had kept a closer eye on me on the job?

"I didn't come here for a psychoanalysis," my father says.

"No?"

"I came here," he says, "because I have a way out of this for you."

EIGHTY-FIVE

"A WAY out of this," I say slowly, repeating Pop's words. "How?"

"Not a question of how," he says. "A question of where."

"A question of..." A moment before it clicks. "Are you telling me to run?"

He takes a breath, shuffles his feet. "If you want to," he says, his eyes on the pavement.

"You're kidding."

He looks up at me again, a brisk shake of the head. "I'm not."

"You put up your house for my bond," I say. "If I left, you'd lose—"

"You think I give a rat's ass about my *house?*" he spits out. "They can have my damn house. Don't need it anyway, not anymore. I'm a widower in a five-bedroom—"

"They'll put you in prison."

Pop looks up at the sky, scratches the razor burn on his face.

I step back, appraising him. "You're serious," I say.

"I've never been more serious in my life, son. We can get you out tonight. Get you out of the country. Mexico, I was thinking, for starters. A retired cop down there has a place outside Playa del Carmen. We start there. Probably move you to South America."

"I surrendered my passport."

"Yeah, you did. But we can get you papers. And then we'll have to—"

"I don't want to hear this, Pop. I don't even wanna—"

I freeze, midsentence.

"Who's 'we'?" I ask.

Pop nods to his Toyota, across the street. I hadn't noticed it parked along the curb. I can just make out Goldie in the front seat.

Pop and Goldie, willing to put their careers and freedom on the line. It hits me in the throat how much this must be affecting them. That the casualties aren't limited to the dead bodies or to me, the one facing prison.

"Billy, we can do this. Tonight. I can get you a car and identification, and you can get across the border before they know you're gone. I have some money. Not a lot, but some. Enough. We'll both have burner phones so we can talk, coordinate it. It can be done, son. You know it can."

While he's been speaking, I've backpedaled. I throw up my hands. "And what happens to you?"

"Don't worry about what happens to me. I'll..." His shoulders rise and fall. "They'll suspect me. I know that. We just have to be smart. Not leave a trail." He nods. "I'm willing to take the chance."

"And Patti? I don't even say good-bye to Patti? I never see her again?"

Pop looks off in the distance, wincing. When he shows pain, he reminds me of my sister.

"Your sister would rather see you living on some

beach, tending bar and banging the local women, than visit you through a glass window in Stateville the rest of your life. She'd be happy that you have a life."

I pinch the skin above my nose, let out some kind of noise.

Freedom. Like a warm breeze. I can taste it on my tongue, feel it flow through my blood. Another chance. A new life.

And then my father is on me, his hands gripping my biceps.

"Let me do this for you," he whispers, trying to hide the tremor in his voice. "You came back for a reason, son. You could've died in that bedroom. You should've died. But you didn't. You fought all the odds and came back. You didn't do that so you could spend the rest of your life in a concrete cell. You have a second chance. *I* have a second—"

I break away from him.

Above us, murmurs from the sky, the first hint of unrest, the clouds darkening.

He clears his throat, wipes at his eyes with his sleeve, collects himself, letting the emotions recede once more to their familiar hiding place.

"You have no case," he says. "You're going to lose. The judge'll have to give you life. If you run and get caught, what's the difference? They can't give you more than life."

It's not like we both don't know it. My case is shit because I can't remember anything. I'm crippled. I'm being pushed into the boxing ring with both hands tied behind my back.

"It's what your mother would want," he says.

"No, don't—don't." I raise a finger. "Mom wouldn't want me to admit to something I didn't do."

My father drops his hands, looks at me the way he did when I was a child—a kid who had done something that completely exasperated his parent.

His expression slowly changing from frustration and pleading to something darker and colder. Something haunted and profoundly sad.

"How do you know you didn't do it?" he whispers. "How do you know?"

EIGHTY-SIX

STATE'S ATTORNEY Margaret Olson stands before the jury, buttons the jacket of her soft gray suit. There is standing room only in the courtroom. It is utterly silent, crackling with anticipation. It is late in the day, after a morning and early afternoon spent picking the jury. There will be time today only for the prosecution's opening statement.

Olson angles herself slightly, allowing her to gesture in my direction. She will point at me, Stilson warned. She will point at me and accuse me.

"Detective William Harney was a crooked cop," she says. "A dirty cop who knew he was about to be caught. So he tried to cover it up the only way he knew how. He killed the star witness, he killed fellow police officers who were on to him, and he killed the prosecutor in charge of investigating him."

She turns and points at me, her wrist snapping down, her index finger extended. "The defendant killed four people, and he is charged with four counts of murder."

I shake my head, not in an exaggerated, *I swear I didn't do it* fashion but rather in bemusement, as though her claims are so preposterous that they aren't deserving of a reply.

"The defendant ran one of the oldest scams in the book," she says. "He was offering protection. If you're a cop, and someone's doing something illegal, you tell them: throw a little money my way, and I'll make sure nobody busts you. I'll protect you."

She nods, lets that sink in for the jurors. Convincing a jury of Chicagoans that a city cop is crooked is about as difficult as convincing Donald Trump that he's an impressive guy. And half these jurors come from suburban Cook County. A lot of suburbanites just assume that everything we do in Chicago is corrupt.

Olson tells them about the brownstone brothel in the Gold Coast, shows them a picture, reminds them of what they already heard play out in the media over the last year about the former mayor, the archbishop, and all the rich and famous clients.

"The defendant was protecting that high-end house of prostitution," she says. "He was *this* close to being caught." Her index finger and thumb are an inch apart. "The Cook County state's attorney's office—my office—was investigating that brothel. The lead prosecutor in charge of the investigation was a woman named Amy Lentini."

Olson places an enlarged photo of Amy in professional attire, a pleasant smile on her face, on an easel.

"Amy was about to break it wide open. She was about to raid the brothel. We will show you the request for a search warrant she was drafting. It will show you what she was looking for, above all else: records. A little black book. You run a business, you need to keep records, right?"

Several jurors nod in agreement.

"But it's an *illegal* business," she continues. "You're

accepting money from clients for sex. You're doling out some of the money to a cop for protection. All of it illegal. Not the kind of records you file with an accountant or share with the IRS."

A couple of the jurors laugh. I've always viewed Margaret Olson as having a stick up her ass, but I can't deny that she's drawing in this jury, speaking to them plainly, a nice blend of drama and folksiness. She's a good politician.

I underestimated her, and I couldn't have picked a worse time to do so.

"Amy had information that the manager of this sex club was keeping records right there in the brownstone—that she had a little black book. Amy was only days away from raiding that brothel and getting her hands on it—days away from having the proof that she needed against a corrupt Chicago cop." Olson takes a step to her right. "We will show you the request for a search warrant that Amy was preparing. You will hear from one of the other prosecutors assigned to the investigation. But you won't hear from Amy, the prosecutor in charge of the investigation. You won't hear from her because the defendant made sure nobody will *ever* hear from Amy again."

She turns and glares at me. Then she slowly nods her head.

"The defendant was smart," she says. "Very smart. He learned about the state's attorney's investigation. He knew we were about to raid that sex club. So what did he do? He did something very, very clever."

A dramatic pause while the jury wonders what I did that was so clever.

"He raided it first," she says. "That's right: the defendant, a *homicide* detective—someone whose job and rank had absolutely *nothing* to do with vice or prostitution or anything close to it—suddenly raided that brothel himself and arrested everyone inside."

She opens her hands. "It was brilliant. It accomplished two goals, really. One was misdirection. Of all the cops in the world whom you might suspect of protecting a house of prostitution, the *last* one you'd suspect is the person who raided it, who exposed it—right? It made him look innocent."

Several jurors nod, scribble in notepads.

"Smart," says Olson. "And the second goal, which was even more important, was to find the brothel's records. By storming into that brownstone before Amy could, the defendant beat her to the little black book. He stole it and destroyed it."

Jurors nodding, the pieces coming together.

"But there's still the sex-club manager herself, right? I mean, even if the little black book is gone, the manager can still testify about her payoffs to the police. Ramona Dillavou was her name. Ramona Dillavou ran that brothel."

She puts an enlarged photo of Ramona Dillavou, taken at some party, on the easel next to Amy's picture, part of the parade of victims.

"Ramona was still a threat to the defendant. More than ever. But Ms. Dillavou will not take the witness stand in this case, either. Because the defendant silenced her, too."

I do another head shake, but I know—everyone in the courtroom knows—that Margaret Olson is doing a masterly job of pinning me down.

A lawyer once told me that 90 percent of trials are won or lost in the opening statement.

Olson holds out her hand, counts off on her fingers.

"Fact," she says, popping her thumb. "The defendant was under investigation for corruption.

"Fact: the defendant used his position to break into that brownstone before the investigators could, and the most damning piece of evidence up and disappeared.

"Fact: the lead prosecutor investigating him was murdered.

"Fact: the principal witness who could testify against him was murdered."

Margaret Olson takes a moment, nods.

"And we're just getting started," she says.

EIGHTY-SEVEN

"I TOLD you the defendant was smart," says Olson to the jury. "Very, very smart. He knew Amy was on to him. He knew she suspected him of stealing that little black book. You will hear from the chief law enforcement officer in this city, the top cop—police superintendent Tristan Driscoll. He will take that witness stand, he will swear an oath, and he will tell you that Amy accused the defendant of stealing that little black book when she questioned him after the brownstone was raided."

Olson strolls a step or two to one side for a segue. For someone who spends more time in a political campaign office than a courtroom, she's doing very well. It's obvious that somebody prepared her. She is performing like a seasoned pro. She is giving her opening statement to the jury at my trial, but she's also giving her closing argument to the media and the public in her campaign for mayor.

"So what did the defendant do? This very smart, clever man? He struck up a relationship with Amy. He charmed her. He seduced her. You know that old saying 'Keep your friends close and your enemies closer'? The defendant took that to heart. He kept his enemy closer. He kept tabs on Amy and her investigation. The relationship became sexual, and it became very intense. Amy fell in love with the defendant." Olson puts a hand on her chest. "You won't have to take my word for it. Amy's mother, Mary Ann Lentini, will take that witness stand and tell you that Amy told her all about the defendant. Amy told her mother that, for the first time in her life, she had fallen in love."

The words hit me like a punch to the gut. I look away from Olson and the jury, as if doing so will somehow distance me from her words.

"Keep it together," Stilson mumbles to me.

"But was it a real relationship? Did the defendant really have feelings for Amy, or was it all a con, a scam, just to keep an eye on her investigation? Well, ultimately, that's for you to decide. But consider this: Amy wasn't the only woman the defendant was taking to bed. He was sleeping with another woman, too. Guess who that was?"

Olson places an enlarged photograph of Kate on the third easel.

"Detective Katherine Fenton, his partner," she says. "His partner for more than six years. All those years it was strictly platonic. A close relationship, sure, but not romantic, not sexual. But then there was the raid of the brownstone. Katherine was with him the night of the raid. Of course she was. She was his partner. And afterward, she was in that room in the state's attorney's office when Amy accused the defendant of stealing the little black book. Katherine even knew that *she* might be under the umbrella of suspicion. Sure. Guilt by association, right?

"So Katherine Fenton started looking into things on her own. And she began to believe that maybe her partner wasn't what he seemed, that maybe what

Amy was saying was true. Maybe the defendant *had* stolen the little black book."

Olson claps her hands together. "And how did the defendant respond when he realized his partner was having second thoughts about him?"

She turns and looks at me.

"Same way he responded to Amy," she says. "He seduced her. He started a romantic relationship. Also a very intense relationship. You will see and hear evidence that, at least to Katherine, the relationship grew *very* intense."

Smart. Taking our defense and flipping it, shoving it down our throats.

"But ultimately his charms weren't enough," she says. "Amy Lentini was a good prosecutor who kept investigating. Katherine Fenton was a good detective who kept investigating. As much as each of them cared for the defendant, the evidence against him was lining up. And finally Detective Fenton confronted the defendant at Amy's apartment. You will see the last exchange of text messages between Katherine and the defendant, only minutes before the defendant killed both women."

Olson uses a fourth easel, next to the photographs of the three victims of my crimes, to post a blowup of the message Kate had sent me.

Fenton: Need to talk to u

Harney: Not now

Fenton: I'm right outside her door open up

Harney: You're outside Amy's apt?

Fenton: Yes open door right now

Harney: Why would I do that

Fenton: Bc she knows u idiot. She knows about u and so do I

State's attorney Margaret Olson lets it all sink in, gives the jurors time to read the exchange on that poster board, watching their eyebrows arch and their mouths drop open as it all comes together for them.

"'She knows,'" says Olson, drawing out the last words on that poster board. "'She knows about you... and so do I.'

"The defendant was cornered by the two women he tried to distract, the two women he tried to charm into turning a blind eye to his crimes. He was cornered, and he had no other choice. He killed them both, within minutes of each other.

"Now let's talk about the physical evidence we will show you," she says.

And there is plenty of it. But it's simply the icing on a delicious cake Margaret Olson has just baked. I can see from the way the jurors react to her words, from the nasty glances they shoot in my direction, that I already have one foot in the grave. And each juror is holding a shovelful of dirt.

EIGHTY-EIGHT

THE NEXT morning, my lawyer, Stilson Tomita, gives our opening statement, just as he previewed it in his office. Kate was the classic "woman scorned." There are seven women on our jury, and my biggest concern is how it will play with them. Patti insists—and my wife once said the same thing to me—that nobody is more critical of women than other women. Maybe. But when the criticism comes from a man? I'm not so sure. Stilson uses the evidence he has—the sexy photos and the messages, including the implicit threat "You had your chance; remember that I gave you the chance."

But they don't look convinced. They spent all last night thinking about what Margaret Olson said to them—that I was devious, manipulative, that I seduced Kate to keep an eye on her, to keep my enemy close. And every piece of evidence Stilson shows them, solidifying our claim that Kate had become irrational and desperate in her pursuit of me, is likewise more proof that my manipulation had worked.

And then it's back to the prosecution. Margaret Olson parades in witnesses over the next three days, carefully building her case.

Ngozi MacNamara, an assistant state's attorney, a

smartly dressed young African American woman originally from Johannesburg, South Africa, who with that last name probably married an Irishman here in town.

"I assisted in preparing the complaint for the search warrant for the brownstone," she says. "I did so at Amy Lentini's direction."

Margaret Olson nods. "And the first sentence of the third paragraph of that document. Could you please read that into the record, Ms. MacNamara?"

MacNamara looks at her copy. "'The undersigned has been advised by a CI that handwritten records of the prostitution activity and the extortion payments made to Chicago police are contained within that residence.'"

"And what does 'CI' mean?"

"It means confidential informant."

"And under whose signature was this complaint going to be filed?"

"Under Amy Lentini's," MacNamara says.

"So Amy had a confidential informant?"

"She did. Her informant told her that Ramona Dillavou was keeping a handwritten record book inside that brownstone. We were particularly interested in records of payoffs to the Chicago Police Department."

"Did Amy tell you the identity of her confidential informant?"

MacNamara smiles at the memory, shakes her head. "You couldn't have pried it out of her with the Jaws of Life."

"No?"

"I mean, eventually she would've had to reveal the source to the judge issuing the search warrant.

But until that moment? Amy would take it to her grave."

Olson casts a look at the jury. "And as far as you know, she *did* take it to her grave, didn't she?"

Police superintendent Tristan Driscoll, my old pal, in full-dress uniform—as if he's ever spent a day on the streets of this city, getting his hands dirty—his chin raised, clearly and coherently explaining that Amy Lentini had become convinced that I had stolen the little black book after raiding the brownstone.

"Ms. Lentini made the obvious point that a homicide detective had no reason to be making an arrest for prostitution," he says. "And I agreed. It made no sense."

"And how did the defendant respond?"

"He became very agitated. Near the end of the conversation, he stormed out of his chair and got within inches of her. At first I thought he was going to physically attack her."

"Objection," says Stilson, justifying his fat hourly rate. "Move to strike."

The judge strikes that last jab Tristan threw in, but how do you unring that bell? *Pretend you didn't hear that, members of the jury—wink, wink, even though we all know you did!*

Mary Ann Lentini, Amy's mother, with many of those same dark features, tearfully recounting that her daughter came for a visit to Appleton, Wisconsin, and confided that she had met someone. "Amy said that for the first time in her life, she found someone she could imagine a future with," says her mother. "She said she was in love with a cop named Billy Harney."

Mark Madison, an evidence technician for CPD, squat and thick, an unfortunate attempt at a dye job coloring the little bit of hair remaining on his head. I've known Mark for years. The last place he wants to be is on a witness stand testifying against me. He can't even bring himself to look in my direction.

"Yes," he says. "I was present in the basement during the search of Billy's home. I did not personally find the weapon—or weapons."

"But as one of the evidence technicians, was the discovery of the weapon called to your attention?"

"Yes, ma'am. I was first called to a room in the basement that looked like a storage room. A firearm was found in a cigar box on one of the shelves."

"Is this the weapon you've just described?" Olson says, showing him the gun in a clear bag.

"Yes, it is," says Mark. "I bagged it and tagged it."

"You—"

"I inventoried it," he says.

Olson nods. "What about other weapons?"

"There was a knife, a regular old kitchen knife, discovered underneath the lid of the basement toilet," he says. "I inventoried that, too."

"Is this the kitchen knife?" Another bag, holding the knife.

"Yes, it is."

"As far as you know, did you receive these weapons from the individual who discovered them?"

"As far as I know, yes."

"And who was that?" Olson asks. "Who discovered the firearm and the kitchen knife in the defendant's basement? Was it the same person?"

"It was the same person," says Mark. "It was Lieutenant Paul Wizniewski."

EIGHTY-NINE

DR. JACQUELINE Collins-Lightford, a forensic scientist with the Chicago police crime laboratory, a number of initials after her name, even more initials of the peer groups with which she is affiliated, fancy words and acronyms flying from all directions. By the time she explains all her credentials, we've covered the entire alphabet several times over.

This witness is being handled by one of Olson's assistants, a prosecutor named Loretta Scopes, whom I've seen around the courthouse but never met. She looks the part—serious, strident, no frills, just the facts.

"Doctor, how do you determine if there's blood on an item of evidence?"

"Two separate tests," she says. "The first, a screening test—a preliminary test, if you will—is called the Ouchterlony test, or OT for short. That test tells us whether the stain is blood. And if that test is positive, I'll do a Hematrace test to confirm that the sample is blood and that its species origin is human."

The prosecutor nods. "Did you perform those tests on people's exhibit 4, this knife?"

"Yes."

"And what were the results?"

"I did confirm the presence of blood. And the blood was human."

(There goes our theory that the knife was used in the ritual sacrifice of a billy goat.)

"Doctor, did you collect a sample of that blood for DNA testing?"

"Yes."

"Did you also prepare a blood sample obtained from the victim, Ms. Ramona Dillavou, via search warrant for DNA testing?"

"I did."

"Did you compare these samples?"

"Yes."

"How did you do that?"

That answer, basically, takes up most of an afternoon. Everybody knows what DNA is. But then again, nobody does. Only people in lab coats really get it—the processes, the intertwined sciences, the flaws. So one of these witnesses takes the stand and provides a ninety-minute tutorial on DNA analysis, throws out phrases like *short tandem repeats* and *amplified fragment length polymorphism* and *polymerase chain reaction,* and we pretend that these jurors could possibly understand what the hell is going on. Would we let a juror perform cardiovascular surgery after a two-hour class? Would we let a juror inspect the ears of a *dog* based on that training? Hell, no. But do we let a juror find someone guilty of murder and send him away for the rest of his life after a crash course in deoxyribonucleic acid fingerprinting? Sure! No problem!

The punch line from Dr. Collins-Lightford: the blood on the knife found in my basement was consistent with that of Ramona Dillavou and would be consistent with only one in 3.6 quadrillion white females.

Since there aren't 3.6 quadrillion white females living on this planet, it sounds like a match for Ramona Dillavou's blood.

The juror in the far left corner, a retired physics professor, seems to be thinking the same thing as he shoots a frosty look in my direction.

Ballistics comes next, a forensic scientist with the Illinois State Police named Spencer Lipscomb.

"Grooves are the spiral cuts made in the barrel of the firearm at the time of manufacture," says Lipscomb. "Grooves are cut into the barrel with a spiral direction either to the left or right. The purpose is to put a spin on the bullet and aid its stability in flight. The uncut surface inside the barrel is called the land. When a bullet is discharged through the barrel, the lands and grooves will impress themselves on the bullet. So a bullet exhibiting five lands and grooves with a left twist couldn't be fired from a weapon, for example, that has *six* lands and grooves and a *right* twist."

"Sure."

"We call these rifling characteristics."

"Okay. Did you find that the bullets recovered in the shooting of Amy Lentini and Katherine Fenton contained rifling characteristics consistent with the service weapon registered to and owned by the defendant?"

"Yes."

"So what did you do next?"

"I examined the striations on the surface of the projectile. Scratches, basically. If you look at the surface of a barrel under high magnification, you see that it resembles the edge of a saw. These microscopic protrusions make contact with the bullet and cause microscopic scratches. So if you have the weapon, as we do, you test-fire a bullet and compare its striations under high magnification to the bullets found at the scene of the crime. Basically, you compare the bullets to see if they have the same scratches."

"And did they?"

"Yes."

"So what did you conclude?"

He concludes that my gun was used to shoot Amy and Kate. We retained an expert to do his own test, and he came to the same conclusion.

"And what about the bullet that killed Detective Joe Washington, Doctor? Did you test that bullet to determine whether it was fired from the weapon found in the defendant's basement?"

He did, of course, and he reached the same conclusion: the gun discovered in my basement was used to kill Camel Coat.

Again, our expert doesn't disagree. So we won't fight it.

So my gun killed Kate and Amy. We already know that.

The knife found in my basement killed Ramona Dillavou, and the gun found in my basement killed Camel Coat. But that doesn't mean I was the one who used those weapons. We could offer up more than one person who might have done so and then stashed the weapons in my basement.

One of them is Kate, who is dead.

Another is the person who discovered those weapons in my basement. And he is very much alive.

"The people call Lieutenant Paul Wizniewski," says Margaret Olson.

NINETY

"PLEASE STATE your name and spell your last name for the record."

"That's W-i-z…" He should stop there. *Everybody calls me the Wiz,* he should say. *But it's not meant as a compliment. Most people think I'm a self-righteous dick.*

The first topic: the raid of the brownstone. Olson gets to it quickly.

"I tried to impress on Detective Harney," Wizniewski says, "that it was very odd for a homicide detective to bust up a house of prostitution. We have Vice for that. I told him he should call in Vice. He shouldn't do it himself."

Bullshit. Wizniewski's only objection was that the people inside were major players like the mayor and the archbishop—meaning that there could be political blowback for me and, more important, for him.

"And how did the defendant respond?" asks Margaret Olson.

The Wiz takes a breath and turns to the jury. "He made it very clear that it had to be him who did it, and it had to be that night."

"Did the defendant say why it was so important that he personally conduct the raid? Or why it was so important that he do so that night?"

"No, he did not. It made no sense."

Olson nods, pauses, looks at her shoes.

"This brownstone he was talking about raiding," she says. "Was this the first time this brownstone had come to your attention?"

"No, it was not," he says.

I sit forward in my seat, something catching in my throat.

"I believed that this brownstone was being protected," he says. "I was investigating the possibility that Chicago police officers were engaged in a protection racket."

I look at Stilson. First I've heard of this. Stilson sees my look and writes on a piece of paper, taps the words with his pencil. No emotion.

"And the target of my investigation was Detective Billy Harney," he says.

I bite down on my lip, turn my head away. So I was investigating my boss while he was investigating me while the Cook County state's attorney's office was investigating all of us? You need a Venn diagram to keep track.

"For the last eighteen months," he says, "Detective Harney had been pulling old arrest reports. It wasn't part of any active investigation. It certainly had nothing to do with homicide."

Right, because I was investigating you, Wiz. I was pulling all the arrest reports in cases where people seemed to magically escape prosecution, many times finding that the chain of command ended with you. And I was doing it surreptitiously, you prick, because I was undercover for Internal Affairs.

"I believe these were records of people he was protecting," says Wizniewski. "People arrested for various offenses who were released before referral to the state's attorney. People who got sprung right away for no apparent reason."

They were records of people you were protecting, Wizniewski.

Feeling my blood boil, my legs bouncing under the table.

My lawyer tapping those words on the page again. No emotion.

"I'm confused, Lieutenant," says Margaret Olson, who is anything but confused. "Why would he pull arrest records that show his corruption?"

The Wiz nods. "See, when you pull old arrest reports, it generates a record. You have to sign them in and out. It's right there on the jacket of the file. You have to put your name and star number next to each request. And you can see who else has made a request."

"You can see all previous requests?"

"Yeah, of course. You can see the entire list of people who have requested these records before you."

Olson nods. So do several jurors, for whom the picture is becoming clearer.

"I believe Detective Harney was pulling those reports to see if anybody else had been pulling those reports," says the Wiz. "He wanted to know if anybody was on to him."

Brilliant. I can't deny it. My teeth grinding together, my hands in fists, sitting in a courtroom having to stay composed while fireworks go off inside me.

But—brilliant. Wizniewski is using my undercover investigation against me, to make me look like the guilty party.

Stilson leans in to me, out of character for him.

"You have got to keep a lid on yourself," he whispers, each word like a dart.

"Did you report your suspicions to the higher-ups?" Olson asks.

"I did, sort of," he says. "I had a conversation with the head of Internal Affairs, Lieutenant Michael Goldberger."

I turn back to the Wiz, catch my breath.

"Internal Affairs? Is that in your chain of command?"

He lifts his shoulders. "From time to time I've passed on information, let's put it that way. I didn't officially work for IA, if that's what you mean."

"All right. So did you go to Lieutenant Goldberger's office?"

"Oh, no, nothing like that. We were at one of the copper bars. The Hole in the Wall, off Rockwell."

"Tell us about the conversation."

The Wiz says, "I threw it out there. I said I'd been wondering about Billy Harney, why he always seemed to disappear on the job and seemed to be nosing around in places where his nose didn't belong, nothing to do with solving murders."

"And what did Lieutenant Goldberger say, if anything?"

"Oh, he shut me down right away. He told me Billy Harney was a righteous cop. He said he's known him his whole life, and Billy was straight as an arrow."

That's my Goldie.

But Olson doesn't want the image of me as a good cop lingering for too long.

"Lieutenant Goldberger has known the defendant his whole life?"

"Yeah. Thick as thieves, those two. Like a second

father. So I knew right then that Goldberger would be no help to me. He was biased."

Olson opens her hands. "So what did you do?"

"I went to the only place I could," he says. "I went to the state's attorney's office."

He went to…he went to the—

"I was Amy Lentini's confidential informant," he says.

NINETY-ONE

THE SCREEN comes alive, a fuzzy black-and-white video of the subway tunnel.

"This individual here," says Wizniewski, standing away from the witness stand and using a pointer, "is Billy Harney."

It shows me acting like I'm waiting for the subway, like everyone else.

"And this gentleman approaching, in the beige coat—"

I prefer Camel Coat.

"—is Detective Joe Washington."

"And where were you, Lieutenant, at the time?"

"I was across the tracks, on the other side. Trying to conceal my face. Trying to watch them without them knowing."

"You followed the defendant to this location?"

"Yes, I did."

"So what happened next?"

"Well, as you can see..."

Wizniewski narrates for the written record, but the jury doesn't need his words. They can see it for themselves. The screen shows Camel Coat approaching me and stopping, without any acknowledgment between us. Just two guys waiting for the train. I'm on the phone—a fake phone call—and then I turn my back to the camera and to Camel Coat.

Then, as we had rehearsed ahead of time, Camel Coat sneezes, and he, too, turns his back to Wizniewski and the camera. Both our backs turned.

Then an envelope passing from Camel Coat to me.

Olson freezes the screen there, so that the image sticks with the jury. Wizniewski returns to the witness stand.

"Do you know what information Detective Washington passed to the defendant?" asks Margaret Olson.

"No. I very much wanted to know. I already suspected that Harney was covering his tracks, and now he was secretly meeting with someone from Internal Affairs."

Right, because we were trying to flush *you* out, Wizniewski. We were trying to flush out my tail, the person who'd been following me.

The whole thing in the subway was a ruse, intended to *look* like a surreptitious meeting so we could catch my tail. But to the jury, it looks like I really *was* meeting secretly with Camel Coat.

Once again, the Wiz has turned my undercover work against me, making me look guilty instead of him.

He has played this brilliantly.

"Lieutenant, did you ever find out what was inside the envelope that Detective Washington handed the defendant on that subway platform?"

"No, I did not."

"Why not?"

"Because later that night, Joe Washington was murdered." He turns and looks at me, an icy stare.

"By a gun we later found in Billy Harney's basement."

I return his stare.

I still don't remember what happened the night that Kate and Amy and I were shot. Or for two weeks before that time. But I don't need to. Not anymore.

He knew I was investigating him. He needed to stop me. What better way than to turn the tables? He became Amy Lentini's confidential informant. He got them to start investigating *me*. And then he set me up for murder.

It was Wizniewski, all along. All of it.

But I can't prove it. And now it's too late.

"Your Honor," says Margaret Olson, "the prosecution rests."

NINETY-TWO

I LIE in bed, curtains pulled tightly closed, dark as ink in my bedroom.

Squeezing my eyes shut, begging for sleep, pleading for peace, praying that the demons will quiet their devious cries, that the dread filling my chest will ease, that my breathing will return to normal. My body utterly depleted, desperate for rest, but my brain malfunctioning, as though wires have been crossed, thoughts still careening about, memories and fantasies, flashbacks and concoctions, fact and fiction, the past rushing forward to the present and mixing together like dirt and water, an indiscernible sludge—

She knows about you and so do I.

You had your chance. Remember that I gave you the chance.

Stewart, patting my shoulder in the ICU.

Amy laughing, a ghoulish, clownish expression. *You shot me, Billy!*

You killed me, and you don't even remember!

Wizniewski, talking me out of raiding the brothel. *You fuck this up, it could be the last arrest you ever make.*

I was Amy Lentini's confidential informant.

The knife found in my basement, used to kill

Ramona Dillavou. The gun found in my basement, used to kill Camel Coat.

A door opening, a soft click, a release of pressure like a gentle sigh.

Kate's head whipping to the right, surprised, then not surprised. Nodding.

What are you doing here?

A door opening, a soft click.

Kate's head whipping to the right.

A door opening. A soft click. The whiny groan of an old door. A door my wife thought was charming when we first moved in but that she later begged me to replace because of all the noise it made.

The back door of my town house.

My eyes open now. No more dreams.

Now reality: somebody is in my house.

All senses on high alert. My heart thumping so hard it might burst out of my body and smack against the ceiling, raining down blood and tissue.

I reach for my gun on the nightstand, feel relief when my fingers brush against the cold, smooth polymer frame. I grip it in my hand, curl my finger around the trigger.

I slip off my bed, my foot lowering gently to the soft rug, my body weight slowly transferring downward until I'm in a crouch.

The images still bombarding me, the echoes of noise and human voices.

Amy: *You can trust me, Billy.*

I have the little black book.

Patti: *There is no little black book.*

Kate: *She knows about you and so do I.*

Footsteps, a groan on the floorboard near the staircase. He's coming upstairs.

Kate's head whipping to the right, surprised.

Then not surprised.

Nodding.

What are you doing here?

There is no little black book.

I have the little black book.

"No," I whisper to myself, shaking my head. No no no no—

It's not that you can't remember. You don't want to remember.

My body inching forward along the rug, my weight quietly shifting, nudging forward like a caterpillar in the darkness of my bedroom.

The soft tap of a footstep.

Holding my breath now. My gun poised in front of me, my hands trembling, sweat dripping off my face, into my eyes, my skin on fire—

The soft tap, each step a negotiation with the floorboards in the hallway. He's getting close now.

A rush of white noise between my ears, a freight train of pressure.

"No," I whisper so quietly that the air barely escapes my mouth.

The figure appears in the doorway, dim light from a hallway window framing the vague outline of a man.

A man looking into the pitch darkness of my bedroom.

Dark turtleneck, ski mask: Stranger Danger.

His foot planting on the bedroom carpet, feeling emboldened. Easier to walk on carpet than on hardwood.

Two confident steps, then raising his gun and aiming it at the bed—toward the pillow, where my head would normally lie.

Pause. His eyes adjusting to the darkness. Something wrong. His target isn't there.

Just like that, he spins in my direction, in the corner.

Kate's head whipping to the right.

What are you doing here?

I squeeze the trigger once, twice, three times. Tiny muzzle flashes, little bursts of fire interrupting the darkness. Four, five, six. I don't stop until the magazine is empty.

Return fire from his gun, muzzle flashes far bigger, clouds of orange dancing downward in the blackness like falling comets, until Stranger Danger smacks the floor and lies still.

I drop my Glock and brace myself, my fingers digging into the carpet as if holding on for dear life against a tidal wave of memories.

Memories. Not dreams.

Memories, vivid and specific, sights and sounds and smells, fear and hatred and pure horror, knocking me this way and that, stealing my breath, sending fire through my chest.

I find my oxygen, taking in delicious breaths in deep gulps, wheezing, gagging, unable to speak.

And when words return to me, all I can say is no.

No no no no no no—

"No!"

NINETY-THREE

THE FOG lifted, replaced with white noise, the buzz of evidence technicians and police officers milling about.

"Let's get you out of here." Patti, a hand under my armpit, pulling me up. "Let them do their work."

We step carefully around Stranger Danger, lying still on my bedroom carpet, the .45 still in his hand, his black sweater ripped open with bloody holes.

His ski mask raised to his forehead. A white male, late twenties or early thirties. A day's growth on his face, a scar along the cheek, vacant eyes staring upward. He was dead before he hit the carpet.

"We'll get his ID," Patti says. "I'm sure he has a sheet."

My father and Goldie standing in the hallway as the evidence technicians do their work inside the bedroom and along the hallway, tagging and photographing and dusting. Pop has his arm out as I approach, taking me in a half hug, Patti on my other side, the two of them propping me up like I was an invalid.

We go downstairs into the family room. A detective takes my statement. I don't have much to tell him: I heard the rear door open, I hid in the corner of my bedroom, I unloaded on the intruder. An intruder I've never seen before.

My two brothers, Aiden and Brendan, who have come into town for the trial, try to fix the locks that have been busted tonight—the one on my back door, which was removed by the intruder, and the one on the front door, which the responding officers busted through.

My lawyer, Stilson Tomita, arrives a couple of hours into it, finding Patti and me on the couch.

My father and Goldie, talking to the responding detectives about the investigation and demanding round-the-clock protection for me.

Through it all, I sit on the couch with my head back on the cushion, my eyes closed. People are speaking quietly around me, assuming I'm asleep, hoping I'm asleep, that I'm having a few moments of peace.

But I'm not asleep. And I'm not at peace.

I'm thinking. Thinking about what happened upstairs.

Not Stranger Danger. Not the shooting. No, I'm thinking about the thoughts and images that came before him and after him, the ones that steamrolled me, that took my breath away.

Now they have hardened, turned to ice, forming solid, jagged blocks inside my chest.

"Billy," Stilson says softly, nudging me.

I raise my head and open my eyes. Behind Stilson, through the window, the first sign of sunrise—lazy, blurry light.

"We'll get a continuance," Stilson says. "After what just happened to you, the judge will grant it."

"No," I say.

"You need to rest," Patti says.

"Listen, here's the other thing," Stilson says. "I know what happened tonight was terrible—but we can use it. It shows that somebody wants to keep you quiet."

I look at Patti, then start to push myself off the couch.

"Where are you going?"

"I'm gonna take a shower and get dressed for court," I say.

Patti and Stilson say, "Whoa whoa whoa," as if in sync.

Stilson steps in front of me, blocking me. "Billy, it had to be Wizniewski. This is all Wizniewski."

I nod at him, pat his shoulder.

"But we need time," he says. "We need time to prove it. To put it all together. After what just happened here, we can make the case for more time."

I push past him. "I don't need any more time," I say.

"Billy, you're not right," says Patti. "You can't go to court like this. You can't testify like this. How are you going to testify?"

I turn and look at my twin sister, the person who knows me better than anybody.

I thought I knew *her* better than anybody.

I thought we trusted each other.

"Stilson, you need to get home and shower. See you at the courthouse."

I raise a hand as Patti and Stilson protest, and I walk away and head upstairs to shower and change.

Today, in just a few short hours, I will testify at my trial.

And I will tell the truth.

NINETY-FOUR

TWO HOURS later, I'm in court. Everyone looks surprised to see me. They've all heard what happened in my house last night. The judge tells Stilson that he will give us a continuance. I instruct Stilson to say no. The judge presses Stilson, makes him affirmatively waive the court's generous offer of a continuance so the judge can protect his record on appeal.

"He wants to testify now, Judge," says Stilson, shrugging. "Against my advice," he adds, protecting his own record.

I walk up to the witness stand, my legs wobbly, my body trembling.

But my mind, for the first time in a very long time, is clear as day.

"Do you solemnly swear to tell the truth, the whole truth, and nothing but the truth, so help you God?"

I do. I will tell the truth.

I will testify, truthfully, that I didn't remember anything about what happened in the bedroom with Kate and Amy.

And then I will testify, truthfully, that I remember now.

It all came back. It all came back when I heard my back door creak open, when I listened to a man sneak up the stairs and tiptoe down the hallway to kill me. The chaos, the terror, the adrenaline—it didn't just unlock the door in my brain. It barreled through it, ripping it from its hinges.

I remember everything.

"Mr. Harney," says Stilson. "You stand accused of killing four people."

"Yes."

"Mr. Harney, did you kill those four people?"

"No," I say. "I didn't kill Ramona Dillavou. I didn't kill Joe Washington. I didn't kill Kate. And I didn't kill Amy."

I look at Patti, sitting in the front row, straight as an arrow, holding her breath.

This is not going to be easy for her.

"I didn't kill those people," I say. "But I know who did."

PAST AND PRESENT

NINETY-FIVE

THE PRESENT

STILSON TOMITA flips through his notes, trying to keep up with me. It's not his fault. He didn't know what I was going to say today. Hell, *I* didn't know what I was going to say today until a few hours ago, when it all came rushing back.

The jurors, even after a full morning of testimony in which I recounted every detail leading up to the murders, are listening with rapt attention, leaning forward, eyes narrowed.

As is everyone else. The media, furiously taking notes and typing on their phones, tweeting out revelations drip by drip. My sister, wound tight, looking as if she hasn't taken a breath for three hours.

"So someone left a photograph on your doorstep of Amy Lentini walking up the steps to the brownstone," says Stilson, repeating the last thing I said. This is the best he can do to keep this in Q-and-A format as opposed to just letting me talk nonstop for hours on end. "So what happened next?"

"Well, after I saw that photo—which had the same angle, the same positioning, the same everything as the photos Kim Beans had been publishing every week in her online column—it seemed clear to me that it was taken by the same person who was slipping Kim those photographs."

"So what did you do?"

"I confronted Amy. I asked her what the heck was going on."

"And... what did she say?" asks Stilson, as curious as the jury.

"She told me about the investigation," I say. "She finally told me that the state's attorney's office was investigating the possibility that the brownstone was making payoffs to Chicago cops for protection. And whoever had left that photo of Amy at my doorstep was probably the same person who had been slipping the photographs to Kim Beans for her weekly column."

"So—"

"But I asked myself, who would leak those photographs to a reporter? And then I finally realized why someone would do that."

"When... when did you realize that?"

"When Margaret Olson announced her candidacy for mayor."

Maximum Margaret, posture already erect, seems to steel herself all the more. Hands flat on the table, about to rise and object. Behind her the spectators buzz, low mumbles of surprise. The sheriff's deputy barks out a call for order in the courtroom.

"Congressman Tedesco was the presumed front-runner for the mayoral job," I say. "He had a lot of money and everyone's support. It would've been his job for the taking. And suddenly he drops out and endorses the state's attorney? I mean, c'mon."

"Your Honor, object to relevance and speculation," says Margaret Olson.

Stilson, bless his heart, does his best, even though he's winging it. "He's explaining the course of his investigation, Judge. He's not saying it was true."

"Yes, I am," I say.

The judge—and Stilson—glare at me.

"The testimony is permissible as far as it relates to what the defendant suspected and how it affected his investigation," says the judge, a brittle old guy named Bradford Beatty. "It is not to be considered something the defendant knew for a fact. And Mr. Tomita," the judge adds, wagging a finger, "assert some control here or I will. Even a defendant testifying to his theory of innocence has his limits."

"Anyway," I say, "that's what I was thinking. That the state's attorney was using these photos to blackmail Congressman Tedesco. She had a photo of him. Because the congressman was a client of the brownstone brothel."

"Okay," says Stilson. "So what—"

"So I tailed the reporter, Kim Beans, in order to discover her source. For three days I stayed on her. I even saw her wait for several hours at a restaurant, the Twisted Spoke, where it sure seemed like she was waiting for someone. But nothing came of it. The source never showed." I nod my head. "The source knew I was tailing Kim. Someone had tipped off the source. But that didn't make sense to me. The only person in the world who knew I was tailing Kim, besides me, was Amy."

Stilson's chin rises. "Okay. So what hap—"

"So naturally, that made me suspicious of Amy," I continue. "Because Amy was a top aide to Margaret Olson. She was her number two. Amy had sworn to me up and down that Margaret Olson had no designs on the mayoral job. And then suddenly I'm watching the state's attorney announcing her candidacy for mayor. I…I didn't know what to think."

Stilson nods, waits to see if I have anything else to say. Lawyers like to prepare well in advance, rehearse and rerehearse, for testimony like this. Stilson doesn't have the slightest idea what will come next. He's been relegated to asking the basic *What happened next?* question so many times that the jurors could ask it for him.

"So what happened next, Billy?"

"That day, the day that Margaret Olson announced her candidacy for mayor, nothing happened," I say. "I was just in a fog. I didn't know whom to trust, whom to believe, whom to suspect."

I nod to Stilson to indicate I'm done, a little signal we seem to have informally worked out.

"What about the next day?"

Stilson, and presumably the jurors, know that the next day was the day that Amy and Kate were murdered.

"The next day," I say, "Amy called me and asked me to come to her apartment."

NINETY-SIX

THE PAST

I DROVE to Amy's condo, the traffic heavy, talk radio breathlessly discussing the new revelation in the Chicago mayoral race. Congressman Tedesco had bowed out. State's attorney Margaret Olson was now the front-runner.

The announcement had been made yesterday, and it had thrown me just as it had thrown the media, but for different reasons. I'd wanted so badly to confront Amy about it. But I hadn't reached out to her, not yesterday—I needed time to process it. She'd promised me that Margaret had no desire to run. And suddenly she was running—with Tedesco's blessing, with his endorsement.

It all pointed to Amy and Margaret from the beginning. The reason they were so sensitive about the little black book. The reason that somebody had been slipping Kim Beans those photographs of the brothel's clientele. It had been a veiled warning to Congressman Tedesco that *his* photograph could be next if he didn't behave like a good little boy.

And if it was true, it was brilliant. They'd taken down the mayor and blackmailed his would-be replacement so that Margaret could have the job all to herself.

I thought about it all last night. I thought about it all day today at work. It meant that the Amy I knew *wasn't* the Amy I knew. It meant that the Amy I knew was capable of not only blackmail but also of murder.

I need to talk to you, Amy had said over the phone five minutes ago. That was it. Nothing else. I'd protested, thrown out some sarcastic remark, but all she kept repeating was *I need to talk to you.*

And the reason I went to her apartment? The reason I didn't just punch off the phone or cuss at her or accuse her?

Simple. Because I wasn't ready to believe any of it. Because I wanted to believe that the Amy I knew really *was* the Amy I knew.

I'll be right over, I told her. It wasn't the smart play. I had no element of surprise on my side. I didn't know what was waiting for me at her apartment. I was falling straight into whatever trap she had set.

I pulled up to her apartment building and walked up to her front door, under the awning outside. I knew this building well enough. There were other ways in. There was an underground parking lot serviced by an elevator that went straight up past the lobby. There was a back door by the garbage bins, too. There was a stairwell, if you wanted to avoid elevators. There were surreptitious means of access if you needed them.

I could picture myself doing it. Slipping in one of the other entrances, picking the lock on her door, and employing at least *some* element of surprise. Not a lot, but a little.

But I didn't. Because I had made a choice. A choice to give Amy the benefit of the doubt.

I pushed the buzzer, and her voice came through the speaker.

"It's me," I said.

The buzzer came next, the front door releasing pressure with a soft *whoosh*.

I opened the door, walked through the foyer, and took the elevator up to her floor.

I walked down the empty hallway. Reached her door. Stopped and listened.

Then rapped my knuckles against the door.

She opened the door a crack, those angelic eyes peering at me. And darting around, looking to see whether I was alone.

I was alone.

My weapon was loaded and secure, but I was alone.

I didn't know if I could say the same for her.

NINETY-SEVEN

AMY OPENED the door a crack and backed away from it.

I walked in and closed the door behind me. I didn't lock it. You never know when a quick exit might be necessary.

I threw off my winter coat and tossed it, leaving me in my sport jacket and blue jeans—what I wore to work today.

Amy took another step back.

"Where is it?" she said to me, her voice trembling.

I didn't catch her meaning.

"The little black book," she said. "Where is it?"

I shook my head. "Seems like we're right back where we started, Amy."

"That's not an answer."

"Me first," I said. "My question first."

She didn't like it, narrowed her eyes. Hurt, confusion, maybe fear across her face.

"Why didn't Kim's source show up this week?" I asked. "Kim went to the meeting place to get her weekly incriminating photograph. I watched her. But the source never showed. Why didn't the source show?"

Amy cocked her head at me. "How should I know?"

I walked over to the breakfast bar by her small kitchen, ran my hands underneath it. Picked up the sugar bowl resting on it and looked inside it. Felt behind the photograph of Amy and her parents posing on a beach somewhere warm.

Did the same thing in the rest of her kitchen. The counters, the coffeepot, the spice bottles, the cookbooks. Felt my hands around and inside everything, like it was foreplay.

"What are you doing?" Amy asked.

"Somebody tipped off Kim's source," I said as I ran my hand over the top of the refrigerator. "The source knew I'd be watching."

Amy gave me a wide berth as I passed her and walked over to the couch, giving it a once-over with my hands, feeling the cushions and pillows, picking up the flower vase and emptying out the fake flowers, then returning them to the vase. Looking at each of the framed photographs on the coffee table, feeling each of them.

"Oh, I get it," said Amy. "The only person who knew you were following Kim was me. So I must have tipped off Kim's source. Which means I knew who the source was in the first place. Which means I'm behind this whole thing."

I looked at Amy, saw the hurt in her eyes. The woman I loved with all my heart. The woman I wasn't sure I could trust.

It was like I'd stolen the wind from her. She remained silent. A long moment passed. I didn't want to believe it. I wanted to trust her so badly my bones ached.

Neither of us knew what to say. It was so quiet in the room that I heard the tick of the clock on the wall behind me as the minute hand inched forward.

I turned and looked at it. An ornate little clock hanging on the wall. It had a picture of a rooster on its small porcelain face and Roman numerals in a fancy font.

I walked over to the clock. Reached up to it with both hands, my jacket hiking up accordingly.

"You brought your *gun,*" Amy said, seeing the holster.

I pulled the clock off the wall, gently lifting the wire over the nail. A decorative piece, a French-country design that fit the decor of the place, running on a battery. I flipped it over and found it.

A small square thingamajig. Even if it were seen—and it was never supposed to be seen—it could pass as some kind of battery compartment or something.

A bug. A wireless recording device.

I suddenly hated myself.

Amy *wasn't* the only one who knew I was tailing Kim. Whoever was on the other end of this eavesdropping device heard our whole conversation when we hatched the plan, right here in this room.

That person heard a lot of other conversations, too.

I removed the bug from the back of the clock and held it in the palm of my hand. Amy's eyes widened when she saw it. She knew what it was. She had been a federal prosecutor for years, and the feds love these things.

She frowned. Put a hand to her chest. The realization, dawning on her, that someone had invaded her privacy, that someone was listening to everything she said in this apartment.

I dropped the bug on the floor and crushed it with my boot. "I'm so sorry," I said. "I should have trusted you."

I started toward her. I thought of touching her, embracing her, caressing her, but I could see how cold she was, how unsure. We were still negotiating a truce. I had just figured out what I came here to learn. I had answered my question. But Amy still had a question for me. She was still a few steps away from fully trusting me.

"If you trust me now," she said, "then why do you still need your gun?"

I nodded, reached behind my back, and removed my firearm. Held it with my thumb and index finger, the weapon dangling upside down, and placed it on the coffee table near her.

She looked at it, then looked at me.

Then in one movement, she took a step backward and picked up the gun, holding it awkwardly in her hands, pointing it at me.

"Okay, now back to my question," she said. "Where's the little black book?"

NINETY-EIGHT

AMY, STILL spooked by the recording device I'd found in the living room, probably worried that there was more than one in that room, motioned me toward the bedroom. She made me go first, keeping her distance, still aiming my gun at me.

When we reached the bedroom, Amy looked around. She had the same thought I did—this room could be bugged, too. She walked over to an iPad resting on the windowsill and pushed a button. Some music came on, symphony music, strings. She turned it up—it was loud enough to run some interference but not so loud that we couldn't talk.

Amy fixed the gun on me again. It was time to get back to business. Though the way she held the gun made me think it might have been her first time handling a weapon.

"I had a copy of the little black book," she said to me.

"You—you had a copy of it all along, and you—"

"Not all along," she said. "I got it yesterday. After your sister, Patti, paid me a visit at my office."

She laid it out for me. Yesterday, after Margaret Olson had announced her candidacy for mayor, Patti confronted Amy as she was leaving the Daley Center.

"Patti explained her whole theory," she said. "That Margaret was blackmailing Congressman Tedesco. That Margaret had a copy of the little black book, and it named Tedesco as a client. Maybe she even had one of those incriminating photographs of Tedesco going into the brownstone, like the other ones Kim Beans published. That the whole thing was a scheme so Margaret could remove the mayor from office and take his place, with Tedesco not only getting out of her way but also actually endorsing her and giving her his money."

"Sounds right to me," I said.

Obviously not to Amy.

"You didn't want to believe it," I said, "but you couldn't deny that it made some sense."

Amy nodded with reluctance. "Right. So I went back up to Margaret's office. I have a key. There's a safe under her desk. It's been there since the 1970s, when whoever was state's attorney wanted to keep some sensitive papers private or something. Anyway, nobody knew about the safe but Margaret and me."

"You broke into it," I said.

"I...I knew the combination. She opened it in front of me once. She was running late for a refinance, and the closing papers were in there. I didn't mean to pay attention, but she sort of sang out the number to herself, and I heard it. 9-2-1-6-0; 9-2-1-6-0. It's her sister's date of birth, September 21, 1960."

The music from the iPad, violins and cellos, the notes dancing about, rising and falling in crisp, short strokes, adding a dreamlike quality to the whole thing.

"You opened it," I said, "and you found the little black book."

"I found a thumb drive. I brought it back here and booted it up on my home computer last night. And yes," she said. "It contained a PDF of the little black book." She swept a hand. "And now it's gone. It was inside my desk drawer last night, and now it's not. Somebody broke into my apartment today and stole it."

That was a concern, a major one. But there were more immediate concerns on my mind.

"Amy," I said, "was Congressman Tedesco's name in there as a client?"

Amy closed her eyes and nodded. "Yes."

"So Margaret *was* blackmailing him."

She didn't answer. She didn't need to.

"Did the little black book list payoffs to cops?"

Amy nodded, her eyes moving away from mine. "One cop," she said. "One name, over and over, once a month, for the last three years."

NINETY-NINE

I FELT something stir inside me. It was what we had thought—that the real value, and the real danger, of the little black book lay not in the names of the clients but in the name of the crooked cop who was receiving extortion payments from the brownstone.

The name of the cop was in that book.

"What name?" I asked. "Which cop?"

And then I felt a buzz in my pocket.

I pulled out my phone. It was a text message from Kate:

Need to talk to u

Now was definitely not the time. I texted back:

Not now

I lowered the phone and looked at Amy. "So whose name was it?" I asked.

Amy didn't want to answer.

"Amy," I said, "whoever's name is in that little black book is probably the same person who bugged your apartment. It's probably the same person who stole the little black book from your apartment today. It's probably the same person behind *all* of this."

Amy nodded slowly, as if she already had figured that out.

"How long before they come here looking for you?" I said.

My phone buzzed again. I raised the phone to see Kate's next message:

I'm right outside her door open up

"Shit." I lowered the phone. "It's Kate. She's out in the hallway right now."

Amy's eyes widened in panic. "Kate's *here?* You brought her here?" She backpedaled, the gun trembling in her hands. As if her worst fears had just been realized.

"No, I didn't. She must have followed me or something."

"Oh, shit. Oh, God. Oh, shit." Amy's eyes cast about the room. She was coming unglued. She had the gun on me, not the other way around, but she was feeling a loss of control, and her fear was overtaking her.

"I'll try to get rid of her." I typed a quick response:

You're outside Amy's apt?

Her reply shot back in an instant:

Yes open door right now

I replied, trying to stall for time:

Why would I do that

But I was running out of time. Kate wasn't going to take no for an answer. She'd break through the door. She could do it. And she'd be armed.

"Amy, give me the gun," I said, reaching out my hand, wiggling my fingers.

Amy shook her head furiously, but I could see her uncertainty. Wanting to believe me, but afraid of being wrong.

"Amy, like it or not, Kate's coming in. And she'll have a gun. You don't know how to use that thing."

"No." Amy's face contorted, tears flowing, her voice thick with emotion. That gun dancing around in her hands. "No."

"Amy, you can trust me. You can—"

I stopped on those words. My phone buzzed again, another text from Kate, but I didn't look at it. I watched Amy carefully. I could see that Amy simply didn't, couldn't, trust me.

"Whose name was in that black book?" I asked. "Whose name was listed as receiving the payoffs?"

The music through the speakers, one song coming to a violent, triumphant climax of violin and cello. Another song beginning, the bass playing solo, moving slowly and cautiously, like a snake through the grass, a warning of a storm.

All that was missing was a drumroll.

"Your name," Amy said. "It was your name in the little black book."

"What?" My phone fell out of my hands. On impact with the carpet, the face of my phone lit up, showing the last message from Kate, which I had yet to read.

I picked it back up to make sure I read it correctly.

Bc she knows u idiot. She knows about u and so do I

Then I remembered that I never locked Amy's front door after entering.

And then I turned and saw Kate walking into the apartment, her weapon drawn.

ONE HUNDRED

"KATE, TAKE it easy," I called as she walked toward the bedroom. I held out my right hand as a signal to stop. I held out my left to Amy. "Amy," I said, "give me the gun."

"No." Amy shook her head, steeled herself through her tears, aimed the gun toward the doorway into the bedroom.

"Amy, I know how to use that thing. You don't. You'll get us all killed."

Kate approached with her weapon in both hands, held at waist level in front of her, walking on the balls of her feet. She could hear what I was saying. She knew Amy had a gun now.

As Kate approached, I moved into the space between Amy and the doorway, where Kate now stood with her weapon aimed at Amy and, by extension, at me.

"Amy," Kate barked, "drop that gun or I'll put you down. Drop it right now or I'll shoot."

The way she said it. I'd heard that voice before, that no-fucking-around tone. Amy was a prosecutor, not a cop. She wasn't cut out for this.

"Do it, Amy," I said, remaining between them. But it wouldn't matter. If Kate wanted to shoot Amy, she would.

Then I heard it behind me, the sound of the gun releasing from Amy, the soft *plunk* as it fell onto the nearby bed. I saw it in Kate's eyes, too, that hint of relaxation.

But only a hint. Kate was keyed up, her eyes on fire.

Amy wasn't sobbing anymore, either. I had my back to her, but I knew she was no longer upset. The only emotion she was experiencing now was pure terror.

"Both of you, against that wall." Kate motioned with the gun. We complied, moving to the far wall. Kate retrieved my weapon off the bed, training two guns on us now. Then she shuffled back toward the doorway and gave us another command, the smart move, the one I would make if I were giving the orders.

"Both of you, on the bed," she said.

I took the lead, sitting down on the edge of the bed. I hoped that would be enough. But again, if Kate was smart—and she was—it wouldn't satisfy her.

"Scootch back all the way on the bed," she said. "Back against the headboard, hands on your thighs, feet on the bed, ankles crossed."

That was the smart move. Make us as immobile as possible. We couldn't rush her this way. In the time it took us to uncross our ankles, push ourselves off the bed, drop our feet down on the carpet, and make a move toward her, she'd have time to empty her magazine and probably reload. She had us completely under her control.

Amy and I sitting on the bed, Kate standing at the opposite end of the small bedroom. I had nothing for a weapon other than my phone, which I put next to me on the bed. I wasn't a good enough aim to skull her with it, and even if I succeeded, it wouldn't do more than momentarily stun her. She'd recover in time to riddle me with bullets.

Satisfied that we were sufficiently subdued, Kate lowered the guns in her hands.

"Was she a part of it, too?" Kate asked me, gesturing toward Amy.

"A part of what?" I asked, though it wasn't hard to tell what she meant.

"The bribes. The payoffs. I know it was you, Billy."

"It wasn't." But I remembered what Amy had said to me. *It was your name in the little black book*. "Somebody set me up," I said.

Kate glared at me, worked her jaw. "It's gonna be like that, is it? Just deny everything up and down?"

"Don't bullshit a bullshitter," I said. "Don't turn this around. It was you, Kate."

Her face showed no sign of anything but disgust. "I trusted you," she said. "I fucking *loved* you, Billy."

With those words, her expression broke. She didn't cry, but she choked up nice and good, the fire still in her eyes but now showing real pain.

She took a deep breath and said, "You're under arrest, Billy Harney."

It didn't register with me. It didn't make sense.

She was going to...*arrest* me?

That's when I knew.

Kate wasn't the dirty cop.

If she were, I'd be dead. Amy and I both. Arresting me made no sense. I could still fight back. I could hire a lawyer and prove my innocence. I could prove that she was the dirty cop, not me. If she had been the dirty cop, she would have killed me, just as she killed Ramona Dillavou and Camel Coat—whatever she needed to do to maintain her cover-up.

It wasn't Amy, and it wasn't Kate.

And it sure as hell wasn't me.

"Kate," I said, "listen—"

And then we all listened, we all heard it. The soft *click* of Amy's front door opening.

Kate's head whipped to the right, surprised.

Then not surprised.

"What are you doing here?" she said to whoever it was.

With Kate momentarily distracted, I reached for my phone, held it in my hand. Using it as a weapon felt like a million-to-one shot.

But that didn't mean I couldn't use it in other ways.

I heard his voice from the living room.

And I dropped my phone back on the bed, just before Lieutenant Mike Goldberger walked into the bedroom.

ONE HUNDRED ONE

KATE TOOK a step back to clear some space as Goldie walked into the room.

My mouth opened, but I couldn't speak.

"Nobody's arresting anybody," he said. "We just need to talk this out."

He seemed almost amused, seeing me and Amy lying on the bed, our feet up and legs crossed. He looked at Kate. "Oh, put the guns away, for Christ's sake," he said. "This is *Billy* we're talking about. I'm sure he can explain this."

Kate lowered her weapon to her side. Goldie took my gun from Kate.

"That's better," he said. He walked over to the windowsill and punched out the music on the iPad. "That damn music," he said. "Drowned out a perfectly good recording device."

Then Goldie walked toward the bed, facing me, his back to Kate. "So Billy," he said. "Let's figure this out."

"There's nothing to figure out," said Kate. "I'm taking him in, Goldie."

"No, you're not, Katie."

"The fuck I'm not."

Goldie looked at me. He heaved a deep sigh.

Then he spun and aimed my gun at Kate. He fired

a single shot. Kate had no chance to react. The bullet hit her above the right eye. She dropped in her tracks, falling to the carpet.

Amy let out a horrified gasp and reached for me. I drew her in. I didn't know—I didn't know what to—

Goldie spun back around, probably to make sure I wasn't making a move on him.

"I can't believe..." I tried to say. "I can't..."

"You can't what? I'm cleaning up *your* mess, pal. Because you wouldn't leave well enough alone."

Everything was racing through my mind. Trying to fit together pieces of a puzzle that hurled at me from all directions—

"It was you," I said. "You set me up. You made Kate believe it was me."

"I...needed to keep Kate guessing, yeah," he said. "But I wasn't gonna let this fall on you." He angles his head. "I admit I didn't expect her to come here on her own and try to arrest you. We can't have that. Nobody arrests nobody. Keep the whole thing a mystery, am I right?"

I moved forward on the bed, enough to shield Amy, who couldn't speak, who was shaking uncontrollably.

"You'll never get away with this," I said.

"Get away with what?" he answered. "My name's not in the little black book. And this thing with Kate? Hey, I was never here." His smile never reached his cold eyes, appearing and disappearing from his lips. "Here's what happened, Detective, and listen carefully, because your life depends on it." He raised a hand. "Kate walked in and caught you and Amy together. She was jealous. She pulled out her gun to kill you both, but you got off a shot first. You killed her in self-defense." He looked down at Kate. "That's a story everyone will believe. I'll make sure they believe it. They won't even charge you."

He walked back over to the bed, watching Amy and me.

"And Ramona Dillavou?" I said. "And Joe Washington?"

His head bobbed back and forth. "Desperate times call for desperate measures. But they won't come back to me, either, my friend. If you push things, I think what you'll find is that those murders will come back to *you*."

"You framed me for those, too?"

He shrugged. "Insurance," he said. "In case you got too nosy. I don't want you in prison, pal. I want you by my side."

My mind was racing, looking for angles, anything. We were sitting ducks on this bed, unarmed and unable to make any meaningful attempt at fighting back.

"So that's out of the way," he said. "Then there's the matter of the little black book. Somebody took a copy from Margaret Olson's safe last night. And Margaret tells me that only one person had a key to her office, and that same person knew that Margaret had a safe hidden underneath her desk."

Goldie turned his gun—my gun—and trained it on Amy. "That would be you, Ms. Lentini. So do me a favor and hand it over, if you would."

ONE HUNDRED TWO

GOLDIE GESTURED with the gun and said it again. "The little black book, Amy. If you please."

I realized that Goldie hadn't heard what Amy told me tonight in the apartment. I had destroyed the bug I'd found in the living room, and the music Amy had turned on in the bedroom blocked out the bug in here.

So Goldie didn't know that somebody had broken into Amy's apartment and stolen the little black book.

He thought Amy still had it.

"I made copies," Amy said, which was smart of her but unlikely to work on a guy like Goldie.

He snickered, showed some teeth. "Sure you did," he said. "And if you don't say the word by midnight, copies are going out to all the news stations in town, right? C'mon, now, Amy. Give it up. Or I'm gonna have to do the same thing to you that I did to Kate."

It was clear to me then that he was going to do that anyway. He couldn't let Amy live. Not after this. He might think he could convert *me,* but Amy?

"Don't tell him," I said to Amy. "The moment you do, you die."

"No." Goldie, showing the first sign of angst. "No. If I get back the little black book, she can live. She can't hurt me. She'll have nothing. My word against hers. Margaret's word against hers." He looked squarely at me. "*Your* word against hers."

"Not mine," I said. "I'm not lying for you."

I started to push myself off the bed. Goldie shook his head and pointed the gun at me. "Don't move, Billy. Not until I can talk some goddamn *sense* into you."

"You kill her," I said, "you'll have to kill me, too."

"Jesus Christ, kid! Why should I have to do that? Just give me Amy's copy, and I have the original. There won't *be* a little black book anymore. Don't you get it? Everything will work out fine. Margaret's going to be mayor. She's going to dump that idiot Tristan Driscoll and appoint..."

He stopped on that.

"Appoint who?" I asked. "She's going to make you the new police superintendent? Was that the deal you cut with Margaret?"

Goldie's shoulders rose and fell. "Didn't have much of a choice. I didn't want to cut *any* deal with that bitch. But I didn't have a choice. *I* didn't give her the damn thumb drive."

Right. I got it now. "Ramona Dillavou did," I said. "She was trying to cut a deal for immunity with Margaret. Ramona admitted it to you after you tortured it out of her."

Goldie smirked. "Ramona—she was a tough broad," he said. "Held out a long time."

"Then why didn't Margaret just make it public once she had it?" I asked. "Tedesco's name was in that book. He'd be ruined."

Goldie shook his head. "Smart a guy as you are, kiddo, you never did think like a politician, did you?"

Amy cleared her throat. "If Margaret made it public and outed Tedesco, then Tedesco wouldn't endorse

Margaret," she said. "And he wouldn't give her his campaign war chest. Margaret couldn't win without those things. The little black book was more powerful as a threat, as blackmail."

Goldie wagged a finger. "See? There you go, Amy. You're a politician already. I'm sure Mayor Margaret Olson will have a nice cozy spot for you in the office." He drew a breath. "Yeah, I went to Margaret. I had the original, and she had the only copy. So we made a deal."

He seemed almost proud of it.

"Enough," he said. "Amy, I need that thumb drive. Give it to me, and we all live happily ever after. You both have great careers ahead of you. You'll get married and have beautiful babies, and everything will be swell. On the other hand, you *don't* tell me, well, I gotta put a bullet in Billy's kneecap."

"No!" I said. "Don't tell him."

"And you don't tell me after that, I put one in his other kneecap. We keep going 'til your boyfriend looks like a fucking piñata."

"Don't, Amy," I said. "No matter what, don't tell him."

Goldie looked at each of us, his bravado wavering. He gave me a cross look and shook his head.

"I'll cop to it," I said. "I'll say I was the dirty cop. I took the payoffs from Ramona Dillavou. I'll admit it, Goldie. Just let Amy go. Let Amy walk out of here, and you have my word, on my daughter's grave, that I'll take the fall. You already have my name in the little black book, anyway, right?"

A wave passed through me. I thought about what I'd just said, and it didn't make sense. I could see Goldie doctoring the little black book and putting my name in it to frame me, sure—but that didn't account for the copy Ramona had made on the thumb drive. Ramona had given Margaret that copy. And she did it without Goldie's knowledge. Goldie only found out about it later, after he tortured Ramona. So how could Goldie have doctored the copy that Amy had found in Margaret's safe?

How could my name have been in the copy?

"Not your name specifically," Amy said. "You never let me finish."

I wanted to turn to her, but I couldn't take my eyes off Goldie.

"There were no first names in the book, only last names," Amy said. "The cop taking the payoff had the last name Harney. That's all it said. 'Harney.'"

I closed my eyes a moment, sucked in a breath.

Not Billy Harney. Just Harney.

That's when I knew who had broken into Amy's apartment and stolen the little black book.

It was Patti.

Goldie raised his chin, turned his head toward the window. His voice louder, he said, "We're not getting anywhere. You better come in here and talk some sense into him."

ONE HUNDRED THREE

THE PRESENT

I TAKE a breath and pause. The clock over the jury box says it's almost noon. Right about now, the judge should be looking for a logical point to take a break so the jurors can have their lunch—and, more important, so he can have his own lunch.

But the judge has hardly moved, his eyes narrowed in concentration, fixed on a space somewhere between me and my lawyer. The jurors are all leaning forward; some of them have been filling their notebooks with scribbles, but most of them have dispensed with the note taking and have settled into positions best suited for viewing the horror show. It's so quiet inside this courtroom that you can hear the breathing from the spectators' gallery, the collective inhales and exhales.

Lieutenant Mike Goldberger, initially shaking his head in mock disbelief, has slowly transformed during my testimony, his eyes now cold, his shoulders drawn in, his fists clenched. He is trapped in the courtroom, essentially. If he runs away, he looks guilty. He looks pretty damn guilty right now anyway, but I know what he's thinking: *This is only Billy's word. His word against mine*. That's Goldie. It always was. Always calculating. Always seeing every angle.

My father, sitting next to him, eyes me intently, some fingers covering his mouth, unsure how to act.

Margaret Olson, like Goldie, even more so than Goldie, is a prisoner in this courtroom. She's the prosecutor, after all. She can't just storm out. She has essentially never stopped shaking her head during my almost three hours of testimony as she watches her political career swirl down the toilet, as she considers every possible angle to salvage it. Ultimately, I assume, she's thinking the same thing as Goldie. *It's his word against mine. The word of a desperate defendant looking at life in prison who will say anything, no matter how far-fetched, to save his own ass.*

My lawyer, Stilson, has forgotten his role and has listened along with the jurors, the reporters, and curious onlookers. "So Lieutenant Goldberger said, 'You better come in here and talk some sense into him'?"

"Yes," I answered. "He was saying it to someone not in the room. He was speaking toward the recording device in the room, wherever it was."

Stilson, whose first instinct all morning has been to simply ask what happened next, instead cocks his head. "You said you knew at that moment that it was Patti who stole the thumb drive from Amy's apartment?"

"Yes."

"How?"

I looked at her, my twin sister, as still as a statue, but I could see it in the sheen of her eyes, the single tear that had fallen. I could almost see the bubble over her head saying, *I'm sorry; I'm so sorry.*

"Because Patti would have seen the name Harney on that page of the little black book and assumed it was me," I said. "Her first instinct would have been to protect me, to steal the little black book and destroy it."

Fresh tears stream down Patti's face.

"This whole time since the shootings, while I was in a coma, when I came out and slowly recovered, as I considered how to defend myself against these charges, she's thought I was the dirty cop. This whole time she's been trying to protect me. Even though she was sure I was guilty, she tried to protect me."

I choke up on those last words. Take a moment. Clear my throat.

"She loves me, and she'd do anything for me," I say, "but she *worships* our father. She never in a million years would have considered the possibility that the name Harney could mean another cop. She never would have suspected that the chief of detectives, Daniel Harney, was the dirty cop."

Patti jumps out of her seat in the front row, her mouth open, pure horror on her face. She turns to my father, whose eyes are now focused on the floor before him.

A second chance, Pop said to me the other day when he tried to persuade me to flee the jurisdiction, to escape to Mexico. *You have a second chance. I have a second chance.*

I'd like to think he was sincere when he said that—that he really was going to try to slip me out of the country to Playa del Carmen, then South America. That he wasn't going to put a bullet in my brain somewhere between Chicago and the Mexican border.

I'd like to believe that he was hoping for that second chance.

But I didn't take it. And so he sent someone to my house last night to try to kill me for the second time.

And now I'll never know for sure. Because I will never speak another word to him.

ONE HUNDRED FOUR

THE PAST

BY THE time my father walked into the bedroom, joining Goldie, I knew that Amy would never get off that bed alive. They might think they could co-opt me into going along with a plan, but Amy? She had seen too much. She'd spent her career being a by-the-book prosecutor, straight as an arrow. And she wasn't blood, wasn't family. They couldn't trust her to keep quiet. They couldn't let her live.

"I'm so sorry I ever doubted you," Amy whispered on a trembling breath.

"I'm sorry I doubted *you,*" I said. "I love you, Amy. I love you so much."

My father entered the bedroom then, looked down at Kate as he walked in, the way he might glance at a homeless person he passed on the street. I didn't expect him to be surprised. He had obviously been listening to everything through the eavesdropping device planted in the room. He shook his head as if disappointed.

"Congratulations, Pop," I said. "Let me guess. Margaret's going to make you the superintendent. And the deputy superintendent will be Mike Goldberger."

My father blinked several times. Always the stoic demeanor. "If you're going to ask me to apologize for providing for my family all these years, I won't."

"Providing for your family through bribes and extortion?"

"Son, you don't—"

"And last I checked, Mom's been gone for years, and all your kids are grown up. So who the fuck have you been providing for other than yourself?"

My father wasn't kidding; he wasn't going to apologize. Not because he didn't have regret. He just didn't like to show weakness.

He put out a hand. "I...didn't want it to turn out this way. But it's not too late for you, son. It's not too late for *us*. Goldie was right. You can have any job in the department you want. You and Amy, you can be happy together."

He might have had more success had he left out that last sentence, the lie about Amy staying alive. But deep down, if he knew me at all, he knew I wouldn't go along with him and Goldie. Which meant these words weren't meant as a plea to me. They were meant as salve for his guilt, so he could tell himself, before he killed me—after he killed me, for the rest of his life—that he gave me one last chance.

I moved directly in front of Amy, put out my arms behind me to barricade her in.

"They're going to kill me either way," she whispered into my ear. "But they don't want to kill you. Save yourself, Billy. Say whatever you have to say."

"No," I whispered, shaking so hard I could barely speak.

"Patti needs you, son," my father said. "You know how she relies on you. She's always leaned on you. Don't make me do this. Get on board here."

My eyes bored into his. I should have felt fear. Instead I felt nothing but pure hatred. "Never," I said.

Amy's head resting between my shoulder blades, her heartbeat pounding into my spine. Her entire body hidden behind mine, my arms behind me, trying to envelop her.

"I love you so much," she whispered to me, the only time she'd ever said the words to me, as my father moved toward Kate and lifted her gun from her dead hand.

My father moving closer, holding Kate's gun. Goldie next to him, holding mine.

Goldie had already laid out the plan, the jilted-lover theory. It would still work for them, I realized—Kate barging in in a jealous rage, a gunfight ensuing. But my father, holding Kate's gun, would have to shoot me. They couldn't sell that story if I were shot with my own weapon.

I moved one hand from Amy and reached for my phone, touched it. My father's eyes moved to it.

"His phone," said my father, not to me but to Goldie. A reminder that they'd have to dispose of it, take it with them or smash it to pieces.

"Move away from the girl," my father said. "It doesn't have to be both of you, son."

"Never," I said again.

"Jesus, Billy. She's worth that much to you, huh? So much that you're willing to die along with her?"

I looked into my father's eyes. Had he ever known love? Love that went beyond love for himself and his own advancement? I didn't know. I hoped so, for my mother's sake. I never would know for sure. All I knew was that I had found Amy, and I couldn't ever let her go. I couldn't live without her.

"You always were the softhearted one," Pop said to me. "I never understood it."

Behind me, Amy scooted sideways, separating herself from me. I reached for her, grabbed her arm, tried to stop her, but she had moved out from behind me before I could. She was doing what they wanted. Making it easier for them to kill her but not me. We looked at each other for a moment, probably only one tick of the clock by any objective measure, but it felt like we held that stare forever. So much courage in her eyes, so much love.

"Shirt off, Amy," said Goldie.

She did what they asked. It would make the story easier—we were in bed, fooling around, when Kate stormed in. I didn't want her to help them, but we were stalling, hanging on to precious seconds. And I needed the distraction.

Because I had one last move. It was a long shot. The way I was seated on the bed, my legs out in front of me, made my ability to spring forward almost nonexistent. And Pop wasn't dumb enough to get so close to me that I could reach out and grab the gun.

But I was out of good choices. I clenched the muscles in my calves and thighs, tried to shift my balance forward without being too obvious, while Amy pulled her shirt over her head.

I thought of my beautiful little daughter, taken so young, those angelic eyes beaming up at me, and told her that I would see her soon.

Then I placed my hands on the bed and prepared to spring off it. There was only one way this could possibly succeed. I was counting on one thing and only one thing.

I was counting on my father not being able to shoot his own son.

ONE HUNDRED FIVE

THE PRESENT

I STARE at the floor as Stilson Tomita struggles for the next question. I don't want to look at Patti, who was ordered by the sheriff's deputy to sit back down.

I don't want to look at my father, either.

"He didn't hesitate," I say. "He knew I was going to make a move on him. He shot me before I had the chance. Amy must have—she...probably turned away by instinct, and my blood spattered on her bare back. For their purposes, it laid the scene out perfectly."

I wipe at my face. The courtroom rings with utter silence.

"I wish I'd died right then."

But I didn't.

"They killed Amy, too," says Stilson, a choke in his voice.

I nod.

Eventually, so the doctors tell me, my brain and heart clicked off for a while before I came back to life, but I didn't check out right away. I heard what they did to Amy. I couldn't see anything at that point, but for some reason I could still hear.

"Amy, this can still turn out okay for you," said Goldie. "They shot each other. You were an innocent bystander."

"Just give us the thumb drive, and we're on our way," *said my father.*

I heard her voice as though it were far away, a muted, low mumble. I could hear Amy's desperate whispers:

"Incline, O Lord, thine ears to our prayers, in which we humbly beseech thy mercy, that thou would place the soul of thy servant Billy, which thou hast caused to depart from this world—"

"Amy! Work with me here. Focus. Give us the little black book."

But Amy was no longer listening. As these two predators closed in on her, ready to steal away her life at any second, Amy wasn't thinking of herself.

She was thinking of me. She was praying for my soul.

"We don't want to shoot you, Amy."

I had forgotten how to pray after I lost my wife and daughter. I had rejected God and lost my faith. But now I prayed. Inside my wrecked brain, I prayed that Amy's death would come quickly and without pain. I prayed that God would take Amy into his kingdom and surround her with all the love she deserved.

"She's not gonna talk," said my father. "It's in here somewhere. We'll find it. Just get on with it."

I felt no pain. I felt nothing but Amy's love wrapped around me, the warmth spreading through me. I didn't feel the touch of her hand or her breath on my face or her lips on mine. I felt all of her, all at once.

I heard the gunshot, the startled gasp escaping Amy's mouth.

And then I heard nothing at all.

I look up at Stilson Tomita through blurry eyes, my face soaked with tears, unable to speak, my heartbeat banging against my shirt.

Right now I feel her again; I am filled with her. A

feeling that wants to be pain, but I won't let it hurt. She wouldn't want that. Amy would want me to feel the joy of her love, not the sadness.

I will never forget you, Amy. I will move on, because I know you want me to. But you will always be part of me.

Stilson Tomita clears his throat, wipes at his eyes.

"No further questions, Your Honor," he says.

ONE HUNDRED SIX

"MAXIMUM MARGARET" Olson moves from the prosecutor's table and slithers toward me, her eyes on me, filled with hatred. This trial has been about me. I've had to fight for my life. But now this trial is about something else, too. It's about Margaret Olson, front-runner in the race for Chicago mayor. In every way that counts, she is now fighting for her life, too.

"That was quite a story, Mr. Harney. Lots of revelations!" She makes a show with her hands. "Little black books and cover-ups! But let me see if I understand this."

She stops only a foot away from me, puts her hands on the wooden frame of the witness stand, bracing herself, leaning forward toward me. I'm half expecting a serpent's tongue to lash out and pluck out my eyeballs.

It's all I can do not to lunge forward and grab her throat. Margaret didn't commit murder, but her ambition and corruption were part of this, too. She is just as much to blame as my father and Goldie.

"Amy Lentini isn't here to corroborate your testimony, is she?"

I inhale and exhale. I am in a court of law, and I

am still on trial. I think of Amy, and what she would want, her by-the-book, respect-the-law way.

Fine, Margaret. I can hurt you without ever laying a finger on you.

"No, Amy is not here," I say, drawing out the words.

"Neither is Kate Fenton, is she?"

"No."

"Now that they're dead, you can say whatever you want about them, can't you?"

"If you say so."

"And I assume that two of the most decorated members of the Chicago Police Department, Chief of Detectives Daniel Harney and the chief of the Bureau of Internal Affairs, Michael Goldberger, can—"

"I'm sure they'll deny everything," I say.

She didn't expect me to agree so readily. "And when the police searched the crime scene afterward, they didn't find any eavesdropping devices, did they?"

"No. They would be easy to remove."

"The point is there's no evidence of that, is there?"

"That's correct, Ms. Olson."

She nods. Feeling a little adrenaline now. Scoring some points. Finally getting to fight back after I testified for four agonizing hours.

"And nobody ever found a little black book, did they? I mean, there's no proof it ever existed, is there?"

I look over at my sister, Patti, in the front row, who has her face in her hands. At this last question, her face pops back up, and peeks at me through her splayed fingers.

I say, "I don't have a copy of the little black book, if that's what you mean. My guess is that both the original and the thumb drive have been destroyed."

"How convenient," Olson says.

"Not for me, it isn't."

"So no witnesses to corroborate, no little black book to corroborate."

"Correct."

"So this whole thing," she says, and with that her hands leave the witness box, and she turns toward the jury, toward the gallery, toward the reporters who have breathlessly tweeted out these juicy, scandalous revelations, "this entire thing you've just told us—we only have *your word* to take for it."

She pauses on that.

I clear my throat.

"Margaret, I recorded the whole thing on my smartphone."

She does a half turn in my direction, as if afraid to fully confront what I've just said.

"My sister was good enough to install an icon on my phone so I can just hit one button and start recording. I hit it when Goldie first walked into the apartment and Kate's head turned away from me for a moment. One touch, and it started recording. And just before my father shot me I touched the icon again, to stop it."

By now, Margaret has retreated to the prosecution's table, where she is huddling with her team. They're showing her something in a manila folder, whispering to her feverishly. Finally she looks up at me. "Your phone was smashed in the bedroom," she says. "Destroyed. Nothing could be recovered from the physical phone. Right?"

"Right."

"You're aware that we tried very hard to penetrate that phone and couldn't."

"Yes."

"And you didn't have one of those save-to-the-cloud functions, did you? The platform that allows you to store records in cyberspace?"

"No, I didn't. I'm pretty clueless when it comes to those phones. If it wasn't for the icon Patti installed, I never could have recorded anything."

"So this…this recording you tell us about…it wasn't recovered from your physical phone, and it's not on any cloud."

"Correct."

"So once again, Mr. Harney," says the prosecutor, fully recovered, her arms out in a theatrical gesture, "we have only *your* word to take for these claims you've made here today."

I look three rows back in the gallery and make eye contact with Stewart's daughter, Grace, who was kind enough to show up today after I called her this morning. Grace gives me a sweet smile. Her father, my good friend Stewart, had died by the time I made the recording in Amy's bedroom. With Stewart deceased, and with my having no memory of recording what happened in the bedroom, nobody else in the world would have bothered to check that private Facebook page that Stewart and I shared, the one to which I uploaded all my jokes and comedy routines with one click of an icon. I certainly wouldn't. Why would I want to listen to a bunch of my old jokes? And Grace wouldn't; there were no memories of her father on that page—just a bunch of one-liners and humorous observations and sometimes a few minutes of stand-up at the Hole in the Wall. It was between Stewart and me, nobody else.

All this time, the audio recording was posted right there on that private Facebook page.

I think Grace enjoys the fact that, even after his death, Stewart was able to lend me a hand in my moment of need. I do, too. I feel his presence now, the man who comforted me while my daughter was dying, the man who was more of a father to me in the short time I knew him than my real father ever was.

The courtroom erupts when I mention my smartphone's automatic link to Stewart's Facebook page—when the reporters and jurors realize that sometime soon they are going to get hold of that recording and be able to listen to what transpired, blow by blow, in that bedroom.

Needless to say, Margaret Olson, Goldie, and my father don't take the news very well.

ONE HUNDRED SEVEN

"WITH 27 percent of the precincts reporting in the special mayoral election, WGN News is now projecting that County Commissioner Estefan Morales will become the first Latino mayor of Chicago..."

As we stand in my family room watching the TV, we four Harney kids clink our beer bottles together and take a congratulatory swig. We don't quite smile at one another. We haven't done a lot of smiling in these last three weeks. We've cried, argued, denied, and questioned. We've mourned, accused, and hugged. And we've drunk enough beer to fill a small reservoir.

"...the tremendous fall of Margaret Olson, the Cook County state's attorney and onetime favorite in the race, finishing in a disappointing sixth place..."

It's not exactly a huge shock that Margaret didn't win. The polls were suggesting as much. I mean, it's kind of hard to run a campaign with the slogan "I didn't kill or blackmail anyone, I swear!" You have to admire Margaret for having the brass to continue the campaign at all after my trial and the release of the audio recording.

"...wasn't just the contents of that audio recording, Mark. I think what really did Olson in was that she didn't act on it over the last three weeks since it surfaced. She didn't file charges against the officers implicated on that recording."

"...agree with Linda, Mark. I think voters thought Margaret Olson was dragging out any further investigation until today, hoping that her denials would be enough to get her through this election."

"Let's turn to the newest member of our team, Kim Beans. Kim, no reporter was closer to this scandal than you. Your thoughts?"

Kim Beans, looking well scrubbed and beautiful, having benefited mightily from the suffering of many, looks into the camera.

"I think you're all correct to an extent," she says. "I do think Margaret Olson still had a hope of pulling out this election. But the real reason she did basically nothing about this audio recording over the last three weeks? More than anything else, what was the real reason?"

"She wanted Pop and Goldie to run," I say.

"I think Margaret was hoping that Officers Daniel Harney and Michael Goldberger would run," she says. "She wanted them to flee the jurisdiction, which they were perfectly free to do as long as they hadn't been charged with a crime. She wanted them to run so there was no evidence against her other than a vague audio recording. She didn't just want to win an election. She wants to stay out of prison."

Patti runs a hand through her hair and blows out air like she's inflating a balloon. Dark circles prominent under her eyes. Our sister was particularly crushed by our father's betrayal. Aiden and Brendan had never had as close a relationship to Pop, and they didn't follow in his footsteps as a cop or even stay in

Chicago. Whatever grief they're feeling they've channeled into helping Patti. It's like when your first parent dies and all focus shifts to the surviving parent.

So we've made Patti our project. Aiden, the musclehead, always trying to tussle with her or lift her off her feet, which makes her laugh only because it's so juvenile, or maybe because it reminds her of our childhood; Brendan, with the off-color humor that Patti always enjoyed. The three of us have made an unspoken pact over these last three weeks to stay near her, one of us always keeping an eye on her. It's been our assignment. The distraction has been helpful. It's easier to focus on someone else's grief than cope with your own.

I put my hand on her shoulder and lower my head, look directly into her eyes. I want to tell her *We'll get through this* or *It's gonna be okay,* but I don't have to say the words. It's a twins thing—that's about the only way I can put it.

My sister kept a lot of secrets and did a lot of things, all to protect me. Did she enjoy it, on some level, being the strong one for once? Being the one to help me instead of the other way around? I'm sure she did. But it doesn't change the fact that she was there for me. She thought I was the dirty cop, the "Harney" in the little black book, and she thought I was guilty of four murders—but she still stood by me. We are family, and we always will be.

"Where do you think they went?" she whispers under her breath, words intended only for me, not Aiden or Brendan.

I shrug. "Does it matter?"

The audio recording I had made—which, by the way, has now received more than three million hits on the Facebook page put up by my lawyer, Stilson—should have been all Margaret needed to arrest both Pop and Goldie. But she dragged her feet, refusing to comment, citing the old "ongoing investigation" excuse. Kim Beans, on television just now, was spot-on about that: Margaret dragged her feet to give Pop and Goldie a chance to run. It would be hard to make a case against Margaret based only on that audio recording; if the star witnesses were sunning themselves on a beach in South America, she could probably avoid being prosecuted.

And it worked. A few days after the audio recording surfaced, Pop and Goldie went adios. They picked a Friday night, when the workweek was over and they wouldn't be missed at the office.

Smart. They were always smart.

Patti gives me a long look, takes a deep breath, and releases. Maybe it's just another twin-intuition thing, but it seems like something has lifted off her shoulders.

"You're right. It doesn't matter where he went," she says. "He's gone either way."

"Hey!" Aiden shouts. "Enough of the serious whispering. Time for another group hug!"

He's big enough by himself to draw the three of us in. Patti rolls her eyes, but she enjoys it, I know.

So the four of us Harneys draw together in a tight embrace. For just that moment, it feels like we're kids again, in our backyard, when everything was simple and the future limitless.

ONE HUNDRED EIGHT

"UNITED STATES versus Michael Leonard Goldberger," the clerk calls out. "United States versus Daniel Collins Harney."

Margaret Olson had given Pop and Goldie a head start on an escape, but there is another gang of prosecutors in town who wear federal badges. The US attorney's office loves to prosecute local cops. No way they were going to pass on this case.

Federal agents found Pop and Goldie in Playa del Carmen, Mexico. The word is that when the marshals kicked in the door, Pop was halfway out a bathroom window, and Goldie was hiding under the bed.

From a side door, Goldie and my father appear, dressed in orange jumpsuits, escorted by federal marshals, their hands in shackles. Patti draws a quick breath. So do I.

Goldie has shaved his head altogether and grown a goatee. His eyes briefly scan the room before they move downward.

And my father. His hair is a different color, a bright red, and it's the first time I can remember seeing a rough blanket of whiskers on his face. His eyes are so dark, it's as if he's wearing a mask. His shoulders are stooped, as if literally wilting under the weight of recent events.

And it goes beyond physical. His eyes remain on the floor. My father never walked into a room with his eyes down. Chief of Detectives Daniel Harney always held his chin up, the proud figure of authority and morality.

A shudder passes through me. It's like our father is already gone, just as Patti said. I take Patti's hand and squeeze it.

"Don't feel sorry for him," Patti whispers. We are both fighting that instinct. Pop brought all this on himself. He deserves the fall he has taken, the humiliation, the disgrace, every last bit of it. But he is still our father. He is still our blood. We are tied to him forever. You don't flip a switch and turn that off.

How could you do it? I want to ask him. *How could you shoot your own son?*

I want so much to understand it. To see things through his eyes. I know I am dreaming of something impossible. There is no justification. I only had a child for three years, but I would have done anything for her. I would have taken a bullet for her.

Why didn't you feel the same thing for me?

"Judge, with the obvious risk of flight and the corruption and murder charges that make the defendants eligible for the death penalty, the government requests no bond."

One of them, if not both, will cop a plea, I assume, and they'll give up Margaret. The feds like busting local cops, but they *love* getting local politicians. Whether it's Goldie or my father or both, whatever deal they cut, they'll still spend the rest of their lives incarcerated, but they could avoid the death penalty and might get their choice of prisons.

Pop and Goldie, standing before the judge, their

backs to us, two broken, defeated men, listen as their lawyers express outrage at the notion of a no-bond order. The judge, on the other hand, doesn't seem so bothered by the thought. With a bang of the gavel, he orders each of them held without bond.

And then, just like that, it's over. My father and Goldie are led from the courtroom. The whole thing took less than twenty minutes. The clerk calls the next case.

The reporters rush out, one of them passing by us, already on her cell phone, calling in to her newsroom. "No bond," she says into her phone. "Held until trial. Which means these boys will never see the light of day again."

The way she said that, it hits both of us. Pop will spend the rest of his life in a federal penitentiary.

We are both quiet, taking that in, as everybody else files out of the courtroom, leaving Patti and me alone. The room feels odd like this, without a judge or lawyers or spectators, like a naked tree in the winter.

Then Patti says, "Well, on the bright side, it'll save us some money on Father's Day presents."

I look at her, stunned. Then I burst out laughing. Don't ask me why. There's no script for how to handle shit like this. Patti and I will have plenty of ups and downs going forward. There will be lots of dark days. We have both changed and will never be the same. But we are still here, we are still standing, and we are still family.

ONE HUNDRED NINE

THE HOLE in the Wall, once my home away from home. Being here feels weird on many levels, one of which is that I'm here without Kate, my longtime partner, my friend, for a brief time more than that. My feelings for her, my memory of her, will always be complicated. She made life difficult for me at the end, but her heart was in the right place, even if her head was not. We never should have slept together. We never should have breached that wall. It colored everything. It made it harder for us to see what was going on around us. She deserved better.

Patti spins on her bar stool and gives me the once-over as I approach.

"How're you doing?" she asks.

I shrug. "I'm a washed-out cop with a questionable future."

She points a finger at me as she raises her beer. "But still a cop," she says.

She seems happy that I've come out of this thing in one piece. Patti is always a mixed bag, a lot of work, but in the end, she was always looking out for me. Did she enjoy it, on some level, being the one helping me instead of the other way around? I'm sure she did. But in the end, what's the difference? She was there for me when it counted.

Soscia, wearing a Hawks jersey, is so far into his pints that he can hardly stand. He falls into me and drapes an arm around my neck. "This guy," he slurs to whomever is listening, which is nobody. "Best cop I know."

"You're a good egg, Sosh," I say, then I catch someone else's eye.

She walks up to me with a coy smile, her eyes down.

"Well, well, well," I say. "Kim Beans, as I live and breathe."

She looks up at me, the smile a bit brighter. "You heard about Margaret, I take it."

"Of course I heard." It was Goldie. My father is too proud to admit anything. But Goldie caved. The feds took the death penalty off the table, and he gave up Margaret. The FBI perp-walked her out of the Daley Center four hours ago.

"Congratulations," she says.

I raise my eyebrows and smirk at her.

She nudges me with an elbow. "Ah, you're not still sore at me, are you?"

I put a hand on my chest. "Sore? Why would I be sore? Because you were receiving those weekly photographs from Margaret Olson and forgot to mention it? Even though it would have cleared me?"

She wags a finger at me. "Just exercising my rights under the First Amendment," she says.

"Yeah?" I lean into her. "Tell you what, Kim. Maybe someday you and I will meet in a dark alley, and I'll exercise *my* rights under the *Second* Amendment."

She deserves that, and she knows it. What does she

care? This whole case rebuilt her career. She's back on TV and has a great future.

"Fair enough," she says. "But if your attitude ever adjusts, Detective, you've got my number. This time it will be off the record."

She gives me one last come-hither glance and walks away.

Did she just come on to me?

Whatever. I'm not touching that hot stove. I'm done with dangerous women.

Never again.

Not for a few weeks, at least.

The truth is, in that particular department, I'm in a weird sort of limbo. My memory is back, which means my feelings for Amy have returned. I remember and feel it more than ever now, how deeply I cared for her.

But it feels like another life to me. Like she's a warm, loving memory, but without the piercing heartache. It feels like I'm starting over now, a clean slate, for whatever that's worth.

The crowd around me is filled with familiar faces, but in some ways foreign. There are nods and averted glances. Nobody knows how to deal with me. The scandal that has rocked the department will be felt for years. That's because of me. Three very popular cops—Kate, Goldie, and my father—are gone now, and in different ways they're all connected to me. I'm not exactly a pariah; nobody can really blame me for anything. But I'm a symbol of the disaster, the last remaining freight car in the train wreck.

My eyes fall on Lieutenant Paul Wizniewski, nursing a glass of rye at a table, the stub of an unlit cigar in his mouth. When our eyes meet, he pauses. Removes the cigar from his mouth. Takes a deep breath.

The Wiz will always be an insufferable, self-promoting jackass, but he wasn't a crooked cop. I thought he was. And he thought *I* was. We were both reporting our findings to Goldie, the head of Internal Affairs. Goldie played each of us against the other, a virtuoso puppet show.

I nod to the Wiz. He nods back. We will never be bosom buddies, but there is room for both of us in the department.

And then I find myself climbing onto the stage and picking up the microphone.

I click the mike on and stare out at the crowd. It takes a while for the noise to die down, but eventually it does, a nervous stillness hanging in the air, all eyes on me, the comedian, the guy whose name they used to chant.

"I just want to be a cop again," I say, surprising myself. "That's all I ever wanted. You guys okay with that?"

Silence.

I don't have anything else to say. I start to drop the mike, then I hear somebody in the crowd clap his hands.

Then someone else claps. Then others join in, a trickle of applause slowly gaining momentum.

Pretty soon they're all on their feet, cheering and clapping. I wasn't expecting a standing ovation, but I'm getting one.

I don't know if I'm going to get back to where I was before this all happened. I'm not sure I want to. But wherever I am right now—a roomful of cops letting me know that I'm one of them again—is just fine with me for the present.

"Listen, I can't stay long," I say, raising a hand to

quiet the crowd. "I'm meeting Margaret Olson for drinks later."

They like that, howls of laughter. It probably helps that half of them can't stand Maximum Margaret and the rest of them are so drunk they couldn't spell their own names.

"Just kidding," I say. "But I have to say, my love life is doing okay these days. I'm losing track of all the women. In fact, you know what I could use . . ."

I look out over the crowd.

"I could really use a little black book."

Laughter, even louder, hoots and shouts.

"I've been looking all over for mine," I say, "and I'll be damned if I can find it."

ABOUT THE AUTHORS

James Patterson holds the Guinness World Record for the most #1 *New York Times* bestsellers, and his books have sold more than 355 million copies worldwide. A tireless champion of the power of books and reading, Patterson created a children's book imprint, JIMMY Patterson, whose mission is simple: "We want every kid who finishes a JIMMY Book to say, 'PLEASE GIVE ME ANOTHER BOOK.'" He has donated more than one million books to students and soldiers and funds over four hundred Teacher Education Scholarships at twenty-four colleges and universities. He has also donated millions to independent bookstores and school libraries. Patterson invests proceeds from the sales of JIMMY Patterson Books in pro-reading initiatives.

David Ellis is a Justice of the Illinois Appellate Court and the author of nine novels, including *Line of Vision,* for which he won the Edgar Allan Poe Award, and *The Hidden Man,* which earned him a 2009 L.A. Times Book Prize nomination.

BOOKS BY JAMES PATTERSON

FEATURING ALEX CROSS

The People vs. Alex Cross • *Cross the Line* • *Cross Justice* • *Hope to Die* • *Cross My Heart* • *Alex Cross, Run* • *Merry Christmas, Alex Cross* • *Kill Alex Cross* • *Cross Fire* • *I, Alex Cross* • *Alex Cross's* Trial (with Richard DiLallo) • *Cross Country* • *Double Cross* • *Cross* (also published as *Alex Cross*) • *Mary, Mary* • *London Bridges* • *The Big Bad Wolf* • *Four Blind Mice* • *Violets Are Blue* • *Roses Are Red* • *Pop Goes the Weasel* • *Cat & Mouse* • *Jack & Jill* • *Kiss the Girls* • *Along Came a Spider*

THE WOMEN'S MURDER CLUB

The 17th Suspect (with Maxine Paetro) • *16th Seduction* (with Maxine Paetro) • *15th Affair* (with Maxine Paetro) • *14th Deadly Sin* (with Maxine Paetro) • *Unlucky 13* (with Maxine Paetro) • *12th of Never* (with Maxine Paetro) • *11th Hour* (with Maxine Paetro) • *10th Anniversary* (with Maxine Paetro) • *The 9th Judgment* (with Maxine Paetro) • *The 8th Confession* (with Maxine Paetro) • *7th Heaven* (with Maxine Paetro) • *The 6th Target* (with Maxine Paetro) • *The 5th Horseman* (with Maxine Paetro) •

4th of July (with Maxine Paetro) • *3rd Degree* (with Andrew Gross) • *2nd Chance* (with Andrew Gross) • *1st to Die*

FEATURING MICHAEL BENNETT

Haunted (with James O. Born) • *Bullseye* (with Michael Ledwidge) • *Alert* (with Michael Ledwidge) • *Burn* (with Michael Ledwidge) • *Gone* (with Michael Ledwidge) • *I, Michael Bennett* (with Michael Ledwidge) • *Tick Tock* (with Michael Ledwidge) • *Worst Case* (with Michael Ledwidge) • *Run for Your Life* (with Michael Ledwidge) • *Step on a Crack* (with Michael Ledwidge)

THE PRIVATE NOVELS

Princess (with Rees Jones) • *Count to Ten* (with Ashwin Sanghi) • *Missing* (with Kathryn Fox) • *The Games* (with Mark Sullivan) • *Private Paris* (with Mark Sullivan) • *Private Vegas* (with Maxine Paetro) • *Private India: City on Fire* (with Ashwin Sanghi) • *Private Down Under* (with Michael White) • *Private L.A.* (with Mark Sullivan) • *Private Berlin* (with Mark Sullivan) • *Private London* (with Mark Pearson) • *Private Games* (with Mark Sullivan) • *Private: #1 Suspect* (with Maxine Paetro) • *Private* (with Maxine Paetro)

NYPD RED NOVELS

Red Alert (with Marshall Karp) • *NYPD Red 4* (with Marshall Karp) • *NYPD Red 3* (with Marshall Karp) • *NYPD Red 2* (with Marshall Karp) • *NYPD Red* (with Marshall Karp)

SUMMER NOVELS

Second Honeymoon (with Howard Roughan) • *Now You See Her* (with Michael Ledwidge) • *Swimsuit* (with Maxine Paetro) • *Sail* (with Howard Roughan) • *Beach Road* (with Peter de Jonge) • *Lifeguard* (with Andrew Gross) • *Honeymoon* (with Howard Roughan) • *The Beach House* (with Peter de Jonge)

STAND-ALONE BOOKS

Fifty Fifty (with Candice Fox) • *Murder Beyond the Grave* (with Andrew Bourelle and Christopher Charles) • *Home Sweet Murder* (with Andrew Bourelle and Scott Slaven) • *Murder, Interrupted* (with Alex Abramovich and Christopher Charles) • *All-American Murder* (with Alex Abramovich and Mike Harvkey) • *The Family Lawyer* (with Robert Rotstein, Christopher Charles, Rachel Howzell Hall) • *The Store* (with Richard DiLallo) • *The Moores Are*

Missing (with Loren D. Estleman, Sam Hawken, Ed Chatterton) • *Triple Threat* (with Max DiLallo, Andrew Bourrelle) • *Murder Games* (with Howard Roughan) • *Penguins of America* (with Jack Patterson with Florence Yue) • *Two from the Heart* (with Frank Constantini, Emily Raymond, Brian Sitts) • *The Black Book* (with David Ellis) • *Humans, Bow Down* (with Emily Raymond) • *Never Never* (with Candice Fox) • *Woman of God* (with Maxine Paetro) • *Filthy Rich* (with John Connolly and Timothy Malloy) • *The Murder House* (with David Ellis) • *Truth or Die* (with Howard Roughan) • *Miracle at Augusta* (with Peter de Jonge) • *Invisible* (with David Ellis) • *First Love* (with Emily Raymond) • *Mistress* (with David Ellis) • *Zoo* (with Michael Ledwidge) • *Guilty Wives* (with David Ellis) • *The Christmas Wedding* (with Richard DiLallo) • *Kill Me If You Can* (with Marshall Karp) • *Toys* (with Neil McMahon) • *Don't Blink* (with Howard Roughan) • *The Postcard Killers* (with Liza Marklund) • *The Murder of King Tut* (with Martin Dugard) • *Against Medical Advice* (with Hal Friedman) • *Sundays at Tiffany's* (with Gabrielle Charbonnet) • *You've Been Warned* (with Howard Roughan) • *The Quickie* (with Michael Ledwidge) • *Judge & Jury* (with Andrew Gross) • *Sam's Letters to Jennifer* • *The Lake House* • *The Jester* (with Andrew Gross) • *Suzanne's Diary for Nicholas* • *Cradle and All*

• *When the Wind Blows* • *Miracle on the 17th Green* (with Peter de Jonge) • *Hide & Seek* • *The Midnight Club* • *Black Friday* (originally published as *Black Market*) • *See How They Run* • *Season of the Machete* • *The Thomas Berryman Number*

BOOK**SHOTS**

The Exile (with Alison Joseph) • *The Medical Examiner* (with Maxine Paetro) • *Black Dress Affair* (with Susan DiLallo) • *The Killer's Wife* (with Max DiLallo) • *Scott Free* (with Rob Hart) • *The Dolls* (with Kecia Bal) • *Detective Cross* • *Nooners* (with Tim Arnold) • *Stealing Gulfstreams* (with Max DiLallo) • *Diary of a Succubus* (with Derek Nikitas) • *Night Sniper* (with Christopher Charles) • *Juror #3* (with Nancy Allen) • *The Shut-In* (with Duane Swierczynski) • *French Twist* (with Richard DiLallo) • *Malicious* (with James O. Born) • *Hidden* (with James O. Born) • *The House Husband* (with Duane Swierczynski) • *The Christmas Mystery* (with Richard DiLallo) • *Black & Blue* (with Candice Fox) • *Come and Get Us* (with Shan Serafin) • *Private: The Royals* (with Rees Jones) • *Taking the Titanic* (with Scott Slaven) • *Killer Chef* (with Jeffrey J. Keyes) • *French Kiss* (with Richard DiLallo) • *$10,000,000 Marriage Proposal* (with Hilary Liftin) • *Hunted* (with Andrew Holmes) • *113 Minutes* (with Max DiLallo) • *Chase* (with Michael Ledwidge) • *Let's Play Make-Believe* (with James O. Born) • *The Trial* (with Maxine Paetro) • *Little Black Dress* (with Emily Raymond) • *Cross Kill* • *Zoo II* (with Max DiLallo)

Sabotage: An Under Covers Story by Jessica Linden • *Love Me Tender* by Laurie Horowitz • *Bedding the Highlander* by Sabrina York • *The Wedding Florist* by T.J. Kline • *A Wedding in Maine* by Jen McLaughlin • *Radiant* by Elizabeth Hayley • *Hot Winter Nights* by Codi Gray • *Bodyguard* by Jessica Linden • *Dazzling* by Elizabeth Hayley • *The Mating Season* by Laurie Horowitz • *Sacking the Quarterback* by Samantha Towle • *Learning to Ride* by Erin Knightley • *The McCullagh Inn in Maine* by Jen McLaughlin

FOR READERS OF ALL AGES

Maximum Ride

Maximum Ride Forever • *Nevermore: The Final Maximum Ride Adventure* • *Angel: A Maximum Ride Novel* • *Fang: A Maximum Ride Novel* • *Max: A Maximum Ride Novel* • *The Final Warning: A Maximum Ride Novel* • *Saving the World and Other*

Extreme Sports: A Maximum Ride Novel • *School's Out—Forever: A Maximum Ride Novel* • *The Angel Experiment: A Maximum Ride Novel*

Daniel X

Daniel X: Lights Out (with Chris Grabenstein) • *Daniel X: Armageddon* (with Chris Grabenstein) • *Daniel X: Game Over* (with Ned Rust) • *Daniel X: Demons and Druids* (with Adam Sadler) • *Daniel X: Watch the Skies* (with Ned Rust) • *The Dangerous Days of Daniel X* (with Michael Ledwidge)

Witch & Wizard

Witch & Wizard: The Lost (with Emily Raymond) • *Witch & Wizard: The Kiss* (with Jill Dembowski) • *Witch & Wizard: The Fire* (with Jill Dembowski) • *Witch & Wizard: The Gift* (with Ned Rust) • *Witch & Wizard* (with Gabrielle Charbonnet)

Confessions

Confessions: The Murder of an Angel (with Maxine Paetro) • *Confessions: The Paris Mysteries* (with Maxine Paetro) • *Confessions: The Private School Murders* (with Maxine Paetro) • *Confessions of a Murder Suspect* (with Maxine Paetro)

Middle School

Middle School: Escape to Australia (with Martin Chatterton, illustrated by Daniel Griffo) • *Middle School: Dog's Best Friend* (with Chris Tebbetts, illustrated by Jomike Tejido) • *Middle School: Just My Rotten Luck* (with Chris Tebbetts, illustrated by Laura Park) • *Middle School: Save Rafe!* (with Chris Tebbetts, illustrated by Laura Park) • *Middle School: Ultimate Showdown* (with Julia Bergen, illustrated by Alec Longstreth) • *Middle School: How I Survived Bullies, Broccoli, and Snake Hill* (with Chris Tebbetts, illustrated by Laura Park) • *Middle School: My Brother Is a Big, Fat Liar* (with Lisa Papademetriou, illustrated by Neil Swaab) • *Middle School: Get Me Out of Here!* (with Chris Tebbetts, illustrated by Laura Park) • *Middle School, The Worst Years of My Life* (with Chris Tebbetts, illustrated by Laura Park)

I Funny

I Funny: School of Laughs (with Chris Grabenstein, illustrated by Jomike Tejido • *I Funny TV* (with Chris Grabenstein, illustrated by Laura Park) • *I Totally Funniest: A Middle School Story* (with Chris Grabenstein, illustrated by Laura Park) • *I Even Funnier: A Middle School Story* (with Chris Grabenstein, illustrated by Laura Park) • *I Funny: A Middle School Story* (with Chris Grabenstein, illustrated by Laura Park)

Treasure Hunters

Treasure Hunters: Quest for the City of Gold (with Chris Grabenstein, illustrated by Juliana Neufeld) • *Treasure Hunters: Peril at the Top of the World* (with Chris Grabenstein, illustrated by Juliana Neufeld) • *Treasure Hunters: Secret of the Forbidden City* (with Chris Grabenstein, illustrated by Juliana Neufeld) • *Treasure Hunters: Danger Down the Nile* (with Chris Grabenstein, illustrated by Juliana Neufeld) • *Treasure Hunters* (with Chris Grabenstein, illustrated by Juliana Neufeld)

OTHER BOOKS FOR READERS OF ALL AGES

The Candies' Easter Party (illustrated by Andy Elkerton) • *Jacky Ha-Ha: My Life Is a Joke* (with Chris Grabenstein, illustrated by Kerascoët) • *Give Thank You a Try* (with Bill O'Reilly) • *Expelled* (with Emily Raymond) • *The Candies Save Christmas* (illustrated by Andy Elkerton) • *Big Words for Little Geniuses* (with Susan Patterson, illustrated by Hsinping Pan) • *Laugh Out Loud* (with Chris Grabenstein) • *Pottymouth and Stoopid* (with Chris Grabenstein) • *Crazy House* (with Gabrielle Charbonnet) • *House of Robots: Robot Revolution* (with Chris Grabenstein, illustrated by Juliana Neufeld) • *Word of Mouse* (with Chris Grabenstein, illustrated by Joe Sutphin) • *Give Please a Chance* (with Bill O'Reilly) • *Jacky Ha-Ha* (with Chris Grabenstein, illustrated by Kerascoët) • *House of Robots: Robots Go Wild!* (with Chris Grabenstein, illustrated by Juliana Neufeld) • *Public School Superhero* (with Chris Tebbetts, illustrated by Cory Thomas) • *House of Robots* (with Chris Grabenstein, illustrated by Juliana Neufeld) • *Homeroom Diaries* (with Lisa Papademetriou, illustrated by Keino) • *Med Head* (with Hal Friedman) • *santaKid* (illustrated by Michael Garland)

For previews and information about the author, visit JamesPatterson.com or find him on Facebook or at your app store.

JAMES PATTERSON

RECOMMENDS

JAMES

"Patterson has mastered the art of writing page-turning bestsellers."
—*Chicago Sun-Times*

PATTERSON

1ST TO DIE

#1 NEW YORK TIMES BESTSELLING AUTHOR

A WOMEN'S MURDER CLUB NOVEL

1ST TO DIE

Have you met my ladies? By "ladies" I mean the first ladies of crime fighting, a.k.a. the Women's Murder Club. Detective Lindsay Boxer and her closest friends—some of the most respected criminal justice professionals in San Francisco—got sick and tired of kowtowing to their male bosses in order to close cases. So they banded together and formed the WMC. But they'll need to stick together to hunt down a serial killer with a sweet spot for murdering newlyweds. Because at the rate the killer is getting busy, no couple is safe. You'll want to grab a glass of wine and a baseball bat while reading this one. It's so fun it might scare you to death.

JAMES PATTERSON

HONEYMOON

2005 International Thriller of the Year

& HOWARD ROUGHAN

HONEYMOON

Seduction and danger. One of my favorite combinations. Nora Sinclair embodies both and much, much more. Mysterious things keep happening to the men around her, which is why the FBI sends Agent John O'Hara. But he'll have to figure out if he's pursuing justice or the woman he's investigating. Especially when he realizes just how dark Nora's desires really are. I love putting my well-meaning characters in compromising situations. In a story like HONEYMOON, you just never know what they're going to do…

THE #1 BESTSELLER and
THE 1st ALEX CROSS NOVEL

ALONG CAME A SPIDER

JAMES PATTERSON

ALONG CAME A SPIDER

Before the movies and before Alex Cross became a household name, there was ALONG CAME A SPIDER. This is the story that started it all: Alex Cross's game of cat-and-mouse with the deadly serial kidnapper Gary Soneji. He's one of the most terrifying villains I've ever created: the soft-spoken math teacher who makes you feel comfortable enough to entrust your children with him. Until they go missing. If you want to know what the Alex Cross series is all about, there's no better place to start than at the beginning.

THIS BOOK
WILL MAKE YOUR
JAW DROP

INVISIBLE

THE WORLD'S #1 BESTSELLING WRITER

JAMES PATTERSON
& DAVID ELLIS

INVISIBLE

When I started writing INVISIBLE, it seemed like every other TV network was telling the same kind of police stories, robberies, and crime twists. So I wanted to tell a different kind of suspense story, one that would really make your jaw drop. In the novel, Emmy Dockery is a researcher for the FBI who believes she has stumbled on one of the deadliest serial killers in history. There's only one problem—he's invisible. The mysterious killer leaves no trace. There are no weapons, no evidence, no motive. But when the killer strikes close to home, she must crack an impossible case before anyone else dies. Prepare to be blindsided because the most terrifying threat is the one you don't see coming—the one that's invisible.